AND SO IT BEGINS...

Ludwig ducked as he rode under the boughs of the tree, but the hulk of a man following failed to see the obstruction. His grunt of pain as a wayward branch slapped his face solicited laughter from the third member of their party.

"Not funny!" shouted Siggy. "I could've poked an eye out."

"Come now," said Cyn. "It's only a branch." She pulled her horse up beside him and caressed his cheek. "Shall I tend to your grievous injury?"

The large warrior blushed despite his grin. "Later. We must get out of this cold first." He raised his voice. "Tell me again, Ludwig, how much farther it is?"

The plan was to reach Verfeld before winter set in, but the weather had other ideas. They now rode through snow and ice, although admittedly, not much of it.

"We should be in Drakenfeld soon enough," said Ludwig. "With any luck, we'll be there before nightfall."

"You've been saying that for three days. Are you sure we're not lost?"

"This is definitely the right road. I recognize the Redwood."

"The Redwood?"

"It likely has something to do with those." Cyn pointed at a copse of trees. "You know, the enormous trees with the red bark?"

"It does," added Ludwig. "Which means we're very close. All we need to do is keep those to our west, and we'll soon be within the baron's lands."

"And this baron," said Siggy. "He's a friend of yours, is he?"

"Lord Merrick? No. I've never met the man, but my father has mentioned him."

"And you just assumed he would welcome us?"

"Of course. Is it not the custom in the Northern Kingdoms for nobles to offer shelter to their peers?"

In response, Siggy laughed. "You're asking the wrong person." Ludwig turned to Cyn.

"Don't look at me," she responded. "I've been a mercenary my entire life."

ALSO BY PAUL J BENNETT

THE BEAST OF BRUNHAUSEN

A PLAGUE IN ZEIDERBRUCH

WARRIOR LORD

POWER ASCENDING: BOOK FOUR

PAUL J BENNETT

DEDICATION

To my wife, Carol, who gave me wings to let my imagination fly.

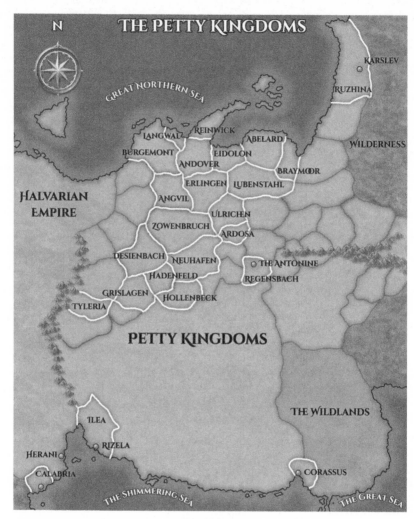

Map of Erlingen

Regional Map

BATTLE OF HARLINGEN

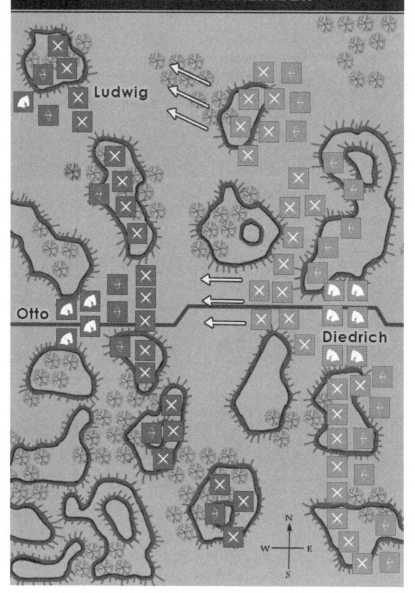

Battle of Harlingen

1

ON THE ROAD

WINTER 1095 SR* (SAINTS RECKONING)

L udwig ducked as he rode under the boughs of the tree, but the hulk of a man following failed to see the obstruction. His grunt of pain as a wayward branch slapped his face solicited laughter from the third member of their party.

"Not funny!" shouted Siggy. "I could've poked an eye out."

"Come now," said Cyn. "It's only a branch." She pulled her horse up beside him and caressed his cheek. "Shall I tend to your grievous injury?"

The large warrior blushed despite his grin. "Later. We must get out of this cold first." He raised his voice. "Tell me again, Ludwig, how much farther it is?"

The plan was to reach Verfeld before winter set in, but the weather had other ideas. They now rode through snow and ice, although admittedly, not much of it.

"We should be in Drakenfeld soon enough," said Ludwig. "With any luck, we'll be there before nightfall."

"You've been saying that for three days. Are you sure we're not lost?"

"This is definitely the right road. I recognize the Redwood."

"The Redwood?"

"It likely has something to do with those." Cyn pointed at a copse of trees. "You know, the enormous trees with the red bark?"

"It does," added Ludwig. "Which means we're very close. All we need to do is keep those to our west, and we'll soon be within the baron's lands."

"And this baron," said Siggy. "He's a friend of yours, is he?"

"Lord Merrick? No. I've never met the man, but my father has mentioned him."

"And you just assumed he would welcome us?"

"Of course. Is it not the custom in the Northern Kingdoms for nobles to offer shelter to their peers?"

In response, Siggy laughed. "You're asking the wrong person." Ludwig turned to Cyn.

"Don't look at me," she responded. "I've been a mercenary my entire life. It's not as if I spent any time amongst the wealthy."

"Well," said Ludwig, "it's definitely the custom in Hadenfeld."

"And he won't mind having us to look after?"

"Of course not," said Ludwig. "You're part of my retinue."

Cyn sat up in her saddle. "Retinue. I like the sound of that, although I fear our attire is not appropriate."

"Nonsense," said Siggy. "We're his bodyguards. What else would we wear if not armour?"

"A dress?"

He laughed. "I'd look pretty silly in a dress."

She gave him a stern look. "I was talking about me!"

"You? In a dress?" Siggy, suddenly noting the seriousness of her manner, struggled to find the right words to rescue the situation. "I think you would look marvellous in a dress."

"You've never seen me in a dress."

"True, but you look marvellous in anything."

She smiled. "There he is, the silver-tongued rogue I fell in love with. The Continent is restored to normality once more."

Ludwig chuckled. "And about time, too. I've had enough war to last a lifetime."

"Speaking of which," said Siggy, "do you truly believe the Duke of Erlingen will keep the peace, or will he use his new-found success to take on his neighbours?"

"That's no longer my concern. The duchy is a long way from here, and I've more local matters to deal with."

"Such as?"

"Reconciling with my father. I'm afraid I didn't leave on the best of terms."

"You're his only son, aren't you?" asked Cyn.

"Yes, although I do have a stepbrother, Berthold. My father remarried a widow, and he came as part of the deal."

"The deal?" said Siggy. "I assume the marriage was arranged?"

"It was," said Ludwig. "By King Otto himself, apparently."

"Apparently?"

"Yes, I don't know the details. I didn't know my father was getting married when he set off for Reinwick."

"How curious," said Cyn.

"What is?"

"That he was married in the north, and we were in the same general area ourselves."

"Yes," added Siggy, "but his father was there years before us, else how would Ludwig even be aware of it?"

Ludwig looked back at the two of them. "You're both correct."

"And what's he like, this brother of yours?"

"I must admit to never having warmed to him, although his mother proved a nice enough woman in the end."

"The end?" said Cyn. "Are you saying she died?"

"Not at all, but I left shortly after learning of her softer side."

"Then at least you've got something to look forward to. I don't remember my own mother. She died when I was very young."

"What about you, Sig?"

"My mother was a most generous woman," the man replied, "with an appetite for life and a heart the size of a horse."

"I assume she's no longer with us?"

"No, I'm afraid not. She succumbed to a fever some years ago. I suppose we should've seen it coming, living as we were in the swamps."

"You lived in the swamps?"

"Oh yes," said Siggy. "After the rebellion in Abelard failed, we were on the run. The swamps were the only place we could avoid the king's wrath. She wasn't the only one to die there, but, by the Saints, I miss her."

"How long ago was this?"

Sigwulf shrugged. "Years. After her death, I had no family left."

"I thought you had a sister?"

"I did, or rather I do, assuming she's still alive, but she left us long before our mother died."

"Is that when you became a mercenary?"

"Aye. What else could I do? It's not as if I had a trade to fall back on."

"Well," said Cyn, "I'm glad that's the life you chose. Else I never would've met you. What about you, Ludwig? Is there a woman waiting for you back home?"

"No," said Sigwulf.

"And how would you know?"

The great man smiled. "He lost his love to the Church."

"She became a Holy Sister?"

"No, it's even better. She became a Temple Knight."

"Truly?"

"Yes," said Ludwig, fondness lingering in his voice. "Her name is Charlaine deShandria."

Cyn shook her head. "You can't love a Temple Knight. They take vows."

"I resigned myself to the fact that we shall never be together, but I will never stop loving her."

"You should adopt a more pragmatic approach."

"Meaning?"

"You're the son of a baron. You'll need to wed to continue the family name, and you can't do that with a Temple Knight."

"They can leave the order, you know," suggested Siggy. "Perhaps it will end well after all?"

"I wouldn't get his hopes up," said Cyn. "It serves no purpose."

She was about to say more, but a dull thud to her left interrupted, a crossbow bolt now protruding from a tree.

"Ambush!" she yelled. Another bolt flew past, striking Sigwulf's saddle.

"Into the woods!" shouted Ludwig, urging his mount off the road.

A yell came from behind them, and then six men rose from their concealment in the long grass. Ludwig dismounted, letting his horse, Clay, trot farther in amongst the trees. Cyn and Siggy soon joined him, weapons in hand, crouching in the snow as their attackers drew closer.

"How do you want to do this?" whispered Siggy.

"Rush in," replied Ludwig. "Ready?"

They both nodded, and then all three charged forward as two of their foes reloaded their crossbows while the other four drew swords.

Ludwig quickly knocked an opponent's lighter sword aside, efficiently plunging his own into the fellow's arm, causing blood to spring forth. He followed this with a second attack to the head, the sheer force of the impact breaking the man's neck.

Beside him, Cyn's mace struck a helmet with a muffled crash, reminding Ludwig of the sound a bell might make if someone tried to dampen it.

On the other side, Sigwulf rushed in, slamming his full weight into his opponent, sending them both tumbling. He quickly scrambled to his feet, looming over his foe as he took the man's life with a quick slice to the throat.

Ludwig, spotting an archer aiming his crossbow, ducked. The bolt sailed overhead, and then the man turned, dropping his weapon in his haste to escape. Cyn finished hers with a second strike to the head—enough to break their enemy's morale. Those still alive quickly fled.

Sigwulf stepped forward, throwing his sword spinning through the air towards a target, only for it to fall short and send snow spraying upwards.

Cyn looked at him. "What in the name of the Saints are you doing? Trying to invent a way to disarm yourself?"

The big man shrugged. "I thought I might've been able to trip him up. In any event, I doubt we'll be seeing any more of those filthy bandits." He spat on the ground.

Ludwig stood, staring down at the three bodies.

"Something wrong?" asked Cyn.

He knelt, taking in everything. "These are no ordinary bandits."

"Meaning?"

"Look at their weapons." He pulled on one of the dead men's cloaks, exposing a chainmail shirt. "How many bandits do you know who can afford armour like that?"

Siggy, having retrieved his sword, returned to his friends. "Those look more like soldiers than thieves."

"Yes, and what kind of bandit attacks without demanding coins first?"

"What are you suggesting?" said Cyn. "That these are foreign soldiers?"

"Unlikely."

Siggy crouched. "I've seen this sort of thing before."

"You have?" said Ludwig.

"Yes. After the rebellion, King Rordan of Abelard sent men like this to hunt us down."

"That would suppose they knew we were coming, wouldn't it?" said Cyn.

Ludwig met her gaze. "I sent word ahead."

"And you told them which road we'd be taking?"

"No, but there are only two roads that lead to Erlingen, and one of those goes through Neuhafen. No Hadenfelder in his right mind would go through that traitorous land."

"I'm not sure I understand," said Cyn.

Ludwig stood. "Neuhafen used to be part of Hadenfeld, but the barons rose in rebellion."

"Much like Abelard," added Siggy.

"Aye, but here they were more successful. They didn't win the kingdom but held their own against King Otto, forcing a truce. There's been bad blood ever since."

"How long ago was this?"

Ludwig shrugged. "Before I was born, in the early days of Otto's rule. I suspect his ascension triggered the rebellion in the first place, although admittedly, I'm no expert in such things."

Cyn dug through the dead men's clothing.

"Honestly," said Sigwulf. "Is that all you can think about—taking their coins?"

"Of course not. I'm looking for anything that might give us some idea of who they worked for." She retrieved a small pouch, dumping its contents into her hand and holding them up to Ludwig. "Recognize these?"

"Those are Hadenfeld coins. Whoever employed them was local to the region."

She began stripping off the armour. "Give me a hand, Siggy. This armour may bear a maker's mark, and even if it doesn't, it ought to fetch a tidy sum."

"Surely we're not going to bury them in this weather?" asked Siggy.

"No," said Ludwig. "We'll strip them and leave them to rot in the woods."

"You know, it would've been handy to take at least one of them alive."

"Let's just be thankful none of us was hurt, shall we?"

It took some time to remove the armour from the bodies. In addition to the chainmail, they retrieved two helmets and a trio of manageable swords. Ludwig was all for ditching them, but Siggy felt it was a waste of resources to let them rust in the snow.

They were on their way again by late afternoon, but the delay cost them. Snow began falling, lightly at first but thickening as the day wore on. Eventually, a keep appeared in the distance as they topped a rise. The sight warmed them, despite the weather, and they renewed their efforts to arrive before dark. They passed through empty fields, the farmers having abandoned them for the warmth of their homes.

Sigwulf looked around as he rode, intrigued by the layout. "Are all farms so spread out in Hadenfeld?"

"Of course," said Ludwig. "It's mostly a peaceful country. Why do you ask?"

"A man would be hard-pressed to defend these farms if attacked."

"War seldom comes here."

"Yet you spoke of insurrection, did you not?"

"True," said Ludwig, "although that was not the work of outsiders, but the treachery of some of the barons."

"As far as you know," added Sigwulf.

At first, Ludwig reacted with irritation but quickly realized the great warrior was earnest. "You think outsiders provoked it?"

"I think it almost assured. Outside funds drove my family to support the usurper back in Andover. We know how fractious the Petty Kingdoms can be. Who benefited most from this civil war you described earlier?"

"Any of our neighbours, I suppose. Before the creation of Neuhafen, Hadenfeld was one of the biggest kingdoms around."

"And wealthy?"

"Aye, until fighting the rebellion drained the coffers dry."

"Then you have your answer."

"Hardly," said Ludwig. "And in any case, how would we even find out the true culprit?"

"Likely, we won't, but chances are whoever was behind it would still have influence in the area. Now that you're home, I would be wary of any foreigners you meet."

"I'm not home yet, and I might remind you that you and Cyn are foreign to these lands."

"Ah, yes," added Cyn, "but aren't we more like family?"

"Yes, I suppose you are. Sorry, I meant no offence, but I do see Sig's point."

"How do you think your father will greet you on your return?"

He considered her words before answering. "I really have no idea. Things were strained when I left. I doubt it's gotten much better in the last year."

"But you did tell him we were coming?"

"Yes," said Sigwulf. "He mentioned that earlier, remember?"

"I know," she replied, "but he didn't speak about the letter's tone."

"Tone?"

"Yes," said Cyn. "Was it apologetic or accusatory?"

Both of them looked at Ludwig for an answer.

"Neither, if truth be told. I said I'd matured in the last year and wished to return home but didn't indicate when. That was before I learned of his illness, of course. His letter begged me to return with all haste."

"I'm a little confused," said Sigwulf. "I thought you wanted to hide where you were?"

"I did, but after the battle, the Duke of Erlingen discovered who my family was and sent a letter to my father. Realizing he had revealed my location, I wrote home. I intended to remain in Erlingen for a while, but after receiving word of his illness, I decided to head home. My experience during the war made me realize the heavy burden a baron must carry."

Sigwulf shook his head. "You're meant to be a leader, my friend, not some lazy noble who spends all his time cooped up in a keep."

"And I will be, someday. I promise you. But right now, my father needs my help."

"And what about us?" asked Cyn.

"I'll convince him to hire you if you wish. Of course, if you're determined to move on…"

"Move on? To where? You know full well we'll hire on, providing you're going to stick around."

"I am," said Ludwig.

"Good. Now tell us more about your home. You said you were near a city?"

"Yes, the free city of Malburg."

"I'm still not sure I understand how that works," said Sigwulf. "How can a city be free?"

"He means," said Cyn, "that the city runs itself rather than being under the control of a noble."

"How is that even possible?"

"They elect a council," explained Ludwig. "Although, I suspect the guilds play a large part in decision-making. Of course, they still pay taxes to the Crown. Far more coins than the nobles, it would appear. I suppose that's to be expected, considering the amount of commerce going through the place."

"And how close is Malburg to the keep?"

"Less than a morning's ride. You can see it from the top of the keep on a clear day."

"But not from the ground?"

"No," said Ludwig. "The ground is uneven in those parts, but you can usually see the smoke from their fires."

"And your father's lands surround it?"

"They do. There are five villages, all pledging fealty to my father."

"How is it," said Sigwulf, "that the city is so close?"

"It's built on the ruins of an old Therengian village. At least that's the story the elders like to tell."

"Are there Therengians in Verfeld?"

"I suppose so, not that I ever gave it much thought. However, you can bet I'll pay more attention to such things in the future."

"I hope you're not going to mention my background to your father."

"No, Sig. Rest assured, the only thing I'll be telling him is that you're both mercenaries. Not that it's likely to impress him. His opinion of soldiers for hire isn't exactly what I'd call enthusiastic."

"Why's that?"

"It's simple accounting," explained Ludwig. "They are more expensive than homegrown warriors."

Cyn laughed. "Homegrown? You make them sound like some kind of melon, ripened to be harvested. Just how many warriors does your father employ?"

"It varies, but usually around two dozen. That's all he can afford."

"And does he count horsemen amongst his troops?"

"No," said Ludwig. "Although a few may ride into the villages when occasion demands. The truth is, there aren't enough horses to equip them all, and even if he could afford to, there are other matters that demand the coins."

"So your father is essentially broke?"

"I wouldn't say broke, precisely, but if you're expecting the high life, you'll be sorely disappointed."

Sigwulf smiled. "This keeps getting better and better."

"Hush now," said Cyn. "It will be nice to put down some roots for a change."

2

DRAKENFELD

WINTER 1095 SR

A trio of riders intercepted them as they travelled the road leading to the keep.

"Halt in the name of Lord Merrick," their leader called out.

Ludwig kept his hands away from his sword. "I am Ludwig Altenburg, son of Lord Frederick, Baron of Verfeld."

"My apologies, Lord. There have been reports of strangers in the area. We've been patrolling the roads to keep them at bay."

"Strangers, you say?"

"Yes. At first, we took them for brigands, but it appears they did little but skulk amongst the trees."

"Likely the same group who attacked us," said Ludwig.

"Attacked? I trust you're unhurt, my lord?"

"We are. Thankfully, we killed three of the ruffians before the rest fled. If you're so inclined to locate them, their bodies lie some distance to the north, just off the road."

"I shall send men to investigate come morning, but I'll escort you back to Drakenfeld Keep in the meantime."

"Then lead on," said Ludwig. "We look forward to tasting the hospitality of His Lordship."

The riders turned around and led the way. They passed by more farms clustered closer together.

"Tell me," said Sigwulf, "is this weather typical of the season?"

"Winter has come unseasonably early," replied their guide. "Although it's at least spared us the deep snow. On the other hand, the wind's been bitter these last few days. It's a wonder you're not all frozen."

"Nothing that a nice cup of mulled mead wouldn't fix."

"I'm sure we can manage much more than that, my lord."

"Lord, is it?" said Sigwulf. "I like the sound of that."

"He's merely being polite," added Cyn. "Don't let it go to your head."

They approached the stables, where the stable hands waited to take their horses. Ludwig dismounted and then waited while his companions gathered their battle spoils.

"Come," said their guide, turning towards the keep. "Having seen your approach, the lord and lady eagerly await word of your arrival."

"Is this a common building style around here?" asked Cyn.

"It is," said Ludwig. "This one, in particular, looks to be very much akin to that of Verfeld Keep."

The soldier opened the keep's iron-reinforced door, motioning for them to enter.

"Has anyone ever attacked this place?" asked Sigwulf.

"No, Lord," replied their guide. "The land's been peaceful for many years."

"What about the rebellion?" asked Cyn.

"The fighting never reached Drakenfeld, my lady."

She moved closer to Siggy, keeping her voice low. "I don't know that I'm ever going to get comfortable with that."

"What?" said Sig. "Entering a keep?"

"No, being called 'my lady'. It just isn't natural."

He chuckled. "Wear it as a badge of honour, if you must, but let's not argue its use at this time."

They proceeded down a hallway and into the great hall where their hosts waited. The lord was of a similar height to Ludwig, although slightly older and with a well-trimmed beard. His wife, somewhat shorter, wore a thick cloak to ward off the chill, her brown locks tucked into a long braid hanging down the front of her dress.

"Greetings. I am Lord Merrick Sternhassen, Baron of Drakenfeld, and this is my baroness, Lady Gita."

"Good evening, my lord. My name is Ludwig Altenburg, son of Lord Frederick, Baron of Verfeld." A look of shock passed over his host's features, but the fellow soon recovered.

"I am... pleased to welcome you to my home, Lord Ludwig."

"My apologies if I offended you, Baron."

"Did you come far?"

"Indeed. My companions and I travelled all the way from Erlingen."

"Then I presume you haven't heard the news?"

"News, my lord?"

"I'm afraid there's no easy way to say this. Your father has been called to the Afterlife."

Ludwig staggered to the side as the room spun before his eyes. Only the reassuring hand of Sigwulf prevented him from falling.

"I am sorry to be the bearer of such distressing news," continued Merrick. "Let us withdraw to more private quarters to discuss the matter in more detail."

"I knew he was sick," said Ludwig. "It's why I'm returning to Hadenfeld, but coming all this way and hearing he has already passed is bitter news indeed."

They remained silent as the baron led them farther into the keep.

"This," said Merrick, "is the warmest room we possess. Please, sit, and the servants will fetch you something to eat."

They all took a seat, Sigwulf and Cyn looking particularly self-conscious.

Lady Gita broke the awkward silence. "You say you came from the north?"

"Indeed, my lady," replied Ludwig. "We came from Erlingen."

"And what, might I ask, were you doing there?"

"We were in service to His Grace, the duke."

"I assume you fought?" asked the baron. "We heard of a great battle, although the details have, as yet, failed to make themselves known in these parts."

"The Kingdom of Andover attempted an invasion, my lord."

"Come now. You'll soon be the new Baron of Verfeld. We can set aside formalities, can't we?"

Ludwig took a deep breath. Losing his father was unexpected, but the news he was to be named the baron made him feel light-headed all over again. He knew it was the logical consequence of being an Altenburg, but somehow it had never occurred to him that he would be called on to fill his father's place so soon.

Lord Merrick leaned forward in his chair. "Are you feeling ill, Ludwig?"

In reply, he took a deep breath. "I shall be fine. It's all been rather unexpected. Might I ask how he died?"

"A fever swept through Verfeld."

"How long ago did he pass?"

"We first heard the news last month. It's said the illness ravaged the keep, and your father was not the only one to succumb."

"Yes," added Lady Gita. "Your poor mother took ill shortly thereafter, joining your father in the Afterlife."

"She was only my stepmother," said Ludwig. "Although I'll still mourn her passing."

"Several others passed as well, although I know not their names."

"I should leave for Verfeld first thing tomorrow."

"You can't," insisted Lord Merrick.

"I beg your pardon?"

"You must ride on to Harlingen. The king will want to invest you as baron."

"But Verfeld is leaderless!"

"As it has been for some time now. What matters if it remains so for a few more days?"

"What about the plague?" asked Sigwulf.

"It was a fever, not a plague," said Lady Gita, "and seems to have been confined to the keep. I suspect it would've long since run its course."

"My lord—" said Ludwig.

"Please, just Merrick."

"Very well, Merrick. I should be glad to hear of any other tidings you might have concerning Verfeld."

"I received a missive from the king," the man replied. "It mentioned your father's death and that of his good wife but provided no specifics other than informing us others had died. We were warned not to travel there for at least a fortnight." He looked at his wife. "A wise consideration, considering my wife's delicate condition."

"Condition?" said Ludwig.

Lord Merrick smiled. "Yes, she is expecting our first child."

"My congratulations to you both."

"Thank you. It's not often we get visitors here in Drakenfeld. I would suggest you stay with us for a day or two. It will give you time to think about your new responsibilities. I shall be happy to help in any way I can.

Lady Gita's gaze turned to Cyn. "Is this your wife?"

"Saints, no!" said Ludwig, blushing at his vehement outburst. "My pardon. I forgot to introduce my travelling companions. This is Sigwulf Marhaven and Cynthia Hoffman. We fought together in Erlingen."

"A woman warrior? Are you a Temple Knight, by chance?"

"No," replied Cyn. "A mercenary."

Gita's brief look of disapproval was quickly hidden. "How interesting. I can't say I've ever met your like before. How many women mercenaries are there?"

"I'm afraid I couldn't tell you, my lady, although I admit to meeting half a dozen or so over the years."

"Marhaven?" said Lord Merrick. "That name sounds familiar. Where did you say you were from?"

"Up north, but Marhaven is a common enough name," Sigwulf said quickly.

"I understand my father knew you well," said Ludwig, eager to change the topic.

"Likely, that was my father," said Lord Merrick. "He died just last year."

"I'm sorry for your loss."

"It wasn't unexpected. He was sick for some time. However, he lived long enough to bless our marriage, so at least we have that."

"Might I ask what he died of?"

"Injuries sustained when he fell from his horse if you can believe it. He struck his head and was never the same. In the end, he passed in his sleep, which was a blessing."

"And how did you find the transition to baron?"

"I helped him run the barony in his later years, but even so, it was overwhelming. Thankfully, Gita was more than up to the challenge of looking after the finances while I concentrated on the tenants. Do you have someone to perform a similar service in Verfeld?"

"We do, at least we did, but I don't know if he survived the fever."

"King Otto will have more information for you, I'm sure." Merrick looked at his wife, who nodded. "Look here, you're being thrown into the deep part of the river. What do you say I accompany you to Hadenfeld?"

"What of your wife?"

"She can come with us. We'll take a carriage and some horses."

"I shouldn't like to inconvenience you."

"Nonsense. We've been meaning to visit the capital for some time. I haven't been there since my investiture."

"You make it sound like it was years ago," said Lady Gita, "but it was only a few seasons. Still, it will be nice to see the king again."

Servants brought in food and drink and were passing it around when Lady Gita stood. "You must pardon me, but it's time I went to bed."

Lord Merrick joined her. "I shall accompany you, my dear." He turned to Ludwig. "Make yourselves at home. The servants will show you to your rooms when you are ready. We'll talk again in the morning, and then you can decide what you will do."

Ludwig stood. "Good night, my lord."

The baron raised a finger. "Now, now. Merrick, remember? You and I are to be peers, and I suspect, great friends."

"Yes, Merrick."

"There. That's more like it. Now, good evening to you all."

He took his wife's arm, guiding her from the room. The three of them sat in silence, listening as the footsteps receded.

"What did you make of those two?" asked Sigwulf.

"I like them," said Cyn. "They're friendly for nobles. Not at all what I expected."

"That's because they're still relatively young. They likely haven't had time for the court to corrupt them yet."

"Not all nobles are bad," said Ludwig.

"I didn't mean to imply they were, but you must admit they are far more haughty on average."

"Haughty?" said Cyn, a grin spreading from ear to ear. "Listen to you getting all high and mighty."

Ludwig rose early, thoughts of his future disturbing his sleep. Down deep, he knew this day would come, but Verfeld used to be full of those who could help a baron run his fiefdom. How then, was he to proceed when those very same people might well be gone? The idea terrified him.

He made his way to the great hall, finding the lord and lady of the keep already eating.

"Ah, there you are," said the baron. "Come, fill your belly. We don't stand on ceremony here."

"Thank you. I believe I shall." Ludwig sat down, plucking some bread from a nearby plate.

"I must say, you look like you had a rough night, not that I can blame you, considering the news. Tell me, have you weighed your options?"

"I did."

"And?"

"I'll take you up on your offer of accompanying me to Harlingen."

"And your companions?"

"They are free to make their own decisions," said Ludwig. "Although I hoped they might continue on to Malburg and find out what information they can regarding Verfeld Keep."

The baron nodded. "A clever solution to a difficult problem. They should have a complete report for you once you return home."

"Tell me," said Lady Gita. "Do you have a woman in mind for baroness?"

"No," said Ludwig. "I've been far too busy for such things."

"But you must know some women, surely? After all, you grew up in Hadenfeld."

"Yes, but until recently, I never travelled far from Verfeld."

"Well then, I'll introduce you to the ladies of court when we arrive in the capital."

"Come now," said Merrick. "The poor fellow has only just learned of his father's demise, Gita. I'm sure there's no hurry."

"It is his duty to supply an heir. I'm not suggesting he pledges his troth anytime soon, but introductions will need to be made. After all, he's the baron now."

Ludwig bowed his head. "I will concede to that, my lady, although I cannot promise to entertain any further thoughts regarding marriage at this time."

"A sensible approach," said Lord Merrick, "and there'll be plenty of time to look into marriage once you settle in."

"How far is it to Harlingen?"

"Only about seventy miles. We should be there well before the end of the week. Shall I have my men prepare our horses?"

"Yes, thank you. I, in turn, will make arrangements with my companions."

He found Cyn and Sigwulf at the top of the keep, looking out over the baron's demesne. The stout warrior turned at his approach. "Quite a sight, isn't it?"

Ludwig took up a spot beside them, following their gaze. "Yes, it is. Reminds me so much of home, although there are some differences."

"You're leaving with them, aren't you?" said Cyn.

"I am. I am duty-bound to meet the king and then be sworn in as baron. However, I'd like you two to carry on to Malburg."

"To what end?"

"I need an honest assessment of my lands."

"Can't your servants give you that?"

"Ordinarily, yes," said Ludwig, "but there've been several deaths of late, and I need to know how the place fares."

"Won't your stepbrother be in charge?"

"I believe so, which is what worries me."

"Oh?" said Cyn.

"Back before I left, we disagreed over his collection of the taxes."

"What sort of disagreement?"

"I hate to speak ill of the man," said Ludwig, "but he overcharged the landholders and pocketed the difference. I shudder to think what he might have been up to since my father's death."

"What do you need us to look for?" asked Sigwulf.

"Talk to the city folk; see what rumours they've heard."

"That's it, just rumours?"

"Speak with some of the keep's soldiers, if you can. They tend to hang around the taverns when they're not on duty. Don't try to enter the keep itself though. I don't imagine that would go over well."

"Understood."

"How long will you be gone?" asked Cyn.

"I can't say for sure. It takes at least three days to reach Harlingen, and the trip back to Verfeld shouldn't be more than a week, but while in the capital, I must await the king's pleasure. I'm unsure how long that will take. Do you need funds?"

"I've enough to last both of us for now, but we could be in trouble if you're more than a month."

"I can work within that time frame," said Ludwig.

"Anyone, in particular, we should look out for?"

"Yes, a man named Kasper Piltz. He used to be my father's right-hand man, but I'm not aware if he still lives."

"And what should we expect from your stepbrother?"

"That's another matter entirely. I suspect he might be the one who hired those men to attack us, so take care not to get on his bad side."

"And how does one do that?"

"By avoiding him whenever possible."

"And if we can't?"

"Then flatter him. That should keep him at bay for the short term."

"That's it?" said Cyn. "Just charm him? That doesn't sound too difficult."

"He may project a calm demeanour, but he's a ruthless, calculating fellow underneath. I suspect he's more interested in separating people from their coins than making any real friends."

"So," said Sigwulf, "in other words, he's a lot like your average northern noble."

"I suppose that's one way of looking at it. In any case, you should be wary."

"Does Verfeld control any villages?"

"It does," said Ludwig. "Five, remember?"

"Do you want us to visit them to determine how they fare?"

"Much as I like the idea, I must leave that to your discretion. Even if you don't, the folks of Malburg rely on the outlying villages for food. You'll soon know if the harvest was good."

"How?"

"Easy," said Cyn. "A poor crop means food prices soar. Don't worry about us, Ludwig. We'll find out what's happened in your absence. I'm more worried about you."

"Me? Why in the Saint's name would you be worried about me?"

"You're going to court, which is something new for you."

"Nonsense. I spent time at the duke's court back in Erlingen."

"Yes," said Sigwulf, "and you were decidedly uncomfortable. You complained to no end."

"Agreed, but all they wanted to do was keep congratulating me."

"And you think it'll be any different in Harlingen?"

"It's not the same thing. There hasn't been a battle in these parts for decades."

"True, but you're about to become the kingdom's newest baron. That alone will make you the centre of attention."

Ludwig turned crimson. "I hadn't considered that. Any advice?"

"Yes. Keep your wits about you, and no matter what happens, try not to overindulge."

"Meaning?"

"Don't drink to excess. You never know who might be watching."

"I shall bear that in mind."

3

HARLINGEN
WINTER 1095 SR

Ludwig quickly became accustomed to the capital's narrow and confining streets. From his point of view, the more concerning issue was the stench permeating the place. That, combined with the ankle-deep mud in some areas, made the visit distasteful. The carriage became stuck three times, necessitating hard work from barons and servants alike.

Towering over the city like a guardian, the Royal Keep finally came into view: an impressive piece of workmanship made using the same grey rock that formed the city's walls.

"Interesting, isn't it?" mused Lord Merrick. "They brought in the stone from the Harlingen Hills. Have you ever seen them?"

"The hills?" said Ludwig. "No, can't say that I have."

"They lie just to the east, astride the road to Grienwald. It's been a substantial source of stone for centuries."

"And they lugged all that here? An impressive accomplishment."

"That's nothing. Wait until you see inside."

"And the king lives there?"

"He does, although you'd assume he'd prefer more glamorous quarters. Most kings prefer their estates in the country."

"King Otto isn't like most kings, at least not from what Father told me."

Lord Merrick barked out a laugh. "That's putting it mildly."

"Come now," said Lady Gita. "The pair of you should know better than to belittle our king. You should be ashamed of yourselves."

"Don't blame me," said Merrick. "It's the king who's eccentric."

"Still, you should be more charitable."

"When you say eccentric," said Ludwig, "to what do you refer?"

"I thought you knew?" said Gita.

"I know he's a large fellow. My father used to say that the king could eat more than a prize bull."

"Quite true," said Lord Merrick, "but he sets possibly the best table in all the Petty Kingdoms. Not that I've much experience in such things, mind you."

"Is that why he's considered eccentric?"

"Not at all, my dear friend." Ludwig's host lowered his voice. "They say he has an equally large appetite for women. Not that he's very active these days."

"How old is he, precisely?"

"Ancient. If memory serves, he celebrated his sixty-fifth birthday some two years past."

"Three," corrected the baroness. "If you remember, Lord Morgan's mistress gave him a bastard that same year."

"Oh yes. I remember now; that was his third."

"That's terrible," said Ludwig. "I would think a noble would set a better example."

"He's hardly the first to father a child out of wedlock."

"What did the baroness make of that?"

"Nothing. At the time, she'd been dead for nigh on five years."

"And does he have a legitimate heir?"

"None whatsoever. I imagine he'll likely name one of his bastards to inherit Grienwald, but at this point, no one knows who it will be. You can ask him yourself if you want to. He's visiting Harlingen."

"How can you tell?" asked Ludwig.

"It's the custom in these parts to hang a baron's coat of arms from the Royal Keep when visiting." He pointed. "That's Lord Morgan's over there—the one with the blue background."

"So he's related to the king, then."

Lady Gita smiled. "I see you're familiar with our Hadenfeld traditions. You're related yourself, if I'm not mistaken."

"I am, although somewhat distantly."

"That means there'll be blue in your coat of arms as well."

"Yes, but I'm far removed from any royal duties."

"Just how far down the line of succession are you?" asked Merrick.

"Eighteenth," said Gita. "No, wait, I tell a lie, it's seventeenth; there was a death last year. Of course, the great majority of those are very old."

"And that number can change quickly if a war comes," added her husband.

"There's talk of war?" said Ludwig.

"Not at present, but Neuhafen makes demands every few years. I'm sure you're well-acquainted with them by now."

"Yes, I am. My father's lands share a border with Dornbruck, one of Neuhafen's baronies."

"They're yours now," Lady Gita reminded him, "or they will be once you're officially sworn in as baron."

"Any idea when that will be?"

"It won't be long now that we're here. The king doesn't enjoy leaving a barony empty."

"But won't he need to call his barons to the capital?"

"What?" said Lord Merrick. "All seven of us?"

"You mean six," corrected his wife. "After all, the Barony of Verfeld is officially empty at this moment."

"Not that it matters. The king likes two witnesses for such things, and we've got that covered between Lord Morgan and me."

Ludwig sighed. "This all feels so rushed."

"That's because it is. Your lands have been leaderless for some time."

"I understand my father died, but surely the castellan would've kept things running?"

"Most assuredly, but a barony without a lord is like a ship without a rudder. Lacking constant adjustments, it would soon run aground."

"I see I'll have my hands full for the foreseeable future."

"Don't worry," said Lord Merrick. "We'll help where we can."

Ludwig halted at the door while the servant announced him. Lord Merrick and Lady Gita were told to wait outside for this initial meeting, making him even more nervous.

The court of King Otto was nothing like that of the Duke of Erlingen. Whereas the duke embraced the dressings of wealth, the King of Hadenfeld seemed more restrained.

Six of the barons' banners hung on the walls, along with the king's own flag taking pride of place in the centre. A massive chandelier packed with candles filled the air with the odour of tallow rather than wax—a strange choice for a wealthy king.

A solitary, portly figure sat at the end of the great table, picking away at his plate. He looked up, and their eyes met. A smile slowly formed on His Majesty's face as he recognized his visitor.

"Ah. There you are—the spitting image of your father." He waved Ludwig forward. "Come, my boy. Sit, and we shall have a nice chat."

"Yes, Your Majesty." Ludwig sat, taking in the king's form. Otto was a large man, both in height and girth, yet his face didn't reveal it. While his hair was a little thin on top, he boasted a thick and lush beard. Based on naught but hearsay, Ludwig expected to meet a glutton, but his cousin took great care while eating, maintaining proper decorum—one might even call him fastidious.

"Would you care for some cheese?"

"No, thank you, Your Majesty."

"Come now. We are cousins, you and I. Let us not be so formal."

"How should I address you?"

"Lord or sire will do well enough. Although, to be honest, I'm taken of late with the expression 'm'lord'."

"That's a strange title for a king, isn't it?"

"It is, to be sure. I first heard it from a visiting delegate, a fellow from Talyria, if you can believe it." The king leaned in conspiratorially. "Nasty business, that."

"My lord?"

"Talyria, I mean. Seems the first minister declared himself ruler after the king's demise."

"Had he no heirs?"

"It would appear not, although there are rumours he tracked them all down and had them killed."

"Very well. M'lord it will be, then."

The king laughed. "That's the spirit, lad." He paused to gently place a tidbit of cheese into his mouth and chew on it. "Not the best, if I'm being honest."

"M'lord?"

"Not you, my lad. I was referring to this cheese." Otto picked up another piece and stared at it. "They don't age it like they used to." He turned to Ludwig. "How about you? I hear you aged a bit in the north?"

"I saw battle, if that's what you mean."

"I daresay you did much more than that. The Duke of Erlingen wrote of you in glowing terms, and he's not the type to hand out plaudits where they're not earned. What I want to know is what changed you?"

"Changed me?"

"Yes, before you left, you had the reputation of a womanizing wastrel. When I look at you now, you're the very model of a heroic warrior. Your mother would have been proud."

The mention of his mother brought a lump to Ludwig's throat, leaving him unable to respond.

"What I'm curious about," continued the king, "is what caused that change?"

"The love of a good woman," said Ludwig, bringing a flush to his cheeks.

"Is this the smith you refer to?"

"You heard about her?"

"Of course. I try to keep abreast of everything that happens in my kingdom, especially when it comes to gossip." He smiled. "I know what you're thinking, that gossip is for old women, but this fascination of mine has kept me on the throne for years."

"Through gossip, m'lord?"

"There's always some truth in it, my lad, although it's often difficult to discern the facts. This woman, is she the reason you ran away?"

Ludwig lowered his head. "Yes, Your Majesty."

"Then we must drink to her health." He watched as his visitor sought a cup, but none were to be had. "This will never do," muttered the king. "Wadswurth," he called out. "Fetch another cup and some wine." He set his own vessel down. "We'll toast her once yours comes. Now, where was I?"

"You were talking about gossip, m'lord."

"Ah, yes, so I was. As I was saying, it may seem peculiar, even unpleasant, if you like, but listening is an important part of ruling. My grandfather used to say a king has two ears and only one mouth. Do you know what that means?"

"Yes," said Ludwig. "That one should listen twice as much as they talk."

Otto smiled. "That's it, precisely. I can see you're a clever fellow. It ought to serve you well in the coming years."

"M'lord?"

"Come now. I'm old, and it won't be long before I'm dead and buried. Every time a ruler of Hadenfeld dies, there's a period of unrest, and these days there's the added uncertainty of Neuhafen's response."

"You believe they would invade?"

"I wouldn't put it past the scoundrels."

"Might I ask you a question, sire?"

"Of course," said Otto. "What is it you'd like to know?"

"How is it Neuhafen came to exist in the first place?"

"That's a long and complicated issue, but I'll try to give you the simple version. As you know, the Crown is usually handed down from father to son. However, when there's no son, the situation becomes more complicated. In such circumstances, the nearest male relative is crowned, but our laws concerning such familial links are... what's the word I'm looking for? Ah, yes—obtuse."

"Meaning?"

"Once one gets past nephews, pretty much anyone can claim the throne. I've tried to clarify that by numbering my successors. Take yourself, for example. Admittedly, you are far down at number seventeen, yet some would even dispute your inclusion within the lines of succession."

"But Hadenfeld only has seven barons."

"It does, but that does not prevent others from claiming their spot on the list." He opened his arms to encompass the room. "Look around you and tell me what you see?"

"A room of sparse furnishings, m'lord."

"And do you know why?"

"I assumed it was due to your... thriftiness?"

Otto nodded. "An assumption I expected, but the truth is it takes a lot of funds to keep my extended family in the lifestyle to which they've become accustomed. Do you have any idea how many I am obliged to support?"

Ludwig grinned. "Just shy of seventeen, I would suspect."

The king chuckled. "Well said, my lad, and that would be true were I only counting the male members, but there are almost as many women. It's a wonder I can even afford this table!"

"I had no idea, m'lord."

"Of course not, and why would you? You've got a tremendous advantage over the others, Ludwig, for you have a barony all to yourself."

"Are you suggesting that none of the other heirs possess lands?"

"Well, Lord Morgan is the Baron of Grienwald, and a couple others have estates, but Hadenfeld isn't the kingdom it used to be. Ever since we lost Neuhafen, we're half our size, less, if I'm being honest."

"Less?"

"Yes, when Neuhafen broke away from us, they took eight barons with them, so they technically outnumber us by one. Of course, some are more powerful than others, so that doesn't give us the most accurate picture."

"Is this leading somewhere, m'lord?"

"Aye, it is, and I'm glad you worked that out. It shows you possess a keen mind." He sipped his wine before casting his gaze around. "Where are those drinks I called for?" He looked at Ludwig and lowered his voice. "Here's a little piece of advice for you, my lad—ensure you hire competent servants. It'll make your life so much easier."

"Understood."

"Now, where was I? Oh yes. I need you to return to Verfeld and build it back up to the power it used to be."

"M'lord?"

"Your father was a loyal subject but terrible at running a barony. I'm hoping you'll be more successful."

"I shall do my best," said Ludwig.

"That's the spirit!"

"Is there anything, in particular, you're looking for?"

"Yes, more warriors. The army of Hadenfeld isn't what it once was, and I fear Neuhafen might seek to take advantage of that."

"Any particular types we're short of?"

The king sat back. "I can see your time in the north was well spent. We need everything: footmen, archers, and horsemen, but the latter would soon bankrupt you. Have you bowmen at Verfeld?"

"We didn't when I left, but I suppose my father might've hired some."

"Unlikely. He was always careful with his coins, and as for Berthold…"

"Berthold? You mean my stepbrother?"

"Yes. He's been in charge in your absence. Did you not know?"

"I assumed Kasper Piltz was running things."

"Ah, then you haven't heard. Piltz succumbed to the same fever as your father, along with half the garrison. I'm afraid you'll be rebuilding Verfeld from the ground up as far as people go."

Ludwig fought to keep from panicking.

"Is there anyone to help you?" asked the king.

"I returned to Hadenfeld with two comrades, m'lord, both of them warriors."

"Then you have a good start, at least as far as soldiers are concerned. I suggest you look for a new castellan as soon as possible. That will free you up to work on raising your army."

"Yes, m'lord."

The door opened, admitting an old man bearing a tankard and a clay jug. These he set down before his lord and master, then exited the room.

Otto shook his head and poured the wine. "See what I mean? They're all like that."

"But you are the king."

"You would think that would make a difference, wouldn't you, but all they see these days is an old man worn away to practically nothing."

Otto lifted his cup. "Now, let's have that toast, shall we? What was her name?"

"Charlaine," said Ludwig. "Charlaine deShandria."

"Then here's to the woman who made you into the fine fellow who sits before me this day!"

Ludwig shut the door behind him. "That was certainly not what I expected."

Lord Merrick looked up in surprise. "Oh? In what way?"

"I expected someone much more bombastic. His reputation makes him out to be so."

"He must like you. When I was sworn in as baron, he scowled the entire time."

"Likely due to the ceremony's expense."

"I beg your pardon?"

"Nothing, I was just thinking out loud." Ludwig looked around the room. "Where is Lady Gita?"

"She's arranging things with the Royal Chamberlain."

"What things?"

"Well, your investiture, for a start. They don't organize themselves."

"Doesn't the king have some say in that?"

"And you believe Otto is going to deal with the details?"

"I concede the point."

"Ah," said Lord Merrick. "I hear footsteps. Perhaps that's her now?"

They waited as footfalls approached, and then the door opened to reveal the baroness. "I see you're back, Lord Ludwig."

"I am, my lady. Have you news for me?"

"Yes. Your ceremony is slated for the day after tomorrow. After that, you'll be free to return to Verfeld."

"That's when the actual work begins," added Merrick. "Have you any experience with running a barony?"

"A little," said Ludwig. "My father sometimes had me collect the tithes."

"And did he ever let you see the accounts?"

"He did, which is how I discovered my stepbrother was skimming."

"And where is the fellow now?"

"Still in Verfeld, as far as I know. And that's what worries me."

"How so?" asked Merrick.

"The king told me Berthold was running the barony in my absence. I can only imagine the state he's left it in."

"Come now," said Gita. "We must give him the benefit of the doubt, surely? He is, after all, a loyal subject of the Crown."

"Actually," said Ludwig, "he's from Reinwick, and as far as I know, he's shown no inclination to do anything that didn't benefit him first."

"Then there you have it. He'd have no choice but to look after things, else his standard of living would be affected."

"I would like to believe you, but I won't know until I return home."

"You must have faith," said Gita.

"Will you two join me in travelling to Verfeld Keep?"

"I'm afraid we can't," said Merrick. "We have business to attend to back in Drakenfeld, but we'll visit as soon as we're able."

"I greatly appreciate all you've done for me. I promise you, someday I'll return the favour."

"You're not rid of us yet," said Lady Gita. "There's still the matter of your little ceremony."

"Yes," added Merrick, "and we'll share the road home for a few days. Now, let us go and celebrate your coming elevation into the ranks of the nobility."

4

MALBURG

WINTER 1095 SR

"This," said Sigwulf, "is supposed to be the best place in all of Malburg to find lodgings."

Cyn stood there, taking in their surroundings. The place was packed this late in the afternoon, likely a common occurrence during the winter months. "What did you say they called this inn?"

"The Willow."

"The people of this city must be well-off indeed to frequent such an establishment. Are you sure we can afford it?"

"The funds are there to be used; why not spend them? After all, once Ludwig arrives, we'll be living at the keep, which won't cost us anything."

"Well," she mused, "I always wanted to sleep in a proper bed."

"You slept in a bed back in Drakenfeld."

"Yes, but you weren't in it with me."

"I can't help it if the baroness put us in separate rooms." He took her hand, pushing his way through the crowd. Eventually, he found a serving girl. "Who do we talk to about getting a room?"

"I can help you," she replied. "My father owns the place."

"We need one big enough for two," added Sigwulf.

"For how long?"

"A week at least, possibly more."

"And you can pay?"

"Do you think I would ask if I couldn't?"

The girl placed her hands on her hips. "You wouldn't be the first one to try to bluff their way into a room for a simple tryst."

"Tryst? I'll have you know this is my wife!"

"My apologies, sir, but I must still see your coins if I am to hand over a key."

He brought out his pouch and spilled some coins into his hand. "Satisfied?"

"Come this way," she said, deftly weaving through the crowd.

Sigwulf was big, likely the tallest one in the room, but even he found his progress slow.

The girl said something to the man behind the bar, who then handed her a key. She led them upstairs, where she handed it off to Sigwulf. "Your room is the last one on the left. We serve breakfast at sunup, and dinner is available as long as it lasts."

"Whatever do you mean?" asked Sigwulf.

"We cook one pot of food. Come late, and you risk none being left. Understood?"

"Yes, of course."

The girl sized up the mercenary. "And you only get one bowl; is that clear?"

He nodded, then watched her descend into the madness below. Cyn took the key from him and made her way down to the door.

"Remember now," she chided, mimicking the girl's voice, "only one bowl for you!"

She opened the door and then stepped into the room. Sigwulf hurried to catch up, but by the time he was at the door, she had already thrown herself onto the bed.

"Now," he said, "this is something I could get used to."

Her eyes met his. "Close that door and get over here. I feel like a good ravaging!" He shut the door in record time.

Sigwulf opened the shutters, gazing out at the city, the early morning sun warming his face. Behind him, Cyn stirred, then moments later, her arms encircled his waist.

"The day promises to be splendid," he said, turning to face her. "We should get to work."

"In a moment. I'm still getting used to being your wife."

"I had to tell her something. You heard what she said."

"I like the thought of being your wife." She smiled, then quickly added, "Not that we necessarily need a ceremony or anything."

"Then wife you shall be. There must be a Holy Father in town. We can see to it right away if you like."

"Oh, Siggy, I didn't mean I wanted a ceremony. The last place I want to be right now is at a temple."

"You don't want a ceremony?"

"Who would we invite? It's not as if we have family here in Verfeld."

"We have Ludwig. Wouldn't you consider him family?"

"It's not the same thing. Let's face it, a wedding is just an occasion for family and friends to gather, but there's just the two of us now."

"Then why all this fuss about being married?"

"We're about to be in service to a noble," she replied. "We should at least present ourselves as a married couple, don't you think?"

"Nonsense. We're talking about Ludwig, not some high-born idiot with too much time on his hands. I'm more than happy to consider you my wife if that's what you truly desire."

She threw her arms around his neck and hugged him. "Thank you, Siggy. That means a lot to me."

"Now, where should we begin our search for information?"

"The Willow is nice, but we need to find someplace more... common."

"I'm not sure I follow."

"It's simple," said Cyn. "If you want to know what's happening in town, start with the merchants. They hold the keys to the general mood of the place."

"Sounds good. What type of merchant are we looking for?"

"A dressmaker."

"And they'll have information about Verfeld?"

"No, but they'll be able to make me a dress, and I'm going to need one if we're to stay at the keep." She paused a moment. "On second thought, I think it's a perfect place to start."

"Because of your dress?"

"No. Don't you see? A woman has to remain at a dressmaker's for some time to be fitted and measured. It's the perfect place to exchange gossip."

"And what am I to do while you're being fitted?"

"I would suggest you find a weapon smith or an armourer. Remember, we still have to identify who made that mail we took off those bandits."

"It would be a little obvious, carrying around chainmail shirts all day."

"Then take a sword instead. You might even find the actual smith who forged them."

"Very well, but let's eat something first." He grinned. "I worked up an appetite this morning."

. . .

Dressed in her armour, Cyn stepped into the shop. The patrons all stopped what they were doing, the better to stare at the strange attire of the new arrival.

"Can I help you?" said an older woman.

"Yes. I'm here to purchase a dress."

"For yourself?"

Cyn looked behind her, but no one else was present. "Yes. I'm to be the baron's guest."

A look of disapproval crossed the proprietor's face. "We don't deal with that kind of woman here."

"How would you know what kind of woman he associates with? He has yet to arrive."

"Don't be ridiculous. He took over when Lord Frederick died."

"Ah," said Cyn. "Now I understand the confusion. You're referring to Lord Berthold."

"Of course. Who else would we be referring to?"

"Lord Ludwig."

"Lord Ludwig? But he ran off, didn't he?"

"That may be, but he's back now. Well, I say back, but he went to the capital to meet the king first."

The woman moved closer, taking an intense interest in the mercenary. "And you say he's returning?"

"Indeed," Cyn replied.

"Where are my manners? My name is Romina Straub, and this is my shop.

"Pleased to meet you. And the rest of you are?"

"Miri," replied the taller blonde, "and this is Zira and Lenka. Did you travel with His Lordship?"

"Aye, I did, as well as my husband, but he is otherwise engaged." She paused a moment. "I assume Lord Berthold is not well-liked?"

"Far be it for me to comment on the ways of nobility," said Romina, "but he's known to have certain... predilections."

"Let me guess—loose women?"

"Along with copious amounts of drink, yes."

"Not only that," added Lenka, "but he likes to throw his weight around."

"Never mind that," said Romina. "This woman..."

"Cynthia, Cynthia Hoffman, but you can call me Cyn."

"Cynthia is clearly in need of a decent dress. Now then, what do we know about Lord Ludwig?"

"I'm not sure I understand what you're asking?"

"You are dressing to impress him, are you not?"

"No, not at all. I want something more befitting castle life."

"You'll be staying at the keep, then?"

"Eventually, but for the moment, my husband and I are at the Willow."

"A fine establishment," said Romina. "Now, let me think." She moved across the room to examine several bolts of cloth. "You'll need something warm. I hear keeps like Verfeld can get cold, especially this time of year. I would also suggest some nice thick footwear. What colour do you prefer?"

"I don't know that I've ever given it much consideration. What do you think would suit me best?"

Romina grabbed two bundles of cloth and came closer, holding them up to Cyn's hair. "Ordinarily, I would recommend blue for someone with your colouring, but I'd go for the green in this case. It matches your eyes."

"My eyes are brown."

"Yes, but there are flecks of green here and there, subtle yet unmistakable up close. Yes, I think the green material would work best. Of course, the final decision is entirely up to you."

"Green sounds fine to me."

"Good. Now, let's talk about the design, shall we?"

Sigwulf halted as the sound of a hammer striking an anvil caught his attention. He waited for it to repeat, then struck off, soon finding himself on a road full of artisans of various types. Several hawkers noticed his arrival and quickly directed their efforts to securing his business.

"I'm looking for a swordsmith," he called out. "Are there any hereabouts?"

"There are two," replied an intimidating man with a scar on his face. "Just past that bend in the road, you'll find the smithy of a fellow named Eckhart."

"And the second?"

"A master swordsmith, Tomas deShandria. His place is half a block farther down the street."

"deShandria? I know that name."

"Not surprising. His reputation is known far and wide."

"Thank you. You've been most accommodating."

"When you're done at the smithy, why don't you come back and let me make you some decent boots?"

"I shall certainly consider it." Sigwulf continued on his way, his thoughts weighing over this unexpected turn of events. deShandria was an odd name; what was the likelihood of more than one of them in Malburg?

. . .

He arrived at the second smithy to find an older man working inside, the door left open to allow the cool winter air to circulate through the place.

Sigwulf stepped inside. "Excuse me. Are you Tomas deShandria?"

The grey-haired man who turned was tanned, but there was no mistaking the strength in his arms. "I am. Have you come seeking a sword? If so, I must disappoint you."

"Are you not a sword maker?"

"I am, but I'm afraid I've far too many commissions. Unless, of course, you're willing to wait a few weeks?"

"As it happens, I'm here on other business."

"Oh? And what might that be?"

Sigwulf drew forth a sword and turned the blade, offering it to the smith hilt first. "I recently came into possession of this. I wonder if you could tell me who made it?"

Tomas took the weapon, inspecting it. "It's certainly not one of mine. I would never make something of such poor quality."

"Poor? I would've said otherwise?"

"It's usable, I admit, but the balance is off." The smith moved to a work table and lifted a sword, offering it up. "Try this, and you'll see what I mean."

Sigwulf took the blade, swinging it around experimentally. "It's a fine piece of work, but I fear its cost would be too much for my meagre purse."

Tomas looked once more at the sword his visitor brought with him. "I need to remove the handle and examine the maker's mark. I hope you don't mind?"

"Not at all."

The smith cleared the table and began removing the pommel. "Some smiths put their mark on the blade itself, a technique going back centuries, but in these parts, the custom is to place it on the tang—the piece of metal sitting beneath the grip."

"I know full well what a tang is," said Sigwulf, "but I must admit to some curiosity why it would be hidden."

"There are various reasons, foremost being the desire to remain hidden to casual inspection."

"Why would a smith desire that?"

"Typically to avoid someone finding out they are supplying weapons to less-desirable people."

"Then why mark them at all?"

"Most smiths guilds require it. A swordsmith who's blacklisted by the guild would soon find themselves without work." Thomas paused a moment. "Ah, here we are." He removed the handle, then carried the now exposed tang over to a window, the better to examine it. "Here it is."

"Do you know the mark?"

"I do, in fact." He turned to his visitor, the weapon still held in his hand. "Might I inquire how you came to possess this?"

"A few bandits attacked us, and one of them used that sword."

Tomas moved closer, holding up the weapon for Sigwulf to inspect. "If you look closely, you'll see a stylized letter N with a line through its middle."

"Yes. It looks like an ancient rune of some type."

"If it is, it has done little for the one who used it."

"Is the smith from Malburg?"

"No, but he's not too far away. Goes by the name Nadan Warling, and he works for the baron."

"Are you sure?"

"There can be little doubt. The guild keeps a catalogue of all the various smiths' marks. I hate to say it, but if someone with that sword attacked you, he's likely in service to the barony; not that it surprises me."

"I beg your pardon?"

"I'm sorry. I shouldn't let my personal feelings interfere with your quest for knowledge."

"Clearly, you don't like the baron. Is that because of your daughter?"

The smith was instantly alert. "What do you know of Charlaine?"

"I mean no trouble for you, Master Tomas. I swear."

"Yet you know my daughter?"

"I know OF her, yes."

"How?"

"I am well-acquainted with Lord Ludwig Altenburg, and he is still very much in love with her."

A tear came to the old man's eyes. "And is she well?"

"I'm afraid I can't say. I understand she's a Temple Knight now, but I never met her myself. What can you tell me of the actual story concerning her and Ludwig?"

"They were in love, but Lord Frederick forbade them to see each other. They were planning to run away together when his men intervened. She agreed to join the Church to save her family… her mother and me, from the baron's wrath."

"That explains so much," said Sigwulf.

"And now you say that Lord Ludwig is back?"

"Not yet, but within a week, barring any other interruptions. Can you tell me anything of Verfeld Keep and those in charge?"

"It is currently in the hands of Lord Berthold, who I believe is Ludwig's stepbrother."

"Have you had reason to interact with him?"

"Unfortunately, yes. He still owes me for a sword he commissioned."

"I imagine he's waiting for it to be completed."

"I delivered it to him more than a fortnight ago, yet I've seen nothing of payment." Tomas paused a moment before continuing. "I suppose I should've seen it coming."

"Why do you say that?"

"He's been running up debts."

"If that's true, why don't people refuse to serve him?"

"And risk incurring the wrath of a baron? He may not run this town, but that doesn't stop him from wielding tremendous influence. Why, one word from him, and Malburg could lose its status as a free city."

"And so the merchants must simply submit to this outrageous behaviour?"

Tomas shrugged. "What choice have we?"

"Listen," said Sigwulf. "I know Ludwig is a man of honour. I'm sure he'll honour Berthold's debts."

"I hope it's so, but I hear the barony has fallen on hard times. The fever was devastating due to the close confines of the keep."

"Did any in Malburg fall sick?"

"Thankfully, no, but then again, we took precautions against such an affliction as soon as we heard of it. Fortunately, it's all over now, but as I said, the baron's people suffered greatly."

"Do you know if this smith, Nadan Warling, survived?"

"I believe so. His dues are all paid up."

"Dues?"

"Yes, to the guild."

"Thank you, Master Tomas."

"I'm glad I could be of assistance. Might I ask your name?"

"Sigwulf. I'm a mercenary by trade, although lately, I've been acting more as a bodyguard for Lord Ludwig."

"In that case, I wish you well, Master Sigwulf. Perhaps one day you'll seek a commission of your own?"

"I should like that very much, Master Tomas, but I doubt I could afford your rates." He turned to the smith's work in progress. "Might I ask you a final question?"

"Most assuredly."

"Your name, deShandria—it's rather a unique form."

"It's Calabrian: a nation that lies on the coast of the Shimmering Sea. The original form was Shandria, but the honorific was added to recognize my service to the queen."

"Then you are more properly addressed as 'Lord'."

"No," said Tomas. "Not since we fled from there. Such titles are meaningless here, and in any case, a queen no longer sits upon the throne of Calabria. It's all Halvarian territory now."

"And yet you were a lord once. You impress me, Master Tomas. I hope we meet again. I would very much like to hear the rest of your story."

"I'm always here, at my smithy, should you choose to find me."

"Tomas?" a woman's voice called out. "Who are you talking to?"

"A customer," the smith replied. "My apologies, Sigwulf. My wife takes an interest in all that I do."

"No apologies are necessary. Now I must be off before my own takes exception to my absence."

5

AN OLD FRIEND

WINTER 1095 SR

L udwig shuffled his feet. "These shoes are terribly uncomfortable. Can't I wear my boots?"

"I'm afraid not," said Merrick. "It's tradition, as are the robes."

"Fear not," added Lady Gita. "Once the ceremony is complete, you can change back into your everyday clothes—including your boots."

A nearby guard struck the butt of his spear on the stone floor. "They are ready, my lord."

Lord Merrick approached the door, grasping its handle before taking one last look at his companion. "All set?"

"I'm as ready as I'll ever be," replied Ludwig.

The door opened, revealing a great hall packed with those here to witness the rare ceremony. Merrick held out his arm, Lady Gita grasping it tenderly, and then they advanced into the room, moving gracefully.

Ludwig followed behind them, maintaining a respectful distance. He kept his gaze forward, but out of the corner of his eye, he spotted a riot of blues and yellows, the typical trappings of the wealthy and powerful of Hadenfeld. Blue was considered the royal colour, but he hadn't expected so much of it. Yellow, on the other hand, was traditionally used to display wealth. If this crowd were any indication, anyone of means was present. The procession in front of him halted.

"Who comes here this day?" boomed out the voice of the king.

"Lord Merrick and Lady Gita of Drakewell, Your Majesty. We come seeking royal recognition of Ludwig Altenburg, son of Frederick Altenburg, late Baron of Verfeld."

"And who here pays witness to this event?"

"I do," came a deep, rich voice, echoing off the walls. "Lord Morgan Bahn, Baron of Grienwald."

"Come forward, Ludwig, that we may see your face."

Merrick and Gita moved aside, allowing the new inductee to advance. Ludwig's pulse quickened, his head swam, and suddenly, the cloak clasp felt like it was constricting his ability to breathe. He closed his eyes for a moment and took a deep breath. When he opened them, King Otto stared back at him, then winked.

"It is I, Ludwig Altenburg, m'lord."

The king grinned, clearly pleased with his reply. "Come closer, that you may receive what is due."

Ludwig advanced to within two paces, then dropped to one knee and bowed his head.

"Be it known to all here that by our decree, Ludwig, son of Frederick, of the house of Altenburg, is hereby recognized as the just and rightful heir of Verfeld. Are there any who would dispute this claim?" Otto's gaze swept over the crowd, but it was merely a formality. He nodded at Lord Morgan, who, bearing a golden circlet, advanced to stand behind Ludwig.

"Do you, Ludwig Altenburg," continued Otto, "promise to swear fealty to the rightful king of Hadenfeld? To defend the kingdom with honour and justice and uphold the king's laws?"

"I do so swear, m'lord."

Lord Morgan placed the circlet upon Ludwig's head. The king drew his sword, holding it out before him, blade down, close to the floor. Ludwig reached out, lifting the tip to kiss the weapon as the ceremony required.

"I swear to faithfully serve the Crown until the end of my days, Your Majesty."

The king sheathed his sword before moving even closer, holding out both hands to raise Ludwig to a standing position. "I name you Lord Ludwig Altenburg, Baron of Verfeld." A brief embrace ended the ceremony, and then music began drifting towards them.

"There," said the king. "It is done. Now is the time for feasting."

"Congratulations," added Lord Morgan, "and welcome as the king's newest advisor."

"Advisor?" said Ludwig.

"Of course. You're a baron now. The only rank higher in Hadenfeld is that of King Otto himself."

"But I hardly have the experience for such things. What if my advice should prove foolish?"

"It's your place to suggest," said the king, "but my prerogative whether or not to follow." He grinned. "Now comes the hardest part of all."

"Which is?"

"Putting up with all the well-wishers." He nodded his head at something behind Ludwig, causing the new Baron of Verfeld to turn just in time to witness a mass of people flooding towards him.

"Don't let him get too wrapped up," the king said to Lord Morgan. "I shall expect you to keep an eye on him."

Morgan bowed. "I will do my best, Your Majesty."

The king departed, leaving Ludwig overwhelmed by unfamiliar faces. Introductions were rapid and numerous, and he soon lost track of who was whom. In response, he merely offered a general greeting to all without recourse to names. He was halfway around the room before he spotted a familiar face.

He broke out into a grin. "Brother Vernan?"

"Father Vernan, now."

"I thought you were going to Eidenburg?"

"I did, but my training was not nearly as difficult as I feared. I was already familiar with most of the ceremonies I needed to know."

"How did you come to be here?"

"They gave me a choice: either Hadenfeld or Talyria, and I seemed to recall there was unrest there. But what of you? Didn't you take up the life of a mercenary?"

"I did, but my heritage caught up with me. I'd decided to eventually return home, but while lingering in the Northern Kingdoms, I received word my father had fallen ill. I returned to Hadenfeld as quickly as I could but was too late to make my peace with him."

Father Vernan nodded. "It is often the case that men leave this mortal realm with unfinished business."

"I never had the opportunity to forgive him for what he did to me," said Ludwig, "and I fear that will haunt me for the remainder of my days."

"You did what you felt best. No one can fault you for that."

"And yet I do. Oh, I know he was an obstinate man, but now I find myself overwhelmed by the magnitude of my new duties as the baron. Had I paid more attention to his teachings, I would've been much better off. In some ways, I think I am beginning to understand him."

"You are struggling with your conscience; that much is clear, but this is not the place to discuss such things. It's time to celebrate. If you want to talk more, seek me out at the Temple of Saint Mathew."

"I shall, my friend. As soon as I can." Ludwig reached out, clasping the man's hand. "It was good to see you again."

"And I, you," the Holy Father replied.

. . .

Last night's feast was a blur. Ludwig ended up drinking far more than he originally intended, for people constantly made toasts in his name. As the celebration's guest of honour, he could hardly refuse to partake. A knocking finally drew him from his bed, and he staggered to his feet, his head still pounding.

"Who is it?" he called out.

"Father Vernan."

Ludwig opened the door to the Holy Father staring back at him. "Are you ill?" inquired the visitor.

"No, merely suffering from the excess of well-wishers."

"Ah. I'm familiar with the feeling."

"You are?"

"Of course. Taking Holy Orders does not preclude an occasional overindulgence of drink, although we try to limit such excesses."

"And do you have a cure for such an affliction?"

"Alas," said Father Vernan, "I wish I did, but I'm afraid those who partake of such are doomed to suffer the consequences."

"Scripture?"

"No, merely common sense, but I fear such knowledge is misnamed, for in my experience, it is not, in fact, common at all."

"Much as I'm glad to see you, is there a purpose for your visit other than to lecture me on my behaviour?"

"My apologies if I gave offence. It was not my intention to berate you. The truth is I came to offer my services."

"Why? Am I dying?"

The Holy Father chuckled. "I know you might feel like it, but no."

"Well then, come in and talk to me while I dress."

Father Vernan stepped into the room. "I see the king has kept you in fine comfort. Does he provide such quarters to all his guests?"

"I have no idea." Ludwig pulled on his tunic. "What are your lodgings like at the temple?"

"Rather sparse, if truth be told, but we do take an oath of poverty. Mind you, we're used to it."

"So you came to Hadenfeld to assume the duties of a Holy Father?"

"That was the original intention, but I've recently learned of an opening elsewhere. That's what I came here to speak with you about."

"Oh? You're leaving us so soon? Where is it you're going?"

"To Verfeld, if you'd allow it."

"Verfeld doesn't have a Holy Father. It never has, as far as I know."

"The Church would like to rectify that situation."

"What makes Verfeld so special?"

"If I'm being honest, nothing. My superiors have been attempting to place Holy Fathers in all the baronies of Hadenfeld. It's thought it would allow us more influence in the ways of King Otto's court."

"So Hadenfeld is suddenly important?"

"Not only Hadenfeld but all the Petty Kingdoms. Not that I'm trying to imply your own lands are not important, you understand."

"And so the Church coincidentally assigned you to Verfeld?"

"Well," said Father Vernan, "I might have done some negotiating. They originally slated me for Luwen, but I suggested my familiarity with the new baron could be used to our advantage, provided you were in agreement, of course."

"And when did you arrange all this?"

"Only this morning. My superiors here were more than willing to make adjustments."

"Does that mean they were going to send someone else originally?"

"It does. A rather stern fellow named Father Calper."

"So it means I am stuck with a Holy Father, regardless?"

Father Vernan blushed. "Yes, I suppose it does."

"Well, if I am to be burdened with such a visitor, I would prefer it be one I am familiar with." Ludwig winked, then laughed. "You're welcome to join me at Verfeld Keep." He was about to say more when a thought struck him. "Say, did your training include any knowledge of finances?"

"Most definitely. As a Holy Father, we're trained to run a Temple."

"I may require your services in running the barony. I hear our old castellan is dead."

"I'm pleased to help in any way I can, but I'm hardly in a position to oversee an entire barony."

"It would only be temporary until I found a suitable replacement."

"Then I shall do all I can to assist. Might I ask when you intend to return?"

"Shortly. I don't want to be stuck here all winter."

"I am ready to travel at a moment's notice."

"Good, then inform your superiors I accept your placement as the baron's spiritual advisor, or whatever it is they call you. We shall leave once I've had a chance to talk to Lord Merrick. He and his wife will accompany us part of the way. I'll send word to the temple when we're ready to depart."

"Excellent. Anything else I can do?"

"Yes. The next time we're in Harlingen, remind me not to drink so much."

Father Vernan laughed. "I shall do my best, but I'm your advisor, not your keeper."

. . .

They set out early in the morning, the crisp air a pleasant change from the cloying stench of the city. The snow-clogged road slowed their progress as they made their way north.

"We should've left earlier," grumbled Lord Merrick. "I doubt the weather will improve much in the coming days."

"There's nothing we can do about it now." Ludwig gazed at the mounted warriors in the lead. "Thankfully, we have your soldiers with us, else we might soon find ourselves off the road."

"Are you sure I can't lend you some men? I hate the idea of you and the Holy Father travelling to Verfeld without an escort."

"Don't worry. I shall meet up with my friends in Malburg."

"I wish you the joy of it, but I fear we shall not be able to visit you till next summer." He drew his horse closer, lowering his voice. "It's Gita, you see. She's having a difficult time of it."

"Her pregnancy?"

"Aye, it's taking its toll. She's never been the healthiest of women, and I suspect this child will be our only one."

"You fear for her life?"

Lord Merrick glanced at his wife. "I pray she'll survive the birth, but I would never risk another such attempt. Better to have her alive than lose her trying to produce an heir."

"And if this one is a girl?"

Merrick forced a smile. "I've got relatives who would lay claim to the barony, have no fear. Who knows? Perhaps you'll get married and produce a son, then we could unite our two houses."

"Steady now," said Ludwig. "I've no desires on that matter at present."

"Still, you must give it some consideration." Merrick glanced once more at his wife. "I think Gita is disappointed you didn't find time to meet any of her friends."

"It couldn't be helped, not with winter firmly at our door."

"Knowing my wife, it's safe to say you'll have letters aplenty come spring."

"Letters?"

"Certainly. It's the accepted way for young ladies to introduce themselves. Surely you had some in your youth?"

"I'm afraid I would never have acknowledged such things in my youth. I was far more concerned with sampling the local hospitality."

"And now?"

"I have matured a great deal."

"Was the war up north responsible?"

"To a certain extent, yes, but the love of a good woman set me on the path."

"She must have been special indeed. Was she a noble?"

"Only of spirit," said Ludwig.

"This doesn't mean you've sworn off women in general, does it?"

"I've tasted the fruit of love. How then, could I accept anything less pure?"

"You'll change your mind in time, I'm sure. And anyway, who says there isn't someone else out there?"

"My father did remarry by the king's order."

"And was he happy?"

"I believe so, although I was bitter about it."

"Were you close to your mother?"

"I was," said Ludwig. "Her death was a great blow to me."

"And your stepmother?"

"I was resistant to her initially but came to appreciate her in time. I only wish I'd taken the opportunity to get to know her better."

"Life is full of regrets."

"Do you regret marrying Lady Gita?"

"Saints, no. That's one of the best decisions I ever made."

"How did you two meet?"

"The king's niece introduced us."

"So your marriage was arranged?"

"Is it so hard to believe an arranged marriage can be happy?"

"I am not opposed to the concept, but my spirit rebels at the idea that I am not free to make my own choices in life."

"We are all victims of our circumstances. Barons we may be, but we are as limited in our choices as the lowest landholders, perhaps even more so."

"Weren't you trying to cheer me up?"

"You have a Holy Father to do that." Grinning, Merrick looked over his shoulder at the carriage that held Father Vernan and Lady Gita. They were both bundled up against the cold in thick cloaks. "How is it you know the fellow?"

"I met him in Erlingen," replied Ludwig. "He helped me in my first and only tournament."

"You competed in a tournament? You must tell me all about it sometime when we have a warm fire and plenty of ale to wash it down with. What other secrets are you hiding?"

"None, I can assure you."

. . .

They arrived at the fork in the road late the next day. Lord Merrick's group headed northwest while Ludwig and Father Vernan took the Malburg road to the northeast. The land here was flat, the Grosslach Hills lying off in the distance to their north. On the third day, a cold spell slowed them as they spent the bulk of the morning huddled around a campfire. They continued on their way and towards evening, reached a roadside inn, taking comfort in its warmth.

A light dusting of snow accompanied their travels for the next two days until they entered the outskirts of the Barony of Verfeld. Ludwig paused as they topped a rise, taking in the distant buildings of the city.

"There it is," he said. "The free city of Malburg."

"And the keep?"

"It lies to the east. On a clear day, you'd be able to see the top of it, but the Saints haven't seen fit to bless us with that today."

"The Saints don't control the weather," said Father Vernan. "They were real men and women, not gods."

"Yet we worship them as such."

"Some might, but it's certainly not the Church's position to do so."

"Then why worship them at all?"

"Because their wisdom guides us. Their words are like a lamp, leading us along our path throughout our lives."

"Controlling us?"

"Does a parent control when they offer their wisdom to a child? Advice is given freely. It's up to the individual to decide whether or not to heed it."

"You've given me much to think on."

"You're more mature than the last time we met. Your experiences served you well. Could it be you've also developed a taste of faith?"

"I've seen a lot since then. I might tease you on the matter, Father, but I've come to believe there's much to be learned from the Saints." Ludwig waited a moment before continuing. "Now, having admitted that, if you repeat it to anyone, I shall deny it."

Vernan laughed. "So be it!"

6

THE SMITHY
WINTER 1095 SR

"Malburg is bigger than I thought it would be," said Father Vernan as he pushed his way through the crowded streets. "How are we ever to find your friends?"

"If I know Cyn and Sig, they'll be at a tavern somewhere."

"How many taverns are there?"

"At least a dozen, but don't worry, I know them all." Ludwig slowed his horse and waved. "Then again, we may not even have to do that. There's Sig now."

There was no missing the huge man, for he was a head taller than everyone around him. It didn't take long for him to spot his friend.

"Ludwig," Siggy called out as he pushed through the crowd, Cyn by his side.

"What's this, now?" said Cyn. "Collecting Holy Brothers, are we?"

"That's Holy Father," corrected Vernan.

"Good to see you again, Father. What brings you to Malburg?"

"My horse."

"He has your sense of humour, Cyn," said Ludwig.

"Some say it's my most endearing quality," said Vernan. "As it happens, you are looking at the new Holy Father of Verfeld Keep."

Sigwulf screwed up his face. "Verfeld has a Holy Father?"

"It does now," said Ludwig, "but it's not all bad news. Father Vernan has agreed to lend me a hand with the finances, at least for the short term. How about you two? Kept yourselves out of trouble, have you?"

"More or less, but out here in the open is not the right place to talk of such things."

"Shall we head inside?" asked Father Vernan.

"No," replied Ludwig. "I have some business to attend to first, then we'd best be off to Verfeld Keep. I'd like to arrive before dark."

"Business? What type of business?"

"I need to make amends."

"With whom?"

"Master Tomas deShandria. I fear my father wronged the poor fellow."

"I've met him," said Sigwulf. "Why don't you ride on, and Cyn and I will join you at his smithy? It'll give us time to get our horses and settle accounts."

"Good idea." His companions once more made their way through the crowded streets.

"Where is this smithy you seek?" asked Father Vernan.

"Down here," said Ludwig, urging his horse forward. "There are several smiths in Malburg, but deShandria is the only master swordsmith."

"And you have need of a sword?"

"No, but as I said, I must atone for my father's actions."

"What actions might those be?"

"My father threatened to ruin the man's business because I fell in love with the smith's daughter."

"Saints alive. What happened?"

"She agreed to join the Church and leave Malburg to spare them."

Father Vernan nodded. "That's why you left, isn't it?"

"It is. I only hope my father kept his word. I'd hate to find out he ruined the poor fellow."

"Ah, but he didn't."

"How could you possibly know that?"

"Simple. Your friend Sigwulf met the man. He could hardly have done that had he been driven away."

"I suppose that's true," said Ludwig. "When did you become so wise?"

"It's a prerequisite for joining the Church, or at least it ought to be. How much farther is this place?"

"There it is, up on the left." From inside came the sounds of hammering. "Looks like he's hard at work." Ludwig pushed open the door and stepped through. "Master Tomas?"

The hammering stopped, and the old man turned around. Ludwig was the taller of the two, yet somehow Tomas's presence filled the room.

"Master Ludwig," the smith said. "My condolences on the loss of your father."

"Thank you. I returned to assume my duties as Baron of Verfeld."

"As I would expect you to." His harsh words hung heavy in the air. "Have you come here on business? If not, I must ask you to leave, for I have many commissions requiring my attention."

"I came to apologize on behalf of my father."

"I find that hard to believe."

"You accuse me of lying?"

"I think you're ridden with guilt over how things transpired. Your father would never apologize for his actions, so your claim means nothing."

"You're right, of course, but I would settle our differences. I have no quarrel with you, Master Tomas: quite the reverse, actually. You are a man for whom I have great respect and admiration. I only wish there were a way for me to undo what my father did to you and your family."

Tomas stared at the floor, exhaling. "It is not you I should blame, but myself. I gave Charlaine the impression that love can conquer anything, including the gulf between commoner and noble. The truth is we are all victims of our social standing."

"But your family is noble."

"It was once, but such is no longer the case. Yes, we still use the old honorific, but it has little meaning these days. It is a lesson I should've taken to heart instead of giving my daughter thoughts of grandeur."

"Her name did not lead me to her; it was her spirit."

"A spirit that's now far from here, on the southern coast."

"You've heard from her?"

"Not directly, but I received a letter from a Dwarven smith by the name of Torek Stronghelm. He wrote me as a fellow guild member. It seems they assigned her to a commandery in Ilea."

"But you've had no word directly from her?"

Tomas shook his head. "Such messages are deemed unworthy of a Temple Knight. They encourage those who join the order to leave their past behind. I assume you've heard nothing further of her?"

"Sadly, no."

"Then we are united in our grief."

"I can't change the past," said Ludwig, "but I can make amends."

"In what way?"

"King Otto charged me with reinvigorating the army of Verfeld. I shall need arms and armour for such an undertaking."

"The guild will be pleased. I shall see if I can arrange a special price for you."

"Thank you," said Ludwig. "Although I've yet to assess the keep and see what our stocks look like."

"They will likely be low."

"Why? What have you heard?"

"It's no secret your stepbrother has reduced his garrison. I fear you'll have your work cut out for you."

"Wouldn't he have kept the armour and weapons when he dismissed the warriors?"

"No. He gifted them instead of pay—at least that's the rumour."

"A princely gift. That would easily pay them ten times over. It appears I'll keep the smiths of Malburg busy for some time."

"Send me a list of what you require, and I'll arrange things with the guild. Be warned, however, they'll demand payment in advance. Your stepbrother still owes several of them."

"Then I shall honour his debt."

Tomas nodded. "It is good to see you returned to us, Ludwig, but only time will tell if your arrival signals a change for the better."

"I understand, and I'll strive to make things right." Ludwig stepped from the smithy, a smile coming to his lips.

"Good news?" said Father Vernan.

"In a manner of speaking."

"Care to share, or is this only for the baron's ears?"

Ludwig climbed onto his horse. "It appears they sent Charlaine deShandria south to Ilea."

"Is that the woman you were in love with?"

"It is. And if truth be told, I don't think I'm over her."

"You're not considering going there yourself, are you?"

"No, I'm the baron now. My presence is required here, while she now belongs to the Temple Knights of Saint Agnes."

Father Vernan noticed two riders approaching. "It appears your friends have arrived."

"Well?" called out Sigwulf. "Did you see Master Tomas?"

"I did."

"And?"

"It appears we may be busy in the weeks to come."

"Busy, how?"

"Rumour has it Berthold reduced the garrison. He also reduced the keep's armoury by a significant degree."

"Meaning?"

"We shall likely require weapons and armour to equip our warriors."

"All of which costs coins," said Sigwulf.

"What about the barony's finances?" asked Cyn.

"Unknown," replied Ludwig. "But unless I miss my guess, we'll find a depleted treasury and my stepbrother living a life of luxury."

"Come now," said Father Vernan. "He can't be that bad?"

"We shall see," said Ludwig. "We shall see."

Ludwig looked forward to seeing his home as they rode through the city's streets. So engrossed was he that he almost ran over an old woman. He apologized profusely, then continued at a slower pace, determined not to repeat the offence.

"You're distracted," noted Sigwulf. "You haven't even asked what we found out in your absence."

"Sorry. What did you learn?"

"I took one of those captured swords to Master Tomas. I don't suppose you can guess what he discovered?"

"That the blade was foreign?"

"No, quite the opposite, in fact. It appears they bear the mark of a man named Nadan Warling. Does that name sound familiar?"

"Warling? He's the smith of Verfeld, or at least he was when I left."

"And still is, by all accounts."

"Are you suggesting that soldiers from Verfeld tried to kill me?"

"I'm not suggesting anything, merely presenting evidence."

Ludwig shook his head. "No, that must be a coincidence. Tomas said Berthold dismissed many men and let them keep their equipment. My stepbrother is a vain man, but I doubt he'd stoop to murder to achieve his ends."

"It would be dangerous to underestimate him."

"I agree, but I won't condemn him out of hand. He deserves an opportunity to explain himself."

"While he bankrupts your barony?"

"I understand your hesitancy, Sig, but we're not certain if that's due to greed or incompetence. I could be just as bad at handling the treasury, for all I know."

"I somehow doubt that, but you do make a compelling argument. However, you'll pardon me if I take a more pragmatic approach."

"Being?" said Ludwig.

"I'll be sure to keep a close eye on your stepbrother, and I think it prudent to look further into who he might have dealings with in town."

"A wise precaution. Did you find out anything else?"

"Cyn did," replied Sigwulf. He dropped back, allowing her to take his place.

"Well?" said Ludwig. "Are you going to tell me Berthold has sold the keep from under me?"

"No," she replied, "but he appears to have a taste for women and drink, some may even say to excess."

"I hate to say it, but that likely describes half the Continent's nobility."

"There's more," she cautioned.

"Go on."

"They say he's not above throwing his weight around."

"In that, I suppose he's not unlike my father."

"Lord Frederick pushed people around?"

"Oh yes. He threatened to run the deShandrias out of town to get rid of Charlaine. She joined the Church to save them."

"Well," continued Cyn, "it seems Berthold is following in Lord Frederick's footsteps. Not that he's driven anyone out of town or anything, but there are rumours he's been collecting... let's call them favours."

"What kind of favours?"

"Coins, mostly, although some goods have changed hands."

"But he has no jurisdiction here."

"That hasn't stopped him and his men from pressuring people. A free city Malburg might be, but that hardly protects the average commoner from a warrior's sword."

"So he's actually threatening the townsfolk?"

"It seems so, but I could only corroborate the stories through second-hand accounts. No one I talked to would speak of their own troubles, but it's clear they loathed even his name. How do you want to handle this?"

Ludwig brought his horse to a standstill. "I need to think this over carefully. If what you say is true, what kind of reception can I expect at Verfeld?"

"I doubt he'd try anything out in the open," suggested Sigwulf, "especially with us around."

"That doesn't preclude the possibility of poison," suggested Father Vernan.

They all looked at the Holy Man in surprise.

"What..." he said. "Can't I have an opinion?"

"I'm just shocked," said Ludwig. "I would've thought of all people, a Holy Father would preach fairness and trust."

"I may have taken Holy Vows, but that doesn't make me stupid. Berthold is clearly up to something, and your arrival will likely cause him to be nervous. We shouldn't discount that he might consider a more permanent solution."

"We don't know for sure he was behind the attack. Those men could be disgruntled former members of the garrison, hired on by Neuhafen."

"That still doesn't excuse his behaviour in Malburg or his use of threats against honest merchants."

"How well do you know the soldiers at Verfeld?" asked Cyn.

"Not well at all. More's the pity."

"But you saw them in your day-to-day life, surely?"

"I did," admitted Ludwig, "but I'm afraid I paid them little attention. The fact is they all looked alike to me, what with their armour and surcoats all the same."

"That's disappointing," said Sigwulf. "It means there's no one we can really trust amongst them."

"Hold on a moment," said Cyn. "What about the servants?"

"What about them?" asked Ludwig.

"How well do you know them?"

"Quite well. Why? What are you getting at?"

"Servants see everything. Talk to them, and you'll get a good idea of what's happening at the keep and who you can likely trust. What we need is a place to start. Is there one, in particular, you would trust above all others?"

"Yes," said Ludwig. "A man named Carson. He helped facilitate my escape, but I'm not sure if he survived the sickness that overtook Verfeld."

"Well," said Father Vernan, "at least it gives us somewhere to begin, but we must be careful not to tip off Berthold about our intentions."

"What are our intentions, precisely?" asked Sigwulf.

"To find out who we can trust amongst the guards," replied Ludwig. "I've got a feeling we're going to be dismissing more of them as time goes by, which means we'll need to recruit trustworthy men."

"Easy enough. We can recruit them in Malburg. The city's big enough."

"That will require a lot of training," warned Cyn. "Wouldn't it be better to hire professional warriors?"

"Too expensive, and we want people who are invested in the success of Verfeld, not sellswords who'll take off at the first signs of trouble."

"Hey now, did you forget we're sellswords ourselves?"

"Not anymore," said Sigwulf. "Now we're the sworn followers of Lord Ludwig."

"To tell you the truth," said Ludwig, "I don't know if I can even afford to pay you, considering what it sounds like Berthold's been up to."

"But you can feed us?"

"Certainly."

"Then that's all we need, at least for now."

"I have some funds, should we require them," said Father Vernan. "They gave me a stipend with which to establish my congregation."

"But those coins belong to the Church," replied Ludwig.

"True, but rebuilding the barony is good for the Church, and I've got absolute discretion to spend my allowance as I deem necessary. It won't purchase a new army for you, but it should at least see us through the winter."

"Thank you. I may take you up on that offer. Now, let's ride out to Verfeld and find out first-hand what my stepbrother has been up to."

Ludwig looked around the countryside as they left Malburg. "I must remember to make arrangements to visit the villages hereabouts, but only after I've had a chance to see the list of accounts."

"That will all take time," said Father Vernan. "Perhaps it's best not to rush things."

"You feel I should take a more measured approach?"

"I do. Barging in and making accusations would only put Berthold on the defensive. Better, I think, to earn his trust and then slowly make changes. As you suggested earlier, he might be incompetent or in the dark about how things are supposed to be done."

"You're defending him, now?"

"I still don't trust the fellow, but that doesn't necessarily mean he wishes you dead. Give him some leeway, and you may find he turns himself around."

"Or condemns himself," added Sigwulf.

"There is that possibility, which only adds to my argument. Should we begin by making accusations, he may bury the evidence."

"You think there are bodies?"

"No," continued Father Vernan, "but written records can be destroyed, coins hidden, that sort of thing. Has he ever done anything similar in the past?"

"He has," replied Ludwig. "Before I left, I discovered him collecting extra taxes from the tenants—without my father's approval, I might add."

"And was anything done about it?"

"Unfortunately, my father considered keeping peace within the family more important, so he did not return the funds."

"So it may have become a habit. I understand now why he might act the way he does."

"You're not excusing his behaviour, are you?"

"Not at all," replied Father Vernan. "There's a big difference between understanding and condoning. I merely meant to imply I can make sense of his habits. We are all products of how we are raised. What do you know of Berthold's life before he came to Hadenfeld?"

"He and his mother are from Reinwick, a duchy far to the north."

"And his father?"

"A noble of Reinwick, I believe. Why? Is that important?"

"There are different customs in the north. We also don't know how he was raised. Maybe he is merely emulating the behaviour of his father? The point is we don't truly understand the fellow, so we should not condemn him out of hand."

"You've given me a lot to think about," said Ludwig. "I shall try to keep an open mind going forward. Now, enough of this banter. Let's get to Verfeld and finally get to the bottom of all this."

7

VERFELD

WINTER 1095 SR

Verfeld Keep's rectangular design was similar to others in the Petty Kingdoms. The only entrance being on what many would consider the second floor, accessible by a set of stairs ending in a stone platform. With no drawbridge or portcullis for protection, a stout iron-reinforced door combined with the platform's small size at least made entry difficult. Should it prove necessary, oil or boiling water could be let loose from above.

Originally, one of the most significant advantages to Verfeld's defences was its location, for it offered little in the way of strategic value. However, since the founding of Neuhafen, it was now expected to guard the border.

A solitary warrior stood guard, leaning against the wall in a manner suggesting he'd been on duty for some time. As the horses approached, he straightened himself, opened the keep door, and gave a yell.

Ludwig remained in the saddle, stationary for now but curious about what kind of greeting he would receive. Beside him, Father Vernan looked on with interest, but a quick glance behind showed Cyn and Sigwulf were ready to draw weapons should the need arise.

The original guard, now reinforced by three colleagues, came down the steps, the shaft of his spear tightly gripped in his white-knuckled hands.

"Identify yourselves," he called out.

"I am Lord Ludwig Altenburg, Baron of Verfeld."

The guard halted, unsure how to proceed.

"Where is your master?" asked Ludwig.

"His Lordship is within the keep. Shall I fetch him?"

"If you would be so kind."

The man rushed back up the steps and into the keep, his associates keeping a wary eye on the newcomers.

"Not exactly what I was expecting," said Sigwulf. He noticed Cyn staring at the guards at the top of the stairs. "Something wrong?"

"I know that face," she said, nodding upwards. "That one with the moustache was amongst those who attacked us."

"Are you sure?" asked Ludwig.

"Absolutely. He's the one Siggy threw his sword at."

"Ah, yes," added Sigwulf. "I remember now. Shall I place him under arrest?"

"Not yet," replied Ludwig. "Let's not reveal what we know, at least not straight away."

"Are we then to sit here all day?"

"Well, I suppose we could dismount." Ludwig climbed out of the saddle, then waited as his fellow travellers did likewise.

"I'll take the horses," said Vernan, grabbing their reins. "I've got a feeling you lot might need some room to use your weapons."

Out of the keep came Berthold, dressed in a long, flowing robe, complete with gold embroidery on the sleeves—hardly clothes made for fighting. A dour expression settled upon his face as his gaze swept over the group.

"Ah, my dear brother, I see you've returned from the war in the north. Welcome."

Ludwig ascended the steps, his hand naturally resting on the hilt of his sword. Cyn and Sigwulf followed on either side, adopting a similar pose as they reached the top, then halted, leaving a few paces between them.

"Berthold," said Ludwig. "I trust you are well?"

"Why would I be anything but? I must admit your arrival here has taken me completely by surprise. A pleasant one, to be sure, but a surprise nonetheless." His gaze wandered over to Cyn and Sigwulf. "And who are these fine individuals?"

"This is Sigwulf Marhaven and Cynthia Hoffman, two warriors of my acquaintance."

"Warriors, you say? I hope you haven't come seeking revenge for some imagined slight?"

"Why would you suggest such a thing?"

Berthold put his hands out to either side, displaying a waist free of weapons. "Merely a jest, Brother. I didn't mean to alarm you." He noticed his breath hanging in the cool air. "You must be cold. Come inside, and we can warm ourselves by the fire while you tell me of your adventures in the north." He turned to his men. "Take their horses, and bring in what belongings they may have."

The warriors descended, then Father Vernan came up and joined them.

"What's this, now?" said Berthold. "Have you found religion all of a sudden?"

"This is Father Vernan of the Order of Saint Mathew," said Ludwig. "He's come to take over as Verfeld's spiritual advisor."

"Take over? Wouldn't that presume we had one for him to replace in the first place?" He met only a glare from his stepbrother. "Very well. Who am I to argue against the Church's inclusion? We shall gather in the great hall. You do remember the way, don't you?"

"Of course, I haven't been away that long."

Berthold turned and entered the keep without further conversation.

"Follow me," said Ludwig, "but remain alert."

They walked through a large hallway, past doors leading to the guard room and duty room. At the far end was the entrance to the pride of Verfeld Keep—the great hall itself."

"This is quite the place," noted Cyn.

"Indeed," added Father Vernan. "Although it's a little sparse in terms of decoration."

"It's chilly in here," said Sigwulf.

"Yes," agreed Ludwig. "Much more so than I remember." He glanced down at the floor as they walked. "There used to be more coverings, as the stone gets awfully cold this time of year."

"Here we are," announced Berthold. "Home at last. Please, make yourselves comfortable. I'll have someone gather you some food and drinks. You must be hungry."

"You're not staying?" asked Ludwig. "I've got so many questions."

"I shall return shortly, I promise, but I should see to your things first. I'm afraid we're not so flush in the way of servants these days." He abandoned the room, leaving the others alone.

"That was a strange welcome," noted Father Vernan. "Are you sure we can trust him?"

"Make up your mind," said Sigwulf. "One moment, you're telling us to give him the benefit of the doubt, the next, you're accusing him of plotting against us."

"Sorry. I should be more trusting."

Siggy took a seat while Cyn wandered around the room. "Nice place you've got here, but not exactly the warmest of rooms, is it?"

"It would help if the fire was lit," said Sigwulf.

In reply, she moved closer and put a few logs in the hearth.

"Well?" said Ludwig. "What do you make of the keep so far?"

"It's nice," replied Sigwulf. "I can see us spending a lot of time here in the great hall, providing we can warm it up."

Cyn retrieved a torch from a wall sconce and returned to the fire, holding it there until the flames took hold. A wave of warmth drifted towards Ludwig. "Ah, that's better."

"So this is your home," said Father Vernan. "I imagine you know every brick in the place?"

"I do. As a small child, I had free rein and got to know every nook and cranny."

"Anything, in particular, we should be aware of?" asked Sigwulf.

"Like what?"

"I don't know—secret passages?"

"None that I'm aware of. The keep is a very efficient layout. I doubt there's the room for something like that."

"How long ago was it built?"

"They built the foundation a hundred years ago or so."

"Or so?"

"Yes. I'm afraid I'm not well-versed when it comes to the keep's history. There are records, if it's something that interests you."

"Not right now, but I thank you for the offer."

Berthold finally returned, along with a trio of servants bearing trays. Ludwig recognized Carson but not the other two. He remained silent as they served the drinks, then each was given a platter loaded with cold meat and cheese.

"I trust this is to your liking?" asked Berthold.

"Yes, thank you. Come and join us. I'm eager to know what has transpired since last I was here." He waited until his stepbrother sat down. "How did Father get sick?"

"No one knows precisely. We suspect he caught something while visiting Freiburg, but there's no proof. Lord Frederick had it first, followed by two of the guards."

"And Lady Astrid?"

"I'm afraid she insisted on caring for Lord Frederick herself. I advised her to keep her distance, but she was adamant about his care."

"And yourself?"

"I'm still here, as you can plainly see."

"How did you avoid becoming sick?"

"I must confess that at the first mention of fever, I sought refuge in Malburg. Apparently, it worked, or I might've perished like the rest."

Father Vernan leaned forward. "Might I ask the symptoms of this fever?

The study of such things greatly interests me, you understand, purely from a professional point of view."

"You're a healer?"

"Well," said the Holy Father, "I know my way around the odd potion or two. I don't claim to be a physician, of course, or a Life Mage, for that matter, but helping the sick and injured is the calling of my order."

"The fever came on quickly and seemed to hang in the very air itself. Half the garrison was down within a week, along with a similar number of servants."

"Did any of those afflicted survive?"

"I'm afraid that most of those who took sick perished. The baron hung on for almost two weeks, but in the end, he was little more than skin and bones: a most horrid development."

"How would you know?" said Sigwulf. "Not to imply anything, but you mentioned you left for Malburg?"

"Yes," said Berthold. "That I freely admit, but I received regular updates. The baron had possibly the worst case of it. My mother nursed him as best she could, but in the end, it took her as well."

"What of the others?" asked Ludwig.

"Let's see," Berthold mused. "Almost a third of the garrison succumbed to the fever; the rest were spared."

"And amongst the servants?"

"Over half are no longer with us, but most of them fled after the initial outbreak, too scared to remain within these walls."

"Aside from the fever," asked Father Vernan, "what other symptoms were present?"

"An unquenchable thirst along with constant sweating. I'm told that they could keep nothing in their stomachs."

"Any sign of a rash or pustules?"

"None, I'm afraid."

"And in the end, it simply vanished?"

"It did," replied Berthold. "Although it didn't stop all at once. Some of the sick lingered on after the Baron's death, but there have been no new cases for over a month, else I'd still be in Malburg."

"How many of the garrison remain?"

"Eight."

Ludwig had a hard time believing the response. "How many?"

"Eight."

"But there were two dozen men here when I left?"

"Indeed," said Berthold, "but, much like the servants, some left rather than remain and risk the fever."

"And the armoury? Will I find it well-stocked?"

"Ah, I'm afraid I've bad news on that score. Some of the men took equipment with them when they deserted."

"So the rumours are true," said Ludwig. "We find ourselves with no armour and weapons to speak of and little in terms of men."

"The same can be said of the treasury."

"Any other information you'd care to share with me?"

"I wish I had something more hopeful to impart, but I'm afraid running a barony isn't something I was prepared for."

"Did you think to send word to the king and ask for help?"

"Ah," said Berthold. "That, you see, is why you were always better suited to running the place than I. I imagine things would've turned out differently had you been here. I did my best, of course, but I'm afraid it did little good. Now that you're back, you can start rebuilding from the ground up."

"I shall, starting with the garrison." Ludwig turned to Sigwulf and Cyn. "Which one of you wants to be the new guard captain?"

"Siggy," said Cyn. "The men will accept him."

"Very well," said Ludwig, "then I'll name you as his sergeant."

"Sergeant? Just like when I was a mercenary. What am I supposed to do here?"

"Help me train new warriors," said Sigwulf.

"Agreed," said Ludwig. "Although, you first need to assess those who remain. I want you to get started on it tomorrow morning. I'll also require an itemized list of what equipment we need to build the army back up."

"Build up the army?" said Berthold. "But you can't possibly do that? Where will the funds come from?"

"That's for me to decide. Father Vernan and I would like to see the keep's accounts, not to mention the strongbox that serves as the treasury. I trust you have those at hand?"

"They're not here in this room, if that's what you mean, but I shall go and fetch them."

"Excellent. Take Father Vernan with you. I'm sure he'd love to see how we run things. Father, if you would be so kind?"

"Certainly," said the Holy Father. Berthold's face fell, for he now realized the futility of trying to hide what he'd been up to. "Very well, this way."

"What now?" said Sigwulf.

"Now comes the fun part," said Ludwig. "At least for you two."

"Which is?"

"Go and find the guard who attacked us and throw him in the dungeon."

"You have a dungeon?"

"Well, there's only one cell, but yes, we have a place for prisoners."

"Anything else?"

"Yes. Lock your door tonight, just to be on the safe side."

"Very well."

"Hold on," said Cyn. "Where exactly is our room?"

Ludwig stood. "I'll show you right now, if you want. All the bedrooms are up on the top floor. It helps you get away from the stench of this place."

"Stench?" said Sigwulf.

"He means the smell of sweat and unwashed men," explained Cyn, "not to mention other bodily functions."

"I wish I hadn't asked."

After showing his friends their room, Ludwig made his way to the study. His father's desk was still here, leaving the illusion that he had stepped out for but a moment. No, that was wrong—now it was HIS desk.

Ludwig sat down, taking in his surroundings. Ink, quills, and papers littered the area that served as his workspace. Across the room, an arrow slit was shuttered against the cold of winter, but the day's chill still seeped through the cracks in the wood.

In his youth, this hadn't just been his father's study but his sanctum, a retreat from the duties of a baron. At least that was how he spoke of it. Would it now become Ludwig's escape? Somehow, he doubted it.

He wondered how many barons had sat here, but the door opening to his right interrupted him. Father Vernan entered, strongbox in hand, with a leather-bound book balanced atop.

"Is Berthold not with you?"

"Alas, no," replied the Holy Father. "He confessed to being exhausted and retired to his chambers. I made sure he gave me these, though." He placed the items on the desk and then extricated a small key from a chain around his neck. "He gave me this as well."

Ludwig moved the book aside and then turned the strongbox around, revealing the lock. "Now, let's see what lies within, shall we?" He unlocked it and lifted the top. Inside sat a small collection of coins of various denominations.

"How disappointing," noted Father Vernan. "It appears he has left you little with which to operate."

"I fear you have the right of it. Still, the book will give us a better idea of where we stand. Hopefully, he's seen fit to pay the servants, else we'll scarce have funds for food." He opened the book and flipped through the pages, seeking the last entries.

"Any luck?" prompted Father Vernan.

Ludwig frowned. "According to this, they're paid up till the end of the month, which gives us a week before we're required to hand over any more. We need to generate more funds, and we need to do it sooner than later."

"And the tenants' taxes?"

Ludwig scanned a few more pages. "They paid more than their fair share, and with midwinter approaching, I can't, in all reason, expect more out of them."

"Then we are looking at some lean times, my friend."

"So it would seem."

Father Vernan reached into his cassock and withdrew a purse, placing it before Ludwig. "You'd best take this to tide us over."

"I can't," said Ludwig. "It's not right."

"Yet it's freely given. Come now. You can always pay me back down the road."

"How much is in here?"

"More than enough to last out this cold weather."

Ludwig tipped the purse upside down, watching as gold crowns spilled forth. "The Church is most generous. This will restock our stores and then some."

"Glad to hear of it. I might suggest you put some aside to hire and equip your new guards while you're at it. You can't very well leave the place undefended."

"It's a pity the Church couldn't loan us a Temple Knight or two to help look after the place. I don't suppose you can suggest something of that nature to your superiors?"

"Come now," said Father Vernan. "Even I don't have that much influence."

8

THE PLOT

WINTER 1095 SR

That night, Ludwig slept with the strongbox beneath his bed. He awoke several times, afraid someone was creeping into his room to steal the newly restocked treasury, but morning dawned without the threat materializing.

He headed downstairs, locking his door behind him. Sigwulf and Cyn sat in the great hall, eating their breakfast, already dressed for the day.

"You look terrible," said Sigwulf. "Did you even sleep last night?"

"Not much. I was too worried about losing the coins Father Vernan loaned us. By the way, did you arrest that guard?"

"We did. He's rotting away in the dungeon. I was going to interrogate him after breakfast."

Ludwig turned to Cyn. "What are you up to today?"

"I planned to take stock of the armoury, then inspect the few guards we still have. Yourself?"

"I was considering riding out and visiting the landholders, but I might accompany you instead. I'm curious to see what my stepbrother left me to work with."

A servant entered the room. "Ah, you're awake, my lord. May I fetch you something to eat?"

"That would be wonderful, Carson." His gaze came to rest on Sigwulf's bowl. "What about some of that porridge?"

"Most surely, my lord."

"Hold on a moment. I'd like a word with you." Ludwig waved the servant over, then lowered his voice, well aware of how easily sound carried in the great hall. "Tell me, Carson, and be honest about it; what happened when my father died?"

"He was ill for quite some time, my lord. I hate to say it, but we all knew he wouldn't survive. Lady Astrid did her best to keep him in high spirits, but even she lost hope by the end. Of course, it didn't help that she herself caught the fever."

"I presume you laid him to rest in the family crypt?"

"Indeed. Your father wasn't the first to succumb to the fever, nor the last. I myself was stricken with it, but somehow I managed to survive."

"Any idea where it started?"

"Your father had just returned from the village of Freiburg when he came down with the chills. He retired to his room, and the fever soon followed."

"I understand many fell ill."

"You have the right of it, my lord. The truth is, we were hard-pressed to keep things running. It ravaged the kitchen staff, and those able fled, seeking safer pastures."

"I can't say I blame them. Might I ask when Lady Astrid passed?"

"Five days after your father, although she seemed to have more strength than he, particularly towards the end."

"So he wasted away?"

"That would be an accurate portrayal, yes."

"And where was my stepbrother during all of this?"

"In Malburg, my lord. He left the keep at the first sign of illness."

"Are you suggesting he had something to do with all this?"

"No, my lord, I would be the last person to cast aspersions. I merely meant it as a statement of fact. He announced his intention to go to Malburg as soon as he learned of your father's fever."

"So he fled," said Sigwulf. "That doesn't bode well for the man's reputation."

"That's no secret," said Ludwig. "He told me so himself. What I'm looking for is something connecting him with the illness."

"You're not suggesting he's responsible for making your father sick, are you?"

"Not directly, but I wonder if he wasn't aware of the fever in Freiburg to begin with. It wouldn't take much to convince my father to visit the place." Ludwig turned once more to Carson. "Did Berthold ever travel there?"

"To Freiburg? Most definitely, my lord, as he did the other villages. He would often undertake such journeys on behalf of the baron."

"For the collection of taxes?"

"I assume so."

"Thank you, Carson. You've been a great help."

"Shall I fetch your breakfast now, my lord?"

"Yes, by all means." Ludwig watched as the man left.

"Is it just me," mused Cyn, "or are you sounding unreasonably suspicious?"

"Because I'm considering the possibility Berthold was involved in my father's death?"

"His mother died too."

"True enough," said Ludwig, "but we also know at least one of the men from this garrison was involved in the attempt to kill me. How is this any different?"

"Think about what we know of the man," said Sigwulf.

"Which is?"

"He's a coward," said Cyn. "He runs at the first sign of trouble, or at least that's how it looks."

"Could it all be an act?" said Sigwulf.

"Are you suggesting he plotted this whole sickness? You give him too much credit. It would also mean he knew of the fever ahead of time. Wouldn't that risk him being exposed himself?"

The huge warrior gave it some thought before replying. "I hadn't considered that. I change my mind. I think you have the truth of it when you say the man's a coward."

"I can't say I agree," said Ludwig, "but I shall amend my estimation of the fellow."

"How so?"

"He's more of an opportunist. He doesn't want to risk being too close to danger; we know that from the fact that he fled to Malburg. We also know, or I should say suspect, he ordered his men to murder me. Once more, a task done at arm's length."

"Someone else could still be behind the attack," said Sigwulf. "We can't rule out Neuhafen just yet."

"Do you truly believe they could hire a Verfeld guard to carry out the attack? And even if they did, wouldn't his absence be noted? No, Berthold had some part in it; of that, I'm sure."

"But you still haven't ordered him arrested."

"I'm torn," said Ludwig. "He's the only family I have left, even if he is untrustworthy. I can't bring myself to simply lock the fellow up. I need more proof."

"Do you?" said Cyn. "You're the lord and master of Verfeld. You can arrest anyone you like."

"I cannot go down that road, or I'll be just as bad as he is."

"Then what is your plan?"

"The prisoner may yet yield information that would condemn my step-brother."

"It would help if you'd allow me to use more pressure," said Sigwulf.

"You mean torture?" said Ludwig. "No. That will accomplish nothing."

"It might loosen his tongue?"

"More likely he would simply tell us whatever he thinks we want to hear, whether it be true or not."

"Then what do we do with the fellow?"

"Keep him locked up for now. Perhaps in the fullness of time he will decide to reveal the name of his co-conspirators."

The armoury was housed in the keep's lowest level. Locked behind an iron gate, it was little more than a room full of weapon racks and armour stands. As Ludwig stood looking at the near-empty room, dismay threatened to overwhelm him. He unlocked the gate, and they made their way into the chamber.

"Where's all the armour?" asked Cyn.

"Good question," replied Ludwig. "All I see are assorted bits and pieces."

"There's a chain hauberk over here and a mail shirt, although neither is in usable condition."

"They're neglected. There's a rusted gauntlet but no corresponding match for the other hand. How are we fixed for weapons?"

Cyn moved closer to a weapon rack. "There are nearly two dozen spears over here that don't look too bad."

"That's it? Only two dozen? There should be close to a hundred."

"There are some tips on the shelves, but I see no shafts."

"How many tips?"

She took a moment to count them. "Twenty-seven, but most of them are starting to rust. Whoever was looking after this place neglected their duty. It looks like we've got a lot of work ahead of us."

"So it would seem."

"Might I ask how many men we're expected to field?"

"In theory, the barons of Hadenfeld were supposed to hold enough arms and armour to equip twenty warriors. In addition, we're to raise a local militia of one hundred souls. They, of course, are not required to be armoured but must at least have some sort of weapons."

"What about archers?"

"By Royal Decree, there should be twenty within our strength, but they would keep their bows at home instead of here."

"So you're saying you don't know how many you have?"

"That would be an accurate assessment, yes. There are records, of course, but I have yet to peruse them."

"Whose duty was it to look after all this?"

"Ultimately, the baron's, but it's usually delegated to the captain of the garrison."

"Who is?"

"A fellow by the name of Bardulf Schenke. At least it was the last time I was here. Since my return, I haven't seen him, so I suspect the fever got him, which makes it Sig's responsibility now."

"Where would you like us to start?" asked Cyn.

"What would be easiest?"

"I imagine it wouldn't be too hard to get some poles made up for these spearheads. As for the rest, we'll need to know exactly how many warriors your stepbrother left you with."

"Berthold said there were eight," replied Ludwig. "Although I suppose we should say seven since one of them is in the dungeon."

"It'll be less than that once we're done. You forget; three survivors fled the attack on the road, they're likely soldiers too."

"That puts us at five we can truly count on, but therein lies the problem. Which five? And even if we did know, that's barely enough to guard the front door, let alone defend the keep from an attack."

"It seems we may need to recruit sooner rather than later," suggested Cyn. "What about the militia? Can they be called up to serve?"

"Only in the event of invasion or war."

"Do the archers count as militia?"

"No," said Ludwig. "Most are farmers. We could use them for the short term, but they'll have to return to their farms during planting season. Come to think of it, they'd probably like the extra coins."

"How do we go about doing that?"

"We travel to each village and spread the word."

"Must you do that in person?"

"No. I could send you or Sig along with a written proclamation."

"Good. When do we start?"

"Tomorrow. I want to visit the villages to get a good idea of how they're doing. In the meantime, we'll gather up those spearheads. You can take them into Malburg and find someone to make the shafts."

"What about the current garrison?"

"Let's wait and see if Sig finds out anything from our prisoner."

. . .

By mid-morning, Ludwig was back at his desk, poring over documents related to his rights and obligations as a baron. It wouldn't be so bad had they been written in a straightforward and concise manner, but it seemed like anything coming out of Harlingen included an excess of elaborate words and little in the way of substance. He was trying to understand how long he could keep the militia under arms when Father Vernan arrived.

"I hope I'm not interrupting?"

"Not at all," replied Ludwig. "I could use a break. What can I do for you?"

"It's what I can do for you. I took it upon myself to chat with the servants."

"And?"

"They are delighted to see you back in Verfeld. I get the impression they were less than impressed with your stepbrother."

"He mistreated them?"

"Not so much mistreated as overused. He was particularly fond of having them wait on him hand and foot."

"Isn't that their duty?"

"It is, but as your stepbrother was never one to keep a schedule, meal preparation was difficult, and one might add, wasteful."

"How so?"

"Berthold demanded to be fed at odd times of the day or night. To satisfy his needs, they kept food constantly on the go. It's a wonder they didn't use up all the stores. By the way, I took the liberty of informing them we shall have meals at regular times from now on. I hope that's to your liking?"

"Yes, that's fine. Thank you."

Father Vernan looked down at all the papers. "Catching up on some light reading?"

"This collection of notes summarizes my responsibilities as baron, but the Saints alone know how I'm to make sense of them."

"Whatever do you mean?"

"There's no uniform list of duties. Rather, there are Royal Proclamations and letters sent over many years, which are often contradictory. For example"—he lifted a note—"this one informs me I am permitted to raise a force of twenty men-at-arms, yet this"—he stabbed down at another—"informs me I am not to exceed fifteen, else I might upset our Neuhafen neighbours."

"Are these missives dated?"

"Some," said Ludwig. "I would've thought it more prudent to allow a baron to raise whatever warriors he may, especially considering what King Otto himself told me. The problem is, his orders were verbal."

"Tell me, is Otto a man taken with rigid customs?"

"I don't know His Majesty well, but I'd say the opposite from all I heard. Why? You believe that makes a difference?"

"I think you must follow your heart. Were it not for this ponderous collection of papers, how would you proceed?"

"I would raise the number of soldiers commensurate with the income of the barony."

"Then you have your answer."

"And if the king disagrees?"

"Then he is more than capable of telling you so himself. You are one of only seven barons, Ludwig. He can't afford to get on your bad side. I understand the last time that happened, there was a rebellion."

"But he is my king."

"And you, one of his barons. People think of kings as these wealthy and influential individuals who are the most important part of a kingdom. But the truth is, the nobility runs the realm."

"I wish I'd paid more attention to my father's teachings."

"As do we all," said Father Vernan. "Then again, had I done so, I would never have become a Holy Father." He stared at Ludwig a moment, meeting his gaze. "Tell me, do you regret leaving Verfeld?"

"I'm torn. Part of me is glad I left, for it allowed me to find my true self."

"And the other part?"

"Deeply regrets not being here during my father's final days."

"There's a saying as old as the Saints," said Father Vernan. "We cannot undo the past."

"I understand that. I truly do, but when it comes to being baron, I feel so… unworthy."

"You're overwhelmed. Not surprising, considering the circumstances. You came here to visit your ill father only to find he'd passed. Then, to add to the pile, you're informed you will be the new baron, which you were woefully unprepared for."

Ludwig spread his arms out, indicating the pile of papers. "How do I handle all this?"

"Simple," said Father Vernan. He stepped forward and swept his arm across the table, knocking everything to the floor. He pointed at the notes littering the room. "Those do not a ruler make—it's the man inside. Follow your heart, Ludwig, and it will not lead you astray."

"And if I make a mistake?"

"You are Human. Of course you'll make mistakes, but you must learn to live with them. Remember, you are not alone in this. You have friends you can rely on. In the words of Saint Mathew, 'Share the burden, and the weight shall be lifted from your shoulders'."

Ludwig scanned the floor, taking in the mess. "You're right. These serve only to make me second-guess myself."

"There," said Father Vernan. "You've taken the next step in self-determination."

"Now you're getting philosophical."

"A Holy Father's duty is to guide those who seek wisdom."

"I wonder if you might do me a favour?"

"Of course."

"I'd like you to find Sigwulf. Tell him I need the entire garrison assembled in front of the keep."

"You mean to address them?"

"Not particularly, but I am curious to see the state of their equipment."

"I shall seek him out immediately."

"Oh, and if you see Cyn, tell her to meet us there."

The woefully small garrison of Verfeld milled around the keep as Ludwig came down the steps.

"Silence," commanded Captain Marhaven. "Form a line for His Lordship."

"Who are you to give us orders?" spat back a muscular fellow.

Sigwulf moved quickly, slapping his hand across the man's face. "I am your new captain. Talk back to me again, and it'll be the lash for you."

The guard obviously wanted to respond, even going so far as to clench his fist, but he swallowed his pride at the sight of the baron. "Sorry, Captain. It won't happen again."

"Trouble?" called out Ludwig.

"Not at all, my lord," replied Sigwulf. "I was merely having a little chat with the men."

Ludwig halted beside his comrade. "I am Lord Ludwig Altenburg," he announced, "the Baron of Verfeld. Some of you I know, for I grew up here. Others..." He stared at the muscular one. "Well, let's just say you're new to me. This grand fellow beside me is Sigwulf Marhaven, your captain. I have complete trust in him. You will obey his orders as if they came from my own lips." He heard the keep door squeak open and glanced up to see Cyn approaching.

"That," he said, "is Sergeant Hoffman."

Chuckles erupted from the garrison.

"Is something funny?" asked Ludwig.

"I thought you were jesting," replied the muscular man. "That's a woman."

"How observant of you. Yes, she's a woman, and yes, she is your new sergeant."

"You can't be serious, my lord?"

"Can't I? The sergeant's been a mercenary her entire life. I wager she's seen more battle than the rest of you put together."

"But she's so... small."

Ludwig turned to Cyn. "What do you say to that, Sergeant?"

She moved up to stand before the muscular guard, who stood more than a head taller than her. "I tell you what. Let's you and me have a test of skills, shall we? A little melee to see who can better wield a weapon?" She rose up on her toes, staring into the man's eyes as best she could. "Unless you're too scared?"

"I wouldn't want to hurt you, madam."

"Madam, is it?" She backed up. "Come on then, pull out that rusty, old sword of yours, and let's have at it."

The man hesitated.

"Go on," said Sigwulf. "Prove your worth."

"She's unarmed."

"I don't need weapons to defeat the likes of you," she taunted.

He moved forward, hesitantly at first. The rest of the men fell back to give them room to fight. Ludwig looked at Sigwulf in alarm, but the big man simply shook his head.

"What's your name?" asked Cyn.

"Horrick, Asgurth Horrick."

"Come along, then, Asgurth. Use those muscles of yours and do something."

The man drew his sword, then rushed forward, stabbing out as he approached his foe. Cyn dropped to the ground and kicked out, sweeping the legs from under the guardsman. He fell with a loud grunt but kept hold of his weapon.

"Ready for more?" She backed up, giving him room to regain his feet. He charged again, swinging his sword in a wide arc this time. Cyn leaned back, letting the tip of the blade slice through the air, then advanced, grasping his outstretched arm and pulling him forwards, throwing him off balance yet again.

"That's enough," called out Ludwig.

Cyn stood over the man, holding out her hand. "You're fast," she said, "but your moves are easy to counter. With some work, you could become quite the warrior."

He looked up at her, her sudden change in temperament surprising him.

"Come now," said Cyn. "Let us join hands in friendship. After all, we're both here to serve the baron."

He grasped her hand and allowed her to help him to his feet.

"Where did you learn that technique?" he asked.

"I was raised with mercenaries, but my father wouldn't permit me to carry a sword until I was sixteen. I needed to protect myself somehow."

9

LANDHOLDERS

WINTER 1095 SR

L udwig slowed, his horse's breath frosting in the chilly winter air. "Shouldn't be too far now."

"Where is it we're going?" asked Sigwulf. "Freiburg?"

"No, Eramon. You passed through it when you first travelled to Malburg."

"That was a village? I thought it was someone's farm."

"I suppose hamlet might be a better description, but regardless of what you call it, it's still part of the Barony of Verfeld."

"But if that's true, then why isn't Malburg included?"

"Because it's a free city."

Sigwulf shook his head. "It sounds to me like someone wanted to steal some of your lands."

"Never mind him," said Father Vernan. "He's just playing games with you."

"I'll admit I am," said Sig. "Saints know, I've got to do something to pass the time."

"Come now, you shouldn't use the name of the Saints in that manner."

"Saints alive! You're right."

"That's enough, you two," said Ludwig. A shadow descended over his heart as he spotted the village up ahead.

"Something wrong?" asked Father Vernan.

"Only with my thoughts. The last time I made this trip, it was with Charlaine."

Eramon boasted only a dozen homes, backing onto fields covered in snow. Ludwig pulled up to the largest building and dismounted. "If memory serves, this is the home of Deiter Macken, a farmer by trade."

"Isn't everyone here a farmer?" asked Sigwulf.

"Yes, now you mention it, I suppose they are." He knocked on the door, and a young man greeted him shortly thereafter.

"My lord? This is a surprise? To what do I owe your presence?"

"Dolf, is your father in?"

The man frowned. "You know full well he isn't."

"I beg your pardon?"

"He's dead."

"Might I ask how he died?"

Dolf's face turned red. "Your men killed him."

Ludwig was at a loss for words.

"Are you sure it was one of the baron's and not bandits?" asked Father Vernan.

"They wore the livery of Verfeld Keep."

"When was this?" demanded Ludwig.

"This past autumn, right after the harvest came in."

"I'm sorry, I had no idea. I only just returned from the north. May I ask the circumstances of his demise?"

"That depends. Do you want the official version or the truth?"

"The truth, always."

"Then you'd best come in," said Dolf, "along with your friends, and I'll tell you."

They all shuffled in out of the cold. On one side of the room, a woman tended a fireplace. "Marjorie," said their host. "Go and fetch some cider for our guests, would you?"

She quickly nodded, then lifted a hatch, descending into the cellar.

Ludwig removed his cloak and tossed it aside, rubbing his hands together to warm them. The cracked wall beside him had the timbers beneath exposed, and a look above revealed thatching badly in need of repairs. Father Vernan moved closer to the fire while Sigwulf remained near the door.

Marjorie soon returned with a small earthen jug, which she emptied into several cups, then passed them around.

"Like I was saying," continued Dolf, "it was after the harvest. We were loading up the hay onto the wagon to take it into Malburg when they rode up."

"They?"

"Aye, the lord and his men."

"You mean Berthold?"

"Yes, of course."

"How many were with him?"

"Three, my lord. Each a warrior wearing mail."

"Then what happened?"

"My father was always a stubborn man. When the lord demanded more taxes, he refused—said we had nothing more to give."

"I assume that wasn't enough for them?"

Dolf shook his head. "No, it wasn't. He ordered two of his men to search the house for coins, but there were none to be found."

"Was that the end of it?"

"No. They turned the place upside down, finding naught but scraps of bread. The lord flew into a rage and ordered the wagon burned, along with the hay we'd just harvested."

"By the Saints!" shouted Father Vernan. "Why ever would he do such a thing? A cartload of hay would be worth at least a few coins."

"That's what my father said, but the soldiers lit a torch anyway and moved to carry out the lord's wishes."

"And Deiter tried to stop them?" asked Ludwig.

"Aye, he did, though it cost him his life. They threw his body onto the wagon and torched it as well."

Ludwig shook his head. "I would say I'm sorry, but such an apology cannot make up for your loss. Trust me, I shall end this behaviour once and for all."

Sigwulf stepped closer. "Can you describe any of the soldiers there that day?"

"They all wore their mail, although I noticed one of them had a somewhat pronounced nose."

"With a weasely moustache?"

"Yes," said Dorf. "You know him?"

"Indeed I do," said Sigwulf. "Even as we speak, he sits in the dungeon beneath Verfeld Keep. His companions must also be fellow conspirators."

"It makes sense," said Ludwig. "He would only send those he trusts on a mission of that importance."

"Mission?" said Dorf. "What mission is that?"

"Nothing that concerns you," replied Ludwig. "But know that we shall find the others responsible for your father's death, and I will deal with them."

"And your brother?"

"It's becoming more apparent with every passing day that he's overstepped his authority. From now on, this man here will be the only one collecting taxes"—he nodded at Sigwulf—"or his sergeant, a woman named Cynthia. Do you understand?"

"That's easy for you to say, but what am I to do should more soldiers come?"

"Do what you need to do to survive, then send word to me at the keep." He glanced around the room. "Have you enough to last you through the winter?"

"It will be difficult, Lord, but we shall do our best."

"I'll have food sent your way. I leave it to you to share it with your fellow villagers."

"Thank you, my lord."

Marjorie ran forward, embracing the startled baron. "Oh, thank you, my lord. You've saved us!"

Father Vernan pried her loose. "It's a lord's duty to look after his tenants, which is something Lord Ludwig takes seriously."

"Is there anything else you need, my lord?" asked Dolf.

"Yes, there is. Tell me, how was your harvest this year?"

"Modest, my lord. Ordinarily, it would be sufficient to see us through the cold months, but losing the wagon cost us dearly."

"I don't understand," said Sigwulf.

"It's simple, really," explained Father Vernan. "They intended to sell off the excess wheat to stock up for winter. It's a common practice in most of the Petty Kingdoms."

"You seem to know a great deal about farming."

"My father was a landed knight with tenants."

"And you gave that up to take Holy Orders?"

"What can I say? I have two older brothers; it's not as if I was ever going to inherit."

"Yes, but to become a lay brother?"

"You seem to believe it's undesirable, but it's a calling, same as being a warrior is for you."

Sigwulf nodded. "Yes, I suppose it is. I'm sorry if I offended you, Father."

"The path of life is all about learning."

"Who said that? Saint Mathew?"

"No," the Holy Father replied. "That one's all mine."

Ludwig drained his cup, then stood. "I thank you for your hospitality, Dorf, and yours, Marjorie. It's time we were on our way before we outstay our welcome."

"It was our pleasure, my lord," said Dorf.

Ludwig threw on his cloak. "Remember now, should you encounter anything of that nature again, be sure to let me know. And only Sigwulf will collect taxes from now on, or a woman named Cynthia, you understand?"

"Yes, Lord."

"Good. I would deem it a favour if you were to spread the word. There should be no more surprises when taxes are collected, nor should such acts leave you struggling to survive. A barony thrives only when its people flourish."

He nodded at Sigwulf, who then opened the door.

"Off already?" grumbled Father Vernan. "I was getting used to that fire."

"Let your faith warm you," said Sigwulf.

They stepped outside and climbed into their saddles, Father Vernan letting out a slight yelp.

Ludwig was immediately concerned. "Something wrong, Father?"

The Holy Father cleared his throat. "I must admit this saddle was much colder than expected. I fear my voice may be a few octaves higher for the next little while."

They rode on to Roshlag, the village demarking the western extent of the barony. Larger than Eramon, it boasted its own inn, the Ragged Dog, where the travellers halted. They stepped inside a conversation-filled room, but everyone quickly grew silent. Their sour faces informed Ludwig they held no love for their lord and master. A woman approached, bowing her head deferentially.

"What can I get you, Lord?"

"Ale and something to eat for myself and my travelling companions. And a round of drinks for everyone here," he quickly added as she walked away.

The gesture was a small one, yet it had the desired effect. Although they raised cups in his honour, he realized it was only in appreciation for the free drinks. It would require more than a cup of ale to convince these people he had their best interests at heart.

He moved through the room, taking a seat by the fire. Around him, voices slowly drifted back to their previous conversations, although in more muted tones.

"At least this place is warm," said Father Vernan.

"You sound like an old woman," said Sigwulf, "but you can't be more than what—twenty-five?"

"Twenty-seven, if we're being precise, but I thank you for the compliment."

"Isn't that a little young for a Holy Father? All the ones I know are ancient. You don't even have any grey hair yet."

"Mayhap not on the outside," replied Father Vernan with a chuckle, "but inside, I am as pure as new-fallen snow."

"I'm not sure that means quite what you intended." Sigwulf scanned the crowd, then lowered his voice. "These people don't look too happy."

"I can't say I blame them," said Ludwig. "They've likely been overtaxed for some time."

"Still," added Father Vernan. "They seem to appreciate the round you purchased on their behalf."

"That won't last long."

"Not that I mind the warmth, and I appreciate the ale, but precisely what are we doing here?"

Ludwig stood, garnering the attention of all. "My name," he began, "is Ludwig Altenburg. By order of His Majesty, King Otto, I am the new Baron of Verfeld." At their looks of indifference, sweat beaded up along his brow. "I came here today seeking bowmen. According to my records, Roshlag is to provide three archers in time of war. I ask you to tell them that their service is required at Verfeld Keep. Let it be known that, besides their regular pay, they'll be given a signing bonus for presenting themselves by week's end."

"How long will they be needed?" called out a voice.

"At least till the end of winter or possibly until early spring. Rest assured, you shall be back home in time for planting, should that be your desire."

A thin youth of fifteen years or so, stood. "I am no archer, Lord, but I would be willing to learn."

"What is your name?" asked Ludwig.

"Kalen, Lord. Kalen Hasrich."

"Then come to Verfeld with the others, and we'll teach you the ways of archery."

"But I have no bow, Lord?"

"Fear not. We'll find one suitable to your physique."

At the mention of his slight frame, laughter broke out, and the youth reddened.

Sigwulf stood, his size quieting the room. He moved to stand before Kalen. "You might be skinny now, my lad, but once we're finished with you, you'll be the envy of Roshlag. Why, I wager the girls won't be able to keep their hands off you."

The young man turned an even brighter shade of red.

Ludwig cleared his throat. "If any others wish to learn the way of the bow, or take up arms in my service, come to Verfeld, and I shall bear the cost of equipping and training you." Most of the faces looked on with little enthusiasm, but a trio of younger men took an interest. Ludwig sat and called Sigwulf back to the table.

"Did you see those three youths?" asked Ludwig.

"Aye, they're young, but I reckon they'll make decent warriors with a little instruction. Should I approach them?"

"No, let them come to us."

"Are they even old enough to fight?" asked Father Vernan.

"Of course," said Sigwulf. "I was younger than that when I first took up a sword."

"Yes, but these are farmers."

"All the better."

"Really?"

"Of course. Farmers labour in the fields; that usually means they are strong and hardy folk."

"That Kalen fellow looks like he has no muscles at all."

Sigwulf chuckled. "He'll grow into them, don't you worry."

A shadow fell across the table as they noticed one of the youths staring down at them. "Something I can do for you?" Sig asked.

"We want to become warriors."

"Oh, you do, do you?" He turned to Ludwig. "What do you think, Lord?"

Ludwig looked them over. "What's your name, boy?"

"Paran, Lord, and this is Gustavo."

"Gustavo? That's a Calabrian name, isn't it?"

The second youth simply shrugged.

Ludwig took in the third member of the party, noting his grey eyes. "And who are you?"

"Edwig, Lord."

"Ignore him," said Paran. "He's a Therengian."

Ludwig smiled. "Then I would consider myself lucky to have him in my service. Tell me, Paran, would you be willing to put aside your differences?"

"Lord?"

"I can hardly have my warriors fighting amongst themselves. If I take the effort and expense to make you into soldiers, I expect you to get along with each other. Do you think you can do that?"

"Yes, Lord."

"Very well. I shall accept your offer, provided you do two things for me." He waited a moment, staring down each youth in turn. "First, you must seek permission from your parents to enter my service."

"And second, Lord?"

"Present yourselves at Verfeld Keep by the end of the week."

"And you will train us, Lord?"

"Captain Sigwulf bears that honour, along with his sergeant, but I shall take a great interest in your progress. You know the way to Verfeld?"

"Aye, we follow the road east, past Malburg. The keep lies just beyond."

"Good. I would suggest you travel with any archers who accept my offer. Now, let's be clear, becoming one of my warriors requires commitment. I don't want to go to the trouble of equipping you if you're going to run off at the first sign of difficulty."

All three nodded.

"Very well. Now, be off, and I shall see you back at Verfeld Keep by the end of the week."

They fled the scene.

"Ah, the passion of youth," said Father Vernan. "I remember it well."

"Will they last?" asked Ludwig.

"I think they will," replied Sigwulf, "but we won't know for sure until we see how they are with weapons. Merely being strong isn't enough to guarantee a career as a warrior; one must be willing to learn."

"Well said," added Father Vernan.

"I assumed you'd be against this idea, Father?"

"Why in the name of the Saints would you say that?"

"I was under the impression your order abhorred violence?"

"Unnecessary violence, yes, but must I remind you, we have an order of Temple Knights? You might say bloodshed is their stock-in-trade. Better to be prepared to fight than to sit by and watch the destruction around you."

"Are you saying YOU can fight?"

"I can handle a sword if need be, although I admit to a preference for the mace."

"You surprise me," said Ludwig. "That was possibly the last thing I imagined I'd hear coming from a Holy Father."

"As I mentioned earlier, both my father and two older brothers are knights. I could hardly grow up without being taught how to fight, all things considered. You might recall that I also helped you equip yourself for the tournament back in Torburg."

"So you did, and I shall always be thankful for that, even if it did cost me a suit of armour."

"And your warhorse," added the Holy Father.

"Strange how things turn out," said Sigwulf. "Had it not been for your loss, you would never have joined the Grim Defenders."

"The Saints move in mysterious ways."

"I don't believe in fate."

"Nor I, but I must do my best to maintain an air of mystery surrounding my order."

. . .

With their objective complete, they left the tavern, riding eastward, the snow quickly growing deeper.

"At this rate, we'll never get back to the keep," mused Sigwulf.

"Nonsense," said Ludwig. "The road is straight, and we shall be in Malburg long before the roads are unpassable."

"Does that mean we're to stay in the city?"

"Not unless we want to."

"Wasn't Cyn going into Malburg today?"

"She was," replied Ludwig. "She's looking into someone repairing those spears."

"Let's hope she returned to Verfeld before the weather set in."

"I imagine she's been back for some time. It's not as if she'd be making them herself."

"It seems you'll be wanting more armour," said Father Vernan. "At the bare minimum, three mail coats, if those lads sign up."

"Yes," agreed Ludwig. "The armour won't be needed right away, but at least some shields to begin training with."

"How long does it take to make a shield, I wonder?"

"Only a few days, I should think, assuming it's wooden. Metal, on the other hand, would take significantly longer."

"Then which do we acquire?"

"Wood for training. We can work on metal shields for the spring."

10

RECRUITS

WINTER 1095 SR

F ather Vernan looked up from where he was poring over the barony's finances. "I should like to journey to Harlingen. You need a castellan to help you run this place."

"I'm more than capable of looking after it myself," said Ludwig.

"And who is to look after things in your absence?"

"Why would you think I would be absent?"

"Come now, do you take me for a fool? Of course you're going to travel. You must visit the king from time to time, at the very least. Your father had one, didn't he?"

"He did, but I'm not sure I can afford that luxury."

"It's not so much a luxury as a necessity," replied the Holy Father. "You must also entertain the possibility of war; the king definitely considered it likely. You can't run a place like this while marching across the countryside at the head of an army."

"I barely have enough men to garrison the keep."

"Yes, but that will soon change, and a good castellan will help you in ways I cannot."

"Very well, to Harlingen you go. However, I'm curious how you'll find a suitable candidate. It's not as if you can ride up to a shop and hire one."

"I shall make enquiries of the king's household. He has, I believe, a vast collection of relatives."

"I know," said Ludwig. "I'm one of them, remember?"

"Yes, of course, but there are even more who are far removed from inheriting the Crown. In such cases, they're likely to be well-educated, prime candidates for a position of castellan to a baron."

"Shall I make some funds available for your lodgings while you're in the capital?"

"Not necessary," said Father Vernan. "I'll stay at the Temple of Saint Mathew. There are always rooms available to members of the order."

"When will you leave?"

In answer, the Holy Man moved to the window and threw open the shutters. A chilly breeze blew in, causing the poor fellow to shiver. He took a quick peek outside before closing them up again. "It's far too late in the day to leave now. I'll head out at first light tomorrow."

Ludwig chuckled. "Dress warmly, my friend. The winds can be cold this time of year."

"Something that is becoming all too clear with the passing days."

"How long do you suppose you'll be gone?"

"I'll return in time for the Midwinter Feast, don't you worry."

"I'll be sure to have some extra food for you."

"You'd better," warned the Holy Man. "I tend to have quite the appetite on such occasions."

Cyn was the first to spot them—a small group of men approaching from the west. "Looks like we have company."

Sigwulf stopped sharpening his sword and looked up. "How many?"

She leaned farther out the window to garner a better view. "Seven, by my reckoning. Friends of yours?"

"That'll be our new garrison. By my calculation, there should be three archers and four youths."

"The bowmen I can make out, but as for the rest, they're too bundled up to be sure of their age."

"We should greet them." Sigwulf got to his feet, tossing the sharpening stone onto the table. "Close that shutter up, and let's see what we ended up with."

"Didn't you meet them in Roshlag?"

"I did, but for the life of me, I can't remember what they look like."

"That's because you're too busy thinking of me."

He smiled. "I like that."

"Because it's true?"

"Of course! Now, come on. We don't want to be tardy."

She laughed. "Tardy, is it? You're starting to talk like Father Vernan."

"I'm working on bettering myself."

"Why?"

"I don't know." He blushed. "I suppose I feel as if I should do better."

"What makes you think you're not doing well already?"

"I'm a captain now. I ought to act more the part."

She moved closer, placing her hand on his chest. "I like you this way. You must tell me more about your worries later, when we've more time."

"Agreed. Now grab your mace and follow me."

"No," said Cyn, rushing through the door. "You follow me!"

They raced down the southeast tower, their steps echoing off the stone walls.

They burst from the keep, Cyn in the lead, and then slowed their pace, the better to appear calm and collected. Once they descended the stairs, they waited for the new arrivals.

"Greetings," one of the archers called out, an older man with a liberal sprinkling of grey throughout his thick, bushy beard. "We come from the village of Roshlag."

"Ah yes," said Sigwulf. "I remember your face now." He leaned to one side, the better to assess the rest of the group. "I see everyone is accounted for."

"Indeed, Captain. I believe you already know the youngsters?"

"I do, yet your own name escapes me."

"I'm Rikal, and this is Arnak and Konstantine."

"Konstantine?" said Sigwulf. "Are you from the north?"

"My family was," the archer replied, "but we've been here for three generations now."

"Welcome, all of you. Let's get you inside and warmed up, then we'll discuss your duties."

"We brought our bows, Captain," said Rikal, "along with a dozen arrows each."

"How are you at fletching?"

"Arnak here is reckoned the most capable in that regard, but we'll need arrowheads."

"A matter easily arranged."

"I'm afraid this young fellow here, Kalen, requires a bow."

"And he shall have one in time," said Cyn, "but I've yet to go into town to pick one up. There are also shields and spears coming, but your swift arrival surprised us."

"Were we not to come by the end of the week?"

"You were," said Sigwulf, "most definitely, but that's still two days away. Don't worry. There's room for you and food to fill your belly. Now follow me."

He led them up the steps and through the iron-reinforced doors into the keep. They were soon all in the great hall, where the baron sat by the fire.

"You're here," said Ludwig. "That's marvellous news. How were the roads?"

"Cold, my lord."

"Come, stand around the hearth and warm yourselves." He turned to Cyn. "Sergeant, see if you can find Carson and have him fetch some food and drink, will you?"

"Yes, Lord," she said before disappearing through a side door.

Rikal cleared his throat. "Might I ask, Lord, why you require us?"

"Ah, well, that's a bit of a story, actually." Ludwig lowered his voice. "The truth is that before my return, the barony was... how can I put this?"

"A shambles?" offered Sigwulf.

"Yes, I suppose that description would fit. In any case, the king asked me to increase the garrison of Verfeld, which means training more men."

"But you have men to guard the keep, don't you?" said Rikal.

"A few, but a fever ran rampant some while back and decimated the ranks. Don't worry, it's over and done with now, but as a result, we find ourselves short-handed."

"Understandable, Lord, but why archers?"

"The fact of the matter is I'd like a permanent force of professional bowmen on hand. I understand that doesn't necessarily fit in with your plans, but I hoped I might rely on your expertise for training new archers. Interested?"

"I reckon it would be better than standing around in the cold all day long."

"Good. I shall leave it to you and Captain Sigwulf to sort out the details."

"Do you mean Captain Marhaven?"

Ludwig grinned. "Yes, I suppose I do. Sorry, I'm still not used to referring to him as captain."

Cyn reappeared. "Carson will be along shortly with victuals."

"She means food and drink," said Sigwulf. "It's an old mercenary term."

The newcomers all looked at Cyn. "You're saying," said Rikal, "that this woman was a mercenary?"

"And what's wrong with that?" demanded Cyn.

Ludwig quickly intervened before tempers flared. "Both Captain Marhaven and Sergeant Hoffman were mercenaries. I served as one myself in the war up north."

"You've seen battle?"

"We all have. We fought under the banner of the Duke of Erlingen."

"Successfully," added Sigwulf. "That is to say we were victorious."

"Yes," agreed Ludwig. "I suppose that's an important point to emphasize. How about the rest of you? Any questions?" He noticed the Therengian's inquisitive look. "Edwig, isn't it?"

"Yes, Lord. I was wondering what weapons we'll be learning."

Ludwig looked at Cyn. "I believe that's your area of expertise."

She moved closer to the fire. "We'll start you off with spears. Well, actually sticks. Once you show you can move around without accidentally lopping off a limb, we'll switch you to something with a metal tip. After that, you'll learn how to use an axe. Who knows? In time, you may even be able to handle a sword."

"Why not begin with a sword?" asked Paran.

"A sword requires much more skill."

"And shields?"

"You won't need those until we start you in on using the axe. Don't worry. We'll teach you how to use a shield to attack as well as defend."

"Attack? With a shield? I assumed it was for blocking the enemy?"

"It is," said Cyn, "but the edge, if used properly, can be as effective as a second weapon. Trust me; we have plenty of experience with the tactics of melee."

"Will you train us to fight in a big battle?" asked Gustavo.

"Eventually, but let's take it one step at a time, shall we?"

"Yes," added Ludwig. "At the moment, we don't have enough men to form a line of battle, but that will change in time. We'll also be equipping you with armour, but that won't come until you're hardened."

"Hardened?" said Paran.

"He means toughened up," explained Sigwulf. "A well-equipped warrior must get used to the weight of his weapons and armour. You might believe you're strong now, but wait till you have to march around all day with that extra weight."

"That sounds like a lot of work."

"And it is," said Cyn, "but to keep you ready for a fight, we'll be feeding you lots of meat. I imagine that's something most of you haven't had in a while."

"You won't suffer for lack of food," said Ludwig, "not while you're here in Verfeld. As to where you'll be sleeping, the keep maintains a room for that very purpose. You'll be sharing it with the regular garrison for now, but eventually, as your numbers increase, we'll open up other rooms for your use."

Edwig raised his hand. "Excuse me, Lord, but when will we start training?"

Ludwig turned to Sigwulf. "I should think tomorrow would give them time to settle in, wouldn't you?"

"Aye," replied his captain. "We'll get them fed and show them to their room, then visit the armoury first thing in the morning."

Ludwig gazed out the window, where below, Sigwulf led the new recruits as they marched around the keep. A blanket of snow had fallen overnight, making their journey even more difficult. The captain appeared unfazed by the effort, striding through the drifts with little effort, but the others struggled, falling ever farther behind.

Eventually, they rounded the keep's corner, disappearing from Ludwig's sight. He closed the shutters before heading downstairs to see what the day promised. Cyn was in the great hall, laying out weapons on the tables, aided by Carson.

"You've been busy," said Ludwig.

The warrior smiled. "Yes. Master Tomas brought us half a dozen spears this morning, along with two helmets and a message."

"Which is?"

"More are coming. The smith's guild has been pretty enthusiastic about the change in their fortunes."

"I can well imagine. I suppose making armour and weapons is more interesting than nails and horseshoes."

"And more profitable, I'd wager."

Ludwig moved closer, examining a spear. "Did you say Master Tomas came here?"

"He did."

"But he didn't make any of these?"

"No. He said the guild felt it best to choose one person to represent them in all future dealings to simplify matters."

"Is he still here?"

"I'm afraid not," replied Cyn. "He needed to get back to his forge. He left this, however." She passed him a note.

"It acknowledges receipt of payment and says I can negotiate subsequent purchases with only half down." He looked up. "Well, that's a relief. I wasn't too pleased about having to pay for everything in advance, I can tell you."

"Can you blame them? It's not as if... certain people paid on time."

"You mean my stepbrother?"

She adopted a forced smile. "I would never insinuate anything, my lord."

"All right, that's quite enough of that. You should call me Ludwig when the others aren't around." He moved to examine a helmet. "The workmanship on this looks promising. I ought to see about getting one myself."

"You can't wear that," said Cyn. "It's far too plain. You're the baron now. You need something to distinguish yourself on the battlefield. You should see about having some plate armour made."

"Now is not the time."

"Now is precisely the time. Armour of that sort takes forever to make. Leave it too late, and you'll be riding into battle without sufficient protection."

"I did well enough at Chermingen."

"You were lucky," said Cyn. "Not to mention we fought on foot. You're not commanding a group of mercenaries anymore, Ludwig. Now they're your own men, and they need to be inspired."

"And you believe a full suit of plate armour would do that?"

"It certainly couldn't hurt. There's also the matter of prestige. How would you feel, riding to battle when all the other barons wear better armour than you?"

Ludwig shrugged. "To be honest, it wouldn't bother me."

"Well, it would bother me. I'd at least like to have the fantasy that this barony is prosperous."

"Very well. I shall talk to our resident smith this very day." He looked around the room. "Where did Carson go?"

"He disappears all the time. I expect he's about his duties."

"I was going to ask him to fetch the smith."

"That was a jest, surely?"

Ludwig stared back. "Why would you think that?"

"I know you're the baron, but the accepted practice is for you to visit the smith, not the other way around."

"Why is that?"

"Because he has to take your measurements, if nothing else."

"Can't he do that here?"

Cyn shook her head. "Don't be like that, Ludwig. You're more than a stuck-up noble. Show respect for the man's skill and visit him in his workshop."

"Very well, I shall, although it would be more convenient if it were a little closer."

"Have you ever considered enlarging the keep?"

"I'd love to," said Ludwig, "but I doubt we could afford it."

"You should consider it in the future. A nice curtain wall would give you a courtyard for training, not to mention safety for the stables."

"I see what you're suggesting. Then the smith could move his forge to a more spacious location."

"Precisely."

"Of course, that would be years away, even if we could afford it."

"You could always petition the king? I'm sure he'd be willing to invest in strengthening the keep."

"Perhaps, but we still need the income to support it."

"I think you'd find more people amenable to coming here if the defences were stronger."

"Are you suggesting folks would move here?"

"That's what happens in the north. There are plenty of freeholders looking for a safe place to raise their families."

"Freeholders? But Verfeld works with tenants, not owners."

"Take Malburg. That's a free city, and look how prosperous that is. Let me ask you this—what is one thing you have in abundance?"

"Land?"

"Precisely. You offer some of that land up for sale, and I guarantee you this village of yours will double within a year."

"That would give me an immediate increase in the treasury," said Ludwig, "but I'd be losing out in the long term."

"Not at all. You would still charge them taxes."

"The same as a tenant or something different?"

"I'm sure Father Vernan would have a better idea than me, but ideally, you want to keep it low to encourage more people to come here. You'll also need to send someone to other cities to recruit prospective buyers."

"And you think many would take on such a task?"

"Given the right incentive, I believe they would. Who wouldn't like a plot of land to pass on to their children? You give them a family legacy, and they, in turn, provide you with a steady income."

"You've definitely opened my eyes," said Ludwig.

Carson entered the room. "Riders approaching, my lord. They bear the banner of the king."

"Let's see what they want, shall we?"

Ludwig met them at the base of the outer steps. Their leader, encased in furs, made it hard to distinguish his livery, but the king's pennant on the end of his spear was plain enough.

"Trouble?" asked Ludwig.

"Aye, my lord. Several of the barons reported incursions by bandits. His

Majesty feels they may be raiders from Neuhafen and wants you to be extra vigilant."

"And the king sent you all this way just to tell me?"

"No, Lord. He dispatched patrols to all the baronies. We're to remain here to augment your own garrison for the winter. We shall undertake visits to each of the surrounding villages on an ongoing basis." The rider turned, nodding to one of his cohorts, who produced a small lockbox. "The king has also sent funds, Lord, to offset the cost of feeding us."

"Very well. Come inside, and someone will see to your horses."

11

TRAINING

WINTER 1095 SR

Life at Verfeld soon settled into a regular routine. Sigwulf brought the new warriors out for a march each morning, followed by a hearty breakfast. After that, Cyn took over, training them with the spear while the bowmen practiced their archery. In inclement weather, they all remained inside, going over their use of melee weapons in the great hall.

The king's horsemen patrolled the barony's villages every second day, randomizing their destination each time. The plan was to keep any potential bandits on their toes, convincing them it was too dangerous to consider raiding.

Now competent with the spear, the new recruits moved on to axes. Edwig, in particular, proved highly skilled with the weapon and ended up helping with training.

Having finally received a bow, Kalen began the long journey towards becoming a seasoned archer. The steady diet of meat and the intense training schedule filled out the young man's physique. His progress improved notably as a result.

Sergeant Hobson, leader of the king's horsemen, was an active sort, taking his men out in even the worst of weather. Thus, it was quite a surprise when they returned early one day, their horses exhausted.

He entered the study where Ludwig was trying to make sense of his finances without the help of the Holy Father, who was still in Harlingen.

"My lord," the soldier began. "I beg to report a problem in Freiburg."

"What kind of problem?"

"There were sightings of bandits in the area, my lord. We sought to track them down, but the weather moved in, covering their tracks."

"Send word to Captain Marhaven," ordered Ludwig. "We shall take the bowmen with us."

"Lord?"

"These men know how to hunt, Sergeant. That skill could prove useful trying to track these villains down."

"And my men, Lord?"

"I'm afraid I'll need them to return to Freiburg. Any idea on numbers?"

"Half a dozen, maybe less. Some of the locals saw them, but only from a distance."

"And when did this attack occur?"

"Sometime early this morning. It was well over by the time we arrived. We would have found them had it not been for the storm."

"You did right in coming back here. We shall return there as soon as possible and try to pick up the trail."

"Where do you think they'd be heading?" asked Hobson.

"I'll send word to Malburg, but I doubt that's their destination. That would only bring them closer to the keep. No, there are only two areas they can hide in—the hills to the north or the forest to the east."

"What if they're heading to Voslund? They might be looking for better pickings?"

"You have a point," said Ludwig. "Dispatch two of your men to take the south road. They are to reach Voslund with all haste and keep an eye out for strangers. In the meantime, the rest of us will head east to Freiburg."

Ludwig retrieved his weapons and met Sigwulf at the front door. The archers were all present, bundled up against the cold, along with young Kalen.

As they adjusted their cloaks, Gustavo showed up. "Is there trouble, my lord?"

"Yes. Freiburg's been attacked: bandits, most likely. We are on our way to investigate further."

"Shall we accompany you?"

"No. You and the others remain here, but stay on the lookout in case this is a precursor to something bigger."

"You think it an invasion, Lord?"

"No, but it might be an attempt to test our resolve. One thing is for certain, if we don't act now, we'll only be inviting them to try again later."

They moved outside to where their horses waited. Ludwig hauled himself into the saddle before gazing back at the keep. High above, a lone figure watched, his shadow falling over them.

"Berthold?" he called out, but the figure withdrew out of sight.

Ludwig shivered, but not from the cold. He was responsible for protecting his lands, that was true, but suddenly he feared his stepbrother was up to no good.

Sigwulf noted his hesitancy. "Something wrong, Lord?"

"The keep. Something's wrong."

"Cyn is here, Lord. You can trust her to look after things in your absence."

"Yes, I suppose you're right. Lead on, Sergeant Hobson, but maintain a steady pace. We don't want to tire the men."

Freiburg lay only four miles to the east, along a road better described as a mere cart track. During the summer months, it was easy enough to follow. Yet today, a person could pass by the village without even knowing, so fierce was the wind that whipped up the snow, surrounding them in a sea of white.

The horses led the way, creating a path for the archers to travel along. They stopped twice, trying to gauge their position, but it was a hopeless undertaking with the road buried by snow and the sky obscured by the weather.

They took refuge in a cluster of trees after deciding to wait out the storm. Sigwulf broke off a few twigs from the nearby branches, building a small fire to keep them warm. The afternoon wore on, and Ludwig fretted, his mind dwelling on the possibilities. He imagined an army crossing into his lands, burning and pillaging as they went. He would return to Verfeld to find it under siege. Panic rose inside him, and he fought to hold it under control.

Sergeant Hobson returned from checking the horses. "The weather appears to be clearing, Lord."

The distraction pulled Ludwig from his thoughts. "Good. We'll continue on our way. With any luck, we'll soon see Freiburg."

"There," said Sigwulf, pointing north. "That looks like smoke from their chimneys."

"We must've gone too far south in the snow," said Ludwig. He turned his horse towards the distant village. "I only hope we're not too late."

They increased their pace to a trot, leaving the archers to follow along in their wake. Empty fields greeted them, their borders marked by a row of trees.

"Sergeant, you mentioned they saw the bandits?"

"Yes, Lord, to the northeast. A cow was slain, and part of it carried off."

"Could wild animals have done it?"

"I know of no creature that cuts flesh with a knife."

They rode on, eventually arriving at the village's only tavern. Ludwig surveyed the area as he waited for the archers to catch up. "Rikal, you and the others head inside, but be ready to move at a moment's notice. The rest of us will investigate the scene of the attack. There's no sense having you stand around in this weather."

The bowman nodded. "Aye, Lord."

"Now, let's see this carcass, shall we? Lead on, Sergeant."

They passed by a ramshackle hut, then turned east onto an open field. The sergeant pointed. "The farmer who lives back there said his cow got away from him."

"Could they have led it away?"

"I'm not sure what you're suggesting, Lord?"

"Someone could have come right up to the building and taken the beast."

"Why do that if they're only going to kill it?"

"Because killing it would make noise," explained Ludwig. "Not to mention the snowstorm would hide their presence while they butchered it."

The sergeant screwed up his face. "So then it's just bandits?"

"By all accounts, bandits are lazy. They take up a life of crime so they don't have to work. Why would they go to the trouble of butchering a cow?"

"To eat, surely?"

"Easier to steal a chicken," said Sigwulf, "and simpler to cook. His Lordship is right. These were no bandits; they were likely soldiers."

Sergeant Hobson looked stunned. "But why would soldiers be here, especially this time of year?"

"Think for a moment," said Ludwig. "The king sent you to Verfeld because other barons had trouble with bandits."

"Exactly, Lord. That proves my point, doesn't it?"

"What are the chances villains like that could simultaneously coordinate attacks against multiple barons? It has to be something bigger."

"I'm afraid you have me at a loss for words."

Ludwig looked at Sigwulf. "Your thoughts?"

"I think you have the right of it. Likely, it's a group of warriors in the service of Neuhafen, sent to gather information."

"How does that explain the dead cow?" asked the sergeant.

Sigwulf grinned. "Soldiers are used to butchering their own meat. What if the cow wandered off, and they spotted it? A find like that would put food in their bellies. I expect it would have been a hard thing to pass up."

Sergeant Hobson halted. "This is where we found the body, Lord, although, as you can see, it's been removed."

"Likely to recover what was left of the creature," added Sigwulf.

Ludwig remained in the saddle, surveying the area. The storm had obliterated any hope of following the attacker's trail, but he wasn't about to let this go unchallenged.

He pointed to the east. "Over there, the river marks the boundary between Hadenfeld and Neuhafen. Unless I miss my guess, we'll find what we're looking for on the other side."

"How far is it to the border?" asked Sigwulf.

"Three miles, maybe four."

"They're long gone by now."

"Not necessarily. They were carrying a lot of meat and may have stopped to cook it."

"You believe they'd risk discovery?" asked the sergeant.

"I think they feel the storm covered their tracks. In any case, we must do something. Ride back to the tavern and fetch the archers. Captain Marhaven and I will await your return, along with the rest of the men." The king's sergeant headed off.

"I don't like this," said Sigwulf. "We could find ourselves outnumbered."

"The reports indicated only half a dozen."

"True, but it wouldn't be the first time an enemy was underestimated. What if the others remained out of sight?"

"Are you suggesting we withdraw?"

"No, of course not, merely that we should proceed with caution."

"On that," said Ludwig, "we are in complete agreement."

It didn't take long for the king's sergeant to return with the archers. They set out eastward, the forest growing closer with every step. First, an occasional clump of trees, then the woods proper, with a thick nest of underbrush covering the ground.

"How do you wish to proceed?" asked Sigwulf.

"We'll spread out," replied Ludwig. "Each man staying within eyesight of those on either side. Move slowly and try to keep some semblance of a line."

"Could they still be here?"

"I doubt it, but we might find something to give us a better idea of how many we're talking about."

The men dispersed, the horsemen anchoring either flank. At Ludwig's command, they advanced. The going here was rough, requiring individuals to occasionally move to one side or the other to avoid some obstruction. The archers held bows at the ready, with arrows nocked but not drawn. The warriors had their swords in hand, prepared for anything that might rush out of the underbrush, but it proved unnecessary. Despite the difficulties, the small band maintained contact with each other, filling Ludwig with pride.

Rikal halted, raising his hand to indicate he'd spotted something. The rest stopped, and then the woods grew quiet.

The archer pointed ahead and slightly to his right. Ludwig, who'd dismounted upon entering the forest, handed his reins to Sigwulf and advanced, pushing aside some low-hanging branches to reveal a small clearing. In the middle of a circle of rocks sat the remains of a fire. He waved his men forward.

Rikal moved up and placed his hand near the ashes. "It's still warm," he warned. "They haven't gone far."

"It seems luck is with us this day," said Ludwig. "In amongst the trees, the storm could not cover their tracks. Look yonder."

"Looks like three, maybe four went through there."

"How can you be so sure?"

"They walked abreast," said Rikal. "See where they spread out after passing the tree with the bent trunk."

"Listen," said Ludwig. "You can hear the river off in the distance."

"They must be heading towards it."

"Then let us see if we can't intercept them before they make it. Sergeant? Take your men ahead, but keep on the lookout."

"Aye, Lord," replied Hobson.

The attack, when it came, still surprised them. An arrow took one of the king's riders in the side of the chest, causing him to fall forward. His horse, no longer under control, bolted. The poor man tumbled from his saddle, his boot catching in the stirrup, his mount dragging him into the underbrush.

"Ambush!" shouted Hobson.

An arrow struck a tree to his right, but he saw no signs of the enemy. He looked over his mount's head, desperately seeking a glimpse of those responsible.

A sudden rush of feet came up from behind him. Then Rikal was beside him, drawing his bowstring back to his ear, pausing a moment before the arrow flew into the trees. A distant thud echoed back at them, then a body crashed to the forest floor.

"Bastard was in the trees," said the bowman. He nocked another arrow, scanning the area even as his first victim screamed out in pain.

Ludwig moved up, his sword firmly in hand. Suddenly his vulnerability struck him, for in his haste to respond to reports of the raid, he'd neglected to don armour.

The now riderless horse stood ahead of him, its rider lost somewhere in the underbrush. Ludwig caught a movement out of the corner of his eye and turned as a man rushed towards him, axe in hand. He parried just in time, the force of the blow travelling up his arm. Kicking out, he smashed the man's knee, the leg bending back at an impossible angle. The man screamed out in pain as he tumbled to the ground. Ludwig stomped forward, driving his sword into his foe's chest, finishing him off.

The rest of the raiders jumped up from their concealment, running east, desperately trying to reach the river before they were overrun.

Sergeant Hobson advanced, his remaining men following his example. They were soon lost to sight, but the sounds drifting back told the story. Horses splashed in the water, and then another scream, although it was impossible to tell who was responsible for it.

Ludwig picked up his pace, jumping over an exposed root and almost tumbling into the river. Hobson and two of his men were in the water, but the enemy were nearly across, having chosen to swim to safety. The sergeant urged on his horse, sending it into ever deeper water.

"Sergeant," Ludwig called out. "Come back. The river can get awfully treacherous midstream." Hobson's horse stumbled right as he finished the sentence, and both rider and mount went under. The poor beast soon emerged in a panic, struggling to make it back to the riverbank, but its rider was nowhere to be seen.

Ludwig rushed in, heedless of the danger. His first steps were ankle-deep, but he struggled to fight off the cold as the river rose to his waist, then he spotted the glint of metal under the water. Steeling himself, he plunged beneath the surface.

His hands grew numb as he struggled to hold his breath, but then he brushed up against a leather strap. He grabbed it, holding on tightly, and dragged it back towards the bank. The cold had done its worst, though, and he stumbled, unable to take another step. Sigwulf rushed into the water, hauling him back to the riverbank while two others took over his burden.

Sigwulf threw his cloak around Ludwig while others helped the poor unconscious sergeant, his helmet lost, a large cut on his scalp. Their enemies jeered from the other bank, but a few well-placed arrows soon quieted them.

"Get a fire going," ordered Sigwulf. "We need to warm these two up."

Ludwig hobbled into the trees, trying to get out of the wind. Desperate to account for his men, he questioned them through chattering teeth. "W-w-where is everybody?"

"Two were injured," said Sigwulf. "One of the king's men took an arrow, and the sergeant here has a nasty head wound."

"And the enemy?"

"Two down that we know of, likely a couple more wounded. I saw at least one of them clutching his arm as he exited the river. I doubt they'll make it far unless they stop to build a fire. Is there a ford nearby?"

"The only one I know is quite a distance downstream."

"Shall I send riders?"

"No. The last thing we need right now is additional injured. We should return to Freiburg and get someone to look at the good sergeant's wounds."

"In time," said Sigwulf. "We must dry you off first. We don't want you catching your death from the cold."

A small flame burst to life. "We've got a fire," called out Rikal as a thin stream of smoke rose up. "Come, warm yourself. You look terrible, Lord."

Sigwulf grinned. "He means that in the nicest way, of course."

Ludwig moved closer, then sat, his feet almost in the fire. The flames built steadily until the warmth finally permeated his cold skin.

"I dare say they won't try that again any time soon," said Sigwulf.

Ludwig shook his head. "They won't give up that easily."

12

TROUBLE BREWS

WINTER 1095 SR

Sergeant Hoffman easily blocked the blow. "Come now, Edwig. What did I tell you about holding the axe?"

"Hold it farther down?" replied the youth.

"Exactly. Try again."

The youth, proficient with the axe, was having trouble when facing an opponent with a shield. He struck once more, this time carving off a small splinter of wood.

"There, much better. Now, what do you do if someone gets in close?"

"Back up?"

"That's not always an option." Cyn gripped her axe and stepped in, pressing up against him. "What do you do now?"

He blushed at her closeness.

"Put aside whatever ideas are in your head. You're a warrior, not a poet."

He swung with the axe, a clumsy movement lacking any real strength.

"Watch closely," said Cyn. She shortened her own grip until her hand was right beneath the axe head, then pushed it forward, pressing against his surcoat. "If you hold the blade like this, you can make small jabs. It won't cut through armour, but watch this." She jabbed at his face, causing him to recoil. "See? It lets you maintain the initiative. Keep the enemy on the defensive, and you'll always control the fight." She backed up, handing her axe off to Paran. Of course, they were only wooden training weapons and a good thing, too, or several of the new recruits would already have battle scars.

"Keep at it," she urged. "I'm going to step outside to get some fresh air." She quickly regretted her decision as her sweat-soaked clothing froze in winter's icy grip. Turning, about to re-enter the keep, she spotted something moving off to her left. It was only there for a moment, but she was sure she'd seen someone creeping along the base of the keep's wall.

Overcome by suspicion, she ignored the cold and made her way down the steps. She was soon by the keep's northwest tower, peering around the corner.

Farther along the base of the wall stood a man looking up. Cyn followed his gaze to spot another figure at the top of the keep leaning over the battlement. There was no mistaking the fellow up top, for his well-made attire marked him as Berthold. He tossed something from the wall to land a couple of paces away from the man at the base. The stranger quickly picked up whatever it was.

"Stop!" shouted Cyn, running towards him.

Spotting her as she came around the corner, he immediately turned, ploughing through the snow, heading north.

Cyn was determined to catch the villain, sure he was up to no good, but a wind blew up just then, reminding her how unprotected she was against the weather. Her prey, wrapped in furs, easily outdistanced her, disappearing into the swirling snow. She cursed her luck and returned to the warmth of the keep.

Ludwig returned that evening, along with the rest of the garrison. One of the king's men was dead, and Sergeant Hobson's head was heavily bandaged. Cyn dispatched men to take care of the horses as Carson saw to the wounded sergeant.

"What happened?" she asked.

"We found the raiders," said Sigwulf, "but some of them made it across the river. The sergeant hit his head when he fell from his horse."

"Yes," said Ludwig. "He was in the water at the time. It probably saved him in the long run, else he might have bled out."

"And the enemy?" asked Cyn.

"Two dead that we know of. As for the rest, we think we injured a couple."

"And were they bandits?"

"No, they were too well-equipped. I suspect they're warriors from Neuhafen."

"Surely an act of war?"

"No," said Ludwig. "At least not yet. We can't discount the possibility that they were working independently."

"How far away is the Neuhafen town?"

"My father used to tell me it was two days' ride, but most of that is through thick woods."

"Could they be planning an attack?"

"I doubt it, at least not here. The river is a natural barrier, and the forest would make it difficult for an entire army to traverse."

"Well, it's good to see you back here. We had a little excitement of our own."

"You did?"

"Yes, but this is something better discussed in private?"

"Very well, we'll use my study. Sig, look after things here, will you? I need to talk to Cyn."

"Of course."

The two of them made their way up the northwest tower and were soon within the study. Ludwig moved over by the window, opening the shutter slightly to let in some light.

"Now, what is it?"

"While you were gone," said Cyn, "I saw Berthold pass something off to an outsider."

"Can you be more specific?"

"While on the battlements, your stepbrother tossed some sort of bundle down. I suspect a note weighed down by a stone or something of that nature. It landed a few paces from the man at the bottom."

"And what did this outsider do?"

"He was gathering up whatever it was when I charged towards him."

"And then he ran?"

"He did. Northward, to be exact. I tried to follow him, but I wasn't dressed for the cold."

"Did you look for a trail?"

"I took some men and searched the area, but the wind had already covered his tracks. I don't trust Berthold. He's up to something."

"Undoubtedly," said Ludwig, "but the real question is what?"

"Has he not done enough for you to banish him?"

"I'm loath to do so. I owe it to his mother to keep him safe, regardless of my own personal feelings on the matter."

"His mother's dead," said Cyn. "Surely such a debt has long since been repaid?"

"I won't condemn the man out of hand. He has his faults, definitely, but I still believe there's some good in him. He's also the son of a foreign noble. I shouldn't like to speculate what that would do for Otto's alliance if I threw him in the dungeon."

"And in the meantime, he's free to wander the keep?"

"What else can I do with him?"

"What if you sent him to Harlingen? He'd be out of your hair. Saints know he would probably love it."

"I shall consider it come spring, but I don't want him travelling in this weather."

"You rode to Freiburg?"

"I did and nearly froze from diving into the river. There's a lesson in there somewhere."

"Like, don't go swimming in the middle of winter?"

Ludwig chuckled. "Yes, something to that effect."

The next day proved unseasonably warm. Sigwulf brought the archers out to practice at long range while Cyn drilled the recruits.

Ludwig, bereft of anything pressing, wandered outside, determined to see how things were progressing. He selected the bowmen first, moving to stand beside Sigwulf as they loosed arrows in their own time.

Rikal took aim at two hundred yards and let loose. The arrow flew true and, moments later, hit the target.

"He's a natural, that one," noted Sigwulf. "I wish we had more like him."

"And the other two?"

"Better than I'll ever be, I'll grant you, but a little more practice wouldn't hurt."

"And the youngster, Kalen?"

"Doing much better now he has some meat on his bones. I still have him using a smaller bow, but I'm confident we'll be able to move him up to something more powerful once spring arrives."

"How's his accuracy?"

"Good at short range, but he has yet to learn how to take the wind into account when the target is farther out. He'll master it in time; he's definitely enthusiastic about it."

"I'm surprised to hear that."

"Truly?" said Sigwulf. "I would expect no less."

"What makes you say that?"

"I reckon using a bow is far more exciting than feeding slop to the pigs, wouldn't you?"

"I suppose I never thought of it that way."

"Serving a lord is a noble profession. You must admit, the coins aren't too bad, either, especially considering you don't need to pay for food."

"Spoken like a true mercenary. Is that your life's dream?"

Sigwulf mulled it over. "There are three things that give life meaning."

"And they are?"

"Love, food, and the joy of battle, although I assume the last thing wears a little thin as you get older."

"They all do," said Ludwig. "I met plenty of men who overindulged in their youth and paid the price for it later."

"With what, battle?"

"No," said Ludwig. "All three!"

Sigwulf laughed. "Then I suppose we should practice moderation with all of them."

Ludwig turned, watching Cyn taking her people through some drills. She'd planted a series of posts for them to train with, and now they hacked away with their swords, alternating sides.

Two of Verfeld's original garrison stood there, their backs to their lord as they watched their new comrades. Something in their manner annoyed Ludwig, so he wandered over to them, intending to have words. Their conversation drifted to his ears as he approached.

"They'll never make decent warriors," noted Manning, the shorter of the two.

"What do you expect with a woman training them?" said his companion, a man named Ridgeway. "There's no force in their swings."

Ludwig paused behind them. "I suppose you could do better?"

His words made them jump.

"Sorry, Lord," said Manning, blushing at being overheard. "We were just—"

"Disparaging the sergeant?" His statement rang true, for the man turned crimson. "I understand your hesitancy to accept a woman into the garrison, but I assure you she is more than a match for the likes of you."

Clearly, they were insulted, but he pressed on, raising his voice. "Sergeant?"

Cyn turned. "Aye, my lord?"

"These good men would like to try out some of your training. Perhaps a round or two of melee might be to their liking?" He turned to his guards. "Well? Here's your chance to prove your words true. Come now, face her in battle, and let's see who is the greater warrior?"

Manning paled, ever more apparent now after his earlier blush. Ridgeway, however, appeared eager to take up the challenge. He stepped forward, facing Cyn with an air of superiority. "Give me one of those practice swords, and I'll show you how to fight."

Cyn sized him up. "Gustavo," she called out. "Bring me your sword."

The youth passed over the wooden blade as his comrades ceased their own training, moving closer to watch the exchange. It didn't take long for the archers to notice, and they all formed a rough circle in anticipation of the coming melee.

Ridgeway grabbed the sword from Paran and took a few experimental swings. Cyn moved into a slight crouch, her weapon arm somewhat extended, enabling her to parry should the need arise. Ludwig watched with interest. She usually favoured the mace, so he wondered how proficient she was with the sword.

Ridgeway stepped forward, then stabbed out, but his opponent simply backed up, easily avoiding the tip. As he pulled back, she rushed in with a stab of her own, aimed not at his torso but his right leg, which the man had extended as he attacked. The sound of wood hitting his thigh was easily heard by those watching, as was the curse he muttered in response.

"Come on," taunted Cyn. "You can do better than that!"

He struck again, this time a good swing with plenty of force behind it, but she brought up her own weapon at the last moment, deftly deflecting the blow. Ridgeway staggered forward, momentarily off balance, and she tapped him on the elbow.

"Now, now. You're getting sloppy."

His face reddened, and he charged her. There was no denying the man's strength, and had Cyn stood still, she would doubtless be sporting a nasty bruise from the contact, but the guard's intentions were easy to predict. This time she twisted, allowing the blade to sail past her, then used her free hand to grasp his wrist, pulling him into the swing and sending him tumbling to the ground.

She waited as he got to his feet, his face now redder than ever. "You're strong, I'll grant you that, but your moves are predictable."

"I'll show you who is predictable!" he yelled, running towards her, blade raised overhead. She stepped in close, much closer than he'd expected, and elbowed him in the stomach, knocking the wind from him. He stumbled, gasping for air.

"Tell me," asked Cyn. "Have you ever killed anyone?"

"No," replied Ridgeway. "You?"

"More than I care to admit. You have the makings of a fine swordsman, and with a little training, I can help you, but first, you must lose your bad habits."

"And what habits are those?"

"Your temper betrays you, leads you to make rash decisions. Also, your feet give away your movements."

"My feet?"

"Yes. You shift them right as you're about to lunge, and you twist them slightly when slashing. It's a dead giveaway." She moved closer and tapped his leg. "Move this back a bit."

"Why?"

"You're a strong man. You don't require the added impetus of an extended leg. Striking in this manner gives you a greater chance of taking your opponent off guard."

"And the lunge?"

"I would suggest only using it when you're close."

"But then how do I penetrate the mail?"

"You don't need to. The sword's weight is sufficient to bruise, possibly even break a limb with your strength. Remember, fighting isn't so much about killing as defeating your enemy's will to carry on the fight."

Ridgeway bowed his head. "I owe you an apology. You're more than suited to the position of sergeant."

Cyn looked over to where Manning watched the exchange. "Well?"

"Well, what?" Manning replied.

"Are you going to join us for practice?"

Instead of answering, the man looked at Ludwig.

"You heard the invitation," he said. "The decision is entirely up to you."

Manning stared at Cyn. "How many of those training swords do you have?"

That evening found Ludwig, Cyn, and Sigwulf gathered around the hearth. They'd partaken of a heavy meal, and plentiful ale caused their tongues to loosen.

Ludwig's companions were deep in a discussion of tactics when he suddenly remembered something. He waited for a brief moment of silence before interrupting. "Hey Sig, it's been weeks now. Did you ever get any information out of that prisoner?"

"You mean the one in the dungeon?" Sigwulf replied. "I'm afraid he's proven quite stubborn. Why?"

"It just occurred to me we never discovered who his fellow conspirators were, or who was behind the attack."

"I still think a little persuasion would loosen his tongue."

"No. As I said before, we could never trust a confession extracted by such means."

"Maybe it was Neuhafen?" said Cyn. "You guessed they were behind the raid on Freiburg."

"Was it really a raid?" asked Sigwulf. "The only thing taken was a cow."

"True," said Ludwig, "but that proved their undoing. We never would have suspected their presence had they not killed the beast. That reminds me, how is Sergeant Hobson doing?"

"As well as can be expected," said Cyn. "He's awake but suffers from terrible headaches. We might want to take him into Malburg. I'm sure the Temple of Saint Mathew would help him."

"Yes, of course. I should have considered that myself. Is he well enough to ride?"

"No."

"Then we'll see if we can't borrow a cart or wagon from Verfeld village to take him there first thing tomorrow, weather permitting."

"Speaking of the Church," said Sigwulf, "when can we expect the return of our intrepid Father Vernan?"

"That's an excellent question. He promised to come back by midwinter, and that's fast approaching."

"Say," said Cyn, "weren't you thinking of hosting a Midwinter Feast and inviting the local leaders?"

Ludwig sat up suddenly, causing his drink to slosh over the edge of his cup. "That's right, I was. With all the excitement going on around here, I completely forgot. How many days have we got?"

"Eight," said Sigwulf.

"No, seven," corrected Cyn, "but we still have time. I'll talk to the cook, shall I?"

Sigwulf laughed. "What do you know about preparing a feast?"

"Nothing, nor do I need to. That's what the cook is for. My task is to inform her of His Lordship's intention to host it. I'm sure she'll take care of the rest."

"That means laying in supplies."

"Then it's a good thing we've got a wagon going to Malburg tomorrow." Ludwig turned his attention to Cyn. "You should bring the new garrison members with you, and they can help."

"And what, precisely, will you be doing?"

"Trying to get over a hangover, I assume."

"You know," said Sigwulf, "there's something I was meaning to ask you, Ludwig."

"Go on, then."

"Why is it your brother never joins us?"

"That's simple. He doesn't prefer our company."

"It's your fault, Siggy," said Cyn. "You're too noisy."

"I'm not noisy," he roared back, then fell into fits of laughter.

She got to her feet, wobbling slightly. "It clearly falls to the more sober of us to carry on with preparations, so if you will excuse me, I will make my way to the kitchen."

"And with that," said Sigwulf, "it's time to make my own way to bed while I'm still in control of my legs. What about you, Ludwig?"

"What about me?"

"Are you going to bed?"

"To be honest, I hadn't given it much thought. On the one hand, I'm not overly tired."

"And on the other?"

"Well, there's the effect of the ale to consider. How much longer, I wonder, shall I be able to sit here and ponder recent events without feeling the soporific effects of too much drink?"

"You're giving this far too much thought. I say to bed and let sleep claim you."

Ludwig stood, swaying slightly, then sank back down again. "On second thought, I'll just sleep here."

13

THE CASTELLAN
WINTER 1095 SR

Father Vernan finally returned when midwinter was only three days away. With him rode a figure unlike any Ludwig had met before. Tall and lithe, it looked as if a slight gust could blow him over. His uncovered head revealed a thick, long mane of yellow hair, but his face was clean-shaven, rare amongst the people of Hadenfeld.

Father Vernan nodded in greeting. "Good day, my lord. Allow me to introduce Master Pelton Wakefield."

"Good day to you, sir," said Ludwig. "Any friend of the father here is welcome in Verfeld."

"I found him in Harlingen," explained Father Vernan. "I thought he might make an excellent castellan for you."

"Oh?" said Ludwig. "You have experience in running a barony?"

"No," said Pelton, "but I have helped run several businesses in my time. A thorough understanding of finances has always been one of my strengths."

"Are you from Hadenfeld?"

"No, I was born up in Zowenbruch but found myself stranded here when a business venture fell through."

"Might I ask the details?"

"I arranged with an acquaintance to set up a warehouse in Harlingen. I intended it to serve as a place to gather goods for export, but I arrived to find he'd made no such arrangements. In fact, exactly the opposite, for my colleague absconded with the funds. I then visited the Temple of Saint Mathew to contemplate my next steps."

"He was praying when I found him," said Father Vernan. "It appears the Saints have blessed us with his presence in our moment of need."

"You say you have experience with matters pertaining to finances?" asked Ludwig.

"I do," replied Pelton. "And have for some years now. My father was a trader, as was his father before him. You might say it runs in the family."

"Yet here you are hoping to settle down. It hardly seems to be the type of thing you would enjoy."

"Actually, I'm looking forward to having some stability in my life. I've spent most of my time travelling the Continent. It would be nice to have a place to call home. Who knows? Maybe I'll find a wife and settle down here, assuming you're willing to hire me on."

"You certainly sound promising," said Ludwig, "but I cannot commit to such a long period of service until I know you can do the job."

"Then might I offer an alternative arrangement?"

"What did you have in mind?"

"With your permission, I shall stay here in Verfeld for three months. I will take no payment for that period, but you must feed and house me. If I cannot improve your finances, then send me on my way."

"You're that certain of your abilities?"

"Most assuredly, my lord."

"It appears there's little risk to the offer. I accept."

"And," added Father Vernan, "Pelton here has travelled fairly extensively. That could prove useful in the future."

"Indeed," said Ludwig. "Very well. Carson will take you to your room. Once you settle in, Father Vernan can show you around, then we'll find a time to sit down and discuss what can be done."

The visitor bowed deeply. "You honour me, my lord."

The next day, Ludwig oversaw the servants as they decorated the great hall for the Midwinter Feast. They arranged tables end to end with benches laid out for maximum capacity. The tradition was for guests to join in the celebration with gifts of food and drink. To that end, they allotted extra space on one of the tables.

This year, Ludwig decided to start his own tradition. Once they'd cleared away the great dinner, the servants would have their own meal and be excused for the rest of the evening. On the other hand, the garrison would celebrate the evening before, allowing them sufficient time to recover to assist with the guests' departures, should they overindulge. He was examining an old candlestick when Pelton entered.

"Ah, my lord," said the castellan. "The exact person I was looking for." He stopped short as his gaze fell upon the object of Ludwig's attention. "Is something wrong, Lord?"

"I'm not sure. I'm trying to place this, but I can't remember where it came from?"

"Storage, I would presume."

"No," said Ludwig. "I mean, I don't recall seeing it before, yet it doesn't look new."

"Lord Berthold purchased it last year," offered Carson.

"He did? Why in the name of the Saints would he do such a thing? Go and fetch the silver ones, will you?"

"I'm afraid I can't, Lord. They are no longer in our possession."

"Are you saying someone stole them?"

"Not so much stolen as... sold."

"Let me guess, my dear stepbrother took them into Malburg?"

"He did, my lord."

"Ah. Well, it can't be helped now. We'll just have to make do." Ludwig returned his attention to Pelton. "You wanted to see me. I assume you looked over our accounts?"

"I have, Lord."

"And?"

"Well, it's good news and bad, I'm afraid. Which would you like to hear first?"

"Let's start with the good, shall we?"

"The barony is bringing in enough in taxes to support a modest garrison and the expenses of the keep."

"And the bad news?"

"The records of expenditures are atrocious."

"Can you be more specific?"

"From what I gather, your costs have more than doubled since your father's demise, not that I understand where it's going. There's also a substantial amount unaccounted for."

"That's hardly a surprise."

"Still, this spending must be curtailed, or you'll be in severe difficulty before the coming year is over."

"Is it repairable?"

"Indeed it is. In fact, the last few weeks have shown a marked improvement in reducing costs."

"That would coincide with my arrival here."

"So Father Vernan informed me. Of course, this feast you're preparing will cost a tidy sum, not to mention the one-time expense to equip the new members of your garrison."

"Understood."

"Are there any other expenses you expect to incur in the coming year?"

"Yes," replied Ludwig. "The king has asked me to increase my garrison by a significant degree."

"That being?"

"I'd like to have a full complement of twenty men-at-arms and enough weapons to supply an equal number of archers, along with one hundred militia."

"The footmen are the problem, my lord. It's the armour, you see, terribly expensive stuff. Would it be possible to equip them later, perhaps?"

"You expect them to go into battle without armour?"

"No, of course not, but we are currently at peace, are we not?"

"We are," said Ludwig, "but the king fears war may soon be upon us."

"How long do we have?"

"I suspect a year, maybe two. Why?"

"If you hold off on the armour until next fall, it would greatly benefit you. From a financial point of view, that period represents your biggest income, assuming all goes well with the harvest."

"I'll need men before then, but I suppose we can make do without armour for the foreseeable future. What of the militia and archers?"

"Would they require weapons?"

"They would. There are some spears in our inventory, but more are needed. My understanding is they are not expensive."

"Indeed they are not, Lord. Bows, on the other hand, are costly."

"Not necessarily. We can call up several bowmen from the villages, and they have their own bows."

"Then I see no issues as far as cost is concerned," said Pelton. "Would the militia require armour?"

"Only what they provide themselves. I will, however, have my armourer make them some shields. There's no point in leaving them entirely unprotected."

"That requires further expenditures for raw materials, although admittedly, not as much as it would cost to purchase them elsewhere. On the whole, I see no impediment to your plans other than putting off the armour. However, I would caution you not to indulge in any future feasts until we restore your treasury to a suitable level."

"Father Vernan lent us some. Did you take that into account?"

"I did indeed. With any luck, you shall pay him back in full within two years."

"That's excellent news. Thank you, Pelton. You've been of great assistance."

"I live to serve, my lord." The castellan turned to leave.

"Oh, by the way," added Ludwig. "You'll sit with us at the Midwinter Feast, won't you?"

"I hardly believe it proper for a mere worker to sit at the head table with such august company."

"Nonsense. I insist on it. Captain Marhaven and Sergeant Hoffman will be present, as will Father Vernan. You shall have plenty of people to talk with."

"Very well," said Pelton. "In that case, I humbly accept."

Ludwig knocked on the door.

"Enter," came the reply.

He opened it, revealing Berthold sitting in a chair, reading a book.

"I didn't take you for a reader," said Ludwig.

"What else would you expect me to do here, now that you've returned?"

"You are welcome to assist in the running of the barony."

Berthold pursed his lips. "I fear my lack of skills in that regard would not be helpful."

"You could learn?"

"Indeed, I could, but the effort on your part would be staggering. Your energies are best applied elsewhere."

"We've had little contact, you and I, and I would see that changed."

"Would you, now? I find that a curious thing for you to say. Since your return, you've done little to make me feel wanted. Quite the reverse, in fact. I now find myself skulking around the keep, avoiding contact with you and your cronies."

"I think you'll find they are as willing as I to accept your presence amongst us."

"How decent of them. We are all one merry band of brothers-in-arms, aren't we? Oh wait, I forgot. I am untested in battle. I suppose that means we have nothing in common after all."

"We are brothers," said Ludwig.

"Stepbrothers," corrected Berthold. "And even then, only for a short time."

"But this is our home."

"Correction. This is your home. I never wanted to move to Hadenfeld, but Mother gave me no choice in the matter."

"You're old enough. You could have stayed in Reinwick. Your mother owned land up there, didn't she?"

"She did, but she was forced to sell it off to provide your father with funds."

Ludwig caught his breath. "I heard none of this."

"And why would you have? I doubt your father would reveal how destitute he was."

"But the accounts for Verfeld show it was a profitable barony."

"And so it would have been, had your father not been excessively extravagant."

"My father was not extravagant!"

"Really? Have you any idea of the cost of that sword you like to wear? Not to mention the armour he outfitted you with. Where is that, by the way? The armour, I mean?"

Ludwig reddened. "I lost it in the north."

"Along with the warhorse, no doubt. Yet another expenditure that drained my mother's purse."

"And I suppose now you're going to claim you've been frugal with your own funds?"

"Not at all," replied Berthold. "I am free with my coins, I admit, but I have merely spent what is rightfully mine."

"Your mother agreed to the marriage. She knew that meant giving up her fortune."

"You make it sound as though she had a choice. Grow up, Ludwig. Women have little say in such matters."

"Are you saying she was forced to marry my father?"

"It was an arranged marriage, was it not?"

Ludwig was caught. Lady Astrid admitted as much before he ran away—she'd married his father for his title. In exchange, he received her late husband's fortune. The realization hit Ludwig like a hammer. Where did it all go? Surely his father couldn't have whittled it away in so short a time? He began to suspect it was hidden somewhere within the keep.

"Well?" said Berthold.

"I'm sorry. My mind was elsewhere."

"I was saying it was an arranged marriage."

"So you were. Just out of curiosity, have you any idea what the value of your mother's estate was?"

"She never deigned to discuss it with me, said I needn't concern myself with such things. It must have been substantial, though."

"What makes you say that?"

"We had a country estate in Reinwick, on the outskirts of Blunden."

"Was it large?"

"Large enough to raise horses. I used to love visiting the stables there. And the parties... well, that was the life."

"Did you spend a lot of time at court?"

"We did," said Berthold. "The Baron of Blunden held a ball every full moon, and then we would all travel down to Korvoran for the Midwinter Feast."

"Korvoran? That's the capital, isn't it?"

"It is. The duke's estate was impressive, although I must admit the city itself is not the most pleasant of places. I found it always smelled of fish."

"Will you return there someday?"

Berthold frowned. "I doubt it. Without an estate awaiting me, there's little reason to travel there. I can still remember the day the duke proposed the idea of Mother marrying to cement an alliance. I mean, of all the people she could wed, why a baron from this Saints forsaken place?"

"The duke is cousin to King Otto," explained Ludwig.

"So are the rulers of half the Petty Kingdoms. You would expect it would make more sense to marry her off to someone nearby, like Erlingen or even Eidolon."

"The Duke of Erlingen took up with a woman from Reinwick. It caused nothing but heartache, especially when his wife died under questionable circumstances."

"How is it you're so familiar with the politics of the north? I know you fought in Erlingen, but I hardly took you for a courtier."

"I served as a knight to the Lord Wulfram Haas, Baron of Regnitz."

"A Knight of the Sceptre? I'd no idea you're so well connected. But how can you serve two masters?"

"I don't," replied Ludwig. "The baron released me from my oath once the war was over."

"You should have stayed in the north. You could be living a life of luxury, married off to someone's daughter."

"My duty is here."

"Is it?" said Berthold. "You didn't consider it so when you ran off to find fame and fortune."

"I had to leave. Life here became unbearable."

"Why? Because your father wouldn't let you marry your precious little commoner? I hardly believe that warrants such extreme measures."

"This coming from a man whose own mother was forced into marriage."

"My mother did her duty. That's far more than you!"

Ludwig took a deep breath. "Arguing will get us nowhere."

"Then what did you come here for? To remind me I am now a guest in this wretched keep? Honestly, Ludwig, you treat me more like a prisoner than a brother."

"I freely admit I've ignored you, but can you say you did any less? You are no prisoner here. You have the freedom to go or stay at your leisure. In addition, I have asked nothing of you, allowing you the freedom to do as you wish. Why do you insist on resisting my efforts to include you in the day-to-day running of this place?"

Berthold closed his book, placing it carefully on the table. "My mother was a noble of no import, my father the second cousin to a baron. As a result, I was never taught how to run anything. In fact, I should've been able to live out my days in comfort without raising so much as a finger. And I would have, had it not been for that annoying king of yours. If he hadn't insisted on marriage to cement relations between our two countries, I would still be up there, luxuriating in comfort. Instead, I find myself here, trying to stay warm in this mildew-infested excuse for a keep."

"No one is forcing you to stay."

"But you are, don't you see? I have nothing to my name save for the clothes on my back. I've been trained in no skills, taught no command of battle—for what task am I suited?"

Berthold stopped to draw a breath but wasn't finished speaking. "I have no choice but to remain here in Verfeld, just as you have no choice but to be baron. We are both trapped, though obviously in different ways. You owe your allegiance, nay your whole existence, to King Otto, and I, in turn, owe my sole line of support to you. You assume I am free to leave this place, but that freedom is short-lived, for, without funds or a skill of some description, I am doomed to a life of starvation. It's not a pleasant way to die, Ludwig."

Ludwig stared at the floor, his mind in turmoil. He'd come here expecting to have a frank discussion with his stepbrother, possibly even convince him to leave Verfeld. Now, in the wake of Berthold's admissions, it would be terrible of him to even suggest such a thing.

"You have stated your case most eloquently," he finally said. "You may stay here as long as you wish; I will expect little in return. I would, however, like to invite you to come to the Midwinter Feast."

Berthold stared back, and for a moment, it appeared he might refuse, but then the hint of a smile creased his lips. "Very well. I accept your invitation."

14

MIDWINTER

WINTER 1095 SR

The Midwinter Feast was an annual celebration marking the halfway point of winter, at least in theory. In actual fact, it was seldom an accurate measure of the season's length. Legend had it that the Saints called upon their followers to celebrate their connections with their fellow worshippers on this day, but many knew the old religion had observed the holiday for eons.

Most cared little for the day's history or its more profound, spiritual origins. Instead, they were content to simply revel in the food, drink, and camaraderie.

The tradition in Verfeld, as in most of the baronies of Hadenfeld, was to host people of import on such an occasion. Thus, Ludwig was now seated at a head table that included Prior Yannick, the regional head of the Temple of Saint Mathew. Though based in Malburg, he'd accepted the invitation to attend, even insisting he bless the meal, as was the custom.

Not to be outdone, Prioress Ophelia of the Temple of Saint Agnes was also present. However, she deferred to the prior when it came to saying the traditional blessing.

Filling the remaining seats at the head table were Sigwulf, Cyn, Father Vernan, Berthold, and Pelton Wakefield, the new castellan.

Servants brought the wine round once they all took their seats. Prior Yannick stood, scanning the guests at the other tables. Representatives from all five of the barony's villages, along with Malburg, waited expectantly for the blessing.

"Beloved Saint Mathew... and Saint Agnes," the prior added as his gaze passed over the prioress. "Watch over us this day as we honour your memory and share this meal. Give us your blessing as we dedicate ourselves to those less fortunate, and give us the strength to care for those who cannot care for themselves. You have shown us compassion that we might show likewise to others. Keep us safe, Holy Saints, to allow us to spread your words to others." He paused. "Saints be with us."

"Saints be with us all," replied everyone, save Berthold, who said, "Amen."

They looked at him in surprise, except for Prior Yannick, who merely smiled.

"What?" said Berthold. "It's the custom in the north."

"So I heard," said the prioress. "Up there, they end the blessing with 'amen', although where that particular habit came from is beyond me. Within the Church, we always call on the Saints to be with us."

"We used 'amen' back in Braymoor," said Sigwulf. "But I suppose it matters little in the long run. Either the Saints are with us, or they're not. I doubt a word or two would make much difference."

"Well said," added Prior Yannick. "I often find little differences like that fascinating, don't you? The Petty Kingdoms are full of strange regional customs, and by strange, I by no means speak ill of them."

The prior took a sip of his wine. "You were up there, Lord Ludwig. Tell me, what custom did you deem the most unusual?"

"I think the politics of Erlingen the strangest."

"In what way?"

"The duke allowed his barons to settle arguments by force of arms."

"You mean with duels?"

"No, with armies. A feud between barons was my introduction to battle."

The prior set down his cup. "You must tell us more."

"The Baron of Mulsingen hired the Grim Defenders to siege Regnitz."

"The Grim Defenders?"

"Yes, the mercenary company in which I was employed."

"Are you saying you engaged in battle for pay?"

"Don't look so astonished, Your Grace. Soldiers do it all the time. Even Temple Knights receive recompense for their services."

The prioress smiled. "He has you there, Your Grace."

"In any event," continued Ludwig, "I was surprised the ruler of a country would allow his barons to fight amongst themselves. King Otto would never condone something like that."

"King Otto is smart enough to not want another rebellion," said Ophelia. "Saints know the last one almost bankrupted the country."

"And gave us Neuhafen," added Yannick, "and they've been a thorn in his side ever since. It wouldn't surprise me if there's war in our future."

"Did you hear something we didn't?" asked Ludwig.

"Only rumours. They say King Ruger is old and in ill health."

"King Ruger?" said Sigwulf.

"He's the king of Neuhafen."

"Is that bad news?"

"It is," replied the prior. "His son, Diedrich, wants to claim Hadenfeld and reunite the land, so I expect it will be war once he's on the throne."

"Just how ill is Ruger?" asked Ludwig.

"That is an excellent question. One of my new Temple Knights just returned from Dornbruck, and he suggested the king was merely suffering from old age."

"Yet you indicated he might be ill?"

"That came by way of a travelling merchant."

"You're consorting with merchants, now?" said Ludwig, a twinkle in his eye. "Careful, Your Grace. You're becoming quite the socialite."

"Yes, well, as it happens, the fellow made a substantial donation to the temple. In any case, he'd just come from Neuhafen."

"And?"

"Prince Deidrich has been busy helping his father run the country."

"There's nothing unusual in that, is there?"

"It's not that he's helping that has me worried. No, it's more about what he's been doing."

"Which is?"

"Enlarging the army, not to mention replacing several of the king's key advisors. It all points to the likelihood that he expects to soon inherit the Crown."

"That bodes ill for us," replied Ludwig. "We may be required to accelerate our own plans to expand."

"You're safe here," said the prior. "Any attack from Neuhafen will cross the river at Hasdorf. That's the shortest route to the capital."

"True, but we must still have enough men to come to the king's aid. Not to mention the time to march to the capital ourselves. We don't want to undertake the trip only to find it in enemy hands."

"Not much chance of that. It's heavily defended."

"I doubt they intend to take Harlingen," noted Father Vernan. "Rather, they want to force a battle."

"Like they did years ago?" said Ludwig. "I didn't know you studied our history."

The Holy Father shrugged. "The capital holds many written records, and I had little to occupy my mind when I first arrived. If I recall, the battle that created Neuhafen took place before the very walls of Harlingen."

"It did. But that doesn't mean it would work a second time."

"Hold on a moment," said Cyn. "I see what he's getting at. It's not about capturing land—it's about weakening Otto's grip on the Crown."

"Precisely," said Father Vernan. "A political objective achieved through military might. If Prince Diedrich inflicts enough casualties on Otto's army, he can divide the remaining barons."

"I doubt it would work," said Ludwig. "The barons of Hadenfeld are loyal to Otto. They're not about to turn on him."

"I didn't mean to imply they were, merely that it could be Diedrich's strategy. In any event, even if they don't take the city, they could surround it and deny entry or exit."

"So they'd starve the city out?"

"Yes, and all the while, their men would have free rein to pillage the countryside."

"I'm curious," said Cyn. "What do you think Otto's response to an invasion would be?"

Ludwig mulled it over, but he could conceive of only one strategy. "He'd do the same thing he did in his youth: pull his army back to the capital and meet them in the Harlingen Hills."

"And are there any other roads Neuhafen could take?"

"No. The only bridge is at Hasdorf."

"What about fords?"

"There are a few, but they are easily defended. The only way to get his army through in sufficient numbers to defeat the Baron of Hasdorf is to take that bridge."

"The baron there has a keep, doesn't he?"

"Yes," said Ludwig, "but chances are they'd just seal it off and send the rest of the army on its way. Of course, Otto could choose to reinforce it, but then he risks having them caught in a siege and unable to help at the capital. Ultimately, it all comes down to a final confrontation at Harlingen."

"Let us not panic," soothed Prior Yannick. "Yes, we know King Ruger is old and possibly in poor health, but his son couldn't march as soon as he became king, could he? He'd have to take care of the transition of power, not to mention securing his own possession of the throne."

"I would agree, had it not been for your news of what Prince Deidrich is presently doing. He's preparing for war. It's not a matter of whether or not he's going to attack as it is about when."

"All this talk is disturbing," said Prioress Ophelia. "Perhaps we could turn the conversation towards more pleasant topics."

"Yes," said Prior Yannick. "She is right, of course. Tell me, Lord Ludwig, whatever happened to that smith you were enamoured with?"

"You mean Charlaine deShandria?" said the prioress. "She became a

Temple Knight of Saint Agnes. It was my suggestion, actually. I thought it a good fit, considering she was already a trained smith."

"Her father heard she was in Ilea," said Ludwig, "though he's had no direct word from her."

"That's to be expected. They encourage Temple Knights to leave their past behind."

"And so they must forget the past?"

"Not forget," replied the prioress. "One must never do that. No, it is better to live in the present instead of the past. You, as a warrior, should understand that better than anyone else."

"I must disagree. The past makes us who we are."

"In that, we agree, yet when someone dedicates their life to a cause, it demands their full attention. Would you be able to concentrate on your swordplay if thoughts of family and friends distracted you?"

"It is precisely because of friends that I fight. I didn't serve the Duke of Erlingen out of a sense of duty. Rather, I fought for Sig and Cyn here. They are my brothers-in-arms." He laughed. "Well, I suppose Cyn is my sister-in-arms, but the same still applies."

He paused, considering his own words. "We might march to war out of a sense of duty, but that duty still comes down to comradeship. Stand alone in battle, and you shall, in all likelihood, fall. However, stand by your friends, and you have a better than even chance of surviving."

Cyn wiped her eye. "I don't believe I ever heard it expressed so eloquently."

"Eloquently?" said Sigwulf. "And here you thought I was the one using all the fancy words. Ludwig's manner of speech must be wearing off on you." He took a swig of his wine. "He's right, of course. We fight for our comrades more than a flag or any sense of loyalty to a stranger."

"Ah," said Father Vernan. "That explains so much. That's why Otto's been taking such an interest in each of his barons of late—he wants to breed that familiarity. I imagine it won't be long before he visits Verfeld in person, though I hear he prefers to travel in warmer weather. If I had to predict when, I'd say late summer."

"That's specific," said Ludwig. "Why late summer, as opposed to earlier in the season?"

"I'm sure all this talk of events in Neuhafen has already reached his ears. He'll be eager to see those along the invasion route first. And honestly, Verfeld is about as far from Harlingen as you can get without crossing the border."

"Tell me," said Cyn. "What is the position of the Church on a potential war, Your Grace?"

Yannick stiffened. "I'm afraid we must remain completely neutral in this regard."

"And yet you preach peace."

"We prefer it, yes."

"But you have Temple Knights. Is their sole purpose not war?"

Prior Yannick reddened. "Temple Knights are dedicated to protecting Church property."

"But you sponsor crusades in the east, do you not?"

"You speak of the Temple Knights of Saint Cunar."

"Oh," said Cyn. "I'm sorry. I assumed they were referred to as the Holy Army. Am I wrong in that regard?"

"You are not," interjected the prioress. "The Temple Knights, in addition to protecting the temples, are here to protect us all from the might of Halvaria."

"Ah, there it is at last," said Sigwulf. "The great evil empire. I was wondering how long it would take to bring them up."

"You don't consider them a danger?"

"I think it makes a convenient excuse for your blessed Temple Knights to exist, even if you seldom use them."

"Personally," said the prioress, "I have no experience with Halvaria, but the Temple Knights are in a difficult position as far as politics go. They can't side with one Petty Kingdom over another; the result would likely be catastrophic."

"In what way?" asked Cyn.

"Saints know there is enough divisiveness within the Petty Kingdoms. Imagine what would happen if a ruler could convince the Church to support their claims?"

"Exactly," said Prior Yannick. "And I can assure you Halvaria is not just some excuse. They have a history of expansion at the expense of their neighbours."

"Yes," said Sigwulf, "but they're thousands of miles away."

"I'm sure the conquered lands once thought as you do."

"So if a war comes, the Church will sit by and watch?"

"We shall do our best to help the innocents. They are often the ones who suffer the most in such circumstances."

"On that, we can agree," said Sigwulf. "I'm sorry. I didn't mean to demean the efforts of your order."

"It's understandable considering the situation. I admit it's frustrating to us as well. It's difficult to remain aloof when those you know are in danger, but it is one of the few tenets of the Church strictly enforced. However, anyone offered refuge within Church property is given safe haven."

"Even if they're criminals?"

"If there were such an accusation, the Church would convene a tribunal to judge the matter, but serving a foreign ruler would not, by definition, be classed as a criminal act. Now, if the individual in question was wanted for murder, it would be a completely different situation."

"How so?"

"The decision on whether to grant refuge would rest solely on the shoulders of the senior Church member."

"Meaning you," said Sigwulf.

"If it were in Malburg, then yes, but I might remind you I am not the highest-ranking member of my order in Hadenfeld. That honour lies with the Grand Prior in Harlingen."

"And how many people are above him?"

"Only one, the patriarch of the order who resides in the Antonine, hundreds of miles from here."

"But you have a Primus, don't you?"

The prior smiled. "Yes, but he isn't necessarily a Mathewite. He is elected by the Council of Peers, which consists of one designated representative from each of the six Holy Orders."

"And where do the Temple Knights fit into all of this?"

"Each order, be they Mathewites, Cunars, or what have you, is ruled over by a grand master, who, in turn, reports to the patriarch of their respective order. Thus, the Grand Master of the Temple Knights of Saint Mathew serves at the discretion of the Patriarch of Saint Mathew."

"And who decides who gets to be patriarch?"

"On the occasion of the death of such an individual, the Arch Priors convene a special tribunal to elect one of their own as the next patriarch. It's a lifetime appointment, although injury or infirmity can result in someone stepping down."

"It appears you have everything well thought out," mused Sigwulf.

"We've had almost a thousand years to do so, but it wasn't always so well organized. The Church's early history is a fascinating tale of mistakes and disasters."

"And that," said the prioress, "is the point at which I must insist the current discussion change to something less tedious. Don't get me wrong, I love my church, but if we are to talk of history, we'll be here all night, and we've yet to break bread."

"Of course," said Ludwig. "How rude of me." He turned to his head servant. "Carson, if you would be so kind?"

"Of course, my lord."

Carson called out, summoning others to finally bring in the main course, platters piled high with all manner of delights. They dug in with gusto, and even though the food had cooled in the interim, no one complained about it.

Ludwig did not make it to bed until well past midnight, for the food was delicious and the conversation engaging. By all accounts, he should be exhausted, yet he lay staring at the ceiling, his mind drifting to the threat of war.

He needed more warriors, but he could do little without the necessary funds. His thoughts led him once more to consider Lady Astrid's fortune. It must be somewhere within the keep, but where? Try as he might, he could conceive of no place suitable for such a treasure.

Could his father have given it to someone in Malburg for safekeeping? Ludwig immediately discounted the idea. His father was not a man who made friends easily. Outside of the prior and prioress, he seldom had visitors at Verfeld. To whom, then, would he willingly entrust such a fortune?

The only possible conclusion was that his father would have hidden it himself. That being the case, it must be somewhere within these very walls.

Ludwig had been given free rein of the keep as a child, yet he could recall no single place where a chest of gold might be hidden. Was it possible the fortune lay not in coins but in some other form? Jewellery, for example? The thought opened up a host of new possibilities, for such a prize would be much easier to conceal. He almost convinced himself to begin the search now, in the middle of the night, but the idea of disturbing his guests finally won out, and sleep claimed him.

15

BERTHOLD STRIKES BACK

WINTER 1095 SR

s soon as his guests were on the road, Ludwig gathered his companions, determined to locate the missing fortune.

"Where do we start?" asked Cyn.

"At the top, and work our way down," replied Ludwig. "No stone is to be left unturned. Search everywhere, no matter how small."

"Would that many coins fit in a tiny space?"

"No, but I suspect she may have exchanged them for precious gems to transport it."

"Makes sense," said Sigwulf. "I can't say I'd feel comfortable carrying an entire inheritance in coins halfway across the Continent."

"Excuse my ignorance," said Cyn, "but what kind of gems are we talking about?"

"Expensive ones," said Father Vernan. "Likely diamonds or rubies, possibly even emeralds or sapphires. They will be translucent to the naked eye, each with a distinctive hue."

"So we're looking for pretty rocks?"

"In a manner of speaking, yes."

"How do you know so much about them?" Ludwig asked.

"It was a passion of my father's. He gave my mother a sapphire ring when they were courting. She still has it to this day."

"Sapphire is the blue one, isn't it?" asked Cyn.

"Indeed, it is. Rubies are red, emeralds green, and we're all aware diamonds are translucent, correct?"

"And how many of these things are we expecting to find?"

"I should think," said the Holy Father, "little more than a small pouch."

"So," said Cyn, "not very valuable, then?"

"On the contrary. A pouch of diamonds that fits in the palm of your hand could easily pay for this entire keep."

"How can such a modest collection of stones be worth so much?"

"Their rarity makes them expensive. That and the demand. They're used in making jewellery, you see. Most of the crowns in the Petty Kingdoms hold at least one precious gem within them, sometimes more. That also doesn't take into account all the nobles who enjoy displaying their wealth."

Cyn looked at Ludwig. "He's looking at you, Baron."

"Not me," replied Ludwig. "I only wear a badge of office for special ceremonies, and then I have a ring when I need to seal official correspondence."

"A ring?" said Sigwulf. "In the north, we use a simple stamp. Yet another difference in our customs, it would seem."

"An interesting observance," said Cyn, "but there's a large keep to search, and we've yet to begin."

"Good point," said Ludwig. "You and Sig start in my study, then make your way around to the east. Father Vernan and I will head in the opposite direction until we all meet up."

"What would you like me to do?" asked Pelton.

"I'll need you to track which rooms we've looked through, ensuring we're not doubling up."

"What about me?" came the voice of Berthold.

"I didn't even know you were here," said Ludwig.

"I want to help too. After all, more funds for the keep means I will continue living a life of relative comfort."

"You can come with me and Father Vernan."

Searching the upper floors took the greater part of the morning. As promised, they checked everything from candlesticks to chairs, even moving all the furniture in the hope it might reveal a loose stone or hidden compartment.

Ludwig began to think there was no treasure to be found as they gathered, empty-handed, by the southeast tower. "Time to move downstairs to the main floor, although that would seem a strange place to hide a fortune."

"I have an idea," offered Berthold. "They put my mother's belongings away in a chest after her death."

"And you think the treasure might be there?"

"Doubtful. I assume she gave it to your father when they married, but she might have mentioned how much she brought with her. I know for a fact that she kept a diary."

"Where could we find this chest?"

"Likely in the storeroom, down in the cellar."

"Why there?" asked Cyn.

"The servants wanted it out of sight for fear it carried the fever that killed her."

"Could it still make someone sick?"

"No," said Father Vernan. "If that were true, then half the missions of my order would be overflowing with fevered patients."

"Berthold, go check it out," said Ludwig. "Let us know if you find anything of value."

"I will. I promise." He made his way down the stairwell.

"And what do we do in the meantime?" asked Sigwulf. "Search the great hall? I doubt we'd find anything there."

"Look on the bright side," said Ludwig. "What else have you got to do?"

"I can think of plenty, thank you."

Ludwig was in the great hall, searching the now cold hearth, when Berthold found him.

"Any luck?" asked Ludwig.

"I located her chest, but I'm afraid there was little of interest in it. I discovered this, though." He held out a small bag.

"It's not the gems, is it?"

"No. I regret to tell you it's not. It's some of her jewellery, enough to pay for another guard or two, but hardly the kind of funds you're looking for."

Ludwig took the bag, emptying its contents onto the table. Out spilled half a dozen rings and two necklaces. "I'm no expert, but I don't believe I see anything expensive here. Do you?" He directed this last remark towards Father Vernan.

The Holy Father came over, picking up a necklace and holding it close to a candle. "It's nice, I'll grant you that, but I wouldn't say particularly valuable. It's definitely not what we were looking for."

"Still," said Berthold. "Every little bit helps, doesn't it?"

To everyone's astonishment, Ludwig scooped up the jewellery and placed it back within the bag, then handed it to his stepbrother. "Here. It was your mother's. It's only right you should have it."

"Are you certain? Surely you can put it to better use than I?"

Ludwig shrugged. "One soldier, more or less, will make little difference in the long run. You take it."

"Very well, but only because you insisted."

Cyn collapsed into a chair. "We searched high and low yet found absolutely nothing."

"Not quite," said Sigwulf. "There are still the rooms below, not that there's many of them."

"You two wait here," said Ludwig. "Father Vernan and I will head downstairs."

"I'll come too," insisted Berthold.

That evening, Ludwig lay awake once more. The search had failed to turn up anything of significance, leading him to wonder if he wasn't over-thinking things. Could the funds have already been spent? He tried to put such thoughts from his mind, but they nagged at him.

His father had been a difficult man to deal with. Spending frivolously had not been something Ludwig considered in his character, but then he remembered what Berthold said about his sword. Could he honestly admit his father was frugal when he'd gifted such a blade? He had to consider other alternatives. Could he have lost it somehow or been accosted by bandits on the return from Reinwick? Ludwig immediately dismissed the idea. Had someone attacked them, Berthold would remember it, at the very least.

He rose from his bed, moving across the room to where a cup and pitcher waited. A drink slaked his thirst, but a chill from the cold floor set in. He threw on his cloak and began pacing, then the door rattled.

Ludwig froze, unsure of what was happening. Again, the door shook slightly, and then came the sound of metal on metal. He'd taken to locking his door ever since they'd replenished the keep's strongbox. Now, it appeared someone was trying to pick the lock, perhaps to steal what few funds he still possessed. He retrieved the pitcher on his way to stand beside the door, making certain it opened away from him.

The door clicked as it was finally unlocked. Ludwig waited, his breath held tight. Muttering came from outside, then the shuffling of feet. The door opened a crack, and an arm slowly snaked through. Whoever it belonged to was taking care to make as little noise as possible.

Ludwig heard breathing from whoever was in the doorway and at least another one behind. "Hurry up," whispered a voice. "We don't want to be here all night, for Saint's sake."

The first one came into the room, his attention focused on the bed. The darkness saved Ludwig, for the torch out in the hallway cast shadows everywhere. He waited until a second individual entered the doorway before he struck, bringing the metal pitcher crashing down onto a helmet. Luckily, the force was enough to make the fellow stagger back into the hall.

"Alarm!" Ludwig cried out as he lunged at the man standing by the bed. His foe turned around in time to receive a fist to the face. Blood splattered all over Ludwig's hand as he broke the man's nose. His opponent twisted to avoid the next blow, and Ludwig's fist smashed into the metal coif, knocking the man onto the bed.

Ludwig, cursing as the skin ripped from his knuckles, heard footsteps behind him, and threw himself to the side, narrowly avoiding the thrust of a sword. Another attacker stood in the doorway, brandishing a torch, flooding the room with light. Two of the three men were in mail, but he recognized all as members of the garrison.

"You!" shouted Ludwig, staring at the one in the doorway. "How did you get out of the dungeon?"

The man simply grinned. "Get him, boys!"

The one on the bed rolled off the side while the second followed up with another swing of his sword. Ludwig stepped back, desperate to keep his distance, but the wall stopped him.

"You'll never get away with this!" he snarled.

"Nonsense," said the ringleader. "We'll claim we found you dead and help search for the assailant." He looked as if he was going to say more, but then his head exploded, blood flying everywhere. His body collapsed, revealing Cyn, a bloody mace in hand.

Even though their leader had fallen, the other two rushed the door, intent on cutting her down, but she expected it. Instead of standing her ground, she simply backed up into the hallway.

The first to reach the doorway stabbed out, but he didn't realize Cyn wasn't alone. A sword swung down from beside the door, taking him in the neck and nearly severing it. Like his companion, his body collapsed, leaving only one lone assailant.

"Give up," yelled Ludwig. "There's no escape."

The villain turned his weapon on his original target. "They may cut me down, but your head will roll first."

"You don't need to do this. Throw down your weapon, and I'll spare your life."

The fellow hesitated, which was his downfall. Having witnessed the exchange, Cyn rushed forward, smashing her mace into his kneecap. It bent the joint back at an impossible angle, and the guard fell to the floor, screaming in agony, his sword rattling on the stone. Ludwig picked up the blade and moved closer.

Sigwulf, following in Cyn's wake, stood looming over the pitiful fellow, the tip of his blade at the man's throat.

"Who sent you?" he demanded.

"Berthold," came the reply.

"No," said Ludwig. "It can't be."

The prisoner merely laughed. "Your brother has played you for a fool, Baron."

Sigwulf pushed the blade down, silencing the man forever.

Ludwig looked up at Sigwulf. "You're naked."

The big man blushed. "I was busy. Me and Cyn were... well, you know."

His gaze drifted over to Cyn, clutching her shift. "What?" she said. "I was cold!"

"Rouse the garrison," said Ludwig, "and find Berthold!"

The entire keep was soon awake, servants and all, but it quickly became clear Berthold had left, stealing a mount to make his escape. The king's horsemen rode out after him, but another winter storm blew in, making pursuit a pointless gesture.

Morning found them all in the great hall, exhausted from the night's events.

"What I don't understand," said Sigwulf, "is why now? He had plenty of time to kill you earlier. What changed?"

"I think he discovered the treasure," offered Cyn.

"How? He was with us the whole time."

"Not the entire time," she corrected. "He, alone, went to look at the chest. Remember?"

"You mean Lady Astrid's belongings?"

She nodded.

"That may be," said Ludwig, "but he even brought me her jewels."

"Likely to throw you off the scent. He gave you the impression there was nothing else of value by offering you that token."

"I hate to admit it," said Father Vernan, "but I fear she is correct. You've been fooled; that small gesture convinced us he only had your best interests at heart. I suspect he arranged everything once the gems were in his possession. What I don't understand is how he released the prisoner?"

"That's easy," said Sigwulf. "Berthold obviously gave them a copy of the key. All they had to do was unlock the cell and head upstairs. It's not as if any of the other guards would suspect anything. Most of them were asleep, anyway."

"So, what do we do now?"

Ludwig stood. "What can we do? It's all gone."

"We could still examine that chest," suggested Cyn. "If nothing else, we might discover where the treasure was hidden?"

"Good idea. Come along, everyone. Let's look in the storeroom and see what we find, shall we?"

As they passed the armoury, Sigwulf halted. "Hold on a moment. Bring me that torch." He pushed on the iron gate, and it swung open at his touch.

"What is it?" asked Ludwig.

"I'll tell you in a moment." Sigwulf took the torch from Father Vernan and walked around slowly, holding the light high to illuminate the room. "Nothing's missing," he said. "So why unlock the door?"

Cyn moved in to join him. "Over here," she called out. "These armour stands have been shoved to one side."

Sigwulf crouched. "So they have." He reached forward with his spare hand. "Someone's been digging at the mortar."

Cyn gripped the brick and pulled. The stone came loose, revealing a small space behind it. "I'm guessing this is where it was hidden."

"But how did he even know it was here?"

She looked at Sigwulf as she tried to work it out. "Didn't he say something about a diary?"

"He did indeed," said Father Vernan. "Come, let us continue looking. He could have left it behind in his rush to hide what he found."

"What good will that do?" asked Sigwulf.

"It won't get the treasure back if that's what you're asking, but it might at least answer some of our questions."

"Lead on," urged Ludwig. "The chest should be down that corridor in the old storeroom on the left."

Finding Lady Astrid's belongings was simple enough. The room was full of furniture, for she'd decorated her room in a style familiar to her northern upbringing. A chest sat on a table, its hasp still undone.

"You do it, Cyn," said Sigwulf. "I don't want to rummage through a dead woman's things."

"And you think I do?"

"It's not that she's dead that worries me."

"Then what is it?"

"There might be… unmentionables in there."

She laughed. "Are you afraid her undergarments would attack you?"

He blushed. "No, but it's just not proper."

"Neither was what you were doing to me last night, but I'm not complaining."

Sigwulf turned an even darker shade.

"For Saint's sake," said Father Vernan. "I'll search the chest." He rummaged through, then suddenly stopped. "I have something." He produced a bound book with a flourish.

"It must be her diary," said Ludwig.

"Indeed. Here. It's only proper that you be the one to examine it."

Ludwig took the book, flipping through it quickly. "It looks like someone's ripped out a page or two."

"Likely Berthold," suggested Cyn. "What's just before the missing section?"

"A line of numbers, by the look of it."

"Let me see." Father Vernan scanned the contents. "It is a list of amounts. I'm guessing this is what she got for selling off her estate. Part of the tally is missing, but it appears only a portion was handed over to your father. If I'm reading this correctly, there was still a substantial sum left in her possession."

"And now it's in the hands of Berthold?"

"So it would seem."

"For Saint's sake!" said Sigwulf. "He got away with a fortune. If I ever get my hands on him, I swear I'll kill him!"

"I doubt you'll get the opportunity," said Ludwig. "With a fortune like that, he'll disappear into the Petty Kingdoms, never to be seen again." He moved to the chest, closing its lid. "It's frustrating. We came so close to finding it."

"It is a sad tale, to be sure," said Father Vernan. "But we must try to look on the bright side of things."

Sigwulf snorted. "What could possibly be bright about all of this?"

"We are all alive and unhurt. That, by itself, is good news, but there's more. The treasure is gone, true, but with it goes Berthold. No longer shall he darken this keep with his presence, nor will he be plotting behind your back or taking any more coins from your pocket. Some might even say those funds were never destined for Verfeld since we knew naught of them. In any case, it's a small price to pay to be rid of your stepbrother."

16

PASSING OF THE SEASONS
SPRING 1096 - SUMMER 1097 SR

Thoughts of Berthold's betrayal faded with the arrival of spring. The kingdom was at peace, the weather mild, and optimism spread across the land like a fresh breeze.

Word of King Rugar's improved health circulated as summer approached, reducing fears of an impending war. The kingdoms of Neuhafen and Hadenfeld stepped back from the brink, and people became more optimistic. The threat of war grew more remote as tradesmen once again took to the roads of the Petty Kingdoms.

Heeding Pelton's advice, Ludwig maintained a reduced garrison throughout the summer. As the harvest came in, filling the coffers, his attention turned once more to restoring his complement of warriors.

He'd written to King Otto, seeking advice, and received a reply indicating additional funds were available from the Crown. Ludwig could now afford to increase his garrison to form an entire company of fifty men in total, footmen all, and boost his number of archers.

Lacking the manpower within his own lands, he sought permission from the city of Malburg to recruit there. They resisted at first, but when word came that King Rugar was again bedridden, they ceded to his request.

By the next midwinter, he had thirty-five footmen, and once the snow melted, forty-five. Sigwulf and Cyn kept up the training while Verfeld's smith churned out armour as fast as possible.

In the spring of ninety-seven, Ludwig began training the levy. By tradition, every male of suitable age could be called upon to serve under arms.

They were typically ill-equipped and lacked fighting skills, so they were usually the first to suffer in battle. To help mitigate this, he introduced monthly training. Each village would gather its men on a prescribed date to participate in training exercises.

In the beginning, they saw it merely as a waste of time, but opinions changed when new spears and shields arrived.

Cyn concentrated on individual training, while Sigwulf worked in groups. These people wouldn't prove decisive in battle, but by the Saints, Ludwig would make sure they could at least defend themselves.

He increased the training frequency as the warmth of summer spread throughout the land. His footmen now filled an entire company, his archers half of one. As they favoured archery amongst the barony's levy, he could call upon many more bowmen should the need arise.

On such a summer day, he found himself in the village of Verfeld, just outside the keep. Sigwulf marched the local levy around, ensuring they maintained their formation as they moved, while Cyn watched the bowmen with a keen eye.

The sweltering heat left the men sweating profusely, so he called a halt. As they rested, he noticed a horseman coming down the Malburg road. The rider, upon spotting him, changed course towards him.

"My Lord Baron," he called out. "I bring you greetings from the Electors of Malburg."

"Good day to you," replied Ludwig.

The fellow handed over a sealed letter. "This is a request, my lord, for you to meet with the electors at your convenience."

"Concerning?"

"Alas, I have no knowledge of that, for I am only a humble messenger. I assume the letter might give you some idea?"

Ludwig grunted, then tore open the missive, scanning its contents. Sigwulf and Cyn soon appeared, drawn by the encounter.

"News?" said Sigwulf.

"It appears the Electors of Malburg have a proposition for me."

"What type of proposition?"

"That remains to be seen." He looked at the courier. "Will tomorrow suffice?"

"I'm sure that would be perfectly fine."

"Good. Tell them I'll be there at noon." He quickly scanned the letter again. "Where am I to find these electors?"

"Might I suggest The Willow?"

"The Willow it is, then."

"I shall inform them of your decision, my lord." The rider turned his horse around and rode off.

"What was all that about?" asked Cyn. "Do they know something we don't?"

"Like what?" asked Sigwulf.

"I don't know. Could they have received word that the King of Neuhafen has finally died?"

"No," said Ludwig. "That news wouldn't be so shrouded in mystery, and it definitely wouldn't involve a request to visit the electors. This must be something else."

"Like what?" said Sigwulf.

"I suppose we'll have to wait until tomorrow to find out."

"And in the meantime?"

"Simple. We continue with the training. Now, come. There's much work to be done."

That evening, Father Vernan found Ludwig in his study, poring over a collection of letters.

"I hear you had a visitor today?"

"I did," said Ludwig. "A messenger from the Electors of Malburg. They want to see me about something."

"Are they coming here?"

"No, I'm meeting them in Malburg. Why do you ask?"

"It seems odd, does it not, that they requested you come to them?"

"I'm not sure what you're implying?"

"It's simple," said Father Vernan. "It's a power play. Your going to them makes you the subordinate, at least in their eyes."

Ludwig bristled. "Are you suggesting they intend to demand something?"

"Quite possibly, and if that's the case, it's likely something you wouldn't normally agree to. They seek to force you into an agreement."

"You talk as though you've seen this before."

"I have. I hate to admit it, but it's the same tactic my superiors used."

"I'm not sure I follow?"

Father Vernan smiled. "The Church likes us to believe we have some choice where we're sent, but the truth is the needs of the order outweigh any objections an individual may have."

"So, you're suggesting the electors are putting their own needs above my own?"

"If it were a simple favour, they would come to you, wouldn't they?"

"I suppose," said Ludwig. "Why is it that people think they must play such games?"

"Why, indeed? It's a question I've often pondered."

"And did you find an answer?"

"I think so, yet it isn't what I expected."

Ludwig chuckled. "Care to elaborate?"

"Some desire to rule, while others are content to be ruled."

"In other words, it's all about power?"

Father Vernan nodded. "There are different kinds of power. Military might is one, as is the rule of a king. Others, however, lack these more obvious traits. They learn to influence people through the power of their words and actions."

"And you believe I let them lure me into a trap?"

"Not necessarily. A man who knows it's a trap has the advantage."

"Perhaps you'd care to accompany me to Malburg tomorrow?"

Father Vernan responded with a slight nod. "I should be delighted, my lord."

"Please, just call me Ludwig. We're not at court here."

"Very well, but only if you call me Vernan in response. All of this talk of Holy Fathers is turning me prematurely grey."

Ludwig chuckled. "We all grow old, eventually."

"Agreed, but I see no reason to rush to that inevitability, do you?"

"No, I suppose not. Tell me, how do I prepare for this meeting when I have no idea what they wish to discuss?"

"Keep in mind the king's wishes at all times."

"Which are?"

"That's easy. The last time you heard from His Majesty, what was the topic of conversation?"

"The coming war," said Ludwig. "He sent word he wanted me to increase my garrison."

"Then that's your strength. Anything else is secondary. Remember, you serve the king directly. Better yet, he is your cousin. Use that to your advantage."

"I possess no power over the electors."

"Nor they over you," said Vernan. "And therein lies the crux of the matter. Whatever they ask of you lies well outside your normal duties and responsibilities. Consider any request from them very carefully."

"You've given me much to think on."

"I am only glad I could be of some assistance."

. . .

Malburg was a journey of five miles, but the meeting would likely last well into the afternoon. At Father Vernan's suggestion, they had an early luncheon, arriving at The Willow long before the expected arrival of the electors.

Tomas deShandria's unexpected appearance interrupted Ludwig as he was finishing his meal. The master smith quickly moved closer.

"May I sit?" he asked.

"Please do. I must admit to some surprise at seeing you here. It's not one of your usual haunts, is it?"

"No, not at all, but I'm here in my capacity as an Elector of Malburg."

"You're an elector? Since when?"

"They asked me to fill an unexpected vacancy last spring."

Ludwig leaned back as a serving girl removed his plate. "Can you tell me why I'm here?"

"How familiar are you with Malburg's charter?"

"Not very. Father Vernan here is likely more conversant with it than I. Why?"

"There is talk of war."

"There is ALWAYS talk of war," said Ludwig.

"Yes, but people are slowly coming to the conclusion it's not so much a matter of if, but when. They feel that war with Neuhafen is inevitable."

"As do I, Master Tomas, but what has that to do with the electors?"

"Our charter lays out the city's responsibilities in the event of war."

Ludwig sat forward, his interest piqued. "Which are?"

"Malburg has, in theory, a militia consisting of every man between the ages of sixteen and forty-five." He grinned. "The electors, who are of an age themselves, insisted the elderly be exempt from such service."

"You must have hundreds, then."

"So it would appear, although the reality is something altogether different."

"Meaning?"

"Malburg is a big city."

"Agreed. What is it you're implying?"

"Much of the levy would be required to protect the city."

"How does that concern me?"

"You don't know?"

"No," said Ludwig.

"I do," said Father Vernan. "Unless I miss my guess, they will want to put their men under your command."

"Why would they do that?"

"Because you, as the nearest baron, are the king's representative in the area."

"Exactly," said Tomas.

"And the electors?" said Ludwig.

"They seek assurances you would not leave the city defenceless should war come."

"So they sent you on ahead to negotiate?"

"I'm not here to negotiate," said Tomas. "I am here as a personal courtesy. The electors know nothing of my early arrival, and I would be much obliged if we could keep it that way."

"Your secret is safe with me."

"Good. Then if you'll excuse me, I shall leave The Willow and make my return later with the others."

The smith left the tavern, leaving Ludwig and Father Vernan to mull over the news.

"Well, that was interesting," said Ludwig.

"Interesting good, or interesting bad?"

"That remains to be seen. At the very least, I now know what they want. Time for me to put your ideas to the test."

"My ideas?"

"Yes, they want something from me. I, in turn, can now get something from them."

"Which is?"

"I don't know. I haven't worked that out yet."

"Tell me," said Father Vernan, "and please be as honest as possible. Do you truly believe the army of Neuhafen will try to take Malburg?"

"No. Their objective will be to take the capital, and to do that, there's only one route of attack. Malburg is safe in that regard."

"And the city's desire to keep its levy in place?"

"Misplaced, though I understand their worries."

"It's not easy sending a large portion of your population off to war."

"I think there's more to it. By keeping their levy here, they can continue to work their shops and stalls, only taking up arms if danger threatens."

"Which you suspect it won't."

"Precisely," said Ludwig. "But once war breaks out, I shall need warriors to march to the king's aid."

"And how do you intend to convince them of that?"

"Simple. I'll follow your advice and negotiate. Let's have another ale before the electors arrive, shall we?"

· · ·

There were five electors, each with silver in his hair. Tomas, already known to Ludwig, introduced the others.

"This is Master Gudrun Waltz," he said, indicating a somewhat rotund individual. "He runs the city's granaries."

"Pleased to meet you," replied Ludwig.

"And this," continued the master swordsmith, "is Hendrick Foss, master carpenter." The fellow was easily a head taller than anyone else in The Willow.

"To my left is Stigurd Grossman, master of taxation, along with Hartwin Bengle."

"And your position is?"

"Commander of the levy," Hartwin replied.

"And have you any experience leading men?"

"I was a soldier for twenty years, Lord."

"And who, might I ask, did you serve?"

"The King of Talyria."

"The present one?" asked Ludwig.

"I do not serve usurpers!"

"I assume that answers your question?" said Tomas.

"Yes, quite," replied Ludwig. "Now, let me introduce you all to Father Vernan of the Temple of Saint Mathew. He is here in an advisory capacity."

They all shook hands before taking their seats.

"Might I ask who speaks for you?" said Ludwig. "It would be simpler to hear your requests from one individual instead of a group."

"They elected me to speak on our behalf," said Hendrick.

"Then, please, let's begin, shall we? I'm eager to learn what requires my attention."

"As you're aware," said the master carpenter, "Malburg is required to provide a levy of all able-bodied men for the kingdom's defence."

"I'm well aware." Ludwig held up his hand. "Before we go any further, I've got a question for Master Bengle here."

"Certainly," replied the commander.

"According to your records, how many men can you raise?"

"That is a difficult number to calculate."

"Is it not your duty to do so?"

The man reddened. "Aye, it is." He looked at Hendrick for guidance, but his comrade only nodded.

"Very well," said Bengle. "My calculations put the levy's size at approximately three thousand. Of course, we couldn't hope to arm half of those, so fifteen hundred is a more reasonable number, perhaps even less."

The group fell silent, looking at Ludwig.

"And?" he prompted.

"Well," said Hendrick Foss, "we will need the bulk of those to protect our city."

"So what you're saying is that you brought me here to tell me none will be available to march to the king's aid?"

"Precisely."

"That is a most unfortunate situation."

Foss smiled. "We hoped you would understand."

"Oh, I understand completely."

"Good. It appears our business is at an end."

"Of course," said Ludwig, "but I have one question before you go."

"By all means, Lord."

"Which of you is to go to the gallows for disobeying the king's laws?"

The electors all grew pale, except for Tomas, who seemed to relish the encounter.

"I-I-I don't understand," stammered Bengle.

"It's simple," said Ludwig, warming to the task. "Part of your city's charter is the agreement to provide a levy for the king's use should he should deem it necessary."

"Yes, but as you can see, we don't have the manpower."

"I understand. Truly, I do, but I'm afraid the king won't. In fact, I suspect he'll revoke your charter."

"You believe he'd do that?"

"It makes sense, doesn't it? After all, if you can't hold up your side of the agreement, why should he?"

"Come now," said Foss. "Let's not be hasty. Surely Master Bengle can see a way of allowing some of our men to fulfill their oaths?"

"You mean YOUR oaths," said Ludwig. "Might I remind you the Electors of Malburg signed that agreement."

"Hypothetically speaking," said Bengle, "how many men would you expect to march?"

"I would be satisfied with two hundred, but they would need to be well-equipped."

"Your definition of which would be?"

"Helmet, shield, and spear."

"That would be a great expense to us, Lord."

"More expensive than losing your charter?"

Foss looked at his companions before returning his gaze to Ludwig. "Would you excuse us to confer, Lord?"

"Of course." Ludwig stood. "Father Vernan, would you care to step outside with me?"

"Certainly."

They took their time leaving, halting briefly at the door to look back and see the electors all huddled around the table.

"Are you sure that was wise?" asked Father Vernan.

"You think I pushed too much?"

"Only time will tell, but you took a significant risk. What if they called your bluff?"

"Who said I was bluffing?"

"You believe Otto would remove their charter?"

Ludwig chuckled. "I doubt it, but the threat got their attention."

"You could have asked for more men."

"Agreed, but I'd prefer two hundred well-equipped warriors to a thousand with makeshift weapons. The question now is whether they will agree."

"It looks like we're about to find out," offered Father Vernan. "Here comes Master Tomas."

They both turned at the smith's approach.

"You have their decision, Master Tomas?" asked Ludwig.

"They accept your demands."

"Excellent. Please convey my pleasure with the result. I shall have my captain begin their training in one week."

"Training, Lord?"

"Of course. I can't march them off to war if they don't know how to hold a spear, now, can I?"

Tomas frowned. "The electors won't be pleased."

"Come now," said Ludwig. "It will help Malburg considerably."

"How so?"

"Well, they will need to hire smiths to make all those spears, not to mention the carpenters needed for shields."

The smith's face brightened considerably. "Yes, I suppose they will."

17

SUMMONS
AUTUMN 1097 SR

The weather turned cooler as autumn waned, but weapons practice continued. Between training Verfeld's men and those of Malburg, Sigwulf and Cyn were busy. So much so that Ludwig saw little of them over the following weeks.

His villages prospered again this harvest, which meant more revenue than expected. A letter from King Otto arrived as Ludwig sat reviewing the barony's expenses. The letter's contents were straightforward, inviting him to visit the capital, while the underlying tone indicated this was not so much an invitation as a command.

He dutifully set off for Harlingen the very next day, Father Vernan by his side. They had the fortune of coming across a trade caravan heading out of Glosnecke, which they accompanied, making the trip far more entertaining.

Upon reaching the capital, they left their newfound friends to make their way to the king's keep. Ludwig expected to find the king alone, but he encountered a gathering, the likes of which he'd not seen since his days in Erlingen.

"What's all this?" he asked.

"A celebration," replied the servant at the door, "honouring the harvest."

"It's a bit early for that, isn't it?"

"Maybe, but who would dare disagree with the king's wishes?"

"He's got you there," said Father Vernan, peering inside. "Should I catch up with you later? I wouldn't like to intrude."

"Nonsense. You're here as my guest."

They handed over their cloaks, entering the great hall packed with people wearing expensive clothes and jewellery galore—a far cry from the plain clothes of its newest guests. A familiar laugh caught Ludwig's attention, and he led Father Vernan across the room.

"Lord Merrick," he called out. "So good to see you again. How is Lady Gita?"

"She is well. Unfortunately, she couldn't join me here in the capital. The pressures of motherhood, you understand."

"And the child?"

Lord Merrick beamed. "A boy, if you can believe it. What luck! We decided to call him Kenley."

"An unusual name."

"It is, isn't it? We named him after Gita's grandfather. What about you? Found yourself a wife yet?"

"No, but admittedly, it's not a priority at present."

"I see what you mean. All this talk of armies has my head spinning."

"If it's not overstepping our friendship, I wonder if I might pick your brain?"

"Of course, pick away, although I can't guarantee you'll find much there after all these drinks. What was it you wanted to know?"

"I was curious how many men each baron must raise?"

"That's an easy one," said Merrick. "The king wants each of us to field four hundred; that's not including whoever you leave back at home, only what will march to his aid."

"Four hundred?"

"Yes. When you add that to Otto's own, it gives us a standing army of over three thousand. I should think more than enough to defeat an invasion from Neuhafen."

"And the composition of these groups?"

"That varies considerably. Typically, about half of that is only the local levy, so it's not as impressive as it sounds. Still, I expect each baron has a core group of well-trained men-at-arms."

"And your own contingent?" asked Ludwig.

"My humble force is comprised of a hundred foot and an equal number of bow."

"And the rest?"

"All peasants, I'm afraid, although some, at least, own armour to help protect themselves."

"Armour? How did you afford such a luxury?"

"Well, I say armour, but it's little more than shields and helms, with the occasional padded jacket thrown in. I know it sounds bad, but any enemy would likely be equipped along similar lines. In any event, it's our trained warriors who'll bear the brunt of the fighting."

"Do any of the barons use knights?"

"No, of course not. They're the sole domain of the king. Bruggendorf and Luwen have some mounted men-at-arms, but no more than fifty apiece, if even that."

Ludwig let out a breath. "I must say that's a bit of a relief. Any more, and I'd bankrupt my barony."

"Once you get past the initial cost, it's not so bad," said Merrick. "Just be glad you don't need to pay Otto's men. Now, that would be expensive."

"Good to know."

"Come now," said Merrick. "You must introduce your friend here."

"My pardon," said Ludwig. "This is Father Vernan. He's my spiritual advisor."

"Spiritual advisor? Are you considering taking up Holy Vows?"

"No, but the good father is a wealth of knowledge, and not all of it religious in nature."

"If only we all had such men at our sides. Tell me, does Verfeld prosper?"

"It does now, but it was tough going initially." Ludwig leaned in closer, lowering his voice. "My stepbrother was stealing from my treasury, not to mention ruining the barony in my absence."

"I hope you took care of the rascal?"

"I'm afraid he left Verfeld, taking a tidy sum with him, it turns out."

"How terrible."

Ludwig shrugged. "At least I'm rid of him."

"And the coins?"

"Gone for good, I fear, but we have recovered. One might say we've even prospered of late."

"That is most excellent news indeed."

"How is the king?"

"In excellent health," replied Merrick, "and fat as ever. To be honest, I'm surprised the fellow has lived as long as he has. You'd think all that weight would have killed him by now."

Ludwig laughed. "He has a robust constitution."

"I'll say. Speaking of which, I should take you to him. He likes to welcome each guest himself."

Merrick guided him through the crowd with Father Vernan trying to keep up, but they soon lost him amongst the throng. The next thing Ludwig knew, a massive hand was thrust out to him.

"Ah, there you are, Ludwig. Good to see you."

"And you, Your Majesty."

"I hear you've been busy in Verfeld."

"M'lord?"

"Increasing the garrison?"

"Yes, of course."

"Now, it's time you started looking to the future."

"I thought I was?"

Otto chuckled. "And you are, in some ways, but there's more to life than building an army, as you should well know."

"I'm not sure I follow, m'lord."

The king stared at him for a moment. "Not so long ago, you had the reputation as a womanizer, yet the man I see before me seems quite the opposite."

"I'd like to think I've matured."

"And so you have, but you still have your duty to see to." The king swept his gaze over the crowd. "Come. There's someone I want you to meet." He grabbed Ludwig's elbow, steering him across the dance floor to a group of well-dressed nobles who turned at their approach.

"Lord Ludwig," said Otto. "Allow me to introduce Miss Alexandra Schafenburg, daughter to Lord Meinhard, Baron of Luwen."

Before him stood a young woman in a long white dress, her golden locks cascading over her shoulders. Her blue eyes sparkled as she met Ludwig's gaze, and then she curtsied. "Honoured, my lord."

"Good," said the king. "Now that you're acquainted, I shall steal away Lord Meinhard."

Ludwig watched them disappear into the crowd. "Well," he said at last. "That was awkward. I do hope I haven't embarrassed you?"

"Not at all," she replied. "I've become all too accustomed to it."

"I presume you're not married?"

She smiled. "No, nor are you, I wager, hence the intention behind this introduction."

"I can assure you I had no part in this."

She lowered her voice. "Before we talk at length, I feel I must warn you, my lord. I am not looking for a husband."

"Nor I, a wife. Not that you wouldn't be a suitable candidate, but there are far too many other duties occupying my time at present."

"Then perhaps we can converse without the pressure of feeling obligated to speak of marriage?"

"Yes, that would be wonderful. Thank you." A weight lifted from his shoulders.

"Tell me of yourself," she asked.

"I'm not sure what there is to say. My father was Lord Frederick, Baron of Verfeld. Upon his passing, I became the new baron, but I've not quite mastered the role yet."

"My condolences. Your father died from a fever, did he not?"

"Yes, although I was in the north at the time."

"I know. I heard you fled the country. You and your father didn't get along?"

Ludwig blushed. "We had our differences, but it came to a head back in ninety-four. That's when I left."

"Tell me, I beg you, is the north as wild as they say?"

"Wild?"

"Yes. My father tells me it's a land of constant war and barbarity."

Ludwig laughed. "No more so than here. They have their troubles, but they are not too dissimilar to our own."

"I note you wear a sword."

He glanced down at his scabbard. "So do all the other men present."

"Yes, but you wear it effortlessly, like someone who knows how to use it."

"I'm not sure what you're suggesting?"

"Look around you, Ludwig. Most of the men here, at least those of our age, wear their swords with a certain... bravado. You, on the other hand, carry it as a tool, like a smith might carry a hammer. I suspect you've had reason to use it occasionally."

He hesitated. "I've seen battle, if that's what you mean."

"But you don't relish the experience."

"Killing is not something to be proud of."

"Many here would be happy to boast of it had they the opportunity."

"If you don't mind me saying, you seem particularly skilled in taking the measure of a man, especially for one so young."

"Young? I'm almost twenty."

"And unwed," added Ludwig. "I can't help but suspect there's a story there waiting to be unearthed."

"You surprise me."

"In what way?"

"Most men in their twenties are less observant and far less expressive in their speech."

He grinned. "I picked up a thing or two in the north."

"Was it a woman?"

"I beg your pardon?"

"The reason you fled north?" She blushed. "I'm sorry for being so straightforward, but I've heard the rumours."

"Rumours about me?"

"Who else would I be talking of?"

"Tell me about these rumours."

"They say you wanted to run away with a commoner. A tradeswoman, no less."

Ludwig stiffened. "She was a master smith and far from common."

"So you're saying she was a noble?"

"No. Well, maybe. I'm sorry. I've said too much. The story is not mine to share."

"Now you have me intrigued. Was she a noble or not?"

"It's complicated. Her father was in service to a foreign queen years ago. I'm not sure if that makes her a noble. Not that it matters."

"You still love her," she said, watching him blush. "Don't worry. Your secret is safe with me."

"I do, even though I know she is gone from my life forever."

"Don't say forever," said Alexandra. "No one can predict where our road in life may take us."

"True. Wise words from someone who likes to control the conversation." He smiled.

If she took insult, she didn't show it. "Control?"

"Yes, you changed the topic earlier when I asked why you weren't married."

"Did I?"

"You know you did. Now, out with it. I told you my secret; it's high time you told me yours."

"I, too, have a lost love, although he's no commoner."

"Now you have my interest, not that you didn't before, of course. Who is it? Or is that getting too personal?"

She grabbed his arm and led him farther away from the crowd. "His name's Emmett Kuhn."

"Kuhn? Why do I know that name?"

"His father is the Baron of Dornbruck... in Neuhafen."

"Yes. His lands share a border with mine. How in the name of the Saints did you ever meet the fellow?"

"King Rordan sent a delegation here two years ago. Emmett was amongst them."

"And you happened to be in Harlingen at the time?"

Her boots suddenly seemed to capture her interest. "We met entirely by chance. I was out in the city, and he came to my rescue when a horse almost ran me down."

"And you fell in love."

"Not immediately, but then he took me to a tavern to find something to soothe my nerves. We spent the entire afternoon simply talking. Darkness fell before I realized it, and I needed to return to my lodgings."

"I assume you didn't say anything to your father?"

"No. He would have flown into a rage at the very idea."

"I think I know how this goes. You spent every waking moment together until the delegation left?"

"Whenever we could, yes, but he still had to maintain a presence at court. I was heartbroken when they left. Emmett promised he would never love another, but I've heard no word since."

"Not too surprising, considering the current state of affairs." Ludwig was about to say more, but a thought struck him. "Would you like to get a letter to him?"

"How?"

"As I said earlier, his father's lands lay adjacent to mine."

"I remember, but sending a courier to Neuhafen would be perilous."

"Not if an outsider carried it."

"You have someone in mind?"

"Let's just say I didn't come back from the north without friends."

She smiled. "I would be most obliged, but how would we carry this out without my father suspecting?"

"Write me a letter," said Ludwig, "and place one to Emmett within. When I receive a reply, I shall forward it to you in a similar manner. To all intents and purposes, it will look as though you and I are corresponding; not too strange, considering the king is trying to marry us off to each other."

"How do I know this isn't some trap to ensnare my father in scandal?"

Ludwig looked around the room, finding his target and pointing. "You see that man?"

"The Holy Father?"

"Yes. That's Father Vernan. Speak to him of my character, and he'll tell you I'm a man of my word."

"And if he doesn't?"

"Then write to me and tell me you wish no response."

"You've given me much to ponder. Thank you, Lord Ludwig."

"Please, call me Ludwig."

"Very well. Ludwig it shall be. Now, if you'll excuse me, I'll wander over and say hello to this Holy Father of yours."

She glided across the floor while Ludwig searched for a drink, finally snagging a goblet from a passing servant right as King Otto appeared.

"Well?" said His Majesty. "What did you think?"

"She's a lovely young woman."

"And?"

"And what?"

"Did you find her a suitable match?"

"As I mentioned before, m'lord, I am in no hurry to wed."

"Well, you should be. War is looming, Ludwig, and you need an heir to carry on should something happen to you."

"And if I should die without one?"

"Then I'd be forced to hand over Verfeld Keep to someone with less of a connection to the region."

Otto moved closer, putting an arm around Ludwig's shoulders. "Look here. I like you, and Verfeld is an important barony in my kingdom, but you need to propagate the bloodline. You are a rare breed, Cousin, a true warrior lord in every sense of the word. I'll require that part of you when war finally comes, but in the meantime, I need the dutiful baron doing his bit to ensure the continued survival of the realm. And that, my friend, includes producing an heir." He glanced over at Alexandra. "Tell me, truthfully. Could you see yourself marrying the girl? Be honest with me now."

Ludwig mulled over his conversation with her. Agreeing with Otto would conceal her secret and allow them both to divert the king's attention. "Yes," he finally said. "In time, I believe I could."

Otto slapped him on the back. "That's excellent news, Cousin. I shall insist she saves a dance for you later."

Ludwig paled. "A dance?"

"But, of course, this is a celebration. What did you expect?"

"To be honest, m'lord, I thought everyone would just stand around and talk."

The king barked out a laugh. "Well, I never." He lowered his voice. "Except for that one time back in sixty-three." Again, the laugh, but this time much coarser.

"I hate to admit it, but I don't know how to dance."

Otto looked at him as though someone had slapped him in the face. "You don't?"

"No. My father never taught me, or my mother, for that matter."

"Well, we can't have that, can we?" Otto searched the room. "We need to find you someone to show you how it's done."

"That would take time, m'lord."

"So it will. Well, I suppose we can excuse it for the present, but it's definitely something we must work on. Do you know anyone who could help you in that regard?"

"Lady Gita of Drakenfeld?"

"By the Saints, you're right. I shall have a word with Lord Merrick."

"I'm afraid Lady Gita isn't here in Harlingen, m'lord."

"Then you shall go to her. Arrange it with her husband, and make it a priority. I want you on that dance floor for the Midwinter Feast."

"The Midwinter Feast?"

"Of course," said the king. "I'm inviting all my nobles to join me in celebration this year."

"And by inviting, you mean commanding?"

"Well, I suppose that's one way of looking at it. In any event, I expect you to be here." He lowered his voice. "I'm sure Miss Alexandra will be pleased to accept the invitation."

Ludwig forced a smile. "Then I will be happy to attend, m'lord."

18

LIFE AT COURT
AUTUMN / WINTER 1097 SR

L udwig's foot caught behind his opposite leg, sending him crashing to the floor. Lord Merrick, unable to hold it in any longer, burst out laughing. "You're supposed to be dancing, not falling."

"I am well aware of that, but my feet don't want to cooperate."

Lady Gita held out her hand. "Let me help you up."

"Thank you. At least someone around here has some manners."

Merrick waited until his guest stood up before moving to grasp his wife's hand. "Here. We'll demonstrate the proper technique." He nodded to the minstrel, who strummed out a tune.

Ludwig watched them glide across the room. Three weeks ago, after sending Father Vernan back to Verfeld, he'd come to Drakenfeld to learn how to dance, but his hosts were hard-pressed to fit it in between the needs of parenting and the running of the barony. In the end, it was agreed he would take instruction twice a week, devoting the rest of his time to helping out with Lord Merrick's responsibilities.

Ludwig found learning to dance far more challenging than expected. The problem wasn't a lack of encouragement; it was his two left feet which were in constant disagreement with each other.

"You make it look so easy," he said.

"I would hope so," said Gita. "We've been dancing together for years."

"I thought your marriage was arranged?"

"It was."

"I'm afraid you've confused me. I was under the impression the king's niece introduced you."

"She did," replied Merrick.

"Then how is it you've known each other so long?"

Gita laughed. "It appears poor Ludwig here misunderstood your meaning, my dear." She turned her attention to their guest. "Our parents arranged our marriage when we were both twelve."

"Twelve?"

"Don't look so surprised," said Merrick. "It's common enough in the Petty Kingdoms."

"That seems so young."

"Calm down, my dear fellow. We weren't married at twelve, merely promised."

"And yet you danced together?"

"We were both instructed by the king's sister," explained Merrick. "Saints rest her soul. She was a wonderful teacher."

"And a gifted dancer," added Gita. "I still remember the grand ball the year we came of age. It was the most magnificent sight."

"Yes. The king decorated the entire hall with coloured lanterns."

"The king did?" said Ludwig. "I find that surprising. He doesn't exactly have the reputation as a big spender."

She laughed. "On that, I would have to agree, but occasionally he heeds the advice of his counsellors. Now, let's get back to Ludwig's instruction, shall we?"

"I think that ship might have sailed."

"Nonsense. All you need is the proper partner. Now, come along. Hold up your arms like I showed you."

They stood opposite each other, their arms held high in the air. She nodded at the minstrel, stepping forward as the music began, touching his hands with hers. "Remember. We touch hands and then back up while keeping in step with the music."

He stumbled, then realized he'd been too slow, for Lady Gita was already advancing again, ready to touch hands. He rushed forward and threw up his hands, missing hers entirely.

"Oh, for Saint's sake!" he shouted in frustration.

The music stopped once more. "Don't be so hard on yourself," said Gita, then a sly smile came to her lips. "Imagine I'm someone else."

"Someone else?"

"Yes. Lady Alexandra, for example."

Lord Merrick took note of the name. "Did I miss something?"

"Haven't you heard? The king introduced our dear friend Ludwig to Alexandra Schafenburg."

"Schafenburg? Isn't she the skinny one with the black hair?"

"No, she's blonde, as well you know." Gita's attention returned to her dance partner. "She's who you're thinking of, isn't she?"

"I-I-I..." stammered Ludwig.

"There," said Merrick. "He's as much as admitted it. Why, you scoundrel. Here we thought you'd sworn off women for good, and now you're courting Lady Alexandra."

"We're hardly courting."

"You admit to knowing her?"

"Yes," said Ludwig. "I'll give you that."

"And your cousin ...you know, the king introduced you?"

"Yes."

"Impressive."

"So when is the wedding?" asked Gita.

"By the Saints, they've only just met. Give the man some time before you have him traipsing down the temple nave."

"To answer your question," said Ludwig, "we agreed to exchange letters in the coming months, the better to become acquainted."

"Letters?" said Merrick.

"I think it's romantic," said Gita. "And what's the harm in learning more about a future spouse before taking the plunge?"

"Taking the plunge? You make it sound like they're going swimming." Merrick moved to stand before Ludwig, putting his hands on his friend's shoulders to emphasize the point. "Look here, this is serious business, Ludwig. You must be careful when wooing a woman of her standing. There are certain customs expected of you."

"Are you trying to scare him off?"

"No, of course not, but he needs to be aware of the risks. The last thing he wants to do is start a feud with her father."

"You believe that likely?" asked Ludwig.

"Have you ever met Lord Meinhard?"

"Briefly, but I can't claim to really know the man. Why? Is he difficult?"

"Difficult? I suppose that depends on your point of view. Amongst us barons, he's known as the Bulldog. I imagine you can guess why?"

"Something to do with his stubbornness?"

"Indeed. Once he sinks his teeth into something, it's almost impossible to make him let go."

"That would make sense," said Gita. "I hear he has a temper."

"That's putting it mildly."

"You're not suggesting he takes it out on his daughter?" asked Ludwig.

"No, of course not," said Merrick. "Alexandra's the light of his life, especially since her mother died. That makes him extremely protective."

"Come now," said Gita. "She has to marry sometime, and look what you're doing to poor Ludwig? You're scaring him away."

"What you need to do," continued Merrick, "is get on Meinhard's good side."

"And how do I do that?" said Ludwig.

"You're the king's cousin—use that."

"How? Surely you're not suggesting I stroll up to him and say, 'Hello, I'm the king's cousin. Want to be my friend?' He'd throw me out quicker than a bad piece of barn bread."

"Barn bread?" said Gita. "I'm afraid I don't understand the reference."

"It's a long story," said Ludwig. "In any case, I can't march up to the man and slap him on the back."

"No," said Merrick, "but you could have the king introduce you."

"He's already done so."

"Yes, but only surrounded by the entire court. What you need is a more private affair where the two of you can have an actual conversation. Do that a few times, and then you should ask for his daughter's hand in marriage."

"Merrick!" said Gita. "Don't tease the poor man. Ludwig must find his own way forward."

"Thank you," said Ludwig.

"Very well," said Merrick, "but we've got this minstrel for the rest of the afternoon, so can we at least continue with the lessons?"

Ludwig returned to the capital as the first snows of winter blanketed the land. He'd considered returning to Verfeld, but with the Midwinter Feast only a month away, the last thing he wanted to do was travel all the way home only to have to turn around and make his way back to the capital.

Otto, his keep overrun with relatives, offered up a mansion in the city's wealthier quarter. Ludwig wouldn't be the only guest enjoying the king's generosity, but at least the place was big enough that he needn't worry about intrusions.

One day as he was sitting alone in the drawing room, a servant approached with news of a visitor.

"A visitor?" said Ludwig. "I wasn't expecting one."

"He is here, nonetheless, Lord. Shall I show him in?"

"By all means."

He waited, eager to learn the identity of this new arrival. The servant soon returned with a young man in tow, a tall fellow, mostly skin and bones beneath his elegant clothes. His long black hair was pulled back into a ponytail, as was the custom these days amongst the more fashionable individuals. Ludwig tried to guess the man's age, but it had never been his strong suit.

"May I help you?" he asked.

"Greetings, Lord Ludwig," the man began in a silky, smooth voice. "My name is Lord Darrian Forst. I have the honour of being the son of Lord Harvald, the Baron of Glosnecke."

"Ah, yes. That makes us neighbours. What can I do for you, Lord Darrian?"

The man shifted his feet, sweat dripping from his forehead, but said no more.

"Where are my manners?" said Ludwig, interrupting the fellow's indecision. "Please. Come in and take a seat. Would you care for some wine?"

Relief flooded Darrian's face. "Yes, that would be nice. Thank you."

Ludwig looked at the servant. "Could you fetch us some wine, please?"

"Of course, my lord."

Ludwig returned his attention to his new guest. "I suppose you're here for the Midwinter Feast?"

"Indeed, Lord."

They sat in silence. This man obviously came here seeking him for some purpose, yet now chose to say nothing. Ludwig wondered if someone wasn't playing him for a fool.

The servant finally returned, delivering two goblets of wine before disappearing again. Lord Darrian took a sip, his hand shaking as he held his cup.

"Is something wrong?" asked Ludwig.

"Indeed, Lord." Again, the silence.

"Then speak up, man. I can't read your mind."

The fellow drained his cup, then slammed it down on a nearby table. "I must ask you to keep away from Lady Alexandra."

Ludwig arched his eyebrows. "This is about Alexandra?"

"LADY Alexandra," corrected his visitor. "You should watch your manners, Lord Ludwig."

"I'm sorry. Did you just threaten me?"

"You may take it how you wish."

"I see. I assume you have some designs on Lady Alexandra?"

"I do."

"And is she aware of this?"

"She soon will be," said Darrian.

"So, let's get this straight—you're warning me to stay away from her so you can approach her?"

"I know the king introduced you to her. I saw it with my own eyes."

"And you believe a warning from you will convince me to stay away from her?"

"Either that, or I shall be forced to convince you with the tip of my sword."

Ludwig laughed at the absurdity of the situation. He'd hoped his ruse with Alexandra would make his life easier, yet he was now forced to deal with this insolent young man.

Darrian, noting Ludwig's amusement, stood, his face turning beet red. "How dare you mock me, sir!"

"I do not mock you, Lord Darrian, merely the circumstances I find myself in. Tell me, when did you first come to notice her?"

"I fell in love with her the moment I laid eyes on her."

"And has she given you any indication she feels the same way?"

"No. As I said before, she is not yet aware of my intentions."

"Ah, so we've gone from designs to intentions. Might I ask what they might be?"

"Why, to seek her hand in marriage, of course."

"By your own admission, you haven't even spoken to her."

"She and I are of a similar age. There are few candidates within the realm's borders worthy of her."

"Other than me?"

"Yes," said Darrian. "So you see, I have little choice in the matter."

"So what you're saying is that you should be able to marry her because, other than me, you are the only candidate?"

"Precisely, and I am a baron's son."

"And I'm a baron," said Ludwig. He leaned forward, staring into the man's soul. "I am the Baron of Verfeld, not to mention the king's cousin."

"Nevertheless, I insist you withdraw the offer of your affections."

"And if I don't?"

"Then I must demand we settle the matter once and for all."

"With a duel?"

"Indeed."

"Don't be a fool," said Ludwig. "I'm a battle-hardened veteran. I fought in the north."

"But I have the blessings of the Saints."

"I very much doubt that."

"True love conquers all," said Darrian.

"True love? You haven't even spoken to the woman."

"I shall not back down, Lord."

"Are you sure I can't talk you out of this?"

"No. I am determined to see it through to the end."

Ludwig shook his head. "I have no desire to fight you, Lord Darrian, but you've left me with no alternative. Send me your representative, and we shall make the appropriate arrangements."

His visitor straightened, trying to adopt an attitude of superiority, but his inexperience in such matters shone through.

"Very well," Darrian said. "I'll see myself out."

The fellow rushed from the room, the door slamming behind him. Drawn by the noise, one of the servants entered. "Is everything all right, my lord?"

"No," said Ludwig. "Everything is not all right. I find myself having to fight a duel, all because a hotheaded youth doesn't understand women."

"I fear it's a common malady amongst the youth of today."

A stiff wind blew in from the west, sending snow swirling across the courtyard.

"Thank you for coming," said Ludwig. "I didn't know who else to ask."

"Quite all right," replied Lord Egan. "When I heard that young Darrian challenged you, I thought I'd best be here."

"You know him?"

"I've known his father, Harvald, for years. He was always a hothead when it came to women. Unfortunately, the apple doesn't fall far from the tree."

"I tried to talk him out of it, but he was having none of it."

"Yes. It's an unfortunate side effect of feeling entitled. Still, it couldn't be helped."

Ludwig rubbed his arms, trying to keep the blood circulating. "Any advice?"

"Try to get it over and done with as quickly as possible."

"I harbour no wish to kill the boy."

"Nor do I wish him dead, but sometimes it's the only lesson that sticks."

Footsteps drew their attention, then Lord Darrian entered the courtyard with a slightly younger man at his side. This new arrival came towards them while His Lordship stood silently brooding.

"You are Lord Ludwig Altenburg, Baron of Verfeld?"

"Who else would I be?" Ludwig immediately regretted his words. "Sorry. Yes, I am Ludwig Altenburg."

"I am Lord Gowan Forst, brother to Lord Darrian. Have you come to renounce your claim against Lady Alexandra Schafenburg?"

"Claim? I make no claim. She is free to make her own choices."

"I shall take that as a no. Are you prepared to defend yourself?"

"Does your brother wish to renounce his... whatever this is?"

"No."

"Then I am ready."

"Hold on a moment," called out Lord Egan. "It appears we are to have a visitor this day."

An expensive carriage rolled to a stop, and then Lady Alexandra stepped out, followed by her father.

"My, my," said Lord Egan. "This is unexpected."

Alexandra crossed the courtyard, coming to stand before Ludwig. "Are you all right?"

"I'm perfectly fine," he replied. "Though I don't have a clue why I'm here."

"You are to duel my brother," said Lord Gowan, his voice higher by an octave.

"What nonsense is this?" demanded Lord Meinhard.

"This gentleman, Lord Darrian," explained Ludwig, "lays claim to your daughter's hand in marriage."

"Eventually," called out his opponent, his voice carrying across the courtyard. "But Lord Ludwig must renounce his intentions first."

Lord Meinhard looked at Ludwig. "Your intentions, sir? Would you care to explain?"

"Come now, Father," said Alexandra. "I told you King Otto introduced us."

"Are you trying to tell me you're enamoured of this fellow? Lord Ludwig, I mean?"

She looked at Ludwig, silently pleading with her eyes. It was an impossible situation, one getting worse with every passing day, yet he'd promised to guard her secret. He nodded ever so slightly.

"Yes," she said at last. "I am."

Her father looked Ludwig up and down. "I suppose you could do worse."

"Then you're not upset?"

"Not with you, my dear. This whole state of affairs, however, is another matter entirely."

"I'm sorry," said Ludwig. "I'd no intention of letting it go this far. The duel, that is."

"Nor should it have. I was young once. I know what love is like." He turned to Lord Darrian. "I also realize what an unhealthy obsession looks like." He walked over to the young lord, halting to look him over as he had Ludwig.

"Well," he demanded. "What have you to say for yourself?"

Ludwig couldn't hear the reply, but it was obviously not to Lord Meinhard's satisfaction, for the Baron of Luwen launched into an expletive-ridden rant that echoed off the courtyard walls.

Lord Egan moved to stand beside Ludwig. "Hopefully, this will put an end to all this foolishness."

Lord Darrian slunk away, his younger brother hurrying to catch up. Lord Meinhard took a moment to compose himself before he turned, displaying a most disarming smile. "Lord Ludwig, Lord Egan, might I suggest we retire to my Harlingen estate?" He shot a glance towards his daughter. "It appears there are a few things to discuss."

"Of course," said Ludwig.

"I'm in," added Lord Egan. "Provided you have more of that delectable red?"

Lord Meinhard let out a laugh. "Ah, a man after my own heart. Yes, I have the red. Now come, we shall take the carriage. No one needs to be out on a day as cold as this." He made his way to his waiting carriage, followed by Lord Egan. Ludwig was about to do likewise, but Alexandra held him back.

He turned to face her, and she kissed him on the cheek. "Thank you. I know how hard that must've been for you. I shall be forever grateful."

"I was only doing what I thought right."

"And that means a lot to me, but I must warn you, things are about to get far more complicated."

"How so?"

"We are about to return to our home, and Father will want to know everything about you!"

19

HOME

WINTER/SPRING 1098 SR

Alexandra undertook the task of fine-tuning his dancing skills while he told her tales of his adventures in the north. After Otto's Midwinter Feast, Ludwig had intended to return to Verfeld, yet the weather had other ideas, forcing him to remain in the capital.

He spent a good deal of time visiting the home of Lord Meinhard that winter. The baron was a perfect host, quickly warming to what he perceived as his daughter's suitor. While the visits were pleasant enough, Ludwig felt the weight of his guilt pressing down on him.

The baron even went so far as to allow some private moments between his guest and daughter. The two of them sat and talked about their wishes for the future, soon becoming firm friends. Ludwig began to see her as the sister he never had.

Once the snow melted away, he set about preparing to head home. Otto, however, insisted that he stay for the king's birthday feast, resulting in yet another delay. Finally, with the blossoming of spring, Ludwig managed to extricate himself from the affairs of court and returned to Verfeld Keep.

Alexandra came to see him off, her father joining her, for the two barons had become great friends. Thankfully, Lord Meinhard retired to his carriage after bidding him goodbye, allowing his daughter some privacy.

"I shall miss you," she said. "You're one of the few people I can be myself with." She pressed up against him, pushing a letter into his hands, hiding its presence from her father. "Take this," she whispered. "It's a letter for Emmett."

"I'll do my best to ensure its delivery."

She suddenly hugged him, and he was at a loss for words. Her hair pressed against his cheek, making him think only of Charlaine, and once more, guilt washed over him. They stood there a moment, gazing into each other's eyes. There was no denying her beauty, yet he knew he would never see her as anything other than a friend.

"Write to me," she said. "And perhaps I'll convince my father to take me to Verfeld for a visit."

"I should like that." He lowered his voice. "And, hopefully, by then, I will have further news." He nodded at the letter, then tucked it away. "Now, I'd best be on my way if I'm to reach that roadside inn before dark."

He climbed into the saddle before looking one last time at Alexandra. "Take care and keep an eye on that father of yours. He's getting on in years."

"I shall."

Ludwig turned around and rode off without a further word. He doubted he would return to Harlingen anytime soon, for his lands needed his attention. Still, he hoped it wouldn't be his last encounter with the Baron of Luwen or his remarkable daughter.

The road forked some forty miles from his home, with the north branch leading to Glosnecke, Lord Harvald's keep. While Verfeld was the farthest from the capital of all the baronies in the kingdom, Glosnecke was not much closer to Harlingen.

That, in turn, reminded him of Lord Darrian, and he wondered what the young man was up to. He'd seen naught of the fellow since the duel, or rather the interrupted duel, but court gossip had not been kind. Alexandra said that such things would soon be forgotten, but Ludwig thought otherwise. His own background, that of a womanizer, still haunted him. He wondered if others had such regrets.

The miles passed in a blur, and by the next day, he was on the outskirts of Roshlag, the very edge of his barony. As he passed through the village, they greeted him with waves and salutations, a far cry from his experience when he'd first returned from the north more than two years ago.

Eramon was next, and then Malburg came into view. Here he stopped to eat, continuing on to reach Verfeld Keep just as the sun set. News of his return spread quickly, and Sigwulf and Cyn waited in the great hall to greet him. Ludwig stood before the hearth to warm his hands, for the evening was chilly despite the season. Sigwulf patted him on the back while Cyn insisted on giving him a hug.

"What is it?" she asked, stepping back to look at him. "What's wrong?"

"Who said anything was wrong?"

"Come now, I know when you're hiding something. What happened in Harlingen?"

"I bet it was a woman," said Sigwulf.

"It was," admitted Ludwig, "but not in the way you think."

"I sense an interesting story. This calls for ale!" Sigwulf called for Carson, then as the servant disappeared, he pulled a chair closer to the fire. "Come, my friend. Sit and tell us what ails you."

"Yes," added Cyn, "and what woman are you referring to? Charlaine deShandria wasn't in Harlingen, was she?"

"No," said Ludwig, taking a seat. "It all started at Otto's keep. He introduced me to Alexandra Schafenburg."

"Who is?" she prompted.

"The daughter of Lord Meinhard, Baron of Luwen. She's a few years younger than me, but Otto thought we'd make a nice match."

"Are you suggesting you are to be wed?"

"No," said Ludwig. "At least not yet, but I'll get to that shortly. Like me, she's given her heart to another."

"Is that good news or bad? I'm having a hard time trying to understand your concern."

"It's good, or rather it was. We decided to feign interest in each other to make everyone leave us alone."

Sigwulf laughed. "Let me guess; she fell in love with you."

"No, it's worse."

"Worse, how?"

"Her father's taken a liking to me. Now, all he can talk about is us getting married."

"Ah, yes," said Siggy. "The twisted machinations of court. Still, you're back in Verfeld now. Give it a few months, and he'll forget all about you."

"There's more," said Ludwig. "I need you to carry a letter."

"A letter? Surely you're not encouraging this false relationship with love letters?"

"No, as I mentioned earlier, she gave her heart to another, a fellow by the name of Lord Emmett. Emmett Kuhn."

"Kuhn?" said Sigwulf. "Why do I know that name?"

"He's our neighbour," said Cyn. "Across the river in Neuhafen."

Sigwulf laughed but quickly sobered at the stares from his companions.

"This is no laughing matter, Siggy," said Cyn.

"On the contrary, it's like one of those plays—what do you call them?"

"Tragedies," she replied, "and they seldom have a happy ending." She paused a moment. "Then again, I suppose they wouldn't be called tragedies if they did, would they? In any event, these are real people we're talking about." She looked at Ludwig. "What can we do to help?"

"She sent me a letter for Lord Emmett, but it has to be kept from his father, the baron."

"I'll deliver it," said Sigwulf. "My accent marks me as not being from Hadenfeld."

Cyn stepped forward, putting her hand on his arm. "You can't, Siggy. It's too dangerous. And in any event, how would you deliver a message without the baron finding out in the first place?"

"I'll use a ruse."

"You? A ruse? I'd like to see that."

"What? You don't believe I can fool someone?"

Their eyes locked, but she said nothing.

"Come now," said Sig. "It's not the first time I've had to pretend."

Cyn snorted. "You mean like you did that time my father found us in the same tent?"

That comment grabbed Ludwig's attention. "All right. Now you have to tell the rest of the story."

She turned to the fire, staring into the flames. "Siggy here tried to convince my father a badger had gotten into my tent."

Ludwig laughed. "What is it with you and badgers?"

The big man flinched. "Let's change the subject, shall we?"

"Wait," said Cyn. "We know Neuhafen is increasing its army. What if Siggy tells him he's seeking employment?"

"I can do that," Sigwulf replied.

Ludwig frowned. "What if he takes you up on the offer?"

"I'll tell him all about my mercenary background."

"And if that doesn't dissuade him?"

"Then I'll demand too many coins. The fact of the matter is I only need to be there long enough to pass on this letter."

"And get a reply, if you can."

"Yes. Very well, I can do that. Maybe we'll be lucky, and the baron won't even be there?"

"It's possible," said Ludwig, "but that might hold true for his son as well."

"And if they're not, do I continue on to their capital?"

"I'll leave that up to you, but don't put yourself in any unnecessary danger."

"Is there such a thing as necessary danger?"

"You know what I mean. Don't take chances."

"Yes," added Cyn. "I want you back here safe and sound."

"Very well," said Sigwulf. "When do you want me to leave?"

"There's no hurry. I'd like you to stick around for another day or two until I have an idea of where we are with things here, but other than that, it's up to you."

"Better I go sooner than later. I'll leave by week's end."

"So soon?" said Cyn.

"There's a better chance of finding this fellow at home before summer is upon us."

"What makes you say that?"

"It's planting season. Barons tend to stay close to home during this time of year to make sure there are no problems."

"Like what?"

"Wild animals attacking the farmers, mostly. Back in Abelard, part of a baron's duties were to protect his tenants during seeding. I imagine it's similar in Neuhafen."

"Likely," said Ludwig. "I'll take you out tomorrow to familiarize you with the local fords. I'm afraid the path to Dornbruck will be somewhat difficult. From what I know of the area, there are no roads, at least not on the western side."

Sigwulf grunted. "I'll manage well enough; trees hold no fear where I'm concerned."

"No, only badgers, apparently."

"That was uncalled for."

"Sorry," said Ludwig. "I couldn't resist. Now, enough about that letter. Where are we in terms of warriors?"

Three days later, Ludwig and Cyn accompanied Sigwulf as far as the river marking the border. They parted ways after a brief embrace, Sig off to Neuhafen, while the other two turned around, heading back to the keep.

"The men are in fine form," noted Ludwig. "I was impressed with the manoeuvres you put them through yesterday."

"My father used to drill his men every day, whether or not we were employed. Said it was good for morale."

"And aside from marching them around, what do you make of them? Will they stand in battle?"

"You can never be entirely sure until they come face to face with an enemy, but they're definitely eager."

"And loyal?"

"Of course," said Cyn, "though we let a few go over the winter."

"Trouble?"

"They were only in it for the pay. In my experience, those types usually desert at the first sign of action."

"Does that leave us short?"

"No, in fact, we already replaced them. It seems there's no shortage of volunteers. Had you the coins, we could double the contingent."

"Yes," said Ludwig, "and bankrupt me in the process. Still, it's good to see we're well thought of."

"I'd like to go a little further with their training."

"In what way?"

"You remember the mock battle the Grim Defenders had?"

"You mean where Baldric tried to kill me?"

"That was after the battle, and you know it."

"Yes," said Ludwig, "but that only came about because I thrashed him."

"So, no to the battle, then?"

"No, I like the idea. We just need to keep tighter control over it to ensure it doesn't get out of hand. Anything else you'd like to propose?"

"Yes," said Cyn. "We could involve some of the levy. It would give them a chance to see what proper warriors look like in battle."

"This is getting more complicated as we speak."

She laughed. "True, but it will prepare them for war. We both know it's coming eventually." She paused a moment, staring off into the middle of nowhere as she rode.

"Something wrong?"

"Sorry. I was just thinking." She turned to face him, a sparkle in her eyes. "What if we hosted a tourney?"

"How did you get from training to a tournament?"

"It would be a good way to show off your warriors."

"What would that involve?"

"We'll run it like a scaled-down version of the one in Torburg."

"So, jousting?"

"Yes," said Cyn. "As well as a grand melee and an archery competition."

"And when would we run this thing?"

"In the summer. We'll need time to send word inviting people to Verfeld. We also need to find participants. Do you believe we could convince the king to award the grand prize?"

Ludwig smiled. "I think I can safely say Otto would be delighted."

"Let me think, now. There are, what—seven baronies?"

"I suppose eight if you include the capital, although technically that's the king's lands. Why? What are you proposing?"

"We should invite each baron to send a champion, or at least hire one for the joust. Oh, and they can carry out feats of horsemanship too."

"Such as?"

"You know, spearing hoops, races, that sort of thing. I hear it's particularly liked by the noblewomen. I imagine it has something to do with all that masculinity on display."

"You make it sound like a beauty contest. Are we to crown a prince of the fayre?"

"Yes," said Cyn, "along with a princess. That will get more involved. We'll also invite everyone from Malburg to attend, even some merchants."

"Merchants?"

"They can set up stalls and sell their wares. You saw the tournament in Torburg."

"I'm afraid I remember little of it," admitted Ludwig. "I was too caught up in my own problems."

"Well, now you'll be able to sit back and enjoy it."

"I assume you've seen plenty of them?"

"My father used to take me when I was little."

"And you competed?"

"Occasionally, although admittedly, Torburg was the last. The grand melee has always been my favourite. No doubt that comes from being raised in a mercenary company."

"And now you command a company of your own."

"Siggy's the captain," said Cyn.

"Yes, but now that we possess a company of archers, I need someone to watch over them, Captain."

"But I'm a sergeant."

"Not anymore," said Ludwig. "And by the way, that comes with a pay increase."

"You're feeling generous today."

"What can I say? You inspired me. Now, we're going to need help to organize this tournament."

"Meaning?"

"What if we get the Electors of Malburg involved?"

"You trust them?" asked Cyn.

"There'll be visitors from all over the kingdom, and Malburg is only five miles from Verfeld Keep. Their taverns will be flooded with customers. We might even hold some events there. I'm sure they'd like that."

Cyn smiled. "And here you thought you knew nothing about organizing a tourney."

. . .

They got to work right away. Ludwig sent Cyn into Malburg with a letter for the electors. She would approach Master Tomas first to find out if he could offer any insight into the city's position on such things.

Ludwig, meanwhile, dug out the few maps of the region he possessed, trying to determine the best spot for each event. As Father Vernan entered his office, he looked up from the floor, where he'd laid out his papers.

"Ah, there you are, Father. I was wondering where you'd gotten to."

"I've been deep in prayer."

"Maybe I should try that? It might help me with this mess."

"Which is?"

"I decided to host a tournament over the summer."

"Like in Torburg?"

"Yes, but a bit smaller in scope. We could place the lists beneath the keep's southern wall. What do you think?"

"It's a workable solution."

"But?"

"What makes you say there's a but?"

"Come now, Father. I know you well enough by now. What's bothering you?"

"In a word, you."

Ludwig sat up. "Me?"

"I fear your soul is in peril."

"For hosting a tourney? I heard the Church frowns upon it, but—"

"That is not what I am referring to."

"Then speak honestly. I shall not hold it against you."

"It is the matter of Lady Alexandra. Does it not concern you that the entire story is built on a lie?"

"A lie meant to protect," said Ludwig. "What would her father say, do you suppose, should he learn the truth?"

"That she claims to be in love with the son of an enemy baron? I have no doubt he would object, and rightly so." He moved closer, softening his tone. "Ludwig, he is her father. It's his responsibility, nay his right, to ensure she is matched with someone suitable. By intervening in this, you are upsetting the very traditions of the kingdom, even the entire Continent. It could have dire consequences for you."

"I cannot help it. I, too, was forbidden to marry whom I chose, and it nearly destroyed me. I will not see Alexandra suffer so when it's within my power to help."

"Help? You think your actions help her? Nothing could be further from the truth. You are playing a dangerous game here, my friend, especially when war looms. At the very least, you may incur the wrath of Lord Meinhard. At worst, suffer a charge of treason for entreating with the enemy."

"And what would you have me do? Stand back and do nothing? Let her wallow in her misery as I did all those months?" Ludwig closed his eyes and took a deep breath. "I've grown close to Lady Alexandra these past few months. I will not stand by and see her given away to some arrogant noble when her heart wishes otherwise."

"I am not your enemy," said Father Vernan, "but there are those who would use this against you should it come to their attention. It's already the talk of the keep. How long, do you suppose, before the rumours spread to Malburg?"

"I've told very few about this," said Ludwig, his manner defensive.

"Your servants are not stupid, nor are they deaf. The halls of Verfeld carry sound well. Never forget that."

"I understand what you are saying, but I cannot easily extricate myself without damaging the reputation of Lady Alexandra, and that is the one thing I will not do!"

20

THE LETTER

SPRING 1098 SR

"He's back!" Cyn's voice echoed through the keep, followed by the sounds of running feet.

Ludwig put down the chicken leg he'd been savouring and wiped his hands. "Apparently, Captain Marhaven has returned. I expect he'll be hungry. Please see that a meal is arranged."

"Yes, Lord," said Carson. "Will you be finishing yours?"

"No. I've had enough for now." He pushed back his chair and rose, grabbing the goblet to finish on the way. He halted at the door and gulped it down before placing it on a nearby table.

Sigwulf was handing off his reins as Ludwig exited the keep. He was about to call out a greeting, but at that precise moment, Cyn hit the bottom step, launching herself at the big man. They were still hugging as Ludwig reached them, even though he'd paused on his way down.

"How was your trip, Sig?"

"Very good."

"And you found Emmett?"

"I did. He was the first person I spoke to, as a matter of fact. I came across him completely by accident."

"How so?"

"He was out riding when I entered his lands. Initially, he took me for a vagabond, but I won him over with my charm and good looks."

Ludwig laughed. "I imagine that's all it took."

Sigwulf grinned. "Actually, all I had to do was produce the letter."

"And his father?"

"The baron was away visiting the king. In any case, Lord Emmett invited me into his keep, fed me, and gave me a drink and a room for the night. I set out the next morning with a reply." He fished a letter out of the sack hanging on his horse. "I have it here."

Ludwig took it, examining the outside. A sure hand had written 'Lady Alexandra' on it, an ornate seal covering the back.

"Aren't you going to open it?" asked Sigwulf.

"No. This letter is not for my eyes."

"But you can't forward that to Lady Alexandra, not without raising suspicion."

"Fear not. I shall place this letter within one of my own. In this way, it should make it past Lord Meinhard."

"Clever," said Cyn.

"While I was away, did I miss anything?" asked Sig.

"You did," said Cyn, grinning.

"Well, are you going to tell me or make me guess?"

She looked at Ludwig, who cleared his throat. "It seems it's up to me to inform you of a slight change in our command structure."

Sigwulf knitted his brows. "Which is?"

"I placed Captain Hoffman in charge of the archers."

"Captain now, is it? I suppose that means you'll want a bigger share of the bed?"

"I'll let you two sort that out later," said Ludwig. "Tell me, what is Lord Emmett like?"

"He was not unlike yourself."

"Meaning?"

"He's of a similar stature, although his hair is a bit darker, and he favoured a beard, but admittedly a little on the thin side."

"And his nature?"

"Polite and well-spoken, nothing like I was expecting."

"What's that supposed to mean?"

"You gave us the idea that the people of Neuhafen were bloodthirsty barbarians, but to tell the truth, they weren't much different from those we see in these parts. Why, if I were to place one of theirs in amongst our own, you'd be hard-pressed to notice it."

"And did he appear to respond well to the letter?"

"I'll say. His face lit up when I told him who it was from. He has strong feelings for the woman, although whether that's love or simple infatuation is hard to judge."

"Why is that?"

"The man is reserved."

"You said his face lit up!"

"And so it did, but he composed himself quickly. Mind you, he was in the company of another, a guard by the look of it."

"And when he took you back to the keep?"

"He didn't say much. He was polite, but I got the impression he might've been a little embarrassed."

"You think him ashamed?"

"Not quite. It's like when I was found in Cyn's tent. It wasn't that I felt bad for being there, just for getting caught."

"That makes sense," offered Cyn. "His father obviously has no knowledge of their relationship, and he's afraid his servants might say something. After all, it's his father's keep."

"Let's hope we didn't make things harder for him," said Sigwulf. "In any case, I assured him that the letter would make its way into Lady Alexandra's hands."

Ludwig nodded. "And so it shall. Did he say anything else?"

"Yes. That I was welcome to return should I bring more correspondence."

"That's a promising turn of events."

Sigwulf looked around the area, his gaze falling on the flat ground to the south of the keep, where timbers sat ready for use. "What's going on here?"

Cyn smiled. "We decided Verfeld should host a tournament."

"That's great news."

"Yes," added Ludwig, "but it involves a lot of work, so your return has come at a good time."

"And all this timber?"

"We're going to build a set of stands up against the side of the keep for spectators. Before them will be the lists, where armoured knights will joust."

"And the grand melee?"

"We could host that on the flat portion over there." Ludwig pointed to the southwest. "The drainage is good, so it should stay nice and dry."

"You're remembering all that mud in Torburg," said Cyn.

"I am, but it's not only that. Placing it there allows vendors to set up stalls around its perimeter while leaving lots of room for spectators."

"You've figured everything out," said Sigwulf. "What do you need me to do?"

"I thought you and I could ride out to Erhard's Folly tomorrow. I'd like to stake out a route for the horse race."

"Erhard's Folly? What's that?"

"Legend has it that one of the last Therengian warriors made a stand up in the hills."

"Are you suggesting they're haunted?"

"That's the legend, but I never saw any evidence of it. Then again, a strange keening can be heard when the wind picks up, so maybe there's something to it after all."

Sigwulf shivered. "I don't much like the sounds of that."

Cyn chuckled. "Come now, Siggy. Don't tell me you're afraid of ghosts?"

"We should leave the spirits of the dead in peace."

"Easy enough to do," said Ludwig. "We don't need to go into the hills so much as ride around them, but we can discuss all that tomorrow. Let's get you inside and fed."

Over the next few days, riders left for all of the cities of Hadenfeld, carrying word of the tournament. Cyn went to Malburg to meet with the electors, who were pleased with the idea of a tournament but balked at bearing the cost of any preparations. Thankfully, the smiths guild saw fit to step in, providing the much-needed coins and the services of its members.

The land upon which the keep sat soon became busy with workmen of all descriptions, constructing stands and marking out archery ranges and a host of other details.

They made a path that separated the jousting lists from the melee. This would form the tournament's main thoroughfare and house the merchants' stalls. The castellan, Pelton, came up with the idea of charging each trader for a spot, putting more coins in the barony's coffers.

Ludwig was watching Edwig, one of his warriors, pacing off the vendors' allotments when Father Vernan found him.

"My lord, we have visitors."

"Yes," said Ludwig. "A great many of them, it would seem."

"No, no. I mean important guests. They arrived in a carriage, with an escort, for Saint's sake."

"Very well. Carry on, Edwig. You know what to do." He watched only a moment longer before turning to his spiritual advisor. "Lead on, Father."

They passed by a large wagon bearing timbers, then the carriage came into view. Ludwig smiled. "Merrick," he called out. "This IS a surprise."

The Baron of Drakenfeld poked his head out the window. "I have Gita and young Kenley with me." He opened the door, revealing the two-year-old sitting on his mother's lap.

"Hello," said Gita. "I hope we're not intruding?"

"Not at all. Father Vernan, would you do me a favour and fetch some servants?"

"My men can help," said Merrick. "We brought them with us from Drak-enfeld in case there was trouble on the road."

"We thought we might stay in Malburg," said his wife.

"Nonsense," said Ludwig. "You'll stay here, in the keep. I insist on it."

"Can I help?" came Cyn's voice.

"I would be obliged," said Merrick, "if you would show Gita and Kenley to our rooms. I fear the last few miles were wearing on them."

"He means," said Gita, "that our son is tired. Though admittedly, I could do with a rest myself."

"Come," said Cyn. "I'll take you in." She looked at the warriors milling around. "Well, don't just stand there. Fetch their belongings."

"And who are you who dares to order us around?" one snapped back.

"She is Captain Hoffman," said Ludwig. "One of my senior officers."

The man blushed.

"Carry on," said Merrick.

The warrior took out his frustrations on his comrades, ordering them to gather the chests strapped to the top of the carriage.

"They're good men," explained Merrick, "but the long trip has been hard on them."

"They're garrison soldiers," noted Ludwig. "Not used to marching. You should have them carry out daily manoeuvres if only to keep them from idleness."

"Spoken like a true leader of men. Did you pick up that bit of wisdom in the north?"

"I did." Ludwig chuckled. "You know, it's strange to think about, but I was one of those soldiers not long ago."

"You mean a mercenary, don't you?"

"Well, yes, but when you're a warrior, you try to avoid doing strenuous work. Yet, as a leader, you want your men to do exactly the opposite."

"So much to learn." Merrick glanced around. "Care to give me a tour?"

"I'd be delighted."

"Excuse me, Lord?" called out the driver. "Where am I to take the carriage?"

Ludwig pointed westward at the distant buildings. "That's Verfeld village. You'll find stables and a carriage house there."

Once the men removed the luggage, the driver used the whip to get the horses moving.

"How long are you here for?" asked Ludwig.

"That depends," said Merrick. "How long can you stand our company?"

Ludwig smiled. "As long as you like, although admittedly, I'll be busy for the next little while, what with all the planning."

"Could we help?"

"Have you ever hosted a tournament?"

"I can't say that I have, but I'm willing to learn. Who knows? Maybe I'll host the next one if you pull this off?"

"Then I shall be pleased to accept your offer."

They made their way through the fields, Ludwig explaining the purpose of each venue while Merrick soaked it all in. Finally, they reached the jousting field.

"What have we here?" said Merrick.

"Surely you're familiar with the joust?"

"Isn't that when two knights try to unseat each other?"

Ludwig laughed. "Well, there's a bit more to it than that, but essentially you're correct. I assumed such sport was common. It certainly is in the north."

"Ah, but this is Hadenfeld. Of course, we have tournaments, but they consist primarily of archery and melee competitions. I would have thought you knew?"

"Not at all. The truth is, before going north, I'd never left Verfeld."

Merrick's laughter was even louder than Ludwig's. "And so you naturally decided to host your own tourney? Saints alive, Ludwig. What were you thinking?"

"I'll admit I might've been a little hasty in my desire to organize such an event, but I believe we've fared well enough so far. Now, with you and Gita here to help, how can we fail?"

"Your generosity is only surpassed by your golden tongue, my friend." Merrick stopped as they reached the centre of the field. "What's this railing for?"

"It's used to separate the contestants and stop their horses from colliding."

"And they charge with lances? What stops them from killing each other?"

"They use special lances that splinter on impact, at least they're supposed to."

"Supposed to?"

Ludwig shrugged. "Sometimes things don't go precisely as planned. Mind you, they have armour, but an injury can still occur, even death."

"Death? Doesn't that dampen the spirits of even the most battle-hardened warrior?"

"You would think so, but it has exactly the opposite effect from all accounts. There are even some knights who travel around the Petty King-doms just to participate."

"Attracted by the danger?"

"To a certain extent," said Ludwig, "but also by the promise of wealth. You see, when you defeat an opponent, they pass over a ransom equal to the value of their arms and armour."

"Surely you jest?"

"Not at all. In fact, I hate to admit it, but that's how I lost my original armour, not to mention the warhorse my father gave me."

"You lost your armour?" asked Merrick.

"Well, most of it, anyway."

"You need a new suit of mail made for you, especially if you're hosting this tournament."

"Already taken care of. I have a smith in Malburg working on some."

"Not your own smith?"

"No," said Ludwig. "He's much too busy making weapons and armour for my warriors. In any event, he's not skilled enough for what I need."

"Which is?"

"Well, according to my captains, plate armour sufficiently ornate enough to show off my position as baron." He cast a sidelong glance at Merrick. "How about you?"

"What about me?"

"Do you have a set of plate armour?"

"Saints, no. I'm no warrior."

"Then who will lead your men when war comes?"

"I would be happy to place them under your command, should you be willing?"

"My command?"

"Yes," said Merrick. "We are friends, are we not? And who better to lead the men of Drakenfeld than an experienced commander?"

"In that case, I accept."

"Good. Of course, we'll need to make some arrangements to gather the army. Do I send them here, or will you collect them on the way to the capital?"

"I'm not sure," said Ludwig. "It depends on Otto's strategy for defending the realm."

"Well, we'd better talk to him about it sometime. Is he coming to the tournament?"

"I would hope so. I invited him."

"Good. Then we should ensure we discuss it with him."

"Agreed. Might I ask how many men you intend to field?"

"Close to a hundred foot and an equal number of bowmen."

"And the levy?"

"Another two hundred," replied Merrick, "although their quality is of a dubious nature."

"And your captains?"

"Inexperienced, for the most part. Perhaps I should send them to you for a little seasoning?"

"I'll take you up on that offer, but not until after the tournament."

"This is quite the place," said Merrick. "I can imagine it packed with commoners."

"Not only commoners, the barons will also be here as well. Or at least I hope so; I invited them. There's even a special area marked out for them."

"Splendid. Of course, you know what that means?"

Ludwig was caught unawares. "No?"

"Anytime the king gathers with all his nobles, he'll want to discuss politics."

"Don't they gather all the time?"

"How often have you been in Harlingen with all the other barons?"

"Admittedly, rarely."

"Indeed. And you've been the baron for nigh on two years. Harlingen might be our capital, but the barons seldom gather without cause... until now, that is. Doubtless, they'll all see this as a shrewd political gambit to curry favour."

"That was definitely not my intention," said Ludwig.

"You and I know that, but it's best if everyone else thinks it is."

"Why?"

"It will force them to take you seriously."

"And I need that?"

"Of course," said Merrick. "The last thing you want to be is like me."

"What's wrong with you?"

"I'm a simple man who prefers peace to war. I don't crave power or the adulation of my peers."

"Yet you are a stalwart companion and fast friend."

"I thank you for the compliment, but we both know of all the barons of Hadenfeld, I wield the least power."

"Even the smallest pebble can dislodge a horseshoe."

Merrick laughed. "Are you saying I'm a stone?"

"No, merely that even small actions have large ramifications."

"Thank you, my friend. That means a lot. Now, let's change the subject, shall we, before I am overcome with emotion."

"Most assuredly," said Ludwig. "Do you think Kenley will like the tournament?"

"I should certainly hope so. He's easily enthralled by horses. He'd spend all day watching them if he could."

"Is that a passion of yours?"

"No," said Merrick, "although Gita loves riding. I can manage well enough in the saddle but were it not for her, I'd always travel in a carriage."

"Like you did to come here?"

"Well, we had little choice there. You couldn't ride a horse while carrying a small child, not if you want to have any arms left at the end of it."

"I can well understand the need."

"That reminds me," said Merrick. "There was one more thing I wanted to talk to you about."

"Go on."

"Gita and I wondered if you might consent to be Kenley's guardian should anything happen to us. Once you're married, of course."

"I would be honoured, but I must confess there are no plans for matrimony in my near future."

"Really? I heard you were betrothed to Lady Alexandra."

"Yes, well, that rumour might be a tad premature."

"Have you fallen out with her?"

"No, not at all," said Ludwig, "but this is not the best time to discuss such matters."

"Oh? And when is?"

Ludwig blushed. "My preference would be... never."

21

THE TOURNAMENT
SUMMER 1098 SR

L udwig bowed deeply as King Otto entered Verfeld Keep.
"Your Majesty, you honour us with your visit."

"Ha!" said the king. "You flatter me, but what's all this nonsense about 'Majesty'? What did I tell you?"

"I'm sorry, m'lord."

Otto laughed. "That's better. Now, tell me all about this tournament."

They made their way into the great hall where the other barons had gathered and stood as they entered, leading the king to wave them down. He grabbed a cup from a passing servant before making his way to the head of the table.

"Lords and ladies," he began. "We are gathered here at the invitation of our most noble companion, Lord Ludwig of Verfeld. Let us raise a toast in his honour."

Everyone held up their goblets as Ludwig blushed at the compliment.

"Now," continued the king, "with that out of the way, let's settle down and eat, shall we?"

And with that, the feast commenced. The nobility of Hadenfeld possessed hearty appetites, and luckily, Ludwig had hired additional help from Malburg. He'd always considered the great hall of Verfeld huge, but now, with everyone packed in together, it felt positively tiny.

Otto leaned forward, ripping a leg off a roast fowl, and took a bite, the juice dripping into his beard. "Spectacular. And so tender. You must give my cook your recipe."

"Excuse me, Your Majesty," called out Lord Harvald, "but shouldn't we be preparing for war?"

The king waved back with food in hand, sending grease splattering everywhere. "Nonsense. It'll be years before that upstart takes the Throne."

"You speak of Prince Diedrich?" asked Ludwig.

"Yes, but I received word that King Rugar has rallied yet again. The man has the constitution of a horse. Mark my words, Ludwig; war will not come this year or the next, I warrant, although beyond that, I cannot say."

"And if the king dies prematurely?"

"It would still take time for his son to solidify his hold on the Throne."

"How can you be so sure?"

"I make it my business to be familiar with my enemies, as should you."

"Me? I have no enemies."

The king lowered his voice. "Come now, we both know that's not the case. Why, it wasn't so long ago that you almost fought a duel. Or did you forget the protestations of young Lord Darrian?"

"You heard about that?"

"I know all that transpires within my borders."

"If only the Duke of Erlingen had been so disposed."

"What's that, now?"

"The duke allowed his barons to fight amongst themselves. Not only duels but full-out battles."

"Then I call him a weak leader," said Otto. "Then again, I suppose he's only a duke, so perhaps the weakness can be explained."

"I gather you don't like the man."

"To tell the truth, I never met the fellow."

"But you do know Lord Wulfram?"

"The Baron of Regnitz?"

"Yes," said Ludwig, "that's him. He said he knew you."

"Let me think now. Oh yes, I met him at the court of King Ebert, but that was years before I assumed the Crown."

"I served him."

"Did you? By my reckoning, he'd be ancient by now."

"I believe he is of a similar age to yourself, m'lord."

"Is that your way of telling me I'm ancient?"

"No," said Ludwig. "Merely well-seasoned."

Otto barked out a laugh. "Very well said, my boy." He sobered a moment. "I'm sorry. You're the baron now. I should refrain from such childish affectations. I shall endeavour to remember that in future." His gaze swept the room, taking in all the lords and ladies. "Tell me," he said, once more whispering. "What do you make of this lot?"

"They are a fine set of people," said Ludwig, struggling to ascertain the king's motives for such a question.

"They're all decent folk, I'll give you that, but I want to identify who I can count on to fight when the time comes."

"You don't believe they would refuse the king's summoning?"

"No, of course not, but I need to know who I can rely on. There are few here with any real military experience, yourself excluded. Take Lord Merrick, for example."

"He's offered to place his men under my command," said Ludwig. "Subject to your approval, of course."

"That's a splendid idea. Clearly, the fellow is loyal."

"You have reason to think otherwise?"

"Not for Merrick, but let's just say not every baron has impressed me with their displays of loyalty."

"Why are you telling me this?"

"Because you're family," said Otto. "And if this invasion is anything like the last one, there's a good chance you'll end up closer to the Throne."

"I'm not sure what you mean?"

"Most of the men in my family command my companies. That ensures loyalty, but it can also result in heavy losses once battle is joined. In all likelihood, you will move up the line of succession, assuming you don't perish yourself."

"I have no desire to take over the Throne."

"I didn't ask if you did, but you would have no choice should those above you die." The king took a sip of wine. "You're low on the list, Ludwig, so your chance of inheriting is remote. Still, you must be prepared to do so if the situation presents itself."

"And should something like that transpire, you may rest assured I will not shirk my duty, but I am content to continue as I am."

"Spoken like a true diplomat. Perhaps I should send you to Neuhafen as an emissary?"

A sudden sense of panic seized Ludwig.

"Come now," continued the king, sensing his discomfort. "It was merely a jest. Now tell me, what have you got planned for us tomorrow?"

"I thought to begin the day with the archery contest, m'lord."

"That will do nicely, although I must admit, it's never been a particular passion of mine. Still, it'll be good to see the calibre of bowmen in Hadenfeld. Will you allow crossbows?"

"We decided to forego the option."

"Any particular reason?"

"The intention was to showcase the skill of our archers, and crossbows are a mite too expensive for commoners to afford. We could, however, consider a special category for them in the future."

The king smiled. "Is this to become an annual event?"

"I am considering several ideas. Lord Merrick has indicated a desire to host one next year, assuming all goes well. Perhaps we might have each baron host in successive years?"

"I like that idea. It will keep the martial spirit alive, an important consideration in these times."

"You're thinking of Neuhafen?"

"Not only them. To be honest, war is a common state amongst the Petty Kingdoms. Neuhafen is our present worry, but our other neighbours have been known to cause some concern."

"Like Deisenbach?"

"No, they've been allies for years. I was thinking more specifically about our western border with Grislagen. Should they side with Neuhafen, it would put us in a perilous situation."

"Is that likely?"

"I cannot dismiss it as a possibility, but I've taken steps to dissuade them."

"What steps are those?"

"Diplomatic ones. A country stands and falls on its alliances, particularly when one is surrounded by Petty Kingdoms."

Ludwig chuckled. "We're all Petty Kingdoms."

"Indeed we are," replied Otto. "Yet it would seem some are more petty than others."

Hooves thundered as the two horses charged towards each other. Lances lowered, and then a great crash erupted as the weapons struck home. Splinters of wood flew in all directions, but the knight known as Sir Petrus caught everyone's attention. He'd taken a hit to the chest and now leaned far back in the saddle, his broken weapon discarded.

Like many spectators, the king stood, ostensibly to get a better view of the poor fellow. "By the Saints, that was quite a blow."

The knight's horse slowed, and the gallant warrior slid to the side, servants catching him before he fell to the ground.

"That doesn't look good," said Otto. "And he was doing so well. I had him pegged as the potential champion."

"There are still many more rounds to go," said Ludwig, "and he isn't necessarily out of the competition."

They watched as men carried the limp knight from the field.

The king turned to Ludwig. "You were saying?"

"Maybe it's time we invested in a Life Mage?"

"I'd love to, but where do I find one willing to come here? There aren't many of them to go around, so they have their pick of the Petty Kingdoms. The last time I enquired, it would have cost me more than a hundred men."

"Still, it would be worth it."

"In what way?"

"You consider it an investment," explained Ludwig. "Even a victorious army takes casualties, but the judicious use of a mage like that can save dozens, maybe even hundreds, given enough of them."

"It's an old argument," said Otto. "I'm not convinced by sheer numbers alone. I admit I've never witnessed one in action, but I can't help but presume the stories of their capabilities are greatly exaggerated. Tell me, did you ever see one casting?"

"Only an Earth Mage, and he died rather suddenly."

"An Earth Mage? Where was this?"

"The Baron of Mulsingen employed him to breach the walls of Regnitz."

"And did it work?"

"In a manner of speaking. It allowed me to get inside the courtyard, but they quickly captured me."

"And the mage?"

"The defenders killed him, I'm afraid. He might've been able to manipulate stone, but it didn't help him resist the tip of a spear."

"An interesting tale. I hear Fire Mages are the most sought-after spellcasters."

"Does Neuhafen possess any?"

"Not that I'm aware of," replied Otto. "Then again, the politics of the region are shifting rapidly. If they are plotting to invade, it wouldn't surprise me to learn they hired some."

"You mean like mercenaries?"

"Either that or on loan from another court. Keeping your own mage is an expense few kings can afford."

"I was under the impression they were more common?"

"They are, but I'm yet to determine how they decide which courts to frequent. I suspect there's more to their loyalties than simple coins." The king laughed. "If I unearth that particular puzzle, I shall be sure to let you know. In the meantime, we must satisfy ourselves with protecting the realm the old-fashioned way, with men like this." He nodded at two new knights preparing for their chance at glory.

Everyone sat, the excitement of the previous round having worn off.

"I say," said Otto. "This takes me back to my youth."

"You participated in tourneys?"

"No, but I witnessed a few while I was at the court of King Ebert."

"And you never considered them for Hadenfeld?"

"No. I spent the early part of my reign keeping the rebels at bay. They call themselves Neuhafen now, but they're still giving me grief. When the time comes, we will deal them a blow from which they'll never recover. Then, maybe we can reunite this kingdom once again."

"I shall do all I can to help, m'lord."

Otto glanced around at the other nobles, his gaze resting on Lord Meinhard. "There is something I need to speak to you about, Ludwig, something unrelated to war."

"What is it?"

The king's gaze returned once more to the Baron of Verfeld. "You've had more than enough time to settle in. It's time you took the next step."

"Which is?"

"You know full well what I'm talking about. You need to marry, Ludwig, and produce an heir. What about Lady Alexandra?"

"What of her?"

"Come now, do not take me for a fool. Are you going to ask for her hand or not?"

Ludwig felt panic rising within. "I'm fond of her, naturally, but..."

"As I suspected," said the king. "Well, you can't say I haven't given you the opportunity to plot your own destiny. Your reluctance is understandable, but it now falls on me to make other arrangements."

"M'lord?"

"I still have several potential allies out there in the Petty Kingdoms. Perhaps we can find a match to cement an alliance?"

"You're speaking of an arranged marriage?"

"Naturally. Come now. It can't come as a complete surprise. After all, your father's second marriage fell into that category. Of course, if there's someone else, I'd be happy to keep my nose out of your private life?"

"I..." Ludwig was at a loss for words. He'd been dreading this very thing for some time: had, in fact, arranged the entire ruse with Lady Alexandra for that express purpose, yet now it was all unravelling. He looked around, desperate to escape the conversation, yet he knew he was doomed. Better then, to accept fate rather than fight it and possibly incur the king's wrath.

He finally nodded. "Very well, I shall agree to your request."

Otto slapped him on the back. "Excellent! Now, let us speak of this no more till I make some enquiries." The king returned his attention to the knights. "Who do you favour in this next bout?"

"Sir Heston," said Ludwig. "I had a chance to see him practicing earlier this week."

The officiant dropped the flag, and then the two contestants charged towards each other. Moments later, Sir Heston flew from his seat to land, unceremoniously, on his backside.

The king found the spectacle entertaining. "You're a fine warrior, Cousin, but it appears a poor judge of character when it comes to jousting."

"It must be his horse."

"If you say so. Speaking of horses, you might want to consider raising some mounted men-at-arms. I hear it's all the rage these days."

"Another tactic to drain my purse?"

Otto chuckled. "No one ever said being a baron was easy or inexpensive, for that matter. Do you have the necessary funds?"

"I could probably find them, but it would likely drain a good portion of my treasury."

"Then I shall find you a wealthy wife," said Otto. "I hear the ladies up north have large dowries. I'll have my agents look there."

"You have agents, now?"

"Every king has agents. It's the only way to keep track of what's happening. I say agents, but in truth, it's merely a string of friends and acquaintances. Still, it helps me stay up to date on the politics of the Petty Kingdoms, a difficult thing to do in the best of times."

"Why is it there's so much strife on the Continent? You would think by now we would have settled all our differences."

"And so we should have, but the Petty Kingdoms were born out of the collapse of the Old Kingdom."

"You mean Therengia?"

"Of course. We, as a people, banded together to defeat them, but the seeds of discontent were sown in their collapse."

"I'm not sure I follow."

"The Old Kingdom was said to possess wealth beyond imagining. Countries fought over the remains, eager to take advantage of their destruction. Borders quickly solidified, but there was always resentment between allies, each assuming the other profited more."

"And that's all there is to it?"

"Not quite," said Otto. "The defeat of the Old Kingdom changed everything. Before that, wars were waged between one country and another, but the Great War showed how smaller allies could cooperate to vanquish more powerful kingdoms. It set in motion a rush to build alliances to prevent a similar fate from befalling the Successor States."

"You know so much about all this."

"Of course I do; I'm the king. To do otherwise could endanger the very existence of my own kingdom."

"What I never understood is why you sent my father all the way to Reinwick? Not that I don't understand the concept of marriages to gain allies, but why one so far away?"

"That's a little more difficult to explain. It makes sense to forge alliances with those that are physically close, but a king must look at the bigger picture."

"Such as?"

"Take our own situation. We currently have a problem with Neuhafen. To counter the threat of invasion, it would behoove us to ally with a country that lies on their border."

"Like Ardosa?"

"Precisely. Neuhafen would then search for someone who borders Ardosa—say Ulrichen, for example. Thus, the chain of alliances grows, eventually encompassing the entire Continent."

"The very thought makes my head ache."

"Mine too," said the king. "And this endless chain of alliances can often lead to unintended consequences."

"Such as?"

"It could end up embroiling us in a war in a far-off land. Should such a thing occur, I'd need to send an army, else all our other allies might refuse to honour their obligations to us."

"Wouldn't that mean escalation?"

"Now you understand. All it would take is one war to start, and the entirety of the Continent could become caught up in a massive conflict, the likes of which haven't been seen for nigh on five centuries. I tell you, it's a delicate balancing act. One false move, and a king could find the balance of power tipping against them."

"And so you marry off your nobles to outsiders to tip the scales in your favour?"

"Yes. It requires a skilled hand, so you see why I'll be counting on you to do your part."

Ludwig stared down at his feet.

"Look," said the king. "I know it's not what you wanted, but the kingdom needs this to maintain the peace. Your marriage might be the one thing that convinces Neuhafen to stay out of our lands. Is that such a high price to pay? Who knows? You might even come to love the woman, whoever she ends up being."

"I doubt it," said Ludwig, "but I shall do my duty and marry her all the same."

22

WORD FROM THE NORTH

WINTER 1098 SR

The tournament was a great success, summer soon giving way to autumn, and with the passing of the seasons, efforts turned towards the harvest. Thankfully, the year was good for crops, and Ludwig's barony prospered. All thoughts of war faded from memory, but not the knowledge that King Otto sought a suitable wife for him.

Ludwig travelled to Malburg a couple of times a month to visit his armourer, Master Romaro. Master Tomas had highly recommended the fellow, and he'd proven more than equal to the challenge. The greater part of his armour was finished, only requiring adjustments to the fit. Thus, three weeks into winter, he stood in the armourer's workshop, staring into a large mirror.

Master Romaro was altering the positioning of a shoulder strap when the door opened, admitting a short, bearded fellow wrapped in thick furs. He crossed the room, warming his hands by the forge.

"Good day, Rurlan," said the smith. "I trust your journey was pleasant?"

The visitor pulled back his hood, revealing the face of a Dwarf. "Aye, pleasant enough, although I can't claim to be happy with this weather of late." He took notice of Ludwig. "And who do we have here?"

"Lord Ludwig," replied the armourer. "The Baron of Verfeld."

"Would that be Ludwig Altenburg?"

"It would," said Ludwig. "Why? Do you know me?"

"Only by name. It appears you can save me a trip."

"I'm afraid I don't understand."

"Rurlan here is a courier for the smiths guild," explained Master Romaro. "He carries letters back and forth on our behalf."

"Your guild exists outside of Malburg?"

"Of course," said the Dwarf. "In fact, we're found in most cities of the Petty Kingdoms."

"And is every smith a member?"

"No, some don't like paying a percentage of their profits to us, while others lack the minimum skills to be granted admittance."

"What kind of correspondence do you carry?"

"I'd be a poor excuse for a courier," said the Dwarf, "if I discussed such things with outsiders. Suffice it to say, I am here on guild business."

"Then, if you don't mind me asking, how is it you've heard of me?"

"Give me a moment, and I'll explain." Rurlan removed his furs, then tossed them aside. He picked up his satchel and rooted through it, finally producing a sealed letter. This he held out before Ludwig. "Is this you?"

Ludwig was surprised to see his name written in a fine hand.

"That's my name, yes. Who's it from?"

"One thing at a time," the Dwarf replied. He dug into his bag once more, producing a ring he slipped on, then pressed against the seal, which crumbled. "It's a phoenix ring."

"Which is?"

"A way of making a letter tamper-proof."

"Why would that even be necessary?"

"Don't ask me. I'm only the courier."

Ludwig took the letter, twisting it to examine it from both sides. "Just out of curiosity, what would've happened had I opened it before you used your ring?"

"It would have caught fire."

"I assume that means this contains something important."

"I have no idea. Perhaps you should open it and find out?"

Ludwig unfolded it, only to find another within. It, too, was sealed, but this time the wax bore three waves.

His heart began pounding, for this was the seal of Saint Agnes. This could only mean one thing—Charlaine was trying to contact him! He was eager to read it but knew he should wait until he was alone.

"Something important, then?" asked Rurlan.

"I assume so," replied Ludwig, "but I'll need to return to the keep first." He turned to Master Romaro. "I'm sorry, but you must excuse me."

"Quite all right, Lord. I have all the necessary measurements to make the last few adjustments." He went to say more, but Ludwig quickly began divesting himself of his armour. The smith moved in to help. His task complete, Ludwig picked up his cloak and rushed out the door, letting it slam shut in his haste.

All the way back to Verfeld Keep, Ludwig wondered what the letter contained. He briefly considered halting and reading it, but the more he thought about it, the more he became convinced it held news of great import.

She'd seen fit to send word through the smiths guild. That alone was enough to intrigue him. Added to that, however, was the use of a phoenix ring. She obviously didn't want it getting into anyone else's hands but his. The last he'd heard, she was in Ilea, a kingdom which lay astride the Shimmering Sea far to the south. He suddenly realized three years had passed since he'd returned to Hadenfeld to take up the mantle of baron.

His guards at Verfeld Keep spotted his approach and waited as he halted his horse. He rushed up the steps to the keep's main door without another word and almost collided with Sigwulf.

"Something wrong?" the huge northerner asked. "You seem to be in a bit of a hurry."

Ludwig threw off his cape. "I just received an important letter."

"Regarding?"

"I'm not sure yet. It was sent to me with certain... safeguards to ensure only I could read it."

"Might I ask who it's from?"

"To be honest, I'm not entirely certain. It bears the mark of Saint Agnes though."

Sigwulf noted the excitement in his voice. "You think it's from Charlaine?"

"Who else in that order would wish to contact me?"

"You'd better get up to your study and peruse it. I'll find Carson and have him bring you something to eat."

"Thank you. I'll let you know if this contains anything that may concern you."

It didn't take Ludwig long to reach his study, where he quickly sat down and placed the letter before him, eager to read its contents yet, at the same time, apprehensive. It occurred to him that this might inform him of her demise. The thought sent him into a panic, but then reason took hold. It was not the habit of Temple Knights to notify others of the death of one of their own. Even if that were the case, why the need for such secrecy?

He gathered his nerve and broke the seal, unfolding it with reverence. A sure hand had written it, and instead of starting from the beginning, he glanced down at the signature. Charlaine, it said, then Temple Captain. He couldn't believe his eyes. He'd heard of Temple Captains, but it was said to take years, if not decades, to achieve that rank. Now, here she was, a captain after only four years!

He carefully read the lengthy note. It barely fit on a single piece of paper, yet its import was staggering. A knock on the door indicated the arrival of Carson. Ludwig turned the letter over, hiding its contents.

"I've brought you some ham, my lord, and some wine."

"Thank you."

"Is there anything else I can get you, Lord?"

"Yes. Please find my two captains and tell them to report to me immediately."

"Of course." Carson bowed, then left the room, closing the door behind him.

Ludwig fretted. He read over the letter again, in case he'd mistaken her meaning, but there could be no question as to what she was suggesting. Cyn and Sig soon arrived, both full of curiosity.

"You wanted us?" said Cyn.

"Yes," said Ludwig. "I've gotten some disturbing news, but before I tell you about it, you must promise to repeat it to no others, at least not for the present."

"Agreed," said Sigwulf.

Cyn nodded. "What is it?"

Ludwig held up the letter. "I received this from Charlaine deShandria. She writes to me from Korvoran, up in Reinwick."

"I thought she was down south?" said Sigwulf.

"So did I, but it appears she's been busy of late. They sent her north as a Temple Captain."

"Impressive," said Cyn. "She must be quite the knight to advance so quickly."

"I don't have the details of how she got there, but she dispatched this letter via special courier—a member of the smiths guild."

"Not through the Church?"

"No, and there's more. She had them use something called a phoenix ring."

Sigwulf laughed. "That's a myth. They don't exist."

"I can attest otherwise. I saw one with my own eyes."

"That makes this very important, then," said Cyn. "What else does it say?"

"She sends greetings but then warns of a corruption in the Church."

"You mean a Holy Order? Which one?"

"All of them, it would seem. What do you two know of Halvaria?"

"No more than you," said Sigwulf. "They're an extensive empire, lying far to the west, blamed for all sorts of mischief amongst the Petty Kingdoms. You might say they've grown to be seen as everyone's worst nightmare."

"She writes that they recently tried to cause a war in the north. What's more disturbing is she's accused a court mage of siding with them. Someone named Larissa Stormwind."

"Stormwind?" said Sigwulf. "Are you sure?"

Ludwig looked once more at the letter. "Yes. It's right here. Why do you ask?"

"The Stormwinds are a powerful family of mages."

"What type of mages?"

"Water, if I'm not mistaken."

"I'm confused," said Cyn. "Why would a Stormwind help Halvaria?"

"That's an excellent question," said Ludwig.

"Could she be mistaken?"

"I doubt she would go to all the trouble of sending me this if she wasn't certain."

"Good point," said Sigwulf. "But how did she know to reach you here?"

"I don't know for sure, but if she travelled to Reinwick, she likely passed through Erlingen. It's not beyond reason to assume she might've heard of our exploits. I made no secret that I was heading home."

"That sounds reasonable, but why warn you about all of this? We're a long way from Halvaria's border."

"True, but maybe she feared another Stormwind might seek influence at Otto's court?"

"One rotten apple doesn't spoil the whole harvest," said Cyn. "Just because one Stormwind worked for them doesn't mean they all do."

"I can see why you would assume that, but why would she send this warning if that was true?"

"I think we're missing the point," said Sigwulf. "The real threat is the corruption in the Church."

"How? It's not as if any Temple Knights serve the king. They're forbidden from getting involved in local matters."

"Also true," said Cyn, "but think about it for a moment. What is the purpose of the Temple Knights?"

"To guard the temples?" said Sigwulf.

"No," said Ludwig. "According to Father Vernan, their real purpose is to dissuade the Halvarian Empire from expanding."

"And now Halvaria has allies in the Petty Kingdoms," added Cyn.

"So it would seem. This is dire news indeed."

"What else aren't you telling us?"

"Last summer, I had an interesting chat with King Otto."

"And?" pressed Cyn.

"He told me all about the system of alliances which exists across the Petty Kingdoms. The situation is so dire that any single conflict could snowball into a continent-wide war."

Sigwulf nodded. "That would be to Halvaria's advantage. They could simply wait it out, then march in and pick up the pieces."

"My thoughts exactly."

"So the question," said Cyn, "is what we do about it?"

"What can we do?" said Sigwulf.

"We can pay more attention to what happens at court," said Ludwig. "If there truly is a connection between this Stormwind family and the Halvarians, they'll be eager to start a war, hoping it will soon escalate. I suspect sooner or later, one of them will show up in either Neuhafen or at Otto's court in Harlingen."

"You really believe Halvaria would go to all that trouble? Their army outnumbers the combined might of the Petty Kingdoms by all accounts. Why not simply invade?"

"Every war is a gamble, and their invasion would be the one thing that could unite all the kingdoms. It makes far more sense to have us fight amongst ourselves, then they could swoop in at the end, all in the name of bringing peace to the land."

"And you believe people would accept that?" asked Sigwulf.

"I think people would accept anything that offered an alternative after years of constant warfare."

"How do we stop that?" asked Cyn.

"By avoiding war at all costs."

"But that would mean giving in to foreign demands, wouldn't it? If word got out we weren't willing to fight, the kingdoms bordering us would begin claiming our lands."

"We need a deterrent," said Sigwulf. "An army strong enough that no one dares attack."

"I doubt that would work," said Cyn. "If we raise a large army, our neighbours would have little choice but to do likewise. That wouldn't halt the problem; it would only worsen it."

"Perhaps the Church could make everyone see reason?"

"But the Church is corrupt, remember?"

"What does that even mean?" asked Sigwulf.

Ludwig glanced once more at the letter. "Charlaine says here that people within the fighting orders have their own interests at heart. Some even want to see the Temple Knights become a political force on the Continent."

"But they're already a political force, aren't they?"

"To a certain extent, but they always stayed away from taking sides in conflicts. If what she says is true, that would no longer be the case."

"It would be nice to fight alongside Temple Knights."

"I agree," said Ludwig, "but who decides which side they take? Imagine what would happen if the Holy Army took Neuhafen's side?"

"I concede the point," said Sigwulf. "Do we have any idea of how bad this corruption is?"

"Enough that Charlaine warned me about it. She was particularly concerned about the Cunars."

"And the Mathewites?"

"She doesn't mention them directly, but she did say even her own order revealed signs of outside influence. She suspected the Halvarians were behind it but had no proof."

"I'm still a little confused," said Cyn. "Of all the people she could have contacted, why you?"

"Verfeld is her home... well, Malburg is, and this land falls under my protection."

"But she doesn't know you're the baron, does she?"

"Likely not. The letter is certainly not addressed as such."

"Then why write to you after all this time?"

Ludwig wanted it to be because she loved him, but he didn't wish to say it, at least not out loud. "She trusts me," he finally said, "and with all that's going on, I doubt there are many people she can say that of."

"Will you write her back?" asked Cyn. "Ask for more information?"

"I haven't decided yet. I must give this some thought. The last thing I want is to make things worse."

"What about Father Vernan? Do we trust him? What if he's part of this corruption?"

"I've seen nothing that indicates he has any motives beyond his religious duties, but you raise a valid concern. Just for a moment, let's suppose he's one of these corrupt individuals. What would that mean?"

"Could he be passing information on to his superiors?" said Sigwulf. "Things like how many men you have under arms, for example. The Church could provide that information to the enemy if they were trying to influence the outcome of a possible invasion?"

"Siggy makes a good point," said Cyn. "And the father has visited

Malburg often enough to send off letters to his superiors. How long have you actually known him?"

"About as long as I've known you two. Then again, I only saw him sporadically in Torburg, then, he was off to become a Holy Father. I understand your concern, but I have a hard time believing he has some sort of ulterior motive."

"And you may be right," said Cyn, "but for now, at least, we must leave nothing to chance. Best if we keep this knowledge to just the three of us."

"Very well."

Sigwulf shifted his feet.

"You have something to add?" asked Ludwig.

"I do, though you may not like it."

"Go on, speak freely. I shan't hold it against you."

"How do we know Charlaine is telling the truth? Perhaps she's trying to sow distrust and discontent to further Halvaria's claims herself?"

"I know her," said Ludwig. "She was always a woman of great faith. I have a hard time believing she'd do anything that would damage the Church."

"Yet isn't that precisely what she's doing? She's an insider now. What if she doesn't like some of her superiors' decisions?"

"You haven't met her, so I'll excuse the accusations. Charlaine is not the type to break the rules. She was a swordsmith by trade and a master one at that. You don't rise to those levels by questioning authority. You met her father, Tomas. Do you honestly believe his daughter would pursue a personal vendetta against a superior?"

"I meant no offence," said Sigwulf. "I'm merely trying to see things from all sides. If you believe her to be pure of heart, I shall accept you at your word."

"I do," said Ludwig.

"So what do we do about Father Vernan?" asked Cyn. "Do we watch him?"

"Let's not get carried away by all of this. There's no indication as yet that the corruption is widespread. We can safely assume that the average member of the Church is unaware of these internal struggles. We won't follow the good father around, but I think we should hold off revealing the contents of this letter for the time being."

"Perhaps you should talk to him about the Church?" said Cyn. "Get a feel for whether or not he's encountered anything odd? He might have knowledge that we're lacking."

"If the opportunity presents itself, I shall give it a try, but I can't exactly go up to him and ask if he's aware of any corruption within his order. This requires a delicate touch."

"Delicate," said Sigwulf. "That's definitely not your specialty."

"Hey, now," said Ludwig. "I can be subtle when needed."

"You mean like when you entered the joust in Torburg?"

23

ARRANGEMENTS

SPRING 1099 SR

T he spring of ninety-nine was particularly wet, with storms ravaging the countryside. As a result, the fields flooded, leading to a late sowing.

Ludwig worried it might cause a shortened growing season, but his farmers quickly pointed out that this had occurred many times, to no measurable detriment.

To help things along, he sent some of his warriors to assist with planting the crops. Definitely unusual and beyond anything any previous Baron of Verfeld had done, but the assistance was greatly appreciated.

Ludwig spent his days riding from village to village, ensuring he dealt quickly with any problems that arose. In Freiburg, they needed to drain a flooded field, which took three days to complete. They created a pond for the runoff, which would later be used to water livestock.

By the time the fields were finally sown, he was looking forward to relaxing but noticed a horseman waiting for him as he approached the keep. Worse still, the rider wore the king's livery, indicating more than just a simple message awaited his arrival. As Ludwig advanced, he recognized the knight.

"Sir Petrus, isn't it?"

"It is, my lord."

"I must say, you're looking much better than when I last saw you. How's the leg?"

"Fully recovered, Lord."

Ludwig dismounted. "Come inside, and we'll find you something to eat. Have you travelled far?"

"All the way from Harlingen, Lord."

"I assume you're here for me?"

"I am. I bear a message from His Majesty."

"Bring it with you, then. I'll read it once I'm out of these wet clothes."

They climbed the steps and entered the keep. "Carson?" he called out. "Take Sir Petrus to the great hall, will you? And see if you can't rustle him up something to eat." Ludwig turned back to the knight. "I shall join you as soon as I change."

"Yes, my lord."

Ludwig made his way up to his chambers and quickly changed, only to run into Cyn as he left his room.

"Something up?" she asked.

"Yes. The king has sent a messenger. Where's Sig?"

"Out marching with the garrison. Shall I fetch him?"

"No. Whatever it is, we can tell him about it later."

"We?"

"Yes. I want you with me in the great hall."

"Should I change?"

"No. It's a messenger, not the king himself. And in any event, you know the man—Sir Petrus."

"Wasn't he the favourite to win the tourney," she replied, "but then he took that terrible fall? For a while there, it looked like he might lose the leg."

"It seems he fully recovered. Now, let's go and find out what he wants, shall we?"

They headed downstairs into the great hall, where Sir Petrus sat nibbling away at some cheese. He stood as they entered.

"My lord," he said, bowing deeply.

"I believe you know Captain Hoffman?"

"Yes, Lord."

Ludwig took a seat, then Carson appeared from nowhere, cups in hand, along with wine. Sir Petrus waited until all were served before continuing.

"I bear a letter from the king," he said, digging into his belt pouch. "Ah, here it is." He held it out, and Carson quickly snatched it, delivering it into his lord's possession. It bore the king's seal, but little else hinted at what lay within. Ludwig's hands trembled slightly, and he gripped the paper to hide his discomfort. He suspected this was the letter he'd been dreading, yet at the same time, he knew he could put it off no longer.

Once the seal was broken, he unfolded it, letting his gaze wander over the contents. Otto had a fine hand, or at least whoever wrote it did, for it was more likely to have been dictated. The king's words were flowery and polite but left no doubt that this was a command, not a request. Ludwig finished reading, then folded it back up.

"Thank you, Sir Petrus."

"Have you a reply, my lord?"

"Yes. Please convey to His Majesty that I shall immediately begin preparations for the trip."

"In that case," said the knight, "I have something else for you." He produced a small wooden cylinder typically used for important documents. "It is a letter of introduction, Lord. You'll need it once you arrive at court in Korvoran."

"I assume that means you know the purpose of my visit?"

"Indeed, Lord, although I've spoken of it to no one."

"I'm surprised he would have confided in you," said Ludwig. "My understanding was that this was to be kept secret as long as possible in case anyone seeks to interfere."

The knight stared back, clearly surprised. "Did he not tell you, Lord?"

"Did he not tell me what?"

"I am to accompany you."

"Why would you do that?"

"To see you safe, Lord. The king is worried the roads may not be secure."

"I thought you would take back my reply?"

"I shall ensure the message is sent, Lord, but my duty is to remain by your side."

Cyn looked from one to the other. "Might I enquire what this is all about?"

"The king," said Ludwig, "is sending me to Reinwick to meet my future bride."

She almost laughed, thinking it a jest, but his serious expression told her otherwise. "And who is this mystery woman, if I may be so bold as to ask?"

Ludwig unfolded the letter to glance down at it. "Someone named Lady Charlotte Stratmeyer, daughter of Lord Kurlan, Baron of Blunden. Ever heard of him?"

"I'm not one to take an interest in the politics of the Petty Kingdoms—that's more Siggy's thing, but I have heard of Blunden. I believe it's on the coast of the Great Northern Sea."

"Yes, in the Duchy of Reinwick."

"So your future bride will share the homeland of your stepmother. How interesting. I suppose that means you're going to need a carriage."

"A carriage? I was going to ride there."

"You can't bring her back here on horseback, Ludwig."

"You mean 'Lord'," corrected Sir Petrus.

A flicker of annoyance crossed her face. "Of course. Now, where was I? Oh yes, you need to bring her back in style. After all, she'll become the new Baroness of Verfeld."

"If I may, Lord?" interjected Sir Petrus. "Might I suggest we take a mounted escort?"

"I employ no knights," said Ludwig, "or mounted men-at-arms."

"Surely there are members of your garrison who can ride?"

"There are, but a trip that long would require experienced horsemen."

"I'll go," said Cyn, "or Siggy can." She paused a moment. "Actually, much as it pains me to admit it, you're better off taking him than me."

"Couldn't I take the both of you?"

"You can't. Someone needs to remain here to look after the garrison. And, in actuality, he knows more about the courts of the northern kingdoms than I do."

"Siggy?" said the knight.

"Captain Sigwulf Marhaven," said Ludwig. "One of my captains."

"The large, bearded fellow?"

"That's him. I fought with him and Cyn in Erlingen."

"So you mean to leave Captain Hoffman here in charge of your garrison? Are you sure that's wise, Lord?"

"Are you questioning my decision, sir knight?"

"N-n-no," he said. "Of course not, my lord."

"Good," said Ludwig. He met Cyn's gaze. "I shall make arrangements with Pelton and inform all that you'll be in charge in our absence. Run the place as if it were your own, and don't be afraid to bite someone's head off if they give you any trouble. If you come across anything out of your area of expertise, send word to Lord Merrick, or the king, if it's serious. You know everyone else of import in these parts, so I don't expect any issues with locals."

"When do you want to leave?" she asked.

"In a day or two. I must first head into Malburg and arrange a carriage."

"I'll let Siggy know."

"Then I'll let you go find him. In the meantime, I'll make arrangements with Sir Petrus."

She rushed off, eager to be about her business.

Ludwig turned his attention to the knight. "Your thoughts?"

"You'll need servants and a matron. Naturally, a handmaiden will be required, not to mention—"

"That's quite enough," said Ludwig. "You would have me bankrupt before I even begin."

"But the Lady Charlotte cannot go without servants, my lord."

"I'm sure she already has servants of her own. This is, unless I miss my guess, a wealthy family?"

"Indeed," said the knight. "They say the Baron of Blunden owns a large estate, not to mention an expensive home in Korvoran. It is there we shall be introduced."

Korvoran. Ludwig had heard the city mentioned earlier but failed to make the connection until now. That was the same place Charlaine was garrisoned—at least it was when she wrote the letter.

"Do you know much about the Reinwick capital?"

"It is a port city, my lord. I believe it also hosts contingents of Temple Knights. Recent reports tell of a Holy Fleet stationed there."

"A Holy Fleet? In the north?"

"I admit the news is somewhat unexpected, but we have reason to believe they are little more than rumours."

"Why is that?"

"For the simple reason that the Temple Knights of Saint Cunar deny it. Who else would man the fleet?"

"Who indeed?" said Ludwig. "Could it be one of the other orders?"

"With all due respect, Lord, I find it difficult to consider that the Church would permit any other order that honour."

"That being the case, why even bring it up?"

"It indicates there is great interest in the Church's activities in the north. That may have a reflection on how we're greeted there."

"But we're not representatives of the Church."

"True," said Sir Petrus, "but we are followers of Saint Mathew. Or are you trying to tell me otherwise?"

"No, of course not. Saint Mathew is the Patron Saint of Hadenfeld, but Saint Agnes is also popular."

The knight snickered. "Not much chance of that."

"Why would you think that?" Ludwig demanded.

"Well…" The fellow blushed. "For one thing, we are not women."

"And you believe that only women can worship Agnes? Do you even know what she represents?"

"I…"

Ludwig let the man swallow nervously a couple of times before putting him out of his misery. "You would do well to watch your tongue, Sir Petrus, particularly when we arrive in Reinwick. I understand there's a detachment of Temple Knights sworn to Saint Agnes there."

"There are?"

"Indeed. And enough of them to warrant the employment of a Temple Captain, if my information is correct."

"You have your own sources?"

"I do, although I will say no more of it at this time. As to your earlier suggestion of horsemen, do you think we might find some in Malburg?"

"I can't see why they would have any."

Ludwig smiled. "I thought we might borrow some Temple Knights of our own."

"Why in the name of the Saints would they agree to that?"

"It's not unknown for Temple Knights of Saint Mathew to protect travellers, especially important ones who help support their missions."

"Are you suggesting they can be purchased? They are not mercenaries!"

"Not so much purchased as borrowed. And think of it, what manner of bandit would take on a Temple Knight?"

"I must concede, Lord, it is not something I considered, but your idea has merit."

"Good. Then I shall speak with Holy Father Vernan and see what he can arrange through his order."

"But he's a Holy Father, not a Temple Knight."

"True, but he's well-known to the Prior of Saint Mathew, and who better to ask such a favour?"

"I don't understand," said Sigwulf. "Why do I need to go?"

"You know all about courts," said Cyn.

"Agreed, but someone might recognize my name."

"Don't worry," said Ludwig. "We'll be sure to only address you by your first name."

"Still, if there's anyone of import from Abelard, it could be the death of me."

"I won't let them get a hold of you, Sig. You have my word. In any case, we'll be there representing the interests of Hadenfeld. I doubt our host would permit a foreign noble to haul you off to face trial."

"I was thinking more along the lines of murder."

"Come now," said Cyn. "You were still young when they crushed the rebellion. Who would even know what you look like anymore?"

He finally nodded. "I suppose you're right."

"You suppose? How about you know I'm right?"

Sigwulf smiled. "I wish you were coming with us."

"So do I, but someone has to stay here to keep an eye on things. I don't want all that training of yours going to waste."

"You did just as much as me."

"All right, you two," said Ludwig. "You can dispense hugs and kisses later. There's work to do."

"Very well," said Sigwulf. "What's first on the list?"

"A carriage. I need you to go into Malburg and arrange one."

"Why?"

"To carry Lady Charlotte back here to Verfeld."

"Why not hire it there?"

"I wasn't aware that was possible."

"There are several coach houses spread throughout the north. You can rent their services to go anywhere, provided you have the funds."

"And they're considered trustworthy?"

"They are indeed. They even formed their own guild."

"Who uses their services?"

"Mostly wealthy merchants, but the occasional noble is not above employing them."

"I would have thought nobles would possess their own transport?"

"And they often do," said Sigwulf, "but travelling long distances is a lot of wear and tear on a fancy carriage. It's better to use someone else's and let them take care of the repairs."

"How long have these coach houses been around?"

"I believe they started in Braymoor some hundred years ago but soon spread all along the coast. Merchants often travel by ship from port to port but require transportation when they're ashore. Somebody recognized the need and came up with what they have now."

"Amazing," said Ludwig.

"Not really," said Cyn. "The truth is the Continent is changing dramatically; people just don't see it."

"Changing, how?"

"Merchants are getting wealthier, some even more so than nobles. How long, do you suppose, before they exert their influence at court?"

"But they have no influence, surely?"

"Ah, but they have coins, and coins translate to power. You're the one who told us all about the free city of Malburg. Think of the Continent as simply a larger version of that idea."

"I can't see that going down well with the ruling class," said Ludwig.

"Oh, it doesn't," said Sigwulf. "Many towns have run into trouble with their overlords."

"You mean kings?"

"Kings, princes, dukes, it makes little difference what you call them. People are tired of being pushed around. Amassing wealth gives them a way to fight back. Don't get me wrong; it's not as if every commoner has that type of influence, but times are changing, and many would say it's about time."

"Not that I'm against that sort of change," said Ludwig, "but it couldn't have happened at a worse time. Especially with the threat of Halvaria breathing down our necks."

"You worry too much," said Sigwulf. "Change comes whether we want it or not. We must adjust accordingly."

"So you're a philosopher now?"

Sigwulf blushed. "I might've been reading some of those books in your library."

"What about your armour?" asked Cyn.

"I shan't be needing it in the north," said Ludwig.

"I understand that, but the armourer won't be able to work on it without you here, will he?"

"He only has a few adjustments left. He'll just have to wait until my return."

"Anything else?"

"As a matter of fact, yes, there is. I thought we might be wise to raise some mounted men-at-arms. What do you think, Cyn?"

"Where would you put the horses? It's one thing to raise additional soldiers, quite another to look after their mounts. I hate to say it, but if you want to grow your garrison any bigger, you'll need to enlarge the keep. At the very least, you'll need a walled-in courtyard to protect your stables, and a fortified gatehouse wouldn't go amiss. Of course, all that takes time, not to mention the funds to pay for it."

"Coins don't bother me," said Ludwig. "I'm sure King Otto would lend us what we need. The bigger issue is finding an architect who can design it for us and the stonemasons to actually construct it. And all this at a time when war threatens."

"No simple task," said Cyn. "But I've some ideas on that score. I tell you what; let me look into it while you're away and see what's available."

"Very well, but don't start any actual construction until I return."

"Of course not. I know better than that." An enormous grin broke out on her face.

"I know that look," said Sigwulf. "What's going on inside that head of yours?"

Cyn's eyes lit up. "I'm so excited. I always wanted to build a castle!"

24

THE TRIP

SPRING/SUMMER 1099 SR

"Here comes Sir Petrus," announced Sigwulf, "but who's he got with him?"

"Looks like a Temple Knight of Saint Mathew," replied Ludwig. "It appears Father Vernan's request has borne fruit."

They waited as the riders approached, and then the knight hailed them. "Greetings, Lord Ludwig."

"Good day, Sir Petrus. Who is this you bring with you today?"

"I am Brother Hamelyn," replied the Temple Knight. "I am here to keep you safe on the road to Reinwick. I am also the instrument by which your wife's dowry will be transferred to Verfeld."

"I'm not sure I understand," said Sigwulf.

Brother Hamelyn smiled. "Understandable. My order deals with many financial transactions across the length and breadth of the Petty Kingdoms. We will secure the dowry in Reinwick, and a similar amount will be released here in Hadenfeld."

"I had no idea the Church provided such a service."

"Merchants and the nobility primarily use it."

"Does this mean," said Sigwulf, "that the order benefits in some way for its benevolence in such matters?"

"We take a small percentage to cover the transaction. It is one of the ways in which we keep the order in funds."

Sir Petrus shifted in his saddle. "Shall we begin, my lord? We have many miles to travel before nightfall."

"Yes, of course," said Ludwig. He urged his horse into a trot, the others following his example. Sigwulf rode beside him while the two knights fell in behind.

"It seems," said Sigwulf, "like only yesterday we were heading south, away from Erlingen. Now we find ourselves traversing the same roads, this time in the opposite direction."

"It can't be helped," said Ludwig. "Unless you know of a better way to travel such a distance?"

"We could try a riverboat?"

"A nice idea, but Hadenfeld's great rivers form our boundaries. Such a trip would put us uncomfortably close to the very two neighbours who cause us the most grief. No, it's better this way."

"But expensive, surely. I well remember what you paid out last time for inns."

"There is a simple solution," called out Brother Hamelyn. "In kingdoms friendly to Hadenfeld, we shall seek lodgings at the homes of other nobles. It's a common courtesy on the Continent."

"And in those places hostile?"

"In those instances, we'll avail ourselves of the hospitality of my brethren."

"Fair enough," said Sigwulf. "But your order doesn't associate itself with women, does it?"

"We don't allow women into our commanderies, if that's what you mean."

"Then how would you see to the comfort of Lord Ludwig's wife?"

Hamelyn went silent for a moment. Sigwulf was just about to continue when the Temple Knight finally spoke. "We shall seek assistance from our sisters, the Temple Knights of Saint Agnes."

"Hah," said Ludwig. "He's got you there, Sig." He noted the look of frustration on his companion's face. "You didn't expect that, did you?"

"No. I must concede I did not, but I shall accept the loss with dignity."

"Have you ever been to Reinwick?"

"No," replied the northerner. "You?"

"You know full well I've never been farther than Erlingen."

"Still, your stepmother was from Reinwick. You must have at least some knowledge of the area?"

"Very little," said Ludwig. "My understanding is that it lies on a peninsula jutting into the Great Northern Sea."

"It does," piped in Sir Petrus. "The duke there is Lord Wilfhelm Brondecker. I made a point of learning all I could about him."

"And what can you tell us about His Grace?"

"He's always been a staunch ally of Hadenfeld, although, for the life of me, I can't see why. Our two lands are hundreds of miles apart."

"That," said Ludwig, "is easy to answer—neither represents a threat to the other. But if the duke's such a powerful ally, why the marriage?"

"It sends a message," explained Sir Petrus. "This marriage isn't so much about finding you a wife as it is announcing to the rest of the Petty Kingdoms that we are firm friends."

"Still," offered Sigwulf, "the dowry won't go amiss. Any idea how much we're talking about?"

"Otto wouldn't say," said Ludwig, "merely that it was substantial, whatever that means."

They made good progress over the next few days, first staying at Drakenfeld as the guests of Lord Merrick and Lady Gita, then heading north into the Kingdom of Deisenbach. Sir Petrus planned for them to travel eastward, to Zowenbruch, then up through Erlingen and into Andover. Ludwig suggested they ride through the Duchy of Angvil instead.

"I don't understand your hesitancy," said Sigwulf. "They would fete you as a hero!"

"True," replied Ludwig, "and then we'd pass into Andover, the enemy we helped defeat. My reputation would then work against us."

"Yes, but that's true regardless of how we enter Andover. Like it or not, we must still traverse the place to get to Reinwick."

"Ah, but we shall be less conspicuous coming from Angvil."

Sigwulf shook his head. "I doubt anyone would notice the difference, although I suppose it would be wise to avoid any references to the war. One thing's for certain, though, this land is still on a war footing."

"That," said Sir Petrus, "is unlikely to change. The recent defeat of a Halvarian expedition has put everyone on edge."

"Where did you hear this?" asked Ludwig.

The knight smiled. "I chatted with that innkeeper last night, and he told me some interesting rumours."

"Such as?"

"Ships manned by the Church defeated a Halvarian fleet."

"The Temple Knights of Saint Cunar?"

"They were present," said Sir Petrus, "but only in small numbers. I've heard Agnesites crewed the fleet."

"Doubtful," said Brother Hamelyn. "The Temple Knights of Saint Cunar would never condone such a command."

"I thought the same thing, too, but I'm only repeating what I heard. Still, it would be interesting to get the full story once we reach Korvoran."

"If what you say is even partially true, it will mean only the second time the Holy Fleet has bested the empire."

"Second?" said Ludwig. "When was the first?"

"Back in ninety-six."

"How in the name of the Saints did they manage that?"

"A small group of Temple Knights, led by a sister knight of Saint Agnes, lured them out of port."

"A sister knight, you say? You don't know her name, by chance?"

"I think it was Jermaine," said Brother Hamelyn, "or something to that effect."

Ludwig could hardly believe his ears. "You mean Charlaine?"

"That was it. Why? Have you heard of her?"

The pieces suddenly fell into place. "That's why they made her a Temple Captain so soon."

"Yes," agreed Sigwulf. "Then they sent her north, to Korvoran."

"Korvoran!" said Brother Hamelyn. "That's the capital of Reinwick. Do you realize what that means? We may actually be able to meet her."

A feeling of panic overcame Ludwig. He'd known, deep down, it was a possibility, but what would he say to her? A flood of emotions ran through him.

"Are you all right, Ludwig?" asked Sigwulf. "You look awfully pale."

"I'm fine. I just didn't think about the ramifications."

Sig lowered his voice. "Do you believe she still loves you?"

"I don't know, nor does it matter. She's a Temple Knight now, dedicated to her order. I doubt she even wants to see me."

"If that was the case, she never would've written, let alone gone through the difficulty of getting that message into your hands."

"But I'm going to Reinwick to get married. How can I do that if I still hold feelings for her?"

"You're a baron now. The marriage is one of political expediency, nothing more. I'm sure she'd understand that. Regardless, as a Temple Knight, she's sworn to a life of celibacy, isn't she?"

"Yes, I suppose she is." Ludwig tried to calm himself, but a tremendous feeling of guilt overwhelmed him. Could he go through with this wedding, knowing he could never give his new wife his heart? He shook it off, for there was no future in a relationship with Charlaine. That thought, more than any other, made him grieve the loss of her all the more.

. . .

Spurred on by his conflicted feelings, the next few days dragged on. Eventually, they passed into Andover, and the journey was nearing its end. On their last night in Andover, they intended to stay at the Temple of Saint Mathew, but their late arrival meant no beds were left, leaving them to seek refuge elsewhere. They ended up packed into the close confines of a small inn called the Green Sparrow.

The table around which they sat seemed destined to collapse under the weight of the enormous tankards of ale served, while the chairs were even less sturdy. Sigwulf took no notice of the place's shortcomings, but Sir Petrus made no secret of his disdain. Ludwig tuned out their conversation, instead contemplating what might happen once he reached Reinwick.

"They say she led a massive fleet," a drink-slurred voice interrupted his thoughts. "I don't hold the men of Reinwick in high regard, but that Temple Knight did us all a big favour."

"Temple Captain," corrected his friend, sitting with him at a nearby table.

Ludwig immediately took note. The larger of the two continued, "Captain, schmaptain. She's still a member of the Church and a leader worth following."

"Agreed," said his companion, a sandy-haired fellow. "Though I wonder what misfortune resulted in her being sent to Korvoran in the first place. That place is full of nothing but thieves and murderers."

"Excuse me," said Ludwig. "Are you talking about the Temple Captain of Saint Agnes?"

"We are," replied the larger man. "Why? Who wants to know?"

"I do," Ludwig said, producing a coin. "I wonder if you might regale us with what you've heard?"

The fellow snatched the coin up in his thick-fingered hand. "I'd be delighted." He stood, then shifted, moving his chair to join them, his companion following suit. "They say the sister knights built a fleet of their own."

"That's highly unusual, isn't it?" asked Brother Hamelyn.

"You'd know better than I, Brother. In any case, they caught wind of a Halvarian plot to foment war."

"How?"

"How should I know? Do I look like an Archprior?"

"Definitely not," said the Temple Knight. "Pardon the interruption. Please continue."

"They say the Duke of Reinwick refused to help, leaving everything up to the Church."

"Just like him," added his companion, spitting on the floor. "The filthy Reinwickers are cowards."

"And this fleet," pressed Ludwig, "did a Temple Captain command it?"

"No, of course not. There's another Temple Knight for that, one from Andover, as a matter of fact. No, the captain led the knights who formed the fighting contingent. They say she found a secret base full of untold riches. I'm sure the duke took his share."

"Actually," said Brother Hamelyn, "the duke would've received nothing. A Holy Fleet is beholden to no one save for the Church."

The storyteller burst out laughing. "Well, that's the best news I've heard today. Tell me, Brother, what brings you lot here to The Sparrow?"

"We're on our way to Reinwick."

Ludwig's heart sank. The intention was to avoid such a declaration, especially considering the poor relations the two realms enjoyed.

"Reinwick, you say? What takes you fine-looking gentlemen there?"

"We are merchants," said Sigwulf, cutting off the Temple Knight. "We're hoping to hire a ship to move goods."

"Aye, well, I suppose you've got the right idea, then. I hate to admit it, but Korvoran is the largest port in the area."

"Does Andover not have a port?"

"We do—two, in fact—but trade isn't what it used to be, and word is both have largely fallen into disrepair. Oh, we have our fair share of fishing villages, but that's not the sort of thing you'd be looking for. Still, it must be nice, having that kind of wealth."

"I'd hardly call us wealthy," said Sigwulf.

"Your clothes would beg to differ. And you're travelling with a Temple Knight. One must be important indeed to warrant such a guardian."

"You seem to have sobered, my friend," said Ludwig. "Let's buy you another round, shall we?"

Ludwig was eager for more details, but it soon became apparent the man had little more to offer. Eventually, they tired, making their way to their respective rooms as midnight loomed.

A creaking noise interrupted Ludwig's slumber. He glanced around the room, trying to ascertain the source, only to realize someone was slowly opening his door. Taking only a moment to jump from his bed, he picked up his sword, pulling it from the scabbard.

The door eased open the rest of the way, letting in a sliver of light, revealing two figures: one in the doorway and the other slightly behind. If he harboured any doubt about their intentions, it quickly fled at the sight of the naked blades held in their hands.

"Begone!" he shouted.

The cry startled them both, but they soon recovered, and the stocky one in the lead rushed forward, his long knife slicing out.

Ludwig's sword easily deflected the attack, then he brought his hilt up to smash the fool in the face. It caught the nose, gouging deeply, causing blood to stream forth. The villain staggered back, cursing, his knife discarded as he attempted to stem the flow. Meanwhile, his companion charged in, brandishing a short sword.

The blade scored Ludwig's arm, then he struck back with a lunge that penetrated the fellow's stomach. His attacker uttered a scream of anguish before falling to the floor, his hands clutching the wound in a vain attempt to stop the bleeding.

The attack was over in mere moments. The one with the bloody nose fled, leaving his comrade to his fate. At the sounds of screaming, other voices called out. Soon, what seemed like everyone in the whole place crowded the hallway, desperate to discover what had transpired. Sigwulf entered the room, sword in hand.

"This one tried to kill me," said Ludwig. "There was another, but he fled." The man on the floor went still, his eyes now lifeless. A woman in the hallway began crying, her voice soon rising into hysterics.

Brother Hamelyn entered the room next, followed by Sir Petrus. They both came with weapons in hand but relaxed once they saw the body on the floor and that Ludwig was fine. Not so the innkeeper, whose red face betrayed his anger.

"This is murder," he shouted. "You'll be hanged for this!"

The Temple Knight placed himself between Ludwig and the innkeeper. "It is not he who should be punished. This individual who now lies dead broke the law, along with his accomplice."

Ludwig stared at the shocked innkeeper, thinking maybe it wasn't shock so much as guilt. Had he put these men up to it, or was he just being paranoid?

"The fact remains," continued the proprietor, "that man lies dead, and we have only your word he was the one who instigated this fight."

"Surely you jest?" said Ludwig. "I'm still in my nightshirt, while this fellow is fully dressed."

"It wouldn't be the first time I saw such a thing. I should call the magistrate. I wouldn't be leaving anytime soon, if I were you."

Brother Hamelyn turned to Ludwig. "Get your things, my friend, and we shall be on our way."

"You'll go nowhere!" shouted the innkeeper. "You'll stay until the magistrate arrives."

"This man is under the protection of the Temple Knights of Saint Mathew."

The hallway went silent. It was one thing to accuse an outsider of murder, quite another to involve a Temple Knight. Indecision wracked the innkeeper until he finally tore his gaze from Brother Hamelyn to glare at Ludwig.

"Very well. Take this filth away, and never show your faces in here again, any of you!"

Sir Petrus stared the fellow down while Sigwulf helped gather Ludwig's things. They were soon out in the stables, readying their horses despite the early hour.

"That," said the knight, "was... interesting."

Sigwulf laughed. "Well, no one has ever accused Ludwig of being boring."

"It wasn't my fault! I was lying in bed, minding my own business. Why did they try to kill me?"

"That's easy—coins. That man in the bar last night likely passed on the knowledge that we had some."

"Then I shall endeavour to keep my mouth shut from now on."

"A good idea," added Sir Petrus. "At least we're not too far from the border."

"And by not far," said Ludwig, "what, precisely, do you mean?"

"That we shall cross into Reinwick before first light."

"Assuming we're not attacked in the dark."

"There is always that possibility, so I suggest we remain vigilant."

"You don't think they recognized me, do you?" Ludwig asked. "It can't exactly be a secret that I helped Erlingen beat Andover in the war."

"We were careful to not use your name," said Sigwulf, "but such things can often slip out unintentionally. At this point, I don't suppose it makes much difference. I think Sir Petrus has the right idea. We'll keep on the lookout for any signs of trouble and make for the border as quickly as possible."

"The horses got little rest."

"Nor did we," said Brother Hamelyn, "but they can rest once we're safely in Korvoran. In the meantime, let's get out of this place while we can. I don't trust this innkeeper."

"You think he might try again?"

"No, but I wouldn't put it past him to alert the town watch."

25

KORVORAN

SUMMER 1099 SR

L udwig had read about the sea, but nothing prepared him for the experience of looking at a never-ending horizon of water. They entered the port city of Korvoran through the southern gate. The seagulls' squawking overwhelmed them, while the overpowering stench of the sea was unappealing to anyone used to a landlocked home.

The constricted streets left Ludwig feeling like he was riding through a maze. The only saving grace was the sea's constantly crashing waves, which made getting one's bearings simple enough. A large warehouse sat to their right, blocking all view of the water, but a veritable forest of masts sprang up as they cleared it. Ludwig halted his horse, overcome by the sight.

"Impressive, isn't it?" asked Sigwulf. "Imagine how many trees it took to make all those ships."

"The harbour is immense."

"If you look closely, you'll see two arms stretching out into the sea; those are the jetties. A narrow channel between those arms is the only way into the harbour."

"How do you know all this?"

"Easy," said Sigwulf. "I lived in Braymoor, remember? It, too, sits astride the Great Northern Sea."

Brother Hamelyn interrupted them, pointing eastward. "Look," he said. "Do you see them? A pair of ships flying the banner of Saint Agnes."

"So it's true," said Sir Petrus. "I can't imagine the Cunars are too happy about that."

"Perhaps they possess their own ships?" said Ludwig. He spotted a trio of

Temple Knights, their scarlet tabards leaving no doubt which order they belonged to. "It seems the sisters also patrol the docks."

"This is all well and good," said Sir Petrus, "but before we do anything else, we should pay our respects to His Grace, the duke."

"Any idea where we would find him?"

The knight pulled forth a parchment and unfolded it, staring at it before rotating it ninety degrees.

"Well?"

Petrus rotated it again. "I have a map, but only the Saints know how to read it."

"Let me see that," said Ludwig. The knight handed him the map. "Ah, I see the docks here, marked in red." He looked up, scanning the surrounding area. "Unless I'm mistaken, we should take the road on the left. That should take us directly to the duke's estate. Lead on, Sir Petrus, and let's see if we can leave the stench of the sea behind us."

They pushed through the crowd and onto the road, which ran up a gentle hill. The buildings gradually became more ornate until they were replaced with a series of opulent estates.

"This must be the wealthier area of town," said Brother Hamelyn. "It's likely the barons of Reinwick keep estates here for when they're at court."

"How many barons are there?" asked Ludwig.

"Three or four," said Sir Petrus. "I can't rightly recall if Korvoran has its own baron or if it falls directly under the duke's rule. In any case, I'm sure we'll recognize the duke's estate once we see it."

As soon as the words left the knight's lips, Ludwig gasped, for just down the street was an estate the likes of which he could never have even imagined. Built solely of a brilliant white stone, the massive pillars out front reminded Ludwig of church architecture. He'd seen nice houses back in Erlingen, but nothing that compared to the grandeur of this place. They rode on a circular path leading to the front of the building, slowing their pace to take in the view.

A pair of guards, immaculately attired in livery bearing the duke's colours of yellow and blue, stood at attention. The group from Hadenfeld halted, dismounting as servants rushed to assist with their horses.

"My name is Lord Ludwig Altenburg, the Baron of Verfeld. We are here to see His Grace, the Duke of Reinwick."

One of the servants moved to stand before him. "Greetings, my lord, and welcome to Korvoran. If you'll come with me, I'll take you to His Grace."

Ludwig waited as his companions handed over their reins, then nodded at the fellow, who then led them inside through a series of corridors until they halted before an ornately carved door.

"Beyond there," explained the servant, "is the dining room, wherein sits His Grace, Lord Wilfhelm."

"I shouldn't like to interrupt him," said Ludwig. "Perhaps we should come back later?"

"Not at all. His Grace often entertains in this manner." Throwing open the door, he stepped forward, bowing deeply. "You have visitors, Your Grace. Lord Ludwig of Verfeld."

"Send them in," came the reply.

The group was ushered into where Wilfhelm Brondecker sat, a man well past his prime, although not as far gone as King Otto. While they both shared a portly frame, His Grace sported a generous moustache and beard laced with grey. A vast array of food littered the enormous table before him, far more than he could consume in one sitting, regardless of his appetite or lack thereof.

The duke waved them forward. "Come in, Lord Ludwig. Take a seat, all of you. Please, introduce your travelling companions."

"This," said Ludwig, after sitting down, "is Brother Hamelyn of the Temple Knights of Saint Mathew. With him are Sir Petrus, Knight of Hadenfeld, and Captain Sigwulf, one of my captains."

"And you came to marry Charlaine? I mean Charlotte." The duke chuckled. "The two names are pretty similar, don't you think?"

Ludwig blushed, something the duke mistook for anger.

"I'm terribly sorry. I didn't mean to give offence. It's just that one of my advisors is named Charlaine. I often confuse their names."

"I assume that would be Temple Captain Charlaine?"

"Yes. You know of her?"

"I've met her on several occasions, Your Grace."

"Well, don't tell Lord Kurlan of my mistake, I beg of you, or I'll never hear the end of it."

"My lips are sealed."

"Good." The duke popped a morsel of meat into his mouth, letting the grease drip onto his beard. "Please, help yourself to some."

Ludwig looked at Sir Petrus for guidance, and the knight shook his head. "Perhaps later, Your Grace. Is Lord Kurlan in Korvoran?"

"He is, though not with his daughter. She remains in Blunden for the time being, pending her father's approval of you."

Unsure how to proceed, Ludwig wished he'd paid more attention to his father's lessons on etiquette, missing him all the more for his lack of training. "Should I go to visit him?"

"Not necessary," said the duke. "I'm hosting a little get-together this very evening, and he'll be in attendance. Why don't you clean up and join us then?"

Ludwig bowed his head. "I would be honoured, Your Grace."

"Good. Then I shall let my servants show you to the door. I'd love to sit and chat, but there's too much to do, and I'll see you tonight, anyway. We can talk then."

Ludwig stood. "Thank you, Your Grace."

"Don't thank me quite yet. You've yet to meet Lady Charlotte." The duke's laughter followed them as they left the room.

They found lodging at the Temple of Saint Mathew. Brother Hamelyn introduced them to Father Salvatore, the leader of the Temple Knights of Saint Mathew, and senior member of the fighting orders in Korvoran.

Ludwig was eager to learn more about the Church's position in Reinwick, particularly regarding the Holy Fleet, but they were quickly shuffled off to their rooms.

"We shall have plenty of time to speak with him later," said Brother Hamelyn. "He'll be accompanying us to the duke's get-together."

"And in the meantime?"

"I would recommend we all get some sleep. It's likely to be a long night. They say the duke is one of those who stays up until the wee hours of the morning, and he expects his guests to do likewise."

"I thought," said Ludwig, "that members of the Church retired early?"

"We usually do, and Temple Commander Salvatore will excuse himself earlier in the evening, but I'm afraid you, as the proposed groom, cannot do likewise."

"So you're saying I am to be held prisoner?"

"Not so much prisoner as honoured guest. Tell me, would you insult King Otto by retiring early?"

"No," said Ludwig. "Probably not. I must concede the point."

"Well, I don't know about you," said Sigwulf, "but if the duke's luncheon is any indication, we're in for quite a feast."

"I'm certain we will be," said Sir Petrus. "My information about him indicates he likes to display his wealth, and what better way than by making sure the guests are well-fed."

They assembled in the dark for the trip to the duke's estate. Temple Captain Salvatore wore his finest cassock, eschewing his armour for comfort. With the warm weather, they elected to walk to their destination, giving them a chance to learn more about recent events.

"Might I ask," said Sigwulf, "why you prefer to be addressed as 'Father'? I thought your rank as Temple Commander would be more appropriate?"

"Many outsiders make that assumption. The truth is Temple Commander is my rank, but there are two types of commanders in the orders, those who can administer the rites and those who cannot."

"Ah, now I see. You are ordained."

"Indeed. If I wasn't, you would address me as Brother Commander, so it's primarily a clarification of my role."

"I thought all commanders were ordained?" said Sir Petrus.

"That is a common misconception, at least within the order of Saint Mathew, but each of the other orders has its own practices. For example, as a Temple Knight of Saint Cunar, it is a requirement for a promotion."

"And Saint Agnes?"

"They operate much like us," replied Father Salvatore. "Though the rank of Temple Commander is less common and usually denotes an administrative rather than a field rank."

This intrigued Ludwig. "Are you saying Temple Commanders don't command knights?"

"The only Temple Knights that command in battle are the Cunars. It is they who lead the Holy Army."

"And what of the fleet?"

Father Salvatore smiled. "Well, that has been a subject of discussion for some time. Not many people know this, but years ago, the Holy Fleet in the south was under the Agnesites' control. It is only more recently that the Cunars took over."

"And why was that, if you don't mind me asking?"

"It followed a reorganization of the fighting orders. At that time, they decided it best that the Cunars concentrate on battle, freeing up the other orders to pursue their own prescribed duties. Naturally, some opposed it, but it has mostly worked out for the best."

"And yet the so-called Northern Fleet is NOT run by them."

The Temple Commander looked decidedly uncomfortable. "That is a more recent development. Technically, the ships under their command constitute a fleet belonging to their order, not the entire Church. Temple Knights of Saint Agnes crew it, but we contribute some of our own brothers to each ship to help care for casualties."

"Casualties?" said Ludwig. "But the area is at peace, isn't it?"

"Currently, although there were some problems a while back. Thankfully, we dealt with it, but we still find ourselves fighting pirates and raiders. It is an ongoing problem, but not to the extent it was in the past."

"Are you suggesting seaborne trade is in danger?"

"There will always be those willing to take advantage of others by pillaging goods. In that sense, the sea is no different from the land. Thankfully, the fleet's constant patrols reduced the frequency of such attacks significantly, mostly due to the efforts of Admiral Meer."

"They have an admiral?" said Ludwig. "How does that fit in with the rank structure of the orders?"

"Admiral is a position, not a rank. At sea, the admiral is the supreme commander, but as soon as she steps ashore, she is a Temple Captain."

"Odd," said Sir Petrus. "I would've thought such a position would warrant at least a Temple Commander."

"In time, it likely will, but the fleet is still reasonably small. However, should it increase, I'm sure her order would see fit to promote her. Of course, if that happened tomorrow, she would be the youngest Temple Commander to ever hold that rank."

"Fascinating," said Ludwig. "It would be interesting to meet her."

"Well," said Father Salvatore, "with a bit of luck, you just might."

"Meaning?"

"If her flagship, the *Valiant*, is in port, you'll likely see her at the duke's estate this very evening."

There was clearly more to this story, and Ludwig suspected Charlaine was part of it. His companions kept chatting away, the subject turning to events in the south, but Ludwig pondered the situation here. Their trip through Andover had revealed a deep-running resentment. Why was it that these two neighbours hated each other so much? He considered his own home where the strife between Hadenfeld and Neuhafen was similar. Yet he was unaware of any rebellion here in the north that might account for such hatred.

Ludwig thought back to Erlingen. He himself had been present at the King of Andover's capture. The victory humiliated Andover, yet their anger seemed to point north towards Reinwick rather than south to Erlingen.

They arrived at the duke's estate to be met by servants who led them through the manor into a large, open area behind the building, replete with well-manicured grass and carefully trimmed trees and bushes. Spotting them, Lord Wilfhelm immediately waved them over.

"Come," said the duke. "You must meet Lord Kurlan, Baron of Blunden. Kurlan, this is Lord Ludwig, the Baron of Verfeld."

"Greetings," responded a man of average height with greying hair and a girth suggesting a healthy appetite, although he wore it well. The wrinkles around his eyes bespoke of one who enjoyed life, while the crease marks framing his mouth indicated an excessive amount of worry. This was a man of contradictions.

"My lord," said Ludwig. "It is an honour to finally meet you."

"The honour is mine," said Lord Kurlan. "It's a pity we didn't have a more definitive idea of when you would arrive, or I could've arranged for Charlotte to be here."

"She's not in Korvoran?"

"No. She's at my estate in Blunden. I thought we might travel there after I get to know you a little better."

"Of course, Lord." Ludwig felt as though he'd been given a reprieve. Was the idea of marrying so distasteful? He shook it off. "What can you tell me of Lady Charlotte? Other than her location, I mean."

The baron chuckled. "She is studious and well-read, but let's talk more of you. I hear you made quite the name for yourself back in Erlingen."

"I was fortunate."

"Ah, and modest too!"

"King Otto speaks highly of him," said the duke. "And you know how sparing he can be with praise."

The baron looked impressed. "You must be remarkable indeed to win such accolades."

"Hardly," said Ludwig. "I am his cousin."

"Ah, now I understand. Well, I shan't hold it against you. Saints know half the rulers of the Petty Kingdoms are in a similar situation."

"Is the trip to Blunden long?"

"By land, yes, but we'll be going by ship, saving us considerable time."

"Do you not fear piracy?"

"Not in these waters," said Lord Kurlan, "but we'll be taking one of the Church ships just to be sure."

"A warship?"

"Aye, and a grand trip it shall be."

"How did you manage that?" asked Ludwig. "I thought such ships were only to be used for Church business?"

"Usually they are, but such vessels require upkeep and maintenance. A generous donation helps fund the fleet, and their regular patrol route takes them up the coast. You might say the system is mutually beneficial."

"You have the advantage of me, Lord, for you appear to know all about my exploits in Erlingen. What of your own background? Anything you'd care to share?"

"I am the descendant of nobles, the seventeenth to bear the Stratmeyer name. My family has ruled over Blunden for generations, which allows us to prosper." He lowered his voice. "That means you shall be getting a very handsome dowry."

The duke laughed. "I've never seen you so generous, Kurlan."

"Well," said the baron, "it's not every day a man marries off his only daughter."

"Is she your only child?" asked Ludwig.

"Oh no, not at all. She has two older brothers and one younger."

"And Lady Stratmeyer?"

"She, I'm afraid, is no longer with us. She passed shortly after the birth of my youngest."

"My condolences."

He waved it away. "It couldn't be helped. In any case, she gave me a large family, so I can't complain."

Ludwig was speechless. It appeared the baron held little love for his late wife. Was this to be his fate also? Doubt festered within him.

"If you will excuse me, Lord," he finally said. "I should very much like to make my way around the room and meet the others. However, I promise we shall talk at greater length later this evening."

"Certainly," replied Lord Kurlan. "I look forward to it."

Ludwig meandered through the crowd, his mind elsewhere. A servant walked by carrying a tray of drinks, and he took a goblet. So intent was he on snagging the cup that he failed to notice another guest standing nearby. He twisted suddenly, and their arms bumped, sending most of the wine sloshing onto the floor.

"I am so sorry," said Ludwig, examining the mess. He raised his gaze to see Charlaine deShandria standing before him, the look on her face betraying her own surprise.

"Ludwig? What in the Saint's name are you doing here?"

"I... I'm here at the behest of my king."

She recovered quickly. "Did you get my letter?"

"I did. I wanted to reply, but time seemed to fly by." He struggled to find something else—anything—to say.

"I-I-I need to talk to you," he finally stammered out.

"Not here," she replied. "There are too many ears. Come to the commandery tomorrow."

"I will. I promise."

She looked as if she wanted to say more, but at that precise moment, another woman wearing the scarlet of Saint Agnes touched her on the elbow. "Excuse me, Captain, but Father Salvatore wants to speak with you."

"Thank you, Marlena. Please convey to the Temple Commander that I'll be right there." She turned her attention once more to Ludwig. "Remember. The commandery, tomorrow, as early as possible." She left him without another word.

26

CHARLAINE

SUMMER 1099 SR

T he Saint Agnes commandery was a vast building, two stories high and topped with a peaked wooden roof, architecture typical in the colder reaches of the Petty Kingdoms. The thick walls, reinforced with stone buttresses, were adorned with large matching scarlet banners bearing the three white waves of Saint Agnes. Double doors guarded by two Temple Knights marked the most obvious entrance.

"Identify yourself," one called out.

"I am Lord Ludwig Altenburg," he replied, "Baron of Verfeld. Here to see Temple Captain Charlaine."

"Stay where you are." They conferred in low voices, then one opened a door and disappeared inside.

Ludwig waited, taking time to examine the remaining knight's armour. She was dressed head to foot in plate, a common enough sight in the Petty Kingdoms. Still, the metal plates lacked decoration, which most knights would find unacceptable. Overtop of it all, she wore a scarlet tabard bearing Saint Agnes's symbol that fell to her knees, allowing her legs to remain free of any impediments in a fight.

He'd seen Temple Knights before, even travelled with Brother Hamelyn, but something was different about the woman before him, something that told him she'd faced battle. The door opened, revealing a woman wearing a cassock, the same one who'd interrupted Charlaine last night.

"Sister Marlena, isn't it?" called out Ludwig.

"That's me. Come this way, Lord Ludwig, and I'll show you to the captain's office."

He followed her into the building, or rather the entrance, for the double doors led into an alley. The other end opened into a courtyard, but Marlena took him through a door on one side where a straight corridor ran the length of the building with heavy doors about every two dozen paces.

His host noted his interest. "Those are closed in the event of an attack. They make it difficult for any foe to seize control of the commandery."

They entered a large room with stairs leading up to where they encountered two more knights, who merely nodded at Sister Marlena. They continued down another corridor, past portraits he could only assume were previous captains. Eventually, they came to a door guarded by a single sentry.

"Lord Ludwig is here to see the captain," announced Marlena.

The guard opened the door, and inside sat Charlaine before a large wooden desk. Behind her, sunlight flooded through the windows, giving the Temple Captain an almost saintly glow. She looked up as he entered.

"Lord Ludwig," she said, her face betraying naught of her emotions. "Please, take a seat."

He sat opposite her, his mind in turmoil, his heart feeling like it would burst. Sister Marlena assumed a position by the door, obviously able to hear all that transpired. This was meant to be an official meeting.

"I must admit," he said, "when I was sent north, I wondered if I might run into you. I trust all is well?"

"As well as can be expected considering our last correspondence. The empire has been quiet of late, and our fleet unopposed at sea."

Ludwig glanced at Marlena. "Is it safe to talk openly?"

"As long as you keep the subject to my letter, yes."

"And if I should desire otherwise?"

"This is not the place to speak of such things."

"Very well. I shall abide by your rules. What do you know about the trouble up here?"

"A woman named Larissa Stormwind heavily influenced the duke's court."

"So you indicated in your letter. Are you sure she was working with the Halvarians?"

"Her ship attacked us at sea. There can be little doubt she was aboard when it struck. The real question is whether this indicates her motives were personal or directed by her superiors?"

"Superiors? Doesn't she work for the duke?"

"Court mages don't so much work for a noble as hire on as professionals. The Stormwind family is powerful, and they supply mages to half the courts of the Petty Kingdoms. If this was the work of their family, it would have dire consequences for the rest of the Continent."

"You mentioned a corruption within the Church. Can you be more specific?"

"Danica and I travelled to the Antonine before coming here. While there, we discovered a Temple Commander using the order to further her own ends. We ended her quest for power, but it soon became apparent others were involved. At this point, we don't know how many, but recent decisions by senior Church officials are worrying."

"In what way?" asked Ludwig.

"I received word that funding for the fleet is being reduced."

"But that's a financial decision, surely? It likely costs too much to maintain."

"I'm fully aware of the costs of maintaining a fleet of ships. Someone clearly doesn't want us to have a powerful presence in these waters."

"What will you do?"

She smiled. "We've established a new base of operations in the Five Sisters."

"I've heard of those. They're islands, aren't they?"

"They are indeed. When we defeated the Halvarians, we landed at a place we named Temple Bay. Over the last few months, we've been working on building a more permanent presence there, hidden from those higher up in the Church hierarchy."

"Is that legal?"

"The Grand Mistress herself gave me my orders. Our intention is to become self-sufficient and maintain a large fleet independent of the Petty Kingdoms."

"And if your superiors find out?"

"There will be trouble, but that is a small price to pay to be ready for the Halvarians."

"You believe they'll invade?"

"I know they will. It's not a matter of if but when, although I suspect some years yet. They seem intent on sowing distrust within the ranks of the Holy Army first."

"Do you realize what that would do to the stability of the Petty Kingdoms? We are but an insult away from war at any given point in time. Why, my very presence here demonstrates that." He suddenly stopped talking, keenly aware he may have said too much.

If she noticed anything, she didn't reveal it. "I am well aware of the delicate balance of power on the Continent. This is precisely why we must do all we can to preserve the peace. Should the Petty Kingdoms fall into fighting amongst themselves, nothing would be left to stop the empire."

"How can I help?"

"If I'm being completely honest, I don't know that you can. There are only a handful of people I trust with this information. You just happen to be one of them."

They sat in silence for a time.

"I heard you're now the Baron of Verfeld," Charlaine said.

"I have been for a few years."

"And is all well back home?"

"There is talk of war with Neuhafen, but that's been going on for ages. I did increase the garrison's numbers, though, just to be prepared."

"Perhaps you could do something for us."

"I'm listening," said Ludwig.

"As I mentioned, I trust only a few people, mostly Temple Knights. It would be beneficial to have a safe haven in the Middle Kingdoms where they could discuss matters without fear of discovery. I thought the temple in Malburg could be used. It's not inconceivable that a knight would make the quick trip to Verfeld Keep while they were there, if only to pay their respects."

"I would welcome such a visit," said Ludwig.

Charlaine glanced up at Marlena, who stood behind Ludwig. Her eyes then flicked down to a small piece of paper she pulled from beneath another. She slid it across, placing it before him, and then looked into his eyes. "I trust this meeting has been fruitful?"

He took the note, tucking it into his sleeve. "It has. Thank you, Captain. You have given me much to think on."

Ludwig rose, and Marlena opened the door.

"Come," said Charlaine's aide. "I shall show you the way out."

Ludwig waited until he was outside the commandery before examining the paper. It was an address, along with the words '*tomorrow-noon*'.

He spent the rest of the morning searching the city for the place in question. He assumed she wanted to meet somewhere they could talk in private, but the closer he got, the more he became aware he was in amongst shops.

When the actual building came into view, he realized it was the perfect place. He returned to the temple to think things through for tomorrow.

Unwilling to reveal his clandestine meeting to the others, Ludwig told Sir Petrus that he and Sigwulf would be spending the morning exploring the city. Townsfolk and vendors crowded the streets as they wound their way to their destination.

"This is it," said Ludwig, stopping a little too quickly for the big northerner.

Sigwulf almost tripped in his haste to stop, then looked up. "Here? Are you sure? This is a smithy."

Ludwig grinned. "So it is."

"Ah, I see now. It's just like her father's."

They stepped inside to discover a Dwarf sharpening a sword. A customer wearing a scarlet cassock examined a set of gauntlets. At first, Ludwig took her for Charlaine and moved over to say hello. She turned at the sound of his approach, revealing a young, black-haired woman—most definitely not the person he expected.

"You must be Ludwig," she said.

"I am. And you are?"

"Temple Captain Danica."

"Captain? Aren't you the admiral?"

"I have that honour, yes. I'm also a friend of Charlaine's." She glanced around the room, her eyes falling on Sigwulf. "Is he with you?"

"He is, and I trust him with my life. He knows everything."

Sister Danica turned to the Dwarf. "I'm taking this fellow in back, Barbek."

"Fine with me. I'll keep an eye on things out here."

She led him through a door at the rear of the shop, revealing a workroom not too dissimilar to that of Tomas deShandria. Charlaine stood there, wearing a leather apron as she held a blade in the coals. She looked up as they approached.

"You're here," she said, smiling. "I wasn't sure you'd come."

"I..." His voice trailed off, his eyes going to Sister Danica.

"She knows of our background," said Charlaine.

"I need to talk to you about something. Something unrelated to everything we spoke of yesterday."

"Has this something to do with why you're here in Korvoran?"

"It does."

"Then speak freely, Ludwig. Let there be no secrets between us."

"I still love you." It felt as if a great weight lifted from his shoulders. "There. I've said it."

"And I love you, and always will, but nothing has changed."

"How can you say that? I'm the baron now!"

"And I, a Temple Captain. I'm needed here, Ludwig, just as they need you back in Hadenfeld. We are fated to be forever entwined yet never together, don't you see? It is the will of the Saints."

He cast his gaze to the floor. "I suppose, deep down inside, I knew that, but it's hard for me to acknowledge."

"There's something far deeper going on, I can tell. Ease your burden and speak to me of what ails you."

"I am here to marry," said Ludwig, blushing at his words. "It's been arranged by King Otto."

"And?"

His eyes bored into hers. "How can I marry a woman I don't love?"

"We must often do things we don't wish in the name of duty. Your duty, as baron, is to marry and produce an heir. I wouldn't hold that against any man."

"But I cannot marry her!"

"Because you don't love her?"

"Love her? I haven't even met her."

"Who is she?"

"Lady Charlotte Stratmeyer, the Baron of Blunden's daughter."

"She is a noble, and as such, will understand her duty."

"To marry someone who doesn't love her?"

"Not all marriages are built on love. If you feel guilty about it, talk to her and explain your issues. If she's a reasonable woman, she'll accept your proposal with grace and dignity. In time, you may grow fond of her, even love her."

"And you do not object to this union?"

"I wish you nothing but the best. I will always love you, Ludwig. Nothing can ever change that, but you must get it into your head that we will never again be together. I have a calling now, far more important to me than I ever imagined." She paused, contemplating their futures. "You have one too," she said. "You just haven't realized it yet."

"Me? A calling? Don't be absurd."

"I heard what you did in Erlingen. You're a natural leader, Ludwig. You should nurture that. A time will come when the Continent needs someone like you."

"You're talking about a war with Halvaria."

"I am, though I pray it never happens."

"I shall do as you ask."

"Don't do it for me," said Charlaine. "Do it for yourself and the people you hold dear."

"That includes you."

She smiled. "I accept that. Promise me one more thing?"

"If I can."

"Stay in touch. Send letters by way of the guild. I'm sure my father can show you how."

"Speaking of your father, is there any message you would like me to take to him or your mother?"

"Now you mention it, yes, but I shall need time to gather my thoughts."

"You mean to tell them of the empire?"

"No, merely of my life as a Temple Knight. I would not burden them with worry."

"I'll send you word when I return to Korvoran."

"You're leaving?"

"Only to travel to Blunden, where I must meet my future bride. I believe we'll return here, to the capital for the actual ceremony."

"Then I shall see you at your wedding."

"You will?"

"Of course. All the orders are expected to be present for a wedding of such importance. After all, it's not every day a baron's daughter gets married."

He smiled at the thought. "I will look forward to seeing you there."

"Good. Now, you must go. You have preparations to make."

"I do?" said Ludwig.

"Yes, you do. At the very least, you should buy your intended a gift. Showing up empty-handed is bad luck, or so I'm told."

"I'll show him out," said Danica. "Lord?"

"Very well." He followed the younger woman out into the storefront where Sigwulf was deep in discussion with the Dwarven smith, Barbek.

"Ah, there you are," said the northerner. "Come. Look at this mace. It's magnificent."

Ludwig moved closer. "It has runes upon it."

"Aye," said the smith. "That's Dwarven steel, a tougher metal you won't find unless you have some sky metal lying around that I don't know about."

"We'll take it," said Ludwig.

"We will?" said Sigwulf. "It must cost a fortune?"

"It's well worth it. You can give it to Cyn as a present."

The great warrior grinned. "She'll love that."

"It's not quite finished," said Barbek. "I have yet to finish the grip. Tell you what, why don't you write down this woman's name, and I'll engrave it on the head while I'm at it."

"How long till it's ready?"

"A week, maybe ten days. I could do it sooner, but there are other projects needing my attention."

"That's fine," said Ludwig. "We must leave for Blunden, but I guarantee we'll be back. Shall I pay for it now?"

The Dwarf looked at the Temple Captain, who merely nodded.

"Not necessary. Your word is your bond."

"But you've never met me before?"

"That may be true, but I know the calibre of your friends. Captain Charlaine clearly thinks highly of you, and that's good enough for me."

"Hey, now," said Danica. "Is my word not good enough?"

The Dwarf moved up to her, taking her hands in his. "I count you amongst my closest of friends. Now, let's close up shop, shall we? I have a hankering for some decent ale."

Sigwulf's ears pricked up. "Did someone say ale?"

"I was talking to the captain here, not you."

Ludwig laughed. "Come, Sig. There's work to do."

"But I wanted ale."

"And we'll get some, eventually, but there are other things to take care of first."

"Like what?"

"It has come to my attention that I need to find a gift for Lady Charlotte."

"What kind of gift?"

"You tell me. I'm new to all this."

They stepped outside.

"Let's walk up the street here," said Ludwig, "and see what piques our interest."

Farther up the road, they found a multitude of shops, including a dressmaker, jeweller, and a silversmith. They halted before the jewellers, Ludwig staring at the sign, deep in thought.

"How did it go back there?" asked Sigwulf. "Is everything good?"

"I suppose it depends."

"On?"

"What you define as good."

"Well, you didn't come out of there screaming and swearing. That must mean something."

"It does, doesn't it?"

"Do you regret going to see her?"

"No. For years, I've been living with the memory of her. It's only now that I realize I need to move on. Not that I don't love her. She'll always have a place in my heart, but I feel like that love has matured. It's all very difficult to explain."

"Then let me save you the trouble," said Sigwulf. "You made your peace with her, and now she's a treasured friend."

"Yes, that's it precisely. You, my friend, are an expert when it comes to things of this nature."

"Me? No, that's Cyn's area of expertise."

"Then perhaps she's starting to rub off on you?"

27

CHARLOTTE

SUMMER 1099 SR

L udwig was clinging to the railing when the *Valiant's* deck dropped as it crested the wave, water spraying over him as the ship hit the trough.

"Invigorating, isn't it?"

He turned at Lord Kurlan's voice. "I've never even seen the sea before, let alone sailed upon it."

The baron laughed. "I've taken this trip more times than I care to admit. Still, it's not every day we get to travel on the Holy Fleet's flagship."

"The flagship? I would think such a vessel to be much larger."

"Don't sell the *Valiant* short. Thanks to the admiral, she's the most manoeuvrable ship in these waters."

Ludwig looked over the deck but spotted no apparent signs of why.

"It's the rigging," said Lord Kurlan, "or so I'm told."

"I'm not sure I'm following."

"The *Valiant* used to be square-rigged, but the admiral had her masts reconfigured to take a triangular sail mounted fore and aft."

"And that makes it easier to handle?"

"That's what everyone says. I don't claim to be an expert in such things, but you can't argue with the ship's success. Since we relaunched it, it has accounted for more than a dozen pirates, not to mention the whole debacle with Halvaria. Of course, *Valiant* wasn't the only ship involved in that."

"When was this, precisely?"

"Last summer," said the baron. "Unfortunately, it wasn't all good news."

"Really? I would've thought it would be cause for celebration."

"It was, at least in the short term, but the duke took it to mean the sea was safe. As a result, he reduced his own fleet, doubtless to save his treasury. He now relies on the good sisters here to keep his kingdom safe, at least as far as the sea is concerned. Naturally, he still maintains a decent-sized army, not that we're expecting war anytime soon."

"It's interesting you should mention that," said Ludwig. "When we travelled through Andover, we encountered a lot of... how should I put this?"

"Let me guess... anger?"

"Yes. They don't like Reinwick very much."

"It's an old feud going back more than a hundred years. Reinwick and Andover were always rivals, at least in terms of economics. Back then, there was a race to gain dominance over sea trade."

"And now?"

"We far surpass them in terms of shipping. Then again, we have more access to the sea. You might say we are surrounded by it."

"Have your two countries ever been at war?"

"Not to my knowledge," said the baron, "but many believe it's coming. Resentment grows on both sides of the border, and all it would take would be an incident to make tempers flare. It was that very thing that Halvaria was counting on. War would've consumed us had it not been for the Temple Knights."

"Instead, you now have peace and the Church to thank for it."

"I know. It's all rather strange when you think about it. After all, the Church isn't supposed to take an interest in secular matters."

"Ah," said Ludwig, "but this isn't secular at all. Halvaria threatens all of the Petty Kingdoms, not just Reinwick."

The baron smiled. "You seem to have a firm grasp of politics, along with your military experience."

"I was in one battle."

"I heard two. Or are you not counting the Siege of Regnitz Keep?"

"I have to admit, you have me there."

"I'm told you're a man with an imagination. Who else would have thought to sally forth and capture the King of Andover?"

"It seemed like the logical thing to do at the time."

"And it was a brilliant manoeuvre. I sense an impressive future for you, and I look forward to calling you son-in-law."

"Speaking of marriage," said Ludwig, "can you tell me more about Charlotte? All you've said so far is that she's studious and well-read. Is she tall? Short? Blonde or brunette?"

"She is of average height," said Lord Kurlan, "just a shade shorter than yourself. Her hair is chestnut brown, as are her eyes. In that way, she takes after her mother."

"And what are her interests? Does she ride?"

The baron was momentarily at a loss for words. He gazed out to sea, extending the pause before he finally spoke. "She knows how but avoids doing so unless absolutely necessary."

"She doesn't like horses?"

"She's not afraid of them, if that's what you believe, but she has a weak constitution and finds riding exhausting."

"Is she ill?"

"No, only slight of frame. She's still more than capable of bearing you a son, but you must take pains to keep her healthy."

"Are you trying to reassure me or frighten me off?"

"Merely manage your expectations. I understand the situation isn't ideal, but no other woman in Reinwick would be suitable to cement an alliance of this magnitude. We can't have you marrying a commoner. You might say Charlotte is the only real choice we have for you."

"I would've thought a father more supportive towards his only daughter."

"Daughters are a curse," said Lord Kurlan. "Sons, at least, can rule, but what can we do with a daughter other than marry her off."

The comment left Ludwig with a foul taste in his mouth. Did the man truly believe what he spewed forth? He thought of Charlaine. Her father, Tomas, was always proud of her, and rightly so. Even Cyn had a loving relationship with her father before his death, but Kurlan appeared devoid of love for his daughter.

"If you will excuse me," said Ludwig. "I should like to go and check on my companions. They've not all grown accustomed to seaborne travel."

"By all means," said Lord Kurlan. "I shall look forward to your return."

Ludwig avoided the baron's company for the rest of the trip, claiming seasickness, but he knew he couldn't continue the ruse forever. He loathed the man, so much so that Sigwulf took notice, although he didn't talk of it further until they were safely ashore.

Blunden was similar to Korvoran in that the sea lay to the east, with the wealthier houses on the higher ground to the west. However, the similarities ended there, for the harbour here was much smaller, primarily populated by fishing vessels rather than merchants.

The buildings were also more spread out, and the roads less crowded, leaving the streets to look almost deserted in comparison.

Alerted by the *Valiant's* arrival, the baron's men waited at the dock with a carriage ready to take them to his estate. They gave Sir Petrus and Brother

Hamelyn horses to ride, forcing Sigwulf and Ludwig into the company of Lord Kurlan. They rolled through the streets of Blunden, prompting the baron to regale them with information about the place.

"Saints know I love this place. Have you ever seen its like?"

"You love your home," replied Ludwig, "as do I, but I must admit the smell leaves something to be desired."

"Spoken like a man from the Middle Kingdoms. Yes, it has a rather distinct aroma, but it's a constant reminder of Akosia's gifts."

"I'm surprised to hear you say that. I didn't know they still worshipped the old religion in these parts."

"It's not so much a religion as a turn of phrase. These people"—he gazed out the window—"live lives full of superstition and myth. Even so, they are fine folk, welcoming to any who set foot in this land. I daresay I would put their hospitality up against any in the Petty Kingdoms. What of your home, Lord Ludwig? Can you say the same?"

"I can now, but I must admit when I first returned to Verfeld, I found my presence unwelcome. In my absence, my predecessor alienated them."

"Your predecessor? But that was your father, wasn't it?"

"No. My stepbrother stepped in after my father's death. He threw his weight around, even in Malburg."

"Malburg?"

"Yes," said Ludwig. "A free city within my lands."

Lord Kurlan shook his head. "Nasty business that. Once you give those folk freedoms, society itself falls apart. Mark my words; it will all end in disaster."

Ludwig saw Sigwulf stiffen. The northerner was a firm believer in the concept of self-governance, but now was not the place to argue its merits.

"How far to your estate?" asked Ludwig.

"Not far at all," said the baron. "In fact, it should be coming into view any moment."

The road curved to the south, revealing a well-groomed field with horses running freely.

"Are those yours?" asked Ludwig.

"They are indeed. We've been breeding them for nigh on forty years. It was my father's idea. They imported most of our horses when he was younger, leading to high prices."

"And so he thought to bring the price down?"

"Saints, no! The premise was to put more coins in our own pockets, and it worked spectacularly. We are now the wealthiest family in Reinwick, potentially even more than the duke himself." He leaned closer. "All good news for you, of course. It means a most handsome dowry."

Ludwig believed it wasn't as much a dowry as a bribe to take Lady Charlotte off his hands, but he kept his thoughts to himself. They turned off the road, coming to rest before a spacious manor house.

"Ah, home at last," said Lord Kurlan. He stepped from the carriage and took in a deep breath. "Smell that fresh air. Is there anything like it?"

The baron was obviously a man who enjoyed life. Ludwig resisted the urge to laugh, and instead followed his host towards the building, Sigwulf falling in beside him.

"What do you make of all this?" asked Ludwig.

"It's grand," said Sigwulf. "I'll give you that, but I see no signs of defences. Does he not fear attack?"

"I imagine not. We're in the far northern reaches of Reinwick. Likely the only threat here is from the sea."

"Must be nice."

"Surely you had the same thing in Braymoor?"

"You don't know your geography," said Sigwulf. "Yes, Braymoor has a coast, but the vast majority of it is inland. They have a bigger army than navy, hence the need for mercenaries."

Ludwig lowered his voice. "And what of the land of your birth, Abelard?"

"It has a longer coast, although, in truth, I remember little of it. Our estate was in the south, close to the border with Lubenstahl."

"Yet another kingdom for me to remember. How do you keep them all straight?"

"Do you know all the lands bordering Hadenfeld?"

"Of course."

"Then there you have it," said Sigwulf. "You learn those that are close; anything else is meaningless. Well, maybe not meaningless, but less important in the grand scheme of things."

"I wish it were so," said Ludwig, "but it's fast becoming important, particularly to Otto. All these alliances make for a complicated web to decipher."

The opulence of the estate interrupted their conversation. The baron's family was obviously wealthy, based on the polished stone floor and walls decorated with lacquered wood, and filled with portraits.

"My goodness," said Sigwulf. "I've never seen anything like this before."

"Nor have I," agreed Ludwig.

"And here she is," announced the baron. He stood aside, revealing his daughter. "Allow me to name Lady Charlotte Stratmeyer. My dear, this is Lord Ludwig of Verfeld."

She curtsied but kept her eyes to the ground. "My lord."

"Why don't you take our guest somewhere private so you two can get to know each other. Perhaps your captain would care for a tour of my wine cellar?"

Sigwulf grinned. "I would be delighted." They disappeared down the hall, talking of drink, leaving Ludwig and Charlotte alone.

"If you'll come this way," she said, "we can retire to the sitting room."

The room they entered was meant for entertaining, for chairs were in abundance. Lady Charlotte indicated he should sit in a large armchair, while she chose one opposite him. He watched her arrange and then rearrange her skirts. She appeared uncomfortable, yet he could not fathom why.

"Please," he said. "Don't be nervous on my account."

She kept her eyes downcast, staring at the floor.

He leaned forward, placing his finger beneath her chin, raising her head until their eyes met. "There, that's better."

"It is not my place to meet your gaze, my lord."

"Who told you that?"

"My father."

"Then your father is wrong. If you are to be my wife, I expect you to at least look at me. Better yet, I would have you speak your mind." He watched as her eyes began to tear up. "Come now, am I so hideous as to elicit tears?"

A hint of a smile appeared.

He pressed on. "Tell me about yourself."

"What is there to know?"

"Your father says you like to read?"

She nodded.

"I also like to read," he admitted. "Have you read *The Ferengeld Saga*? It's one of my favourites."

Again, the ghost of a smile. "Is that the one about the travelling knight?"

"It is," he said, trying to sound cheerful, despite his discomfort. "My mother used to read it to me."

"Does Verfeld have a library?"

"It does, though admittedly, it's small. However, should you come to live there, I shall let you enlarge it."

"Are you suggesting we might not marry?"

"That is entirely up to you," said Ludwig. "I won't pretend this marriage was my idea. It wasn't, but we must make the best of our circumstances."

She turned her head. "You find me ugly?"

"Not at all. In fact, quite the opposite. You are a lady of grace and dignity."

"But not the kind of woman you want to wed."

"It has nothing to do with you; it is the concept of marriage itself. I have no wish to be burdened by a bride..." His voice trailed off, and he felt a tightness in his chest. He'd spoken without thinking and only made things worse. He tried to recover. "Look, we only just met. Perhaps, if we learn more about each other, we might find some common ground? We both like to read. That's a good start, isn't it?"

"If you say so."

"What other interests do you have?"

"I... write."

"You do?"

"Yes. Poetry, though nothing that would compete with the masters."

"And what do you write about? Courtly love? Romance, perhaps?"

"Do you suppose that's all women think of?"

"My apologies. I just assumed a woman of your age would enjoy such things. I should have known better. It's certainly not something I've ever heard Cyn talk about."

"Cyn? Is she your mistress?"

"No, not at all. She's one of my captains and a close confidant."

"A warrior? Was she a Temple Knight?"

"No, a mercenary, if you can believe it, but we're getting off-topic. You mentioned poetry, and then I assumed it was about romance. Might I ask what you write of, instead?"

"Nature features prominently, particularly animals, but occasionally I am inspired by other events, such as battles."

"Battles?"

"Yes. I composed one last month to commemorate the recent victory of the Temple Knights."

"I should very much like to hear it."

"Perhaps I shall read it to you," said Charlotte. "But not today. Might I ask your interests?"

"If I'm being honest, I have few. As baron, I've spent most of my time rebuilding my forces."

"My father says you led men in battle?"

"I did," said Ludwig, "in Erlingen. We defeated Andover just outside of Chermingen."

"I've heard of it. They say they captured the king."

Ludwig blushed.

"Was that your doing?"

"Not alone, but yes."

"Then you must be brave, indeed, if the accounts are to be believed."

"I'm sure the accounts were greatly exaggerated."

"It seems you are that rarest of creatures," said Charlotte. "A modest hero."

The door flew open, revealing Sir Petrus. "Sorry," said the knight. "Am I interrupting?"

"Is something wrong?" asked Ludwig.

"That depends on your point of view. Brother Hamelyn and I were delayed, and no one was here to greet us. Where is our host?"

"In the wine cellar, along with Sigwulf."

Lady Charlotte rose. "Allow me to take you to him." She turned to Ludwig. "I trust that meets with your approval?"

He, in turn, stumbled to his feet. "Of course, my lady."

She disappeared, Sir Petrus following, but Brother Hamelyn remained, poking his head in to check on things.

"Are you well, Lord?"

"I'm fine," said Ludwig. "Come, sit down and take a load off your feet."

The Temple Knight moved into the room and jabbed his finger into a seat cushion. "This looks most comfortable." He sat down. "Have you been acquainting yourself with your intended?"

"I have, not that I've learned much."

"You're disappointed?"

"Only with myself. It seems courting is not something that comes naturally to me. I found myself struggling to say the right thing."

"Are you admitting you bear feelings for her?"

"No, at least not yet."

"Then what is the problem?"

"Who says there's a problem?"

"You do," said Brother Hamelyn, "by your manner, if not your words."

Ludwig slumped into his chair. "This was not what I expected at all."

"Then perhaps it might help to talk about it. What did you think would happen?"

"I'm not sure. I suppose I assumed Charlotte would be more like Lady Alexandra."

"I'm afraid I don't know this Alexandra you speak of. Is she a paramour of yours?"

"No, merely a good friend, but she was more outgoing, willing to speak her mind. Charlotte is just so timid."

"Can you blame her?"

His words stunned Ludwig. "Whatever do you mean?"

"I couldn't help but overhear your conversation on the *Valiant*. Lord Kurlan would be a hard man to live with for a son, let alone a daughter. He sees her as little more than chattel. Saint Mathew teaches us we all have value. A lesson, it appears, His Lordship has yet to learn."

"I fear she has been mistreated or ignored, and I know not how to deal with it. I feel sorry for her, yet marrying her would seem like a lie, especially when my heart is elsewhere."

"Then tell her of your concerns and let her decide."

"And if she should refuse the marriage, what then? I don't imagine that would make her father very happy."

The Temple Knight nodded. "I expect you're right, but maybe there is another way?"

"If there is, I'm eager to hear of it."

"Allow her the ability to refuse. You can always claim it was your decision should the baron find it distasteful. In that way, you bear the burden for her."

"Wise words," said Ludwig. "Are you sure you're not a Holy Father?"

28

THE PROMISE

SUMMER 1099 SR

The next few days flew by in a whirlwind of activity. Everyone in Blunden wanted to meet the new couple, resulting in dinner after dinner. And when they weren't eating, they were paraded through town like royalty. After their initial meeting, they were never left alone. Ludwig feared he might never be able to broach the subject of cancelling the wedding.

He finally got his chance when they visited the baron's distant cousin, who owned a large manor house north of the city. After a noon meal, they headed outside to wander the estate and breathe in some fresh air.

As they were walking, Ludwig had Sir Petrus engage the baron in conversation. He waited until Lord Kurlan was deep in discussion before tapping Charlotte on the shoulder and waving her to the back of the procession. He slowed considerably, allowing the rest to gain some distance before speaking.

"Charlotte," he began, "there's something I would like to discuss with you."

"Of course, my lord. What is it?"

"How do you feel about this marriage?"

A look of panic set in. "Do I not please you?"

"This has nothing to do with that. I wish to know whether this is something you want or not. I will not marry someone against their will."

She regained her composure. "I assure you I will not flinch from my duty."

"But if you had a choice, would you still marry me?"

"It is my fate to be married off. What else is there for me?"

"To enjoy life? To experience that which makes you happy?"

"Such things are fleeting, and I have a duty to my father and the duke. Why? Is there some reason you do not wish to wed me?"

He decided to admit the truth. "I don't love you."

"And?"

"That doesn't surprise you?"

"Why should it? Love is not necessary for a successful marriage. True, it sometimes blossoms in the fullness of time, but that is very rare from what I've seen."

"There's more," said Ludwig.

"Then speak freely, I beg of you."

"I love another."

"That hardly matters."

"I would not wed you against your wishes. If you want to marry another or not marry at all, tell me, and I shall refuse the marriage."

"There is no other," she replied, "nor is there ever likely to be. My fate is to be married off for political expediency. If it wasn't you, it would be someone else. You are a decent man, Lord Ludwig. I thank you for your concern, but whether you love me or not is immaterial in the grand scheme of things. I will therefore accept you as a husband, provided that is still your desire."

"Very well," said Ludwig. "And though I am not sure that I can ever love you, I give you my word I will treat you with dignity and respect."

"Thank you. That means a lot to me. I always feared I would marry a man of low morals and beastly manners, but you have proven to be neither."

"I shall take that as a compliment."

"As it was meant. I think we should endeavour to catch up with the others. It seems we have lagged behind to a significant degree."

They sped up their pace. "Might I ask the custom in these parts?" said Ludwig.

"Regarding what?"

"The announcement that we are to be wed. Is that already assumed, or is there an official ceremony to announce it?"

"Have you told my father that you agree to the marriage?"

"Not yet. To be honest, I've been avoiding it until I knew your thoughts on the matter."

"Then we shall confront him together to show we are united in our desire to be wed."

"I'm not sure confront is the word I'd use."

"You don't know my father. He likes to see people fight for what they want. In his mind, it demonstrates they truly desire something."

"When should we do this?"

"This evening, before dinner. He likes some wine before a meal, usually in solitude."

Ludwig smiled. "So we can talk to him without fear of being interrupted by others."

"Precisely."

"You've given this a lot of thought."

"I have," said Charlotte. "For years, I couldn't wait to be free of this place, but at the same time, I was terrified of what awaited me. You now provide me with the very escape I always desired."

"Ah, there you are!" Lord Kurlan came into view. "Sir Petrus and I were just talking about my horses, and he mentioned you're very fond of riding. What do you say we all go out for a ride upon our return?"

Ludwig looked at Charlotte.

"I shall leave you gentlemen to your passions," she said. "As for me, I have reading to catch up on."

"Well, Ludwig?" said Lord Kurlan, ignoring his daughter.

"It appears there is nothing else that requires my presence, my lord. Lead on, and let's see this stable of yours."

It was late in the day by the time they returned. Ludwig made his excuses to his host, then sought out Charlotte, eventually finding her putting words to paper.

"I hope I'm not intruding."

"Not at all. I was just trying my hand at some poetry."

He moved closer, looking at the page before her. "May I?"

She nodded. He picked it up, holding it delicately as if the words might fall from the page.

"This is exceptionally good," he said. "You have a gift for prose."

She smiled. "I'm glad you like it."

"Do you write often?"

"When the mood strikes me."

"And have you ever spoken them aloud for others?"

"No. I'm far too shy for that."

"And yet these words... they're inspiring. Perhaps one day you'll read them at court. Or, if you prefer, someone else can read them on your behalf?"

"Whoever would do such a thing?"

"A troubadour," said Ludwig. "They have them up here, don't they?"

She chuckled. "Troubadour is such an archaic word. We prefer the term 'bard' in the north, but yes, we have them, although I doubt my writing would interest them."

"I beg to differ, but it's your decision." He reread the poem. "These words are full of life. Is all your work so flowery?"

She cast her gaze to the table. "No. I must confess much of my prose is far darker."

"How so?"

"It is not something I wish to burden you with."

Ludwig sat opposite her, taking her hand in his. She raised her eyes to meet his. "We are to be married," he said, "and a burden shared is half the weight."

"I... struggle sometimes."

"Struggle?"

"Yes, to find my place in all of this." She cast her gaze around the room. "I know I shouldn't complain. After all, I live a life of comparative luxury, yet sometimes that is not enough. At times, I feel as though a part of me is missing, like all my joy has been erased from existence."

"And how long does this feeling last?"

"It varies. I've been known to lay in bed for weeks, unable to force myself to rise. On such occasions, the days drag on endlessly. Other times it's as if the Saints themselves inspire me. That's when I'm at my most creative."

"Have you sought help?"

"From whom?" asked Charlotte. "There is no healer in Blunden who knows of such a malady, nor would my father take pains to find one if there were. He believes I am merely being lazy or indolent."

"Then perhaps we shall have better luck in Hadenfeld."

"We?"

"Of course," said Ludwig. "You are to be my wife. I will not hold it against you should you fall ill. Nor should your father, if truth be told, but I cannot dictate his actions. However, I will ensure we find some way to help you deal with this affliction, even cure it, if that's possible. Assuming that's what you would like?"

"Very much so, thank you, though I have my doubts about whether such a cure exists."

"I cannot predict what the future may hold, but there's no denying that inaction changes nothing. At the very least, we can make your new home more comfortable for your peace of mind than your current surroundings."

She held out her hand, and he returned the poem. "I shall put this away with the others."

"Perhaps you'll let me read them someday?"

"Possibly, but we have more important matters to attend to at this moment."

"Being?"

Charlotte chuckled. "We must brave the bear in his cage."

"Ah, you mean your father. I'd forgotten about that."

"Don't tell me the Hero of Chermingen is nervous?"

He grinned. "I would gladly face the hordes of the Underworld on the field of battle, but talking to my future father-in-law? That's a whole different matter."

Lord Kurlan Stratmeyer was sipping his wine, enjoying the solitude, when a knock at his door demanded his attention. He set down his drink, irritated at the intrusion.

"Who is it?" he called out.

"Lord Ludwig, my lord," the servant replied. "Along with Lady Charlotte."

"Very well. Send them in and go and uncork another bottle of wine."

"The white, my lord?"

"No, the red, and be quick about it, for Saint's sake."

The door opened, admitting his visitors.

"Lord Ludwig," said the baron. "You must excuse me. I like to ruminate in solitude before a meal."

"I'm sorry, my lord, but I thought it best we settle things at the first opportunity."

"Settle things? I daresay that sounds a tad ominous."

"Not at all. Lady Charlotte and I are here to inform you we are in agreement that the marriage should go forward."

"That is excellent news and well worth the interruption." He turned to his daughter. "You must excuse us, Charlotte. We have much to talk about, Ludwig and I, things not meant for a woman's ears."

She curtsied, then quickly exited the room.

Lord Kurlan lifted the bottle to pour his guest a drink, but noted not much was left. "My man has gone to fetch some fresh wine. We'll wait until he returns to toast your health."

"It is I who should toast you, my lord, for you are the one who has provided me with my bride."

"Yes, I have, haven't I? Now, let's see. There are several things we must talk about. Let me start by saying you are growing your family substantially. Not only does Charlotte have three brothers, but quite a few cousins as well. In fact, the duke himself is related, although admittedly fairly distantly. What of you? Have you any familial connections to anyone important?"

"As I mentioned before, King Otto is my cousin," replied Ludwig.

"Does that mean you could inherit the Crown?"

"Not unless many died. I am seventeenth in the line of succession."

"Saints alive, that makes you royalty. I had no idea!"

"In Hadenfeld, only the king's immediate family and his designated heir are considered royalty."

"Why is that?"

"It comes from necessity," said Ludwig. "Otherwise, every noble in the kingdom could claim that honour."

"Ah, yes. I see the wisdom in that. If the rest of the Petty Kingdoms did likewise, it would make courtly life so much easier."

"Do you consider the duke as royalty?"

"We do, although our beloved leader is addressed as Your Grace, not Your Majesty. How is Otto addressed?"

"Usually as Your Majesty," said Ludwig, "although he prefers me to call him m'lord."

"Why in the Continent would he do that?"

"I can only assume he has an affection for me. Either that or he's teasing me. I can't tell which."

"Then let us assume it is the former rather than the latter." He looked down at his goblet. "Let's see... where was I? Oh yes, we need to talk about the ceremony. When I first read of King Otto's request, I took pains to make some preliminary arrangements."

"Being?"

"You shall be married in Korvoran, enabling the Archprior to bless the union."

"Of Saint Mathew?"

"Of course. Who else would do it, an Agnesite? Come now, we don't need any of that foolishness."

Ludwig felt his temper building. Did the baron intend to insult just the order of Saint Agnes or all women in particular? He wanted to lash out and argue with the man but knew it would do no good. Instead, he took another approach. "I understand there will be Temple Knights in attendance?"

"Yes. It's common when nobles are wed, and your wedding will help secure our alliance with Hadenfeld."

"And afterwards?"

"We'll all go to the duke's estate. He's hosting a reception in your honour. There'll be food aplenty with enough wine to drown a fish, all paid for from His Grace's coffers. I couldn't have planned it better myself."

Ludwig was stunned. "You didn't make the arrangements?"

"Only those in the beginning. Once the duke got hold of it, I could do little else. Of course, I'll still provide the dowry, so there is that."

"Speaking of which, how much should I be expecting?"

"In terms of crowns, I should imagine eighty sufficient, wouldn't you?"

"Eighty crowns?"

Lord Kurlan laughed. "No, Ludwig, eighty thousand. Saints alive, eighty crowns would barely get you a decent warhorse."

Ludwig could scarcely believe his ears. Eighty thousand crowns was a princely sum. Enough to expand the keep at Verfeld and still have plenty left over. He tried imagining what that amount might look like, and then panic set in. How would he transport it all back to Hadenfeld? He imagined a carriage full of golden coins.

"That is most generous, my lord," he finally replied.

"I know that look," said the baron. "You're wondering how to transport such a sum."

"I am. It would, I imagine, require several wagons."

"Not at all. I shall transfer the funds through the Temple Knights of Saint Mathew."

"Oh yes, of course. Brother Hamelyn told me about how they handle such things. I should have remembered."

"And I should have explained it a bit better. Still, it's nice to picture that much in gold coins, isn't it?"

"And the Church can handle such a sum without difficulty?"

"The Church?" said Lord Kurlan. "I wouldn't trust them as far as I could throw them, and that's not saying much."

"But you just said—"

"I know what I said, but you clearly weren't listening. The Temple Knights take care of such things, not the Church hierarchy. And let's face it, if you can't trust a Temple Knight of Saint Mathew, who can you trust? Now that I think of it, it's all rather strange."

"What is? The knights handling financial arrangements?"

"Of course. Where else but in the Petty Kingdoms would you find a group of knights who take a vow of poverty guarding large sums?" He laughed at his own remarks.

Ludwig doubted the Mathewites would find it amusing, but he had to admit there was a certain irony to it.

"In any event," continued Lord Kurlan, "I will hand the funds over to them once the ceremony is complete, minus some to put in your pocket to cover travelling expenses. Have you given any thought to how you'll return home?"

"I expected to hire a carriage, but I'm not sure I want to take her through Andover. I don't imagine they would appreciate a Reinwick noble passing through."

"I agree. We shall have to see what else can be arranged. What about a boat?"

"Hadenfeld is landlocked, my lord."

"Ah, but there are rivers, are there not? And plenty of smaller craft ply those waters."

"We would still need to traverse Andover."

"Not necessarily." The baron leaned forward, a sparkle in his eye. "You might persuade the sisters to take you westward and avoid Andover altogether. I'm sure such things could be arranged for a suitable donation."

"I'm not sure I would be comfortable with that."

"Don't think of it as paying for personal travel so much as supporting a worthy cause. You get the use of a ship, and they get what they need to expand their fleet. Always assuming that's what they intend, of course. I can put in a good word for you if you like?"

Ludwig warmed to the idea, despite his initial reservations. "No, that's quite all right. I'll make the arrangements myself."

"You have a friend in Korvoran?"

"As a matter of fact, I do," said Ludwig, a smile breaking out. "Someone I've known for many years and who, I might add, has access to several ships."

"That's all well and good, but you'll need warriors to protect you while you're on the open sea. There are no end of raiders in these parts, particularly as you go westward."

"Fear not. The Saints will protect us, and if they don't, there'll be knights aplenty to fend them off."

"Yes. Well, I still think you should talk to the Agnesite captain—what's her name?"

"Temple Captain Charlaine?"

"Yes, that's the one. Once we return to Korvoran, you should try to get on her good side."

29

MARRIAGE

SUMMER 1099 SR

Blaring trumpets announced the arrival of Lady Charlotte Stratmeyer. Inside the Temple of Saint Mathew, Archprior Anders waited with Ludwig at his side. As unusual as it was for a man of Anders' rank to oversee a wedding, this was no ordinary union. These nuptials would cement an alliance between Reinwick and Hadenfeld, presenting a strong and unified front against their enemies.

Ludwig thought it ludicrous. While it was true alliances made a kingdom strong, there came a point at which an excess of such agreements became more of a burden. It was also an empty threat, for Hadenfeld was so far from Reinwick that any conflict would be over long before their army arrived. And it didn't consider that such a force would be required to march through other kingdoms to reach these shores.

Sigwulf stood beside him, looking as if this were just a day like any other. Then again, Ludwig was the one getting married, not Sigwulf, so maybe he had the right of it.

The room fell quiet as the great door at the front opened, revealing the wedding procession led by two Temple Knights of Saint Agnes. Behind them was an older woman clutching an ornately carved staff topped with a pale blue crystal. Another robed individual holding a censer came next, its smoke spreading incense throughout the temple.

Then Lady Charlotte appeared, accompanied by her father, brothers, and various cousins. As they made their way towards the Archprior, these familial guests split off from the entourage, taking their seats on either side.

The Temple Knights paused before the Archprior, bowing reverentially, but the woman holding the staff stood tall, remaining defiant. Ludwig wondered if there was more to the woman's glare than mere tradition.

The cloying stench of the incense enveloped him, but he resisted the urge to cough. His eyes, stung by the smoke, watered, and then, before he realized it, Charlotte was standing there.

"Take your place by the side of your intended," said the Archprior, "and we shall begin the ceremony."

Ludwig moved to stand to her right.

"We are gathered here today to witness the uniting of two noble houses. Lord Ludwig Altenburg comes to us from the Kingdom of Hadenfeld, while Lady Charlotte Stratmeyer is one of our own. Who speaks to this assembly on behalf of Lord Ludwig's character?"

Sigwulf stepped forward. "I, Sigwulf Marhaven, do hereby swear that Lord Ludwig Altenburg, Baron of Verfeld, is a man of honourable character and a follower of the faith."

A gasp from someone in the crowd interrupted the solemnity of the ceremony. Ludwig wondered what had caused such a reaction and was so intent on working it out that he lost track of the Archprior's speech. A nudge from Charlotte brought him to his senses.

The woman with the staff directed someone to approach the couple with a bowl. They'd informed Ludwig what the ceremony would entail, but seeing an actual container of seawater before him still felt strange. Even more peculiar was the fish swimming around within it. Charlotte nodded, and they both plunged their fingers into the bowl.

"As you cleanse your hands," said the old woman, "so, too, do you cleanse your souls in Akosia's waters."

Ludwig couldn't help but glance at the Archprior, noticing the distaste despite the Holy Man's best efforts to hide it. They removed their hands, and a young woman moved closer to dry them with a towel. She then removed the bowl, and with that, the old woman left.

Archprior Anders took centre stage. "We bring these two together this day to join them in Saintly harmony. Since time immemorial, man and woman gathered thus..." His voice droned on.

The man appeared to possess a knack for long-winded ceremonies. Between that and the persistent haze of incense, Ludwig felt drowsy. He risked a glance at Charlotte to spot her eyes also drooping. A gentle elbow startled her awake, but she still looked as if she struggled to remain upright. Concerned for her well-being, he coughed, interrupting the ceremony. The Archprior looked at him in shock.

Ludwig kept his voice low. "Move along, Your Grace, before my new bride faints." Certain he'd overstepped the rules of decency, the redness in the Archprior's face only confirmed it. However, despite the insult, the fellow did as he was bid, bringing forth a silver cup with consecrated wine within it.

"Drink now in health to your betrothed," commanded the Archprior as he passed it to Ludwig. Ludwig took a sip, immediately tasting the brew's potency. This was no ordinary wine, and he suspected someone had decided to spice up the proceedings.

The cup was then passed to Charlotte, who drank in a like manner. Her reaction was more pronounced as she coughed and sputtered, but only momentarily. Those gathered to witness chuckled at her misfortune. Ludwig found their reaction cruel.

The Archprior then took the cup, handing it to an aide, who wiped it out before the Archprior presented it to those assembled. "This cup," he intoned, "symbolizes the union of Lord Ludwig and Lady Charlotte. Let none divide what the Saints have blessed here today." The Holy Man lowered the cup and passed it to Ludwig, who, along with Charlotte, turned to face their guests. Together, they hoisted the vessel into the air to be greeted by applause. Everyone rose, many coming forward to offer their congratulations. Ludwig recognized the utter fear in Charlotte's eyes as the well-wishers threatened to engulf them.

"Sigwulf!" he called out.

The great warrior was soon there, using his bulk to push against the well-intentioned guests. Panic welled within Ludwig, not for his sake but that of his new bride. He tried to back up, but others came from behind them. He was about to scream out in frustration, and then Charlaine was there, along with a trio of Temple Knights.

"This way," she said. "We can leave by a side door."

The mob parted at the sight of armoured knights, and moments later, Ludwig led his new wife outside. Charlotte bent over, gasping for air, her panic visible to all.

"Fetch the carriage," ordered Charlaine. One of her knights ran down the side of the building while the Temple Captain moved beside Charlotte, gently placing her hand on the woman's back. "There, there," she soothed. "It's all over now. Let's get you somewhere you can find some peace and quiet, shall we?"

"To where?" asked Ludwig.

"We'll take her to the commandery. You go on to the duke's estate. We'll join you as soon as she feels up to it."

"And if she doesn't?"

"Don't worry. We'll send word on her condition."

"I should come with her."

"No," said Charlaine. "Your presence is required to reassure your new allies. We'll look after Charlotte." She looked at Sigwulf. "Keep an eye on him. He can be headstrong at times."

"Don't I know it," he replied.

A carriage rolled down the alleyway with a Temple Knight in the coachman's seat. Ludwig helped Charlotte climb into the thing but was loathe to let go of her hand.

"I'll be fine," she assured him.

The carriage moved, leaving his hand empty. Ludwig stared after it until Sigwulf grabbed his shoulder, breaking the spell.

"Come, my friend. It's time we made our way to the duke's reception."

The guests swirled around the dance floor, each movement perfectly timed. Ludwig watched, marvelling at how even relatively simple steps could appear so graceful, especially when repeated simultaneously by so many.

He should've been ecstatic, for the entire reception was in his honour, a fact that had been hammered into him repeatedly, yet he felt no joy. Instead, he was content to watch the jubilation in others, his own thoughts too sad to voice.

His gaze swept the room, and he noticed a familiar face moving through the crowd, her distinctive scarlet marking her as a Temple Knight.

"Sister Danica, have you news?"

"I do," the woman replied. She came closer, lowering her voice to avoid being overheard. "Lady Charlotte is here, within the manor. Captain Charlaine thought you might want to see her."

"Of course." He moved to stand, but she placed her hand on his forearm. "Tell everyone you need to relieve yourself. We don't want people clamouring for her attention."

"Yes. Good point." He waited for the knight to leave, then counted to fifty. Finally, he rose, nodding to Sigwulf. "A call of nature," he explained, then made for the door.

Sister Danica stood there, ready to guide him through the manor to where Charlotte sat on an armchair, her feet elevated. A Temple Knight stood outside the room to prevent any unwanted intrusions.

"My lord," said Charlotte. "I hope I didn't embarrass you today."

"Not at all," he replied, moving to take her hand. "The truth is, I worried the ceremony might prove too much for you. In any case, it's all over now."

"Not quite. I've yet to meet our guests."

"You owe them nothing," said Ludwig. "Tell me you wish only peace, and I shall send them all away."

"No. I must do my duty. My father would wish it, and I would not see his name besmirched."

Ludwig bit back his retort. Lord Kurlan had made it quite plain he wanted to be rid of her. The man didn't deserve the devotion she showed. And all this despite his poor treatment of her. He swallowed his feelings. "How shall we do this?"

"Captain Charlaine has an idea."

Ludwig turned to look at the Temple Knight.

"We'll escort her to the head table. Two sisters will stand behind her, dissuading any who might desire to get too close."

"Won't that cause problems?"

Charlaine smiled. "We shall explain it away as a custom of Hadenfeld."

"But there is no such custom?"

"True, but you and I are the only ones who know that."

"Aren't Temple Knights sworn to tell the truth?"

"We are, but customs must start somewhere, and it is our duty as Temple Knights of Saint Agnes to protect women. Naturally, we knights could not make such a claim. That must be left to you unless you insist on starting such a custom?"

"That's a splendid idea, and it absolves you of the need to be involved with a lie."

"Then we are in agreement," said Charlotte. She slowly came to her feet, the effort looking as if it might break her. "Take my hand, my lord. It will give me strength."

Charlaine led, the mere sight of her presence enough to clear a path as they entered the great hall. All in the room quieted as the couple made their way to the head table, then a voice called for a toast.

The silver cup that symbolized their union sat before them. Ludwig filled it with wine, offering it first to Charlotte. "Don't worry. It's much milder than that horrid stuff they had at the temple."

She took a sip, then placed the cup before Ludwig's lips. He responded in a like manner, and then they both raised it as they had in the ceremony. Everyone broke into a cheer, and then the music resumed.

The mood in the room was celebratory, and even Ludwig felt at ease. Charlotte contented herself with concentrating on the plate of food set before her, only looking up occasionally to give the appearance of interest.

Ludwig remained by her side, ready to assist her in a graceful exit if needed. Guests shouted toasts and drank, then a bard came forth, mandolin in hand.

"Ugh," said Charlaine. "Not this fellow again."

Ludwig looked back in surprise to see the Temple Captain wincing. "You know him?"

"His name is Rascalian, and to be honest, he's a nuisance."

"Are you suggesting he can't sing?"

Charlaine frowned. "It's not his voice that's annoying. It's his choice of songs."

"Now you have me intrigued." Ludwig turned his attention back to the fellow adjusting his instrument.

"A gift for the happy couple," said the bard. "A song to memorialize their wedding." He cleared his throat, strumming a few notes before beginning his work. His voice echoed off the walls, giving it an ethereal quality.

Noble lords and ladies,
And all knights brave and strong,
Gather round and heed my words,
As I sing to you this song.

Here is a tale as old as time,
Of lovers' hearts entwined.
A hero born in foreign land,
In need of love to find.

While far in northern climate cold,
Surrounded by the sea.
A noble lass sat waiting long,
Her heart to Saints did plea.

And then did hero make his oath,
To woo this lady fair.
And she in kind returned his gaze,
And into eyes did stare.

"I pledge my love to you," he said,
"With all my beating heart.
And from this day, forever more,

Us two shall never part."

All was silent for a moment before the crowd burst into applause. Ludwig found the song not quite to his tastes. He looked at Charlotte, who was obviously pleased with the result, and decided to keep his thoughts to himself. Instead, he leaned in close to whisper to her. "If you like, I'll hire a bard to put some of your poetry to music?"

"I thank you for the offer, my lord, but my work is for private consumption only."

"Very well. I shall accede to your wishes, but you must remember to call me Ludwig, not 'my lord'. We are married now, making you the Baroness of Verfeld."

"Do not all ladies refer to their husbands as my lord?"

"Perhaps here in the north, but Hadenfeld has its own customs."

"And why is that, I wonder?" she asked.

"Many of our people came from distant lands, bringing their customs and beliefs with them."

"And so they disdain the show of respect?"

"Not at all, but in the privacy of one's home, I would consider such things unnecessary, wouldn't you?"

A faint smile graced her features. "You have such strange ideas. Tell me, are all men in your homeland this way?"

He chuckled. "I don't claim to speak for all men, only myself. Yet I can't help but feel others would agree with my outlook." He nodded to his right. "Take Sigwulf there. His... well, I suppose you would consider Cyn his wife —he treats her as an equal."

"You're not sure if they're married?"

"Umm... I don't believe they ever had an official ceremony, but they've been together for years."

"Cyn," said Charlotte. "It is such a strange name."

"It's short for Cynthia."

"Oh. I suppose that explains it, then."

An immaculately dressed individual approached the table, walking with determination, something that immediately commanded Ludwig's attention. The stranger halted, glaring at Sigwulf.

Ludwig sensed trouble. "Have you come to offer your best wishes?"

The fellow kept glaring, ignoring the question. Instead, he pointed at the object of his ire. "You, Sigwulf Marhaven, are a traitor and condemned rebel. I order you to surrender yourself for execution."

Sigwulf was about to stand, but Ludwig interjected. "And who are you, sir, to make such an accusation?"

"I am Lord Torsten Walsh, Baron of Saylen."

"Never heard of you."

"I am the emissary from King Rordan of Abelard, my lord."

"Then I suggest you take your seat, sir, for you have no power here."

"This cur," the man shouted, pointing at Sigwulf, "is a traitor to the Crown of Abelard. As such, he has a death sentence on his head."

"Yes," said Ludwig. "I understood your accusation the first time you made it." He stood to emphasize his intent. "How dare you come to my wedding, of all days, to make unfounded accusations against my captain! Were this day not one of celebration, I would demand satisfaction." He looked at Sigwulf, noticing his friend's anger building. "Of course, I would be happy to let you and the good captain settle this matter man to man, should you desire it."

Lord Torsten paled. He appeared willing to have others do his dirty work, but his own skin was more important. "I w-w-withdraw my accusation," he finally stuttered.

"Good. Return to your seat, and we shall hear no more of this." The man slunk away.

"Sorry," said Sigwulf. "I should've used another name."

"Nonsense. Who could predict that a noble of Abelard would be present here in Reinwick?" After feeling a tap on his arm, Ludwig turned to Lady Charlotte.

"What was that all about?" she asked.

He considered lying but decided she deserved to know the truth. "Some years ago, Captain Sigwulf's family was on the losing side of a civil war."

"He must've been someone of import to garner the recognition of the Abelard ambassador."

"His father was one of the leaders of the rebels."

She smiled. "Does that mean he has a claim to the throne?"

He looked over at Sigwulf, but the man simply grinned.

"I suppose it does," said Ludwig, returning his gaze to his wife. "Not that he's likely to act upon it."

Sigwulf leaned past Ludwig, keeping his voice low. "Not anytime soon, at any rate."

She laughed. "You have a rebel amongst your closest confidantes. How exciting!"

"No," corrected Ludwig. "WE have. You're part of this merry crew from this day forth."

"Something I accept with a great deal of pride. However, having said that, I think my time here amongst all these people has worn me out. I need to lie down."

"My knights will escort you out," said Charlaine.

Ludwig watched as the Temple Knights of Saint Agnes guided his new bride from the room.

"Thank you, Charlaine," he said. "You've been of great assistance to us, to me."

"It's what friends do. And I hope you shall always consider me one."

"And I, you."

She smiled, reminding him of fonder days.

"If you're ever in Hadenfeld again," he said, "be sure to drop by."

"I will. And should you find yourself in need of Temple Knights, feel free to contact someone else. We don't work for others." She laughed, and he felt a lightheartedness he'd missed for quite some time.

"It was good to see you," Ludwig said.

"I could say the same. Don't return to being a stranger."

"I won't. I promise."

30

THE RETURN

SUMMER 1099 SR

L udwig stared landward as the port of Korvoran disappeared over the horizon. The coast remained in sight and would be for some days, yet it felt like they were in the wilderness with the city no longer visible.

Admiral Meer came up to stand beside him. "Nice view, isn't it?"

"If you say so. Personally, I'd prefer to keep my feet on solid land."

They stared silently over the ship's rail as a dark shape appeared beneath the water.

"It's a porpoise," she explained. "Along with whales, they're considered a good omen."

"By whom?"

"Worshippers of Akosia."

Her statement caught him by surprise. "That old woman at the wedding? Who was she?"

"Elsbeth Fel, Sacred Mother of Akosia, although I suppose you could call her a priestess. Why do you ask?"

"It's a little strange to have a worshipper of the old Gods at a wedding, isn't it? Especially with an Archprior conducting the ceremony."

"Not as strange as you might think," said Danica. "The nobility all worship the Saints, but many commoners still follow the old ways."

"And you don't find that unusual? I would've thought the Church eager to eradicate such beliefs."

"Not at all. The Saints preached acceptance, and those aren't just empty words."

"Yet the very same Church organizes crusades to kill the Easterlings."

Danica frowned. "We don't all condone such violence, but the Church, like any hierarchy, is comprised of people, and people vary in their beliefs."

Ludwig looked back down the deck to ensure they were out of earshot of any others. "Do you believe the Crusades have anything to do with this corruption within the Church?"

"Possibly, although I haven't given it much thought. The east is a long way from here, and we've had our own problems."

"Fair enough." He watched the porpoise surface before diving beneath the waves. "Can I ask you a question?"

"Certainly, although I can't guarantee I'll give you an answer."

"Do I call you captain or admiral?"

"Either will do. I'm a Temple Captain by rank, but I hold the position of admiral when at sea."

"What's the difference between a rank and a position?"

"Think of it like an army. We generally think of a captain as someone who leads a company. Yet that same individual may need to command even more men in extreme circumstances. In that instance, he would still maintain the rank of captain but would do the work of a commander. It's not a perfect comparison to my present situation, but it's close enough. In any case, we're not much for titles aboard ship. Sister Danica is good enough for me."

"Might I ask how you met Charlaine?"

"We served together in Ilea."

"You knew all about me, so I assume you're close."

"Yes. She's like the older sister I never had and a trusted friend and confidante."

He cast his gaze once more to the water. "You must think me a fool."

"Not at all. You love Charlaine, that's easy to see, but you're also a man who will do his duty. Charlotte's lucky to have you, and you, her."

"You don't think I'm deceiving her?"

"No. I had an opportunity to talk to her back at the commandery. She knows what she's getting into. She also knows that you're a decent man. She could've done far worse in terms of an arranged marriage. Just make sure you treat her with dignity and respect."

"I shall. I promise."

"You surprise me," said Danica.

"I do?"

"Yes. You're more mature than I expected."

"I'm the same age as Charlaine."

"In body, yes, but I'm referring to your behaviour. From what Charlaine said, you came across as a spoiled noble. Yet, I've seen anything but over the last few days."

"It's battle," he replied. "It made me grow up and realize what's important."

"And that is?"

"Friends and family, and not just mine. Everyone deserves the chance to live free from worry about death and famine."

Danica chuckled. "You sound like a Temple Knight. Have you ever considered taking Holy Orders?"

He smiled. "Too late. I'm a married man now."

"Yes, and sooner or later, you must make efforts to produce an heir." She turned to face him. "Charlotte is fragile, Ludwig. Take your time with her. Do you understand what I'm saying?"

"I do, and I promise you I shall heed your words. I'll not touch her unless it is at her urging. I give you my word."

"Good. I trust you to keep it." She turned her gaze seaward once more.

"Can you tell me again where we're going?" he asked.

"Round the tip of Reinwick, then we'll sail down its western coast. We'll take you and your people past Langwal to a kingdom named Burgemont. From there, you can make your way south, back to Hadenfeld."

"Do you suppose we'd be able to hire a coach?"

"Undoubtedly, but you might find it more expedient to take river transport. Where is Verfeld, relative to the rest of Hadenfeld?"

"The northeast corner. Why?"

"If memory serves, that river runs up into Burgemont. It's the same one that forms Andover's western border."

"Andover," said Ludwig. "I never want to see that place again."

"Really? I'm from Andover."

"Ah, you must be the one they were talking about back in the Green Sparrow. What part are you from?"

I was born in a small fishing village on its northeastern shore, but don't worry, I shan't take offence."

"What can we expect in Burgemont?"

"They're close to Halvaria, so they're more cautious about strangers."

"I don't suppose I could convince you to take us home in the *Valiant*?"

"Much as I'd enjoy the trip, I can't. Our orders are to keep the coast clear of enemy warships."

"You mean Halvarians?"

"That's part of it, but mostly we hunt down pirates."

"I hear you have a secret fleet in Temple Bay."

"We do, but you must deny all knowledge if you hear anyone else speak of it."

"And if I wanted to donate to help fund the fleet?"

"You can always send donations to the commandery in Korvoran. The Temple Knights of Saint Mathew would be more than willing to take care of the financial arrangements on your behalf."

"I'll bear that in mind."

"Good. Now, it's been nice talking to you, but I have a ship to run. I shall see you later. After all, it's not as if there's anywhere to hide around here."

They sailed northeast, up the coast of Reinwick for several days, then rounded the tip. Years ago, a massive lighthouse had been constructed to guide ships. Since then, the Dukes of Reinwick continued the tradition of keeping it alight, although now it was simply known as 'The Beacon'. The immense structure was taller than any building Ludwig had ever known, the flame atop it visible for many miles.

The *Valiant* turned west, the wind picking up considerably as The Beacon fell astern. Even though the shore led them more southwest than west, they hugged the coast for protection from the open sea. The land here was uninhabited, save for majestic oak trees, their boughs spreading out like some ancient beast caressing the sky.

The wind often shifted on this part of the coast, making sailing difficult, but the Temple Ship proved equal to the task. They sailed close to two hundred miles before Admiral Meer took them farther out to sea. The Temple Knight spent a lot of time on the foredeck, searching the horizon.

Ludwig found her one day in this position, her expression alert. "Tell me," he said. "Are we expecting trouble?"

"We are north of Langwal, so that's always a possibility."

"I'm afraid I don't understand?"

"There are two islands north of Langwal. We call them The Eyes. They're a frequent hangout for pirates."

"Why is that?"

"There is no navy to speak of in these parts, and such criminals can operate with impunity. Or at least they could until we came along."

"And you think they might attack us?"

"No," said Danica. "No pirate is foolish enough to attack a Temple Ship, but we must be alert, lest we come across a merchant vessel in distress."

"And how long will that take?"

"We'll be clear of it by this evening, assuming the wind holds. After that, we round a cape and reach Vilnitz."

"Is that the capital of Burgemont?"

"No, but it's one of their larger cities. From there, it's easy enough to book passage south on a riverboat or hire a carriage, if you should feel so inclined."

Ludwig chuckled. "From your tone, I gather you don't much like the idea of a carriage?"

"You're travelling through the Petty Kingdoms; banditry is a scourge, particularly at times like these."

"Why? What have you heard?"

"This region is heading for war, either amongst themselves or with Halvaria. People are fearful, which leads to desperate acts, often at the tip of a sword."

"Is there no such thing as river pirates?"

"Those are rare," she said with a chuckle, "and with good reason. They'd quickly be tracked down without a sea to disappear into."

"Couldn't they raid using small boats, then flee to shore?"

"They could, but thankfully, they don't possess your sense of tactics. Also, most riverboats like to employ a few guards to act as a deterrent, not to mention a Water Mage, if they can find one."

"A Water Mage?"

"Yes. They help move the ships faster. Such vessels carry cargo in addition to passengers, and the first to market can often command the highest prices for their goods."

"And how do I go about finding one of these boats?"

"I know several vessels that would suit your needs. We'll just have to wait and see who's in port."

They were well past the first island by noon and closing in on the second when a sail was spotted mid-afternoon, but it proved to be a merchant flying the flag of Burgemont. The *Valiant* sailed close enough to hail them, but there was little news to pass on.

That evening, they rounded the cape, the lights of a fishing village illuminating the shore. Ludwig thought they might anchor for the night, but the crew was familiar enough with the area, so they kept the sails set. By midnight, the lights of Vilnitz came into view, and the *Valiant* reduced sail, slowly making its way into the harbour.

The port here was considerably smaller than that of Korvoran, the number of ships less than a fifth of Reinwick's largest port. They soon bumped up against the dock, and the first part of their journey was over.

Sir Petrus led the way, the green tinge to his features betraying his discomfort with the sea. Brother Hamelyn was sturdier on his feet, although he, too, looked relieved to finally be on solid ground. Sigwulf led Charlotte across the boarding ramp while Ludwig remained to thank their hosts.

"You've been of immense help to us," said Ludwig. "I shall be sure to send some coins your way to support the fleet."

"That would be much appreciated," said Danica. "Now, as to the next portion of your trip, it appears you're in luck." She pointed. "You see that ship over there with the blue sides?"

"Yes."

"That's the *Wren*. Its captain is a large fellow named Vectrix."

"How large?" asked Ludwig.

"Let's just say he could give that captain of yours a challenge. In any case, he has a reputation as a trustworthy sort, and he's a devout worshipper of Saint Mathew. Be sure to mention my name, and he'll look after you."

"I'm much obliged, Admiral."

She smiled. "As you should be. Oh, and one more thing?"

"Yes?"

"Make sure you write. I know Charlaine would appreciate it."

"I will. I promise."

"Excellent. Now, be off with you, and let me get back to the job of pirate hunting!"

He walked across the boarding ramp to where Lady Charlotte waited. She was in a good mood despite the late hour.

"Come," said Ludwig. "Let's find ourselves an inn."

Ludwig woke early, for he was concerned they might miss their chance to board the *Wren*. So much so, he almost made the trip to the boat in the middle of the night. As it turned out, such late-night arrangements weren't possible, for the *Wren* didn't begin taking on passengers until well past mid-morning. It was closer to noon before they finally unfurled the sails.

Their party of five joined three others, all of them remaining on deck for most of the day. Only when a light drizzle came up late in the afternoon did anyone think of taking refuge.

The *Wren* made good progress despite working against the current. On the *Valiant*, they sailed through the night, but here on the Continent, the *Wren* anchored each evening, its guards walking the deck to dissuade any who might do them harm.

The days wore on, the banks of the river changing little. Occasionally, they would come across a tributary. Still, being unfamiliar with the region, neither Ludwig nor Sigwulf could claim any knowledge of their where-abouts. Therefore, it was with some surprise that they learned they were skirting Andover. Eventually, they hit the border of Erlingen, finally making port at Zurkirk, where they unloaded some goods. Shortly after that, they continued on their way, passing into the Duchy of Angvil.

For the most part, the river was a smooth ride, and it became the custom for Charlotte and Ludwig to spend much of the afternoon on the deck, watching the trees as they floated past. The river turned westward, and then they followed the border of Zowenbruch.

Here, the land mainly consisted of overgrown forests with only the occasional glimpse of farmland as they approached towns and villages. On one of these lazy, sun-drenched afternoons, trouble began with a scraping sound, and then the *Wren* came to an abrupt halt, sending many crashing to the deck. Ludwig quickly picked himself up, then helped Charlotte to her feet.

"We hit a sandbank," explained Captain Vectrix.

"Can you float her free?" asked Ludwig.

"That remains to be seen." The captain moved to the ship's railing and was leaning out, trying to get a better view of their situation, when an arrow thudded into the wood just beneath him even as a second flew over-head. The captain let out a curse as he ducked.

Ludwig drew his sword, then remembered Charlotte was beside him. "Get below, and don't come back until I say it's safe."

He crouched, making his way up to Captain Vectrix. "Can you see how many are out there?"

"Less than half a dozen if that rowboat out there is any indication. No doubt, they intend to board and empty our hold."

"Then why loose arrows first?"

"To show us they're in earnest."

"Can we refloat the ship?"

"Not without considerable work. I'm afraid they have us."

"Then let them come aboard," said Ludwig. "My group should be able to handle them."

"If you say so." The captain stood, raising his arms to indicate he had no weapon in hand.

The bandits, excited by the prospect of easy plunder, pushed their rowboat out, making their way to the side of the *Wren*. After hearing the first one start climbing aboard, Ludwig glanced back at the aft deck, spot-ting Sigwulf crouched by the tiller. Sword in hand, Sir Petrus had taken time to don his gambeson while Brother Hamelyn, as was typical for a Temple Knight, still wore his full regalia.

The first bandit set foot on the deck, his eyes darting around, quickly noting the presence of Brother Hamelyn. He went to shout a word of warning, but the Temple Knight put a finger to his lips, and the fellow remained silent. The next in line climbed over the edge to come face to face with the tip of Sir Petrus's sword. He, too, said nothing, although he moved aside as the knight indicated, freeing up room for the third raider.

The next one, however, was more attentive, and as soon as his head cleared the railing, he gave a shout of alarm. Ludwig lunged, jabbing out with his sword but failed to hit his target, for the man let go of the railing to avoid taking a wound and fell back into the boat below.

Ludwig rushed forward, jumping over the railing. In his haste to follow the enemy, he misjudged the distance, landing in the water instead of the boat. To make matters worse, his feet went out from under him, sending him beneath the river's surface. He struggled to gain his footing and surfaced only for someone to stab at him, catching the tip of his ear but only lightly nicking the skin. He leaned back, eager to get out of reach.

Shouts from above drew his attention. Sigwulf, lowering himself over the side of the *Wren*, took a moment to line up before jumping to land smack in the middle of the tiny rowboat.

With the enemy distracted, Ludwig dragged himself through the chest-deep water, finally seizing the side of the enemy vessel. He heaved himself into it, but the fighting was already over. One had fallen overboard, floating down the river face down, while the rest raised their hands in surrender.

Sigwulf laughed as he looked down on his friend. "I didn't know it was the custom in Hadenfeld to bathe before a fight."

"Nor is it," said Ludwig, "but we are on the border of Zowenbruch now, and you know what they say about adopting local customs."

31

BIRTH

SPRING 1100 SR

Footsteps echoed in the halls of Verfeld Keep. The lamps were lit, and the entire household was in a state of alarm, for Lady Charlotte was finally in labour.

They'd returned home in late summer, and now, nine months later, the result of their homecoming was due at any moment. Father Vernan, ever the practical one, had arranged for the Temple of Saint Agnes to provide a midwife, along with two assistants and sister knights who now stood watch at the door as the women did their work.

Ludwig paced, halting only to prevent himself from running into Sigwulf. "What are you pacing for?" he snapped. "It's not as if it's your child."

"I know, but I'm anxious for your sake."

Cyn was the voice of reason. "Calm yourselves, the two of you. Honestly, it's like you're children."

"Easy for you to say," insisted Sigwulf. "You're not the one having the baby." He immediately realized what he'd said and flushed, then tried to repair the damage. "I'm sorry, Cyn. I didn't mean anything by it."

"No," she shot back. "It's quite clear what you meant." She stormed off.

"What's that all about?" asked Ludwig.

"She can't bear children," replied Sigwulf. "We tried long ago, but it proved impossible. The sisters pronounced her barren. It's always weighed heavily on her."

"Then best you seek her out and provide comfort."

"What of you?"

"I'll be fine," said Ludwig. "Now get ye gone, and see to that wife of yours."

"You know, she's not actually my wife, at least not in the eyes of the Church."

"Then perhaps you should see to rectifying that."

"Agreed," added Father Vernan. "It is particularly important for her to have stability in her life, especially if she can't have children."

"Stability?" said Sigwulf.

"Yes, something she can rely on. Without marriage, you could run off at the first opportunity."

"I hate to say this, Father, but even married men can run off. Not to say I ever would. I'm in this for the long haul."

"Then tell her that."

"But she knows already."

Father Vernan moved closer, peering up at the huge man with a finger pointed at his chest. "Have you explicitly told her that? In those exact words?"

Sigwulf blushed. "Well, maybe not in those precise words."

"Then go and do so. Now!"

Ludwig chuckled as the giant of a man fled. "I think you put the fear of the Saints into him."

"The Saints do not work by fear," said Vernan. "Rather, they advise and suggest."

"It appears you can be quite persuasive when the occasion permits. Just out of curiosity, how did you learn so much about women?"

"Believe it or not, it's part of our training. After all, we look after the poor and sick, including women. One could hardly do that if one didn't understand them."

"And here I was thinking you Holy Fathers avoided women at all costs."

"We associate with them. We just don't... you know."

Ludwig chuckled. "No, I don't. Tell me, Father, what is it you don't do?"

"Engage in conjugal relationships."

Ludwig decided to have some fun at the Holy Father's expense. "Conjugal? You mean where you and others are in a financial interdependence?"

"No, of course not. I mean, we took a vow of chastity."

"Oh, that," said Ludwig with a smile. "Of course, I should've realized. My apologies, Father."

The door opened, revealing a matronly figure who exited the room, closing the door quietly behind her.

"Well?" said Ludwig. "Have you news?"

"The Saints have seen fit to bestow on you a child," she replied. "A boy, to be exact."

"And Lady Charlotte?"

She paused before answering, sending Ludwig into a panic. "She is... recovering."

"What does that mean?"

"She had a difficult time of it, I'm afraid. Her Ladyship is a frail woman to begin with, and the birth of a child can be a most traumatic experience."

"But she will recover, won't she?"

"I cannot rule out the possibility of long-term debilitation."

"So you're suggesting she'll be an invalid?"

"It's possible, yes, but only time will tell. Meanwhile, I suggest you let her rest and recover from her ordeal. Oh, and I'm afraid there will be no further children in your future if you want your current wife to survive."

"My current wife? What's that supposed to mean?"

"Calm yourself," said Father Vernan. "She means no disrespect, but it's common amongst the nobility to remarry if more children are desired."

"I shall be more than happy with the one, thank you," said Ludwig.

"Surely you don't mean that," said the matron. "You need an heir and a spare at the very least."

"I need no such thing," said Ludwig. "It matters not who succeeds me as baron of this wretched place. I shall not discard my wife simply to satisfy the whims of kings."

"He is upset," explained Father Vernan, "and emotional. Quite reasonable, considering the circumstances. Wouldn't you agree, Matron?"

"Perhaps," she replied, although her expression of distaste indicated otherwise. She re-entered the room, but when Ludwig tried to follow, she blocked him. "Lady Charlotte must rest," she repeated, closing the door.

"I don't even get to see my son?"

"In time," said Father Vernan. "Let's go down to the great hall for some wine, shall we? A little drink to celebrate the birth of your heir." He tugged Ludwig by the elbow, finally convincing him to leave.

They made their way down the stairs in silence. When Ludwig threw open the door to the hall, he spotted Sigwulf and Cyn locked in a tight embrace.

"Sorry," he said. "I didn't mean to interrupt anything."

"Not at all," said Cyn. "Come in. We were just... hugging."

"Lord Ludwig has a son," announced Father Vernan. He turned to Ludwig. "Have you a name in mind?"

"Several, but I've yet to speak with Charlotte about it. This whole pregnancy has been hard on her."

"As it has on us all," said the Holy Father.

"Pardon me?"

"I meant no offence, my lord, but we've all been worried for her health. As the matron indicated, she is of a frail countenance."

"On that, we are in agreement," said Ludwig.

"Have you given any thought to the lad's future? Will you send him to Otto's court once he's older?"

"I think it's a little early to be making such arrangements, don't you? And even if he were old enough, why would I send him to Harlingen?"

"Why, to learn all about the realm. It is a common practice in the Petty Kingdoms."

"My father kept me here, in Verfeld. He felt it better to be raised amongst one's family."

"When one is young, yes, but if a child is to be raised as a noble, it's imperative he eventually learn the ways of court."

"What do you think, Sig?"

The huge northerner shrugged. "It doesn't seem to have hampered you, Ludwig."

"On the contrary, Lord," said the Holy Father. "You were very uncomfortable in the capital."

"I'll admit you have me there," said Ludwig. "I shall give it some thought, but not until I've had a chance to discuss the matter with Charlotte. Not that it needs anyone's immediate attention when he's only just been born."

He flopped down into a chair, resisting the urge to put his feet on the table. Exhaustion nagged at him, yet he was unable to sleep.

"I know that look," said Cyn. "You're thinking."

"I am."

"What about?"

"The longer I'm the baron here, the more I understand my father. That thought would have horrified me years ago, yet now I'm the one wearing the mantle of baron."

"It's the responsibility," said Sigwulf. "It sobers a person. Thankfully, there is a cure."

"Which is?"

"Ale, of course!"

Late the next day, Carson brought news that Lady Charlotte was awake. Ludwig made his way to her chambers, his mind in a state of worry. The midwife informed him his wife would be bed-bound for at least a week, even going so far as to insist she would return each day to check up on her. She was a stern woman but clearly had the best interests of her charge at heart.

Ludwig knocked, only for the door to be opened by a servant. He peered around the woman to spot his wife lying on the bed, looking pale, her eyes darting about wildly. He moved to stand by her side, taking her hand.

"How are you feeling?" he asked.

"Worn out," she replied. "I can't muster the strength to even hold him."

"The babe needs to eat," urged the servant, "but she won't take him."

"Then go into Malburg and find a wet nurse." He reached out and grasped her hand. "Rest. I'll take care of our son."

She managed a half smile. "What shall we call him?"

"That's a good question. How about we name him after your father?"

"A man who showed me little love? No, I don't think so. What about yours? What was his name?"

"Frederick."

"A fine name and one befitting a future baron."

"Then Frederick it shall be. Now that we have a name, we must see to your health. I'm told the birth was difficult. I'll not expect you to go through that again."

"But you require more heirs—"

"I need no such thing," said Ludwig. "I will not have you risk your life merely for another heir."

"And if Frederick should die young?"

"Then the king can appoint someone else to take my place. It's more important to me that my son has his mother growing up."

"Like you did?"

"No. I lost my mother when I was fifteen, far too soon for such a tragedy."

"Yet you became the man you are today. She would be proud of you were she here to see how you turned out."

"You think so?"

"I know so," said Charlotte, "but I hear your words. I shall do all I can to live long enough to watch him become a man."

"Perhaps one day we'll have grandchildren?"

"One would certainly hope so. I'd hate to think I went through this birth for nothing." She closed her eyes. "Now, you must excuse me. I am exhausted."

"Then we shall let you rest." He brought his gaze back to the servants. "Leave the room."

"My lord? What of the infant?"

"Take him with you. It will allow Lady Charlotte to rest."

"But she is his mother?"

"Of that, I am well aware, but leaving him here when she cannot look after him will do no good."

The woman shook her head, then lifted young Frederick, taking him from the room.

"She's right," said Charlotte. "I cannot even care for my own child." Tears came to her eyes, and helplessness welled up inside Ludwig. He was torn between giving her the solitude she desired and comforting her in her time of need. He decided on the latter, moving close to embrace her. It was awkward to do with him standing beside the bed and she in it, but he somehow managed. She, in turn, clung to him in a desperate embrace.

He wasn't sure how long they stayed this way, but he had to shoo away the servants twice. Eventually, Charlotte's grip loosened, and she sank back into the bed, her eyelids drooping until she finally fell asleep. He remained, holding her hand in his, afraid to leave lest she need him.

Ludwig awoke with a start. A gentle tap on his shoulder made him look up through sleep-bleary eyes to see the face of Cyn.

"They found a wet nurse," she whispered. "Your son is feeding now." She nodded at Charlotte. "How is she doing?"

"Better than I expected, but she needs to rest."

"She seems to do a lot of that."

"It's her illness," he replied. "She told me about it back in Reinwick."

"What can we do to help?"

"Not much, I'm afraid, other than to be there for her when she needs us."

"And when she's in this state, does she eat?"

"She does, although admittedly, not much. I suspect that's part of the reason for her frail health."

"Is it possible your son might suffer the same affliction?"

He looked up at Cyn in surprise. "I hadn't considered that possibility, but it matters little. I shall accept him regardless of his health."

"Of course, I didn't mean to infer otherwise. I merely meant we should be vigilant as he grows and be on the lookout for signs."

Ludwig stood, his back aching. "I feel ancient."

"That's understandable. You've been up here for what seems like forever. You know, Sig and I can help too."

"Thank you. I appreciate the offer."

"But?"

He smiled. "What makes you think there's a but?"

"Come now. I've known you for, what, five years?"

"Has it really been that long?"

"Well, let's see, shall we? We met at the tournament in Torburg, back in ninety-five, wasn't it?"

"So it was," replied Ludwig. "I had no idea so much time had passed. Just think how different things would have turned out had you not pulled me from the saddle."

She laughed, then immediately stifled it for fear of waking Charlotte. "Come. Let's get you downstairs to a nice comfortable chair."

"I won't argue with that." They left the room, closing the door as quietly as possible. As they descended the stairs, they came across Sigwulf.

"I was just looking for you two."

"Something wrong?" asked Cyn.

"A delegation has arrived, seeking an audience."

"From who?" asked Ludwig.

"The villages of your barony. Word of your son's birth spread quickly, and people are coming to pay their respects. Apparently, it's the custom in these parts."

"Is it?" said Ludwig.

"You would know better than I. I sent them to the great hall. I hope that wasn't too presumptuous of me?"

"Not at all." Ludwig straightened, rising to his full height. "There. How do I look?"

"Like a man who hasn't slept in ages, but it'll have to do."

"Then lead on, and let us greet our guests."

They passed by several servants, and Ludwig ordered them to fetch ale. When they finally arrived at the great hall, Sigwulf and Cyn each took a door, opening them on either side to allow Ludwig to make an entrance fit for a baron.

Many rushed forward to offer their congratulations. Ludwig did his best to be gracious but struggled to remember their names. He finally set his eyes on someone he recognized.

"Dolf Macken, I see," he called out. "And Marjorie as well. I didn't expect you to make the trip."

The farmer bowed clumsily while his wife attempted a curtsy. Ludwig ignored their lack of skill, instead grasping the surprised fellow's hand in a firm shake. "How are things at the farm?"

"They are well, Lord."

"Glad to hear it. I'm sorry I haven't been out to Eramon to see everyone, but with the baby on the way..."

"Quite understandable, Lord."

"I was thinking about you the other day."

"You were?"

"Yes. While I was going over my accounts."

The fellow paled. "We are paid up in full, Lord."

"I know you are. That's not the issue."

"Then what is, if I may be so bold as to ask?"

"You raise cows: three, if I remember correctly."

"Four now, Lord."

"Do you think you'd be able to raise more?"

"I can't afford more."

"No, but I can. I thought I would purchase some on your behalf. You raise them, and then, when they're sold off, I'll take back my original investment, and you keep the profits."

"Why would you do that?"

"Because I want to see the land prosper," said Ludwig. "And your village is the smallest of my holdings. We've had great success increasing the population of Verfeld. It's high time we did the same for Eramon."

"It's your land, Lord."

"Yes, but I know next to nothing about farming. I intend to build more houses and encourage others to plant crops, but I need someone to supervise it. Someone who can be there when needed. Of course, I'd pay you, perhaps even Marjorie?"

"Marjorie?"

"She's the one who milks the cows, isn't she?"

"She is."

"Then there you are. Now, the real question is where to find people interested in becoming farmers."

"Easy enough, Lord. There's plenty in Malburg who'd be keen to give it a go, had they the coins, although I can't speak of their ability."

"Do you think you could teach them?"

Dolf nodded. "I'd be willing to give it my best try."

"Good. I'll come out to Eramon next week to discuss specifics. In the meantime, you and Marjorie look around and decide the best place to build houses."

"Yes, Lord."

Ludwig's gaze fell upon Cyn, who was chatting with Pelton.

"You must excuse me, but there's someone I need to speak to." He left Dorf and Marjorie, pushing through the crowd of well-wishers, stopping on occasion to accept congratulations. Finally, he stood before his target.

"Cyn," he said. "You must think me a terrible friend."

She stared back in surprise. "Why would you say that?"

"When we left for Reinwick, you said you wanted to take a stab at designing a castle. Here we are, nearly a year later, and I haven't asked you how you fared."

"You were busy with a new wife," she replied, "and then the baby was due..."

"Which still doesn't excuse my manners. What I am curious about, though, is what happened to that design. Did you finish it?"

"I did and sent it off to Harlingen to a scholar to get his thoughts on the matter."

"And?"

"He made a few recommendations and gave me the name of a castle builder. That fellow, in turn, recommended several stonemasons from whom I was able to make some estimations as to cost."

"Good. Let's get together tomorrow. I'm interested to see what you came up with."

"And then?"

"Why, we begin construction!"

32

THE MESSENGER

SPRING 1100 SR

The Baron of Luwen arrived at Verfeld only a week after Frederick's birth. The visit came as a surprise to Ludwig, but as he went to greet the carriage, he tried to maintain as cheerful a countenance as possible.

"Lord Meinhard, this is a rather unexpected pleasure. To what do I owe this visit?" Ludwig took a quick look in the carriage for Meinhard's daughter, Alexandra, but there was no sign of any others.

"We should go inside," said the baron, without greeting. "We need to talk in private."

The statement piqued Ludwig's interest, but he resisted the urge to probe further. Instead, he led his fellow baron up the steps to the front of the keep.

Lord Meinhard halted at the top, looking at the growing pile of lumber and stone. "What's going on here?"

"We are stockpiling building material for the expansion of the keep."

"To what end? Verfeld is far too distant to be targeted by Neuhafen."

"Neuhafen is on the other side of the river," said Ludwig.

"Yes, but the forest is thick in these parts, hardly the type of terrain an enemy would march through."

"True, but I need more space if we are to maintain a large garrison. At present, we're all crammed into the keep, and it's most unsatisfactory."

Lord Meinhard barked out a laugh. "It's your dowry now, Ludwig. Spend it how you like, but if I were you, I'd look at building a house in Harlingen. That's where all the important decisions are made."

Meinhard's words hinted something had changed, yet Ludwig was loathe to bring it up in public. "Come," he said instead. "We'll retire to my study and talk over some wine. You must be parched after your trip."

"Ah, a man after my own heart. Very well, lead on, and let us waste no further time."

They made their way upstairs, then Ludwig sat at his desk, feeling guilty for not cleaning up. Lord Meinhard took a seat opposite him, but they said little until after Carson delivered drinks and left them in peace.

The baron took a sip of his wine before placing his cup on the desk. "I came from Harlingen at the king's behest."

"That sounds serious."

"Aye, it is. Earlier this month, we received word King Ruger finally passed. I shouldn't need to tell you the ramifications."

"War," said Ludwig. "Any idea when it's to commence?"

"No, but they won't wait long. Ruger was a pain in our backsides but at least smart enough to know war would devastate both our treasuries. I'm afraid his son is far less learned about the political ramifications."

"But an invasion now would trigger our allies to march, would it not?"

"Agreed, but you and I both know that will take time. I'm guessing their new king, Diedrich, thinks he can take the capital before anyone comes to our aid."

"And can he?"

"Otto thinks not, but there are others who disagree."

"And what about you?"

Lord Meinhard took another drink. "It all hinges on Hasdorf and Grien-wald. We'll have time to assemble the army if either of those towns can stall them long enough."

"Why not call up the army now?"

"It's a matter of economics. Put all those troops in the capital, and we shall go broke just trying to feed them. Then all our enemy need do is wait us out until they starve. There's also another problem."

"Which is?"

"The king is only empowered to call on the army when war is actually declared. That means either a formal declaration or enemy warriors crossing the border."

"But surely the barons would be willing to march sooner?"

"You must remember, Neuhafen has been busy in diplomatic circles. They may have allies prepared to take advantage of our situation."

"I see," said Ludwig. "If we move troops too soon, we may find our neighbours invading."

"Precisely. All part of the elaborate chain of alliances that keeps us on our toes."

"How long do we wait?"

"That's the big question."

Ludwig studied his guest's face. "You didn't come all the way here just to tell me this when a courier would have sufficed. What's the real purpose of your visit?"

"The king feels you might be able to help us."

"My men are ready to march."

"That's not what he needs, at least not yet."

"Then, for Saint's sake, get to the point."

"He wants you to go to Neuhafen."

"For what?"

"To see if you can talk some sense into Diedrich."

"What makes him think I can make any difference?"

"You have experience in the north."

"That was as a military leader," said Ludwig, "not a diplomat."

"I was referring to your trip to Reinwick. According to Sir Petrus, you handled the entire situation with great aplomb."

"What situation?"

"You know full well," said Meinhard. "Lord Kurlan has a reputation as a hard man to get along with, yet you won him over. In addition, you impressed the duke so much that he wrote to King Otto, extolling your virtues."

"But I hardly met the duke."

"Perhaps, but you certainly made an impression on the fellow. That's why Otto wants you to go to Neuhafen and plead our case."

"I shall follow the king's wishes, but I doubt it will make a difference."

"Good," said Lord Meinhard. "Otto knew you'd agree. He even provided you with a list of where he's willing to compromise, and more importantly, where he's not."

"It's the king's command. What else could I do?"

"It's not his command, merely a request. Did I not make myself clear?"

"You and I both know it's tantamount to the same thing. When does he want me to leave?"

"The sooner, the better, although the trip is not without risk. There is the very real possibility they might imprison you or even execute you. We know so little of King Diedrich's ways."

"Then I shall put my affairs in order and leave by week's end. Will that suffice?"

"I should think so, yes."

· · ·

Sigwulf sat up with a start. "Neuhafen? Have you lost your mind? Even I know their new king is set on war. What can you possibly hope to accomplish?"

"Peace is always preferable," said Father Vernan. "What Ludwig is attempting is difficult, to be sure, but so is anything else worthwhile in life."

"Then we'll go with you," added Cyn.

"No. I require you all here to keep an eye on things in my absence. If war comes, you'll need to march the men to Harlingen."

"But you can't go alone!"

"I must offer no threat to them, and the presence of guards could be construed as mistrust on our part."

"He's right," said Vernan. "It's his journey and his alone."

"How far do you have to go?" asked Sigwulf.

"I shall cross the river here before picking up the road at Dornbruck. I understand their capital, Eisen, is about seventy miles from that point."

"That close?" said Sig. "I thought it would be clear over the other side of Neuhafen."

"Actually," said Ludwig, "I've spent a great deal of time reading about our friends across the border. The baronies are all found in the western part of Neuhafen."

"Why is that?"

"The eastern area is thickly forested and said to have all kinds of strange creatures beneath its boughs. It's one of the things that contributed to the rebellion in the first place."

"I'm not sure I understand," said Cyn. "How did a forest lead to a rebellion?"

"The eastern baronies struggled to tame the wild woods. They pleaded with the Crown for more help, but the king refused them."

"Was that Otto's doing?"

"His predecessor's, but things came to a head right after his coronation. He could have diffused the entire situation had he given it some thought, but Otto can be stubborn. In this case, it worked against him."

"So they went to war because they weren't getting help?"

"That more or less sums it up. They primarily wanted Royal Troops to help protect them as they cleared the forest, but such things are a drain on the Royal Purse."

"And so they raised their own army," said Cyn. "It's ironic, isn't it?"

"And had you been king," said Sigwulf, "what would you have done differently?"

"It seems to me," said Ludwig, "that the barons should've been invited to sit down and talk things out."

"And Otto didn't offer that?"

"If he did, there's no mention of it. In any case, it matters little now. What's done is done. We can't undo the past, merely work to make a better future."

"And what do you intend on telling this new King of Neuhafen?" asked Father Vernan.

"That Hadenfeld desires peace."

"And what will you give up to secure that peace?"

"That's an interesting question. I know Otto won't give up his Throne, so that's out of the question, and I've been informed he is unwilling to surrender territory."

"That doesn't leave you with much to negotiate with."

"No, I suppose it doesn't. Still, I feel like I must try."

"Why?" said Cyn. "Why not cut your losses and prepare for war. It's going to come anyway. You have a wife and son now, Ludwig. Do you really want to risk losing them?"

"It's precisely because of them that I must try. I don't want to live in a land where war is a constant threat."

"You have little choice, my friend," said Sigwulf. "We're one of the Petty Kingdoms. War is our constant companion."

"But it doesn't have to be, don't you see? Wars seldom solve problems—they only make them worse. The Petty Kingdoms have been around for hundreds of years; and they're still arguing over things that are insignificant in the long run. And every time we go to war, we lose men, men who could be used to stave off an invasion by the Halvarians. In some ways, I believe we would've been better off had the Old Kingdom remained. At least then there would be a united front against the empire."

"You don't need to concern yourself with the Halvarians," said Father Vernan. "The Temple Knights are there to keep us safe."

Ludwig wanted to mention Charlaine's warning but kept silent. Better the Holy Father feel secure than worry about such things. He cast his gaze at Sigwulf and Cyn, but obviously, they felt the same.

"Cyn and I will accompany you as far as the river," said Sigwulf. "From there, you can make your own way. I assume you'll take a horse?"

"Yes, but not Clay. I hate to admit it, but I've become rather fond of the beast. The last thing I want is for him to be lost should I be imprisoned."

"You actually believe they would do that?"

"If they feel I'm a threat, yes."

"One man, a threat?"

"It's not an unreasonable assumption," offered Cyn. "If he arrives at their capital to see they've assembled a large army, that would justify his captivity. After all, they wouldn't want him getting word back to Otto that the army's on the move."

"She makes a good point," said Ludwig. "And for the same reason, I shall not be taking my armour. It was expensive to have made, and I don't think a suit of plate will help me should they decide I'm truly a threat."

"But you'll take your sword?" said Sigwulf.

"Of course. There are appearances to keep up, and what noble worthy of the name travels without his weapon?"

"And should war come, have you any specific orders?"

"I do. As you know, Lord Merrick has agreed to put his men under my command. I intend for you to lead them, Sig, while Cyn leads the Verfeld contingent. You may make other arrangements if you prefer, but should the invasion come, your first priority would be to march the men to Harlingen; the warriors of Drakenfeld will meet you there."

"And what of your family? Do we bring them to the capital with us?"

"No," said Ludwig. "They would be much safer here, in Verfeld."

"And if the war goes ill?"

"Then take them north, into Desienbach. The court there is friendly to Otto, so they'd likely be well-received."

"Come now," said Cyn. "All this talk of disaster is depressing. Let's look on the bright side, shall we? Ludwig will go to Neuhafen and convince them not to invade. Then he'll return a hero, and bards will sing his praises for all the great work he's accomplished."

Ludwig winced. "After hearing that bard up in Reinwick, I'd prefer not to be the subject of a song."

He found Charlotte sitting in the library, reading a book. She looked up at his entrance, a sadness to her eyes.

"What are you reading?" asked Ludwig.

"The *Campaigns of Aeldred*."

"You surprise me. I didn't take you for someone interested in military strategy."

"I felt it would help me understand what you've been through, my lord."

"I was in one battle. That hardly compares to what Aeldred went through."

"Yet it is the basis of your military knowledge, is it not?"

"It is, but it's not entirely suitable reading for one such as yourself."

"Because I'm a woman?"

Her statement caught Ludwig off guard. "A poor choice of words," he replied. "I assumed that such would not be of interest to you."

"On the contrary. I find it fascinating." She smiled, though it looked forced.

"Is something the matter?"

"You're leaving." Her words were neutral in tone, yet still they stung.

"I am," replied Ludwig, choking on the admission, "though not till the morning. How did you know?"

"It's hard to keep a secret in a keep, my lord. There's been talk of little else."

"I'm sorry, Charlotte. The king wants me to go to Neuhafen. He hopes we might be able to avoid war."

"And you think it possible?"

"I must try, no matter how slim the chance. War is not something to be taken lightly."

"If only others thought as you do, my lord."

"Please," said Ludwig, "don't call me 'my lord'. As I've said before, you must call me by my given name. You are my wife after all."

"A wife whose bed you no longer grace, now that you have an heir."

"I did not wish to overstay my welcome. Our marriage was arranged. I would not force you to remain in my company."

"We are married, Ludwig, and I am committed to that. I will never refuse your presence." She paused a moment. "Or is it that you find the very thought of me repulsive?"

"Not at all," he quickly responded. "You are a very attractive woman. Why, any man would be happy to call you his wife."

"But not you?"

His face burned as the guilt raced through him. "I-I-I'm sorry," he stammered. "I promised you I would treat you with dignity and respect, yet I have neglected you. I shall endeavour to do better upon my return."

"It is true ours is an arranged marriage, yet in the short time we've been together, I've come to care deeply for you, Ludwig Altenburg."

The warmth flowing into his heart surprised him. Initially, he'd seen the entire marriage as a political necessity. Yet, now that he'd gotten to know her, he felt sad at the mere thought of leaving. He moved closer, taking her hand in his. "I promise I shall do all in my power to return safely to your side."

"It will be dangerous. I hope you'll bring guards?"

"I thought it best to go alone."

She took in a sharp breath. "Alone? Into the lair of the enemy? Surely you jest?"

"I go to negotiate with the King of Neuhafen, not threaten. Warriors will only make that more complicated."

"He could kill you!"

"I shall be within his court and vastly outnumbered. A few guards of my own would make no difference."

"And so you will simply throw your life away?"

His throat constricted as he knelt, looking deeply into her eyes. "You may rest assured I have no intention of throwing my life away. He might imprison me, true, but execution would set all the rulers of the Petty Kingdoms against him."

"So you would then rot your life away instead. Can you honestly say that is any better? Please, Ludwig. I implore you. Take men with you."

"I'm sorry. My mind is made up. If I am to go to Neuhafen, I must do things in my own way."

"Then I shall pray for the Saints to watch over you."

He squeezed her hand, then stood. Charlotte remained seated, yet he now saw not a woman of delicate health but one with strength and determination to match his own.

"Will you bid your son goodbye before you leave?"

"Of course."

The next morning, Sigwulf and Cyn accompanied Ludwig to the river. Listening to the water wind its way north reminded Ludwig of the ride he'd taken with Charlaine. While true they'd been farther north, her words that day had proven prophetic.

"Something wrong?" asked Sigwulf.

"No, I just remembered another day when Charlaine and I rode to the river. She asked what I thought we'd be like in ten years."

"And?"

"It's hard to believe that was nearly six years ago. So much has changed in such a short time."

"For the good, I hope?"

Ludwig smiled. "Yes, yet neither of us could have predicted the strange paths our lives took. No, I take that back. She once told me she'd join the Church if she couldn't be a smith."

"And you're the baron," said Cyn. "You must have suspected that would happen sooner or later."

"Yes, I suppose I did. Now that you mention it, our paths weren't so strange after all."

"Except for that whole bit about becoming a mercenary!"

"Yes, or making a fool of myself at the tournament."

"You don't have to be so down on yourself," said Cyn. "You're coming back."

He forced a smile. "Of course. I can't let you two run my barony into the ground."

"Hey, now. That's Pelton's job, not ours."

"Agreed," said Sigwulf. "Although it's our responsibility to drain your wine cellar while you're away."

"Well," said Ludwig, "I suppose somebody has to."

Sigwulf's gaze wandered to the far bank. "This is where we must part, my friend. Once you cross the river, head due east, and after half a day's travel, you should come across a path that will take you all the way to Dornbruck."

"Are you sure you want to cross here?" asked Cyn. "There's a ford down-river that would be more convenient."

"The water here isn't too deep," said Ludwig, "and I'm not wearing anything that might weigh down my horse. We'll be fine."

"Then we'll bid you the joy of the morning—once you're safely across."

He was about to object but saw the look of determination. Surrendering to the inevitable, he entered the river, the water quickly rising to his boots. One last wave, and then his mount moved forward and began swimming.

Ludwig had never enjoyed the sensation of riding a swimming horse. Still, the alternative, to find a ford, was a delay he was unwilling to consider.

In the end, he worried for naught. The horse was a good swimmer, and before long, they were on the far bank, with Ludwig wishing he'd thought to remove his boots beforehand. He looked back across the river. "Satisfied?"

Sig and Cyn turned around and disappeared into the woods, leaving Ludwig alone with his thoughts. He headed east, riding deeper into the forest, fully aware there were many more miles yet to travel to reach a decent road.

As he rode, the thick vegetation varied little, yet there were enough clearings to keep his bearings by the sun. He found the path leading east by noon, easing his travel considerably.

In his youth, he'd heard stories of bears, wolves, and other strange crea-tures that defied description. His memories caused him a moment of panic, and then he reminded himself such tales were only meant to frighten chil-dren. Helping him along was the constant sound of birds chirping as they went about their daily business. Surely such creatures would not be present were enemies close by?

After a few hours, the path widened, and he saw his first sign of civilization—hoofprints. The Baron of Dornbruck must regularly send his men into these woods, something he wished to avoid, lest he find himself under arrest before talking to the king. When he heard the distant sound of a horse snorting, he dismounted, walking his mount into the underbrush to evade detection. He kept his hand on the horse's head to calm the beast.

The pounding of hooves approached, followed by the jangle of armour as two mounted men rode past. He waited until the sounds dissipated before coming out from his place of concealment. His next few miles were more cautious, fearing the patrol might return. The sky grew darker, evidence that the day was drawing to a close. He picked a spot out of sight of the path and settled in for the night.

Ludwig rose early in the morning, determined to cover as much ground as possible. The terrain varied little, but the path was easy enough to follow until finally, with the sun near the horizon, he spied Dornbruck Keep. In form, it was much like Verfeld, rectangular with a raised set of stairs leading to an entrance. But, whereas Verfeld possessed a simple door, this keep had a more elaborate gatehouse out the front of the building.

Ludwig had to admit he liked the design. Had he not been in enemy territory, he would have loved the chance to enter the place and discover the inner layout and defences.

Instead, he simply watched it for a while, keeping his distance. This almost cost him his freedom, for as he stared, the patrol returned. Only when his horse's ears pricked up did he realize his danger.

He eased his horse forward, remaining under cover of the trees, and proceeded eastward, soon coming to the forest's edge. Here he waited, his pulse racing. The enemy patrol slowed their gait while wisps of their conversation floated closer on the wind.

Ludwig's hand went to the hilt of his sword, clutching it, ready to spring into action at a moment's notice, having no idea if that would have him running or fighting. It felt like time stood still until the voices finally faded to nothingness. He sighed in relief before urging his horse onto the road to begin the long trip to Eisen.

33

INTO THE LION'S DEN

SPRING 1100 SR

E isen lay astride a great lake, although Ludwig didn't know what it was called. When he arrived at the city gates and informed the guards he was there to speak with King Diedrich, their inattentiveness immediately changed. He thought that was a good thing at first, but when they discovered he came at the behest of King Otto, things grew decidedly frosty.

Despite their obvious distrust, they sent him with an escort to the Royal Keep, a most convenient turn of events since Ludwig had no idea how to get there. The streets of Eisen were even more confounding to him than those of Chermingen.

Eventually, they delivered him to his destination, where servants took charge of him. King Diedrich was holding court at this very hour, with all his barons in attendance and a bevy of other important folk. The servants delighted in telling him so as they cleaned him of the accumulated dirt and sweat from his trip.

Finally, they escorted him to the great hall, where a somewhat portly fellow with a full beard and white hair announced his arrival before ushering him into the room.

Ludwig halted a moment to take in his surroundings. King Diedrich sat at the end of the hall, sprawled upon a throne both ludicrously ornate and of gigantic proportions, giving the royal the appearance of being a small child.

Ludwig kept his eyes on the king, advancing at an even pace, avoiding the impulse to rush. On either side stood the nobles of Neuhafen, falling silent as he passed by them. Diedrich eyed him warily, sitting up straight as this new visitor approached.

Ludwig bowed. "Your Majesty. I bring you greetings from King Otto of Hadenfeld."

The king sneered. "Greetings, is it? Do you dare to tell me you came this way only to say hello? Or is it that you were sent into the lion's den to test the sharpness of my teeth?"

"My king wants only peace between our realms."

"Then he should have had more consideration all those years ago. Had he seen fit to answer our pleas for help, we might be more willing to receive his ambassador, but history has forced us to take a different path."

"Are the people of Hadenfeld and Neuhafen so different? We share a common history. Surely that accounts for something?"

"You are well-spoken," said the king. "I'll grant you that, but I am not my father. I shall not sit back and watch the people of Hadenfeld suffer under the heels of a tyrant."

The words caught Ludwig off guard. Did the people of this realm truly see Otto as a tyrant? He thought the idea absurd, yet the face of King Diedrich revealed it was no jest.

"I can assure you there is no tyranny in Hadenfeld," Ludwig replied. "Perhaps your sources are mistaken?"

"You dare question my sources? You, no more than a lapdog sent to do Otto's bidding!"

Murmurs from the crowd echoed their ruler's sentiments, placing Ludwig in a difficult situation. He realized that he might end up on the chopping block if he couldn't do something to turn things around.

"My apologies, Your Majesty. It is, as you say, not my place to question those who serve you. Rather, I seek to understand.

"Prior to assuming my duties as Baron of Verfeld, my stepbrother may have abused his authority, but I can assure you such is not the case now."

"Liar!" came the response, but not from the king. An unease built within Ludwig as though he were teetering on the edge of a great precipice. He struggled to ignore the accusation, but the voice was familiar.

"This man lies," insisted the accuser. "He's the guilty one!"

Ludwig could resist no longer. He turned to see the face of Berthold emerge from the crowd. At that moment, he knew his fate was sealed. Berthold had vanished four years ago, along with a sizable treasure. He'd obviously spent his time gaining influence in Eisen. How, then, would Ludwig be able to counter the accusations that his stepbrother had been sowing for years?

"What say you to this, Lord Ludwig?" demanded the king.

Ludwig knew he should tread carefully, but the surprise of seeing his stepbrother here dredged up years of frustration he'd long kept buried. "That is quite the accusation coming from a common thief!"

"So you deny the charge?"

"Not only do I deny it, but I also call this man's reputation into question. Berthold took advantage of my father's death to rob the good people of Verfeld, filling his own purse. To add insult to injury, he absconded in the middle of the night, cleaning out my treasury as his last willful act."

"How amusing," said Diedrich. "Two men, both foreigners and relatives, no less, each accusing the other of misdeeds. I'd not expected such delightful entertainment." He rose from his seat. "But enough of this. Lord Berthold, we dismiss you from this gathering, at least for now. I would have words with your stepbrother."

Ludwig heard a growl as Berthold stomped off, but he kept his eyes on Diedrich.

"Enough of these proceedings," ordered the king. "Music!"

Hidden from view, a mandolin struck up a tune, and the room's mood immediately shifted. Voices echoed off the walls, intent on their own conversations, leaving Ludwig and Diedrich to themselves.

"There is clearly bad blood between the two of you."

"With good reason, Your Majesty," said Ludwig.

"Such enmity is of little interest to me. Your presence, on the other hand, is an affront. For years we have sent delegates to Hadenfeld, but Otto has never deigned to send any of his own representatives to us. Why did he send you, and why now?"

"There are rumours of war," said Ludwig.

"And does he always place such faith in rumours?"

"He is a king, Majesty. He cannot afford to do otherwise."

"Do not treat me as a fool," said Diedrich. "I know it is the right, nay the duty, of a sovereign to do whatever is needed to secure the safety of his people, but his efforts are too little and far too late. Still, I wonder why he chose you, in particular, to carry that message? You are the newest baron, are you not?"

Ludwig bit back his response. The king already knew the answer, especially considering Berthold was in this court. He decided to play his part to the best of his ability, nodding slightly. "I am, Majesty. I was made a baron in ninety-five."

"I'm told you spent some time in the north?"

"I did, first as a mercenary, then in service to Lord Wulfram Haas, Baron of Regnitz."

"And did this service include battle?"

"It did, Majesty, at a place called Chermingen. Are you familiar with it?"

"I can't say that I am. Who fought?"

"Andover invaded Erlingen. The duke defeated his enemy and captured their king." He noted how Diedrich stepped backwards to put more space between them.

"I thought you had the look of a warrior to you. If Otto fears invasion so much, would you not have been better employed readying your own warriors?"

"My men are ready to do their duty. They don't need me to lead them."

"So you are here, trying to impress us with your reputation. Well, it won't work." The king looked him over, his gaze lingering on the hilt of his sword. "That's an interesting weapon you have."

"A master smith forged it, Majesty. If you permit, I'll show it to you."

Diedrich nodded, and Ludwig placed his hand on the hilt. Two guards immediately rushed forward, but Diedrich raised his hand to halt them in their tracks.

Ludwig slowly withdrew the sword, then handed it over, hilt first. The king took it, holding it up to examine the cross guard. "A fine weapon, although I must say, the pommel is an unusual design. Is it foreign?"

"Calabrian," said Ludwig.

"Is that one of the Petty Kingdoms?"

"That depends on your definition of a Petty Kingdom. It lies on the western coast of the Shimmering Sea but is now part of the Halvarian Empire."

"Ah, so a conquered people, then. How, might I ask, did this come into your possession?"

"The smith who created it is descended from those who fled the occupation. Her father is also a master smith."

"Her? Are you telling me a woman created this?"

"Yes."

"Perhaps I should invite her to come and forge weapons for my own troops?"

"You'd have a hard time doing so," said Ludwig, "as she no longer works as a smith. She took up Holy Vows."

"From smith to lay sister. How disappointing."

"Not a lay sister, a Temple Knight."

King Diedrich stared, clearly interested in learning more yet reluctant to admit it. He handed back the blade. "An interesting story, if it's even true."

Ludwig elected to remain quiet, for to his mind, arguing with the king would accomplish little.

"You intrigue me," said Diedrich. "That does not, however, mean I agree with your presence here as one of Otto's lackeys. I shall consider speaking with you in the future, but for the present, I'll keep you under guard in guest quarters. Now, off with you. I have more pressing business to attend to."

Ludwig bowed. "Of course, Your Majesty."

A pair of guards moved closer to keep an eye on him, but if they were to take him somewhere, they made no indication of it.

"So, you are Lord Ludwig."

He turned to see a man of similar age to himself. "I'm afraid you have the advantage of me, sir."

"Yet we have so much in common." The fellow grinned. "I am Lord Emmett Kuhn, Baron of Dornbruck."

"Baron? Doesn't your father claim that honour?"

"And so he did until early last year. It seems the winter got the better of him. Mind you, he'd been in ill health for some time." He lowered his voice. "Might I ask how Lady Alexandra fares?"

"I'm afraid I have little information on that score. Since my marriage, the family has had nothing to do with me."

"Yes, I suppose I should've foreseen that eventuality. Do you know if she is still unwed?"

"I've had no news to the contrary," said Ludwig. "I would be pleased to convey a message to her should we meet again."

Lord Emmett smiled. "I'll have to give that some consideration. At this point, a letter might prove burdensome should it fall into the wrong hands."

"Then a verbal message?"

"If that is acceptable, although I need some time to gather my thoughts."

A woman came closer, threading her arm into that of Lord Emmett. "Aren't you going to introduce us, Emmett?"

The fellow blushed. "This is Lady Mina Stormwind, court mage to King Diedrich."

Upon hearing her name, Ludwig was instantly on guard. "Lady Stormwind, you say? Unless I miss my guess, that makes you a Water Mage."

She smiled, displaying perfect white teeth. "I see you are familiar with those of my line."

"What can I say? The Stormwinds' power is renowned throughout the Petty Kingdoms."

"Yet not at the court of Harlingen. Something we must rectify going forward."

"Have you been here long?" asked Ludwig.

"Almost a decade, but time passes quickly in such places."

"She is one of the king's closest advisors," said Lord Emmett. "He seeks her opinions on a wide range of subjects."

"And here I thought her only a mage?" said Ludwig.

"It is a common misconception," the woman said. "The Volstrum graduates are well-trained, and not only in magic."

"The Volstrum?"

"The name of their academy," said Lord Emmett. "It lies up north somewhere."

"Yes," added Lady Mina, "in Karslev, to be exact. Do you know it?"

"I'm afraid I don't," said Ludwig. "Is that anywhere near Reinwick?"

"Karslev lies within the Kingdom of Ruzhina, on the eastern coast of the Great Northern Sea."

"Then how is it you find yourself here?"

"Some time ago, King Ruger requested the family send a representative." She removed her arm from Emmett and moved close enough to Ludwig that the scent of her perfume filled his nostrils. "King Otto could do the same, you know. All it would take would be a request bearing the king's seal."

"And to whom would he send it?"

"To any court that counts a Stormwind amongst its advisors."

"Including this one?"

She smiled. Ludwig found it unsettling in light of what Charlaine had revealed.

"Were circumstances different," she said, "I would be most pleased to forward such a request myself, but I fear, at present, King Diedrich might take such an act as an insult, if not outright treason."

"Sorry. I'm not sure I understand? Do you work for this family of yours or King Diedrich?"

"Both, if you must know. I am a member of the Stormwind family, yet I am currently in service to the King of Neuhafen. You might say the terms of my employment are not unlike those of a mercenary company like the Grim Defenders."

"You seem to know a lot about me," said Ludwig.

"I make it my business to learn as much about the nobles of Hadenfeld as possible, along with those of our other neighbours."

"So you're an information broker?"

"Of sorts, yes. Take you, for example. We've been following your progress for some time. Especially after your visit to Reinwick."

"Now why, I wonder, would that interest you?"

"You distinguished yourself," said Mina. "First, performing a heroic act in battle at Chermingen, then ingratiating yourself with King Otto. All within a very small span of time as well. Very few nobles become the favourite so quickly."

"Favourite?" said Ludwig. "It appears your infallible source of information isn't perfect. The king is a relative of mine. That's why he trusts me to represent him."

She glanced at Lord Emmett, then lowered her voice. "Don't think you can get away with anything here. I'm fully aware of the secret messages passed between you two. King Ruger may have looked the other way at communications between our realms, but Diedrich certainly won't."

"Are you threatening us?"

"No. Merely warning you that things are about to change quite dramatically. Whether that turns out to be in your favour or not largely depends on your actions over the next few days."

She stepped back, bowing to each in turn. "Now, if you'll excuse me, my lords, there are others I must visit." Her eyes locked with Ludwig's. "Perhaps we shall meet again, Lord Ludwig. I would very much like to converse with you in a more intimate location." And with that, Lady Mina Stormwind left them.

"You must be careful around her," warned Lord Emmett. "She is not to be trusted."

"She seemed quite comfortable with you. Is there something you need to tell me?"

"Whatever do you mean?"

"Have you two been getting to know each other?"

Lord Emmett blushed. "No, of course not."

"Yet her actions indicate otherwise."

The Neuhafen lord lowered his voice. "She's like that with everyone. You know the old saying, a little flattery goes a long way."

"Intriguing," said Ludwig, "but I'm still unsure what she does here in Eisen. Is she the king's advisor, or does she work for this Volstrum she spoke of?"

Emmett shrugged. "Who can say? Maybe a little of both. Whoever she works for, she's far more powerful than the usual court mage."

"And you have experience with mages, do you?"

"Not personally, but I heard my father speak of other courts. What about you? Any experience with mages?"

"Yes. A man named Linden Herzog, who unfortunately died getting me into Regnitz Keep."

"I'm sorry to hear that. Was he a Water Mage like Lady Mina?"

"No," said Ludwig. "An Earth Mage."

"Those are rare at courts."

"Why is that?"

"They prefer living in the wild, and most rulers have little use for unsophisticated country types."

"Are Water Mages any better?"

"You forget," said Emmett, "Lady Mina is a Stormwind. She's much more than just a mage."

"So she delighted in telling me, but are they really all that different from other spellcasters?"

"Let's put it this way: All the major courts of the Petty Kingdoms seek a Stormwind, yet they're Water Mages. I'm not trying to be facetious here, but what use is Water Magic to a country like Neuhafen? Are we to presume she can drown Hadenfeld by flooding the rivers? No mage is that powerful. No, she's here because of the influence she wields."

"Are you suggesting she controls the king?"

"I'm sure the relationship is mutually beneficial, although, for the life of me, I can't see what she gets out of this arrangement."

"I'm surprised to hear you say that," said Ludwig. "Surely, as a noble of Neuhafen, you'd be glad for her presence, if only to bolster your kingdom's power."

"I have no quarrel with Hadenfeld," said Emmett, "and would much prefer to see closer ties between our respective peoples than this constant threat of war. Ultimately, all this animosity will get us nowhere except into an early grave."

"You may be right. I'm beginning to fear Otto has sent me on a fool's errand."

"It is never foolish to try to avoid war."

"Perhaps," said Ludwig, "but to do so at the risk of one's own life seems very reckless indeed."

"Yes, you're right, but we are mere barons, doomed to follow our respective sovereigns to the end of our days."

His words rang true, but Ludwig needed to consider if Emmett spoke them in earnest. The fellow held Mina Stormwind in no high regard, yet here he was in Eisen, gathering to pay homage to King Diedrich. Homage Ludwig knew could only lead to war.

"Lord Ludwig?"

Ludwig was shaken from his reverie when the two guards drew closer and demanded his attention.

"Time to go?" he asked.

"Indeed, Lord."

34

INFLUENCE

SPRING 1100 SR

Ludwig lay on his bed, contemplating his next move. King Diedrich hadn't seen him since his arrival two days ago. True, they'd fed him and housed him in a room rather than a dungeon, but the king's silence was not encouraging.

Otto had made it plain he did not desire war, yet the longer Ludwig stayed in Eisen, the more likely such a thing seemed inevitable. He gave some thought to the politics of Neuhafen, in particular, who was really in charge.

Charlaine had warned him about the Stormwinds, but who was using whom? Was Mina Stormwind controlling the king somehow, or was it the other way around?

He shook his head, trying to make sense of it all. He was forced to ask himself whom he trusted. Of all the people he'd ever met, only a handful warranted his complete trust. There were Cyn and Sig and even Father Vernan, although he'd yet to mention the letter from Charlaine.

Charlaine—the very name still brought warmth to his heart. Of all those within his inner circle, she was the one he trusted most. She could've kept her suspicions to herself but chose to alert him to possible danger. The thought struck him that maybe she was trying to manipulate him, much as Mina Stormwind was, but he quickly dismissed the idea. Charlaine was a Temple Knight, one who truly believed in her vocation. She would never lie to further her own ends.

His logic began with her. If all the Stormwinds served this family, it stood to reason they sanctioned the trouble in the north. That, perhaps, was the most disturbing news of all, for Larissa Stormwind had aided the

Halvarians. Did that mean Mina Stormwind was also in league with the empire? If she wasn't, it would make little difference, but if she were, what was the family's interest in the state of affairs between Hadenfeld and Neuhafen?

Hadenfeld was considered a Middle Kingdom, meaning it was quite some distance from the border of Halvaria. It was also relatively small, or was it? He suddenly remembered Hadenfeld used to be one of the largest of all the Petty Kingdoms before the civil war. Was that the secret? Did Halvaria want Hadenfeld and Neuhafen reunited for some reason?

It was an odd hypothesis unless the empire itself sought help in over-running the Continent? The thought sent a chill down his spine. He stood, then began pacing, his mind now in a whirlwind.

Everyone knew the empire would come one day, but most saw it as decades away, perhaps even centuries. Was it possible they sought to move sooner? Or maybe it wasn't allies they wanted, but the mutual annihilation of two armies? The constant risk of war had convinced both kingdoms to maintain large armies. Did they see that as a threat?

The rebellion that led to Neuhafen's founding failed to take over the entire kingdom, splintering it into two realms. Left decimated by the battle that decided the outcome, a war between them had never been considered a serious threat until now.

A knock pulled Ludwig from his musings.

"Who's there?" he called out.

"Mina Stormwind," came the reply.

He opened the door to the Water Mage standing there with a bottle in one hand, and two pewter cups in the other. "I thought you might like some refreshment."

His first impulse was to refuse, but then he realized this was a chance to learn more about what was happening here. He moved aside. "Come in and make yourself comfortable."

She entered, not even deigning to look at the guards outside the door. She glanced around the room before placing the cups on a small table, then poured the wine. "I hope you don't mind a red?" She handed him a cup.

Ludwig sniffed it, noting its heady aroma.

"It's perfectly safe," she assured him with a mischievous grin. "It's not poisoned, I assure you."

He took a sip. "Not bad, but a little on the heavy side."

"Are you an expert in such things?"

"No. These days, my tastes tend more to a good ale."

"Is that a custom you adopted as a mercenary?"

"Yes, although not the only one."

"You intrigue me," said Mina. "Could it be that there's a civilized man beneath that rough exterior?"

"You think me rough?"

"Only in the best possible way." She moved nearer, her hand gripping her cup. "Do you find my countenance pleasing?"

"I beg your pardon?"

She stepped closer still, her eyes staring up into his. "I asked if you found me attractive?"

He had no words. There was no denying she was pleasing to the eye. Yet, the more he stared at her, the plainer she became, as if the allure of power was all that made her appear glamorous.

"No," he replied, watching her stare turn icy at his admission. She was here for a reason. She'd storm out if he was wrong, but she'd try another tactic if he was right.

She backed up a step and took a sip of wine. "You are a most interesting individual, Ludwig of Verfeld. Few men have resisted my charms."

"And yet you're still here. What is it you want, Mina?"

"To give you a chance."

"At?"

"Surviving this war."

"Why would you care? You work for King Diedrich. Surely he wants precisely the opposite?"

"My desires do not always align with his."

"Your desires or your family's?"

"They are the same thing," replied the mage. "For Saint's sake, Ludwig. Surely you know Otto will lose this war. It's inevitable. Wouldn't you prefer to be on the winning side?"

"By betraying my king? I think not."

"And if I could make your side the winner?"

Ludwig caught his breath, for this was precisely what he hoped for—a chance to learn her real motive. "Go on," he urged. "I'm listening."

"The animosity raging between Hadenfeld and Neuhafen can only be satiated by the spilling of blood."

"And yet you now propose to help Otto at the expense of Neuhafen. Why?"

"In the end," said Mina, "peace is what's important, not the person who delivers it."

"You would support Otto in the war against your master?"

"King Diedrich is not my master; he is my employer. Such relationships are... fleeting at best."

"So, you're proposing to change sides? How much would that cost us?"

"You think me so mercenary? Let me put your mind at rest. I am not offering this over a need for coins but to bring peace to a troubled land."

"At the end of a sword?"

"If Otto were to strike now before Neuhafen has gathered its warriors, ultimate victory would be his."

"So I am to convince my king to cross the border on your word alone? I think not."

"Don't be a fool, Ludwig."

"Rather a fool than the man who led the army of Hadenfeld to disaster."

"Disaster? I'm giving you a chance at a glorious victory!"

"No, you're not. You want me to go back and convince Otto to invade. King Diedrich will wait until half our army is across the river to launch a counterattack and slaughter us. Then, you could simply march to Harlingen and install Diedrich as the ruler of a rebuilt Hadenfeld, assuming you don't continue using the name Neuhafen."

"You're making a big mistake. One word from me and Diedrich will have you executed."

"I see. So now we're progressing from words to threats? It won't work with me, Mina Stormwind, so I suggest you save it for another day."

She downed the rest of her wine before moving back to the table to place it gently down. "Very well, but don't say I didn't warn you. I shall leave you now, but feel free to drink the wine. It may not be the ale you so covet, but at least you have the luxury of enjoying it at your leisure. I doubt that will be the case for much longer."

She left the room, leaving the door open in her wake. Ludwig listened as her footsteps receded, and then a heavier set of boots approached. Lord Emmett appeared in the doorway, his attention still on the figure heading down the hall. "Was that Lady Mina?"

"It was," said Ludwig. "Come in." He closed the door behind his guest.

"Anything I should know about?"

"That depends. Where do you stand on this looming war?"

"To tell the truth, I'm not overly thrilled by the idea."

"Don't all the nobles of Neuhafen support their king?"

Ludwig's visitor paused for a moment, considering his words. "Diedrich is not someone you want to get on the bad side of."

"Meaning?"

"Let's just say he has a firm grip on his power here in Neuhafen."

"Are you suggesting he's forcing you to go to war?"

"I suppose that's one way of interpreting it. Ludwig, you need to under-stand that the people of Neuhafen had been fed hatred towards Hadenfeld for decades. It doesn't help that Otto still rules—the very same man who foiled the rebellion."

"Yet some might argue the rebellion succeeded. After all, you created your own kingdom."

"Yes, but that was never the intent. Our predecessors wanted all of Hadenfeld, not just the eastern portion."

"Neuhafen is larger by far."

"True," said Emmett, "but most of that land is inhospitable."

"I've read that, but is it truly as bad as they say?"

"Yes, I've seen it myself. You and I are lucky for the forests in our lands are relatively easy to navigate. However, the area east of Eisen gets very hilly, not to mention the undergrowth, making it almost impossible to travel through. They also say it's inhabited by all sorts of things that would like nothing better than to see us dead."

"Such as?"

"Wild animals, mostly, but there've been reports of savage Orc tribes."

"Have you seen those yourself?"

"No," said Emmett. "I confess I have not, but I have seen enormous creatures in the sky, enough to convince me to turn around and leave."

"Surely you're not suggesting dragons?"

"You cannot deny their existence, Ludwig. We know the Kurathians employ them."

"Only to defend their islands, and even then, we only have their word for it. Do you honestly believe such creatures exist?"

"Don't you?"

"To be honest, I haven't given it much thought. I know the legends must come from somewhere."

"But?"

Ludwig chuckled. "Well, how would such a large creature fly? Its wings would need to be enormous."

"They could use magic?"

"Oh yes? Next, you're going to tell me that donkeys can talk."

"You shouldn't be so quick to dismiss the accounts. True, dragons haven't been seen on the Continent for centuries, but that doesn't mean they don't still exist. The forest in East Neuhafen covers an immense area. By the standards of the Petty Kingdoms, you could hide an entire realm in there."

"Perhaps there are even Elves?" suggested Ludwig.

"Now you're mocking me."

"I'm sorry, but it all sounds so preposterous. Then again, up north, they all fear the return of the Old Kingdom. As if that's ever going to happen."

"You mean Therengia? Yes, I've heard that too. My father used to tell me horror stories about that place. They say it was a brutal empire."

"I doubt there's much truth in that," said Ludwig. "The victors always dictate what stories survive. I've read many accounts of their history, and none of it suggests anything of the type. Likely, fear tainted his stories."

"That would make sense," said Emmett. "After all, his grandmother came from the north. It was all part of an arranged marriage, which we still practice today. I worry King Diedrich wants me to marry some princess from Abelard."

Ludwig chuckled. "I'm married to a woman from Reinwick."

"A princess?"

"No, the daughter of a baron, Charlotte by name."

"And do you love her?"

"I wouldn't necessarily say love, but I've come to hold her in great affection. She gave me a son, but I fear her health will not allow us more children."

"I'm sorry to hear that," said Emmett. "You know, I would've been happy to enter an arranged marriage only a few short years ago, but then I met Alexandra. Had circumstances been different, I would've pressed my suit, but I'm afraid the enmity between our kingdoms is too great an obstacle to overcome."

"Life is cruel," said Ludwig. "Especially when love is ripped from your arms."

"Spoken like one whose heart has been broken."

"It's too late for me, but perhaps not for you."

"What are you suggesting?"

"Consider this," said Ludwig. "This war is coming, whether we want it or not. You and I both know this will end no differently than the previous one. Neuhafen will march on Harlingen, and Otto will make a stand outside the city. The last time that happened, the two armies were so closely matched that it ended in a stalemate."

"A stalemate that allowed the birth of Neuhafen."

"True, but this time we're expecting the attack. Your king has lost the advantage of surprise. Now it's only a question of who can inflict more casualties—you or us."

"Our army is larger."

"Perhaps, but we have the advantage of defending. You must garrison the areas you take while we can gather everything we need in one place."

"You make a compelling argument, but Diedrich won't listen. He's intent on taking Hadenfeld and reuniting the land."

"I know," said Ludwig. "But all I'm asking is that you keep an open mind.

When the dust settles, it'll be time to negotiate. You are, by my account, a moderate compared to your king. That could serve you well once the fighting is done."

"Neighbourly advice?"

"Well, our lands do share the same border."

"So they do," said Emmett. "And as a neighbour, I assure you no warriors of mine will invade your lands, although I cannot make the same promise regarding the rest of your kingdom."

"Understood, and I appreciate your candour. I, in turn, assure you that none of my men will enter yours."

Lord Emmett's gaze flicked to the table. "Perhaps we should drink on it?"

"An excellent idea." Ludwig gathered up Mina's cup and refilled it. He passed it to his guest, then topped up his own. "To neighbours."

They both drank deeply.

"A nice vintage," noted Emmett. "Where did you come by it?"

"It was a gift from Lady Mina."

His guest chuckled. "And you didn't stop to consider it might be poisoned?"

"She drank it as well, from the exact cup you now hold."

"Well then, you can say what you like about the woman, but she has good taste when it comes to wines."

"I sensed earlier you distrust her," said Ludwig. "Might I ask why?"

"I question her motives."

"She works for the king, doesn't she?"

"She does," said Emmett. "At least in theory, but like anyone else who spends their time at court, she has her own motives."

"Such as?"

"I wish I knew. She's skilled at deflecting a conversation and reveals little about such things."

"Little implies you learned something?"

"She has a lot of connections in foreign courts and used them to help Neuhafen build alliances. None who'd commit to helping us retake Hadenfeld, but if we were attacked, aid would soon be on the way."

"And you assume we have no allies?"

"Oh, Diedrich knows all about your agreements, but he's gambling we'll take Harlingen before your allies can muster."

"And if he fails?"

"Then alliances shift their armies around, and war spreads across the Continent like a wildfire."

"Do you believe that could be Mina's intention?"

Emmet laughed. "Why in the name of the Saints would you even think such a thing? That's absurd."

"Is it?"

"Of course it is. Look at it from a practical side. How could she possibly profit from such a war?"

Ludwig wanted to mention Halvaria, but something told him to keep it to himself. "It was mere speculation on my part," he said instead. "Ignore the ramblings of a desperate man."

"Desperate? Why would you say that?"

"I'm here to prevent a war that everyone wants. If that's not the very definition of desperate, I don't know what is."

"I suppose I never looked at it that way, but you never know; stranger things have happened. Look at the Saints. They brought about peace in the Holy Land when everyone thought war was coming."

"I am no Saint," said Ludwig, "and this is no Holy Land."

"Truer words were never spoken. I regret that you and I find ourselves on opposite sides in this approaching conflict. In another time or place, we could've been friends."

"We are friends if only fleeting ones. In any case, I thank you for the visit, Emmett. At the very least, you have kept my trip from becoming a complete disaster."

"I might remind you that your duty is not yet over. You may still get another audience with King Diedrich. Perhaps you'll change his mind, and there'll be peace after all?"

"You and I both know that's extremely unlikely. Still, I'll press Otto's case if given a chance, but I fear my words will fall on deaf ears. Neuhafen is on the road to war, and nothing will alter its course."

"I think you have the right of it. I only hope that Diedrich doesn't take your words personally. I hate to say it, but he can have a bit of a temper at times, and now he's king, there is little to hold him in check."

"Any advice?"

"Yes, watch your words and avoid raising your voice—he is easily angered. Thankfully, you'll be seeing him in full view of his court, so he'll want to project the image of a wise and thoughtful king. That performance, however, will only go so far."

"Anything else you can suggest?"

"Yes, pray like your life depends on it."

35

PLEA

SPRING 1100 SR

A ll was deathly quiet in the room, save for the sounds of Ludwig's boots upon the marble floor. The barons of Neuhafen, along with their captains and knights, stood watching, their armour gleaming in the torchlight. King Diedrich sat straight-backed on his throne; his regal countenance projected power to all who had come to witness the encounter. Ludwig halted three paces from the king, bowing deeply.

"Your Majesty," he began. "Once more, I offer greetings from His Majesty, King Otto of Hadenfeld. Long have we been at peace. Let us not now wander from that position, but continue as we have for decades, in peace and tranquility."

"Peace?" replied Diedrich. "You dare to speak to me of peace? Otto is a tyrant who keeps his people enslaved under his merciless hand. There is no peace for the denizens of Hadenfeld, only endless suffering. Decades ago, a handful of nobles stood up to your oppressive king, trying to bring freedom to those he sought to enslave. The war was long, and though we failed to take the Throne, we earned the right to live free of such rule. Now, the time has come to free our brothers and sisters, to extend to them the same freedoms that we of Neuhafen enjoy."

Diedrich paused, letting his gaze wander the room. His audience was enthralled—none daring to interrupt.

"This man," continued the king, "came here not to beg for forgiveness but to threaten us anew. This shows how desperate and despicable a king Otto is, if nothing else. Rather than come himself, he sends another to do his bidding. I say no to King Otto, no to his false peace, and no to any negotiations. Let us march forth and finish the war which started so long ago!"

The crowd erupted with applause, their cheers echoing off the walls. Though he wished it wasn't so, Ludwig knew his mission had failed. There was no turning back now, no way to stop the madness of war. An immense sadness overwhelmed him.

The king, not yet done with his display, locked eyes with Ludwig. "What say you now, lackey?"

"It is clear, Your Majesty, that the march to war has begun. I ask only that you allow me to return home that I might tell my Sovereign Lord of my failure."

Diedrich laughed. "Do you really suppose I would let you leave here alive? Otto can suffer in ignorance until my army delivers the message in person." He rose from his throne. "Guards! Seize him!"

Two men moved quickly, grabbing Ludwig's arms and forcing him to his knees. The king stepped forward until he was but an arm's length away.

"You fool!" Diedrich shouted. "Did you really believe you could come here and threaten me?"

"I did no such thing," said Ludwig. He wanted to say more, but as his mouth opened, the king slapped him across the face, his ring digging into his cheek.

"You shall pay for the insult. Kill him!"

"Your Majesty," sang out Mina Stormwind's voice. "Might I suggest an alternative to execution?"

The king's head swivelled to take in the Water Mage. "Speak," he ordered.

"The death of this individual, while unimportant in the long-term, seems a waste of your efforts."

"What are you suggesting?"

"That he die in a more eloquent manner, one which might prove entertaining to Your Majesty."

A hint of a smile crept across the king's lips. "Go on."

"Lord Ludwig is said to be an experienced warrior. Why not let him fight for his life? Surely you are not lacking for people willing to challenge him in your name?"

Diedrich's gaze wandered over the room's occupants. There was no lack of volunteers, but he stopped at one in particular, a knight, if his armour was any indication. "You, Sir Ferrand," he called out. "Will you fight for your king?"

"With pleasure." The knight stepped out from the crowd. Ludwig turned to size up his soon-to-be opponent, whose scarred face stared back with a piercing glare. The man's battle-hardened plate armour was a testament to his ability to protect the honour of his king.

"Release the prisoner," ordered Diedrich, who stepped back to give the two combatants room to manoeuvre.

Ludwig regained his feet and drew his sword, his gaze locked with his opponent's. He swung the weapon several times to loosen up his arm before slowly moving to his right, watching for any sign of attack.

Sir Ferrand pulled forth a sword, broader of blade than Ludwig's and longer by a hand span, forcing the Baron of Verfeld to consider the better reach.

The knight swung first, a wild attack slicing through the air. Though easily avoided, it gave Ludwig some concern, for his opponent quickly countered with a vicious backhand that surprised him. Thankfully, he got his blade up to block—steel met steel as the force of the blow travelled up his arm.

He backed up, trying to gain some room to move, but his foe kept at him, striking again and again. Each time Ludwig blocked, his Calabrian blade rang with the blow's ferocity. The next attack drove him back again, but at least now, Sir Ferrand was breathing hard.

Seeing his chance, Ludwig let the knight come at him, then countered with a quick jab that scraped off the man's vambrace, catching him by surprise. Ferrand went on the defensive, using his weapon to do little except block.

Another jab from Ludwig's sword pushed his opponent farther back, and then he struck high, digging into a cheek and drawing blood. Sir Ferrand screamed out in rage, immediately going on the offensive. His blade swung back and forth, all sense of discipline eradicated. Anticipating his impending victory, the onlookers cheered him on.

Ludwig, meanwhile, kept retreating, narrowly avoiding the man's vicious attacks. Constantly on the defensive, he noticed his attacker's regular and rhythmic motions, and it soon became easier to predict the next blow. He waited for one more attack, then he kicked out with all his weight behind it, striking the knight's kneecap. While it did nothing to penetrate the armour, it did snap the leg back with a horrific crack. The man fell to the floor, screaming while clutching his knee, his weapon discarded and forgotten. Ludwig quickly put the tip of his sword at his foe's neck, ready to finish him off.

"I yield," shouted Sir Ferrand.

Ludwig backed up, lowering his blade. King Diedrich stood there fuming, and for a moment, it looked as though he might still order the death of his prisoner, but then he calmed himself. "Surrender your sword, Lord Ludwig. You've earned a stay of execution."

Three guards moved in, and he passed over the blade. They seized his arms once more, binding his hands behind his back. One gave Ludwig's weapon to the king, who examined the blade with interest.

"This has done you proud this day. I thank you for the gift."

Ludwig seethed, but there was nothing he could do about it.

Diedrich moved closer, emboldened by the prisoner's restraints. "You have failed, Lord Ludwig. True, you won the right to live a little longer, but do not, for one moment, think you will ever see home again."

"So," said Ludwig. "You intend to kill me after all. So much for the word of a king."

"I lied to no one. Your death will not be at my hands. It rests with the will of the Saints." He chuckled, amused by his own rantings. "Do you consider yourself a religious man?"

"I do," said Ludwig. "Saint Mathew watches over me."

"Saint Mathew? I would've thought a warrior like you would worship Saint Cunar. He, at least, appreciates a good fight. Your Saint betrays your weakness."

"My Saint will guide me to the Afterlife. You, however, are destined for a far worse fate."

"Even to the end, you threaten me. How amusing." Diedrich walked around Ludwig, taking his measure. Once in front of him again, he smiled, his voice quiet but menacing in its intensity. "You shall be taken to the Forgotten Chamber to rot away the rest of your miserable existence in darkness and solitude."

A collective gasp echoed throughout the hall, but what this foretold was beyond Ludwig's understanding.

"Take him away," ordered the king, "and let no one ever again utter his name in my presence."

Guards dragged Ludwig from the great hall, one holding each of his arms. Behind him followed a guard captain, his sword drawn, its point pressing not so lightly against his back. A fourth led them, stopping in a hallway only long enough to equip himself with a lantern.

They then made their way through a series of corridors, descending stairs twice, moisture forming on the walls as the air grew cold and damp. The ceiling lowered as they entered a tunnel, forcing them to crouch to avoid banging their heads.

The tunnel opened into a circular room, no more than five paces in diameter. In the centre sat a large iron grate locked in place with a massive padlock. Their guide set down the lantern and produced a key from around his neck. He struggled to undo the padlock.

"It's rusty," the man explained, although no one asked him. "Hasn't been used in some time." The guard breathed a sigh of relief as the lock finally sprang open.

The captain stepped back, sword drawn lest his prisoner make a bid for freedom. The remaining two guards released his bonds, then the captain stood before him. "Would you like to take a moment to pray?"

"For what?" asked Ludwig.

The captain shrugged. "Salvation? Once you go down that hole, there's no coming back."

Ludwig peered into the inky blackness but saw nothing. "What is this? Am I to be drowned?"

"Oh no. It's quite safe down there, as long as you don't mind being entombed."

Panic surged through him at the guard's words. "Entombed?"

"Of course. If you prefer, my men can kill you now. It's not as if the king will ever know. You're already as good as dead to him and everyone else at court."

"I don't suppose I could talk you out of this?"

"No," said the captain, "but I guess you could try to fight your way out, in which case we'd have to kill you outright. That's what I'd do if I were you."

"I'm still not sure I understand."

"It's simple, really. We lower you down into that hole. It's basically just a deep pit, but there's no room to sit or lie down, only stand. Then we'll seal you up inside."

"For how long?"

"Why, forever. You'll be nothing but bones the next time we see you."

"Then perhaps I'll take you up on that offer to let me pray?"

"Of course. We're not barbarians."

Ludwig knelt, closing his eyes and placing his hands before him. "Blessed Saint Mathew," he began, "watch over me this day and protect me in my time of need. Give me strength that I might endure what is to come and the serenity to accept my fate. Guide me, oh blessed Saint, that I may pass to the Afterlife knowing I followed thy teachings to the best of my ability."

He stood only to find his legs were shaking.

The captain chuckled. "Don't worry, there's worse to come. Most prisoners would've pissed themselves by now." He directed a guard to retrieve a rope tied with a loop at the end. "Be a decent chap and hold on to that loop. Once we lower you down, you can let go."

"And if I don't?"

"Makes no difference to me. We just toss the other end of the rope in with you. It's not like you could use it for anything. Sooner or later, we'll get it back."

He nodded at a guard, who lifted the grate and pushed Ludwig to the edge before offering him the end of the rope.

"Any last words?"

A calm enveloped Ludwig. He looked at each of his captors in turn. "I forgive you," he said, "for you know not what you do."

His words unnerved one of them, for he turned pale.

"Get on with it!" ordered the captain.

The pale guard quickly recovered, pushing Ludwig forward slightly. "Off you go, then."

Ludwig sat on the edge of the hole, peering down into the darkness.

"Got a good hold of the rope?" asked the guard.

"Yes."

"Excellent."

The captain nodded, and one of the guards pushed Ludwig from behind. He fell the first few feet before the rope went taut, slamming him against the side. Slowly, they lowered him down, the only light coming from above, where someone held the lantern to monitor his descent.

The pit narrowed as he descended, his elbows soon scraping against stone. When he hit bottom, his foot slipped on something slimy, causing his knee to buckle and crash against the side of the pit, sending a spasm of pain up one leg. He let out a grunt, letting go of the rope to feel the injury.

"Haul it up, boys. Our job here is almost done," a voice echoed down from above.

Ludwig looked up, spotting three faces staring down at him. The rope slowly went up and over the lip, disappearing along with the faces. They placed the grating over the top, the screeching of metal on metal echoing down to Ludwig below.

"There we are, all locked up nice and tight. Come along, lads. We're done here."

The light above faded slowly, plunging Ludwig into darkness. He reached out, trying to ascertain the limits of his cell, but his fingers contacted stone almost immediately. He felt to either side before turning around as best he could under the cramped conditions.

His cell, or more appropriately, shaft, was barely wide enough to turn around without scraping his shoulders against the sides. The surrounding stone was cold and damp and would soon sap his strength, then he would likely die as his body lost its heat.

His foot struck something, and he attempted to pick up whatever it was, but hit his head against the shaft. He cursed, then tried using the top of his boot to lift up his discovery. It took him several tries, but finally, he grasped it. Long and smooth, it was difficult to move around without knocking it against the wall. As he gripped it in both hands, he realized he held a bone, clear evidence of the fate of his predecessor.

Panic rose within, and he fought to control it. He wanted to lash out, but such folly would only injure him, making his fate more painful. He closed his eyes and tried to pray, but the walls closed in on him. Was this some diabolical plot to crush him in darkness? He reached out with both hands only to find his prison still intact. His mind must be playing tricks on him.

Ludwig leaned back against one wall before shuffling his feet forward until they hit the far side. He could at least lock his legs in place in this manner, giving him a resting pose. He knew such comfort was fleeting, for, in time, his limbs would succumb to weakness and fatigue, but he felt like he was in control of something.

It didn't take long for the darkness to invade his soul. He wasn't afraid to die, yet the realization he would never again see his family brought him to tears. He thought back to his youth, of the dark-haired smith who'd stolen his heart, then of Charlotte, and it almost broke him. He'd treated her with dignity and respect yet denied her the very love she so rightfully deserved. She'd even given him a son, and now he would never watch him grow up to become the Baron of Verfeld.

More than any other, that thought brought him to his darkest moment. He considered bashing his head against the wall to end his misery, yet something held him back. The memories of Charlaine and her faith gave him hope. Would the Saints spare him as well? King Diedrich said his fate was in the hands of the Saints. The man had meant it as a mockery, but the darkness receded as Ludwig contemplated the king's words.

He never considered himself particularly religious, yet facing certain death, the belief that Saint Mathew watched over him filled him with an inner peace. He'd read the Book of Saint Mathew as a youth, if only because his father insisted. Now, years later, he wished he'd paid more attention to his teachings as he tried to recall what was written. Saint Mathew had been a healer, a man dedicated to using herbs and medicines to help the sick.

At first, many shunned Mathew, some even going so far as to call him out for witchcraft, but he earned their acceptance in time. His followers had spread throughout the Continent in the centuries since, bringing healing and relief to tens of thousands.

Ludwig struggled to remember more. He knew they often worked with the Sisters of Saint Agnes, and the thought brought a smile. Was he now emulating his Saint? Working with Saint Agnes to help stave off the threat of Halvaria? At that moment, a sense of clarity overcame him. He was sure Mina Stormwind was working with the empire, and their plan would plunge the entire Continent into a great war.

Passion burned in his heart, and he swore not to rest until they were defeated. He now understood his life's calling—all he needed do was escape.

36

ESCAPE
SPRING 1100 SR

Trapped in the darkness, Ludwig's breathing was the only indication that time had passed. The cold seeped into his bones while his legs went numb, but worse than the chill was the near-constant thirst.

He attempted to occupy his mind by talking, but that only worsened matters. Muscles ached, his throat burned with the dryness, and he struggled to remain upright. Crouching seemed like it might be an option, but his knees scraped along the opposite wall as soon as he tried. It was then he realized they meant for prisoners to die on their feet. He wondered how long a person could last without food or water, assuming he didn't go mad first.

Buoyed by his faith, Ludwig remained remarkably calm. The Saints had suffered, or at least some of them had. He struggled to recall their history, but it had been years since he read of their exploits.

He tried again to find a more comfortable position, his hand brushing against the stone, only to come back wet. Lifting his fingers to this mouth, he licked them, concerned lest it be blood, but all he tasted was water. In desperation, he reached out again, finding the source, then licked the stone. It wasn't much, but to him, it was a gift from the Saints. He felt around the edge, then used his fingernails to scrape away the mortar. It came loose quickly, likely due to the damp conditions, and his finger found dirt.

The discovery gave him renewed energy, and soon he was scooping out handfuls of mud. Unfortunately, it was not to last, for he struck stone, a massive boulder, one far too large for him to dislodge. However, he'd created a small hole in the wall, one sufficient to allow a place for water to pool.

His thirst now satisfied, he turned his attention to food. From what he remembered of the *Book of Saint Mathew*, it recommended occasional fasting, but only for members of the order, and even then, solely for special occasions. It also warned against doing so for longer than a few days. Naturally, fasting in the name of piety wasn't the same thing as starvation, so Ludwig suspected it would take far longer to die from lack of sustenance. It was hardly productive trying to work out precisely how long, so he focused once more on the idea of escape.

Digging his way out wasn't an option, for his fingers were already sore from what little excavation he'd completed. Even with tools, he doubted he could dislodge the stone he'd encountered, and the complete lack of light didn't help. Briefly, he considered trying to flood the pit, allowing him to float up to the top. He knew he was beneath Eisen, which sat upon the shores of a great lake, so it only made sense that the ground here was saturated. On the other hand, the tiny amount of water pooled in the hole he'd created was barely enough to sustain him, let alone allow him to float anywhere. Assuming he drank none of it, it would likely take weeks, if not months, to flood the cell. Then there was still the matter of the grate sealing the top of his prison. He would drown long before gaining the necessary height to consider dealing with the rusty padlock that lay waiting.

Time wore on. There were no days down here, no moon to mark the night, no meals to break up the sheer monotony of his existence. His mind wandered, and he imagined Verfeld growing into a mighty castle. One day, his son would become the baron. Would Frederick ever learn what happened to his father, or would he simply be lost to the annals of history?

His thoughts inevitably came to Charlotte. He'd promised to treat her with dignity and respect, and even though he'd been honest with her, he now found himself wracked with guilt. Part of him still longed for the companionship of Charlaine, but more and more, he imagined a future with Charlotte by his side. It took a while, but eventually, he realized he loved her. The conclusion shocked him, for it certainly had not been his intention. Yet here, facing almost certain death, he wanted more than anything else to see her one more time.

Others might succumb to despair at such thoughts, but not Ludwig, for they drove him to search for some means of escape. To that end, he once more felt around the close confines of his cell. The walls were made of stone but were uneven. He tried pushing his back against the wall, then placed his feet on the opposite side, the idea being to walk himself up the narrow confines. It took half a dozen attempts to find his footing, but finally, he made some progress.

In the darkness, there was no way to measure his success. He worked for what felt like an eternity until a small stone dislodged, and his foot slipped. Ludwig scrambled to grip the side of the pit, his breathing laboured.

Below him, the stone hit bottom, the delay indicating a significant drop. Strengthened by this revelation, he continued his climb, but his legs began to shake with the effort. His back, already bruised by scraping along the wall, felt damp, and he suspected it was bleeding.

He halted once more to catch his breath, but it cost him dearly, for his legs finally gave out. As he slid down, his knees scraped painfully against the wall. A sharp pain shot up his leg as his feet hit bottom, and he wondered if he might have broken his ankle. He cautiously moved his foot around, but everything appeared to be working properly.

His attempt at scaling the wall proved exhausting, and he now realized that had he reached the top, he still wouldn't have been able to get past the grate. The thought chilled him, for he'd expended considerable strength in the foolish enterprise. He must conserve what energy remained—the better to take advantage should an opportunity present itself.

Hunger gnawed at him, but he could do little about it. He prayed to Saint Mathew to occupy his mind—not to ask for deliverance but to help him bear his torment. Even at his darkest moments, he refused to surrender to despair. As long as he lived, he had hope, which gave him the strength to carry on.

A sound, ever so subtle, broke through the silence. He held his breath, not sure if his mind was imagining things. There it was again, perhaps the shuffle of feet? It grew louder, and then light flooded into his cell. Someone held a lantern above, and the flickering flame danced around his cell. He looked up, his eyes struggling to focus.

"Ludwig? Is that you?" The voice was familiar, but he couldn't place it.

"Yes," he croaked out, surprised by how weak he sounded.

"I'm going to get you out of there. Be patient."

"I can do little else."

There was a crash just before the grate above him disappeared. The figure crouched to set the lantern down before lowering the rope to him. Ludwig grasped it, the rope going taut as his rescuer began hauling him up, but the slow progress left his arms burning with the effort of holding it. He cursed himself for not tying a loop at the end, or even knotting it to make it easier to hang on to. The light grew brighter, and then the lip of the well was there, tantalizingly close.

"Grab the top," said the voice. Ludwig took hold as best he could, and then a firm hand gripped his arm, pulling him upward and onto a stone floor. He rolled over onto his back and stared up at his benefactor, Lord

Emmett, bent over with his hands on his knees, struggling to catch his breath.

"Saints alive," Emmett gasped out. "That was much harder than I imagined."

Ludwig sat up, then tried to stand, but his legs shook beneath him. "W-w-what are you doing here?"

"I couldn't let you die," said Emmett. "Not after all you did for me." He shoved some bread and a wineskin into Ludwig's hands. "Take this. You must be starved."

He wolfed it down.

"I wish it were more," continued the Baron of Dornbruck, "but I would've had a hard time smuggling a full meal out of the kitchen." He reached into a sling bag. "I also brought a fresh set of clothing for you. We can't have you traipsing through the castle looking like that."

Ludwig stripped away his soiled and blood-encrusted clothes. "What next?" he asked.

"The first step will be to get you out of the castle. Then we can worry about Eisen itself."

"Perhaps they'll think I'm still down there?"

"I doubt it. I smashed the lock to let you out, but I suppose we could throw the grate back over the top. That might buy us a little time. Has anyone come to visit you?"

"Not since they imprisoned me. Why? How much time has gone by?"

"Four days. I would've arrived sooner, but the king's been marshalling the army, and we've all had to do our part."

"So it's war, then?"

"I'm afraid so."

"Won't they notice you're missing?"

"I'm sure they will, but I shall plead illness. However, we must concentrate on getting you out of the city."

"You're not supporting the war, are you?"

"That, my friend, is a difficult question. I know war only leads to a tremendous waste of life, but I cannot shirk my duty. I swore an oath to follow Diedrich. I cannot renege on my word even though this could spell disaster for us."

"I'm not sure I understand your reasoning? You will march to war regardless of the fact you expect defeat?"

"It's not only us," said Emmett. "Our two kingdoms will wear each other down fighting, allowing one of our neighbours to march in and pick up the pieces. In the end, neither of us can win."

"Do you think we can stop them?"

"Not unless you have any ideas?"

Ludwig shook his head. "No. Diedrich has convinced himself it's time to act, and Otto won't back down. I'm afraid this will all play out on the battlefield."

"Then let us instead turn our attention to getting you out of here. Can you walk?"

"I think so, although I'm a little weak."

Emmett held out his hand and helped Ludwig to his feet. "Put your arm around me to steady yourself, but grab that lantern first. I can't carry it and you at the same time."

Ludwig held the light aloft, revealing the exit. "This way, I should think."

His rescuer chuckled. "You think? Has imprisonment so addled your mind that you see an alternate escape?" The words echoed off the walls. "Sorry. I didn't mean to insult you."

"I shan't take it personally, but let us not tarry here any longer than we must."

"You're quite eloquent for a man just newly rescued from the brink of death."

"I like to think that though my body is weak, my spirit is unbroken."

They made their way down the tunnel.

"Did you encounter any guards when you came here?" asked Ludwig.

"No. Everyone is far too busy watching the army march off. Even those supposed to be on duty are observing from the walls. After all, it's not every day the army of Neuhafen can be seen in all its glory."

They eventually reached a set of stone steps that spiralled upward.

"Hold a moment," said Emmett. "I'll go ahead and see what awaits us at the top."

Ludwig listened carefully as his benefactor's steps receded. He felt vulnerable, as weak as he was in his present state, not to mention unarmed. All it would take would be for a guard to wander by, and then he'd be doomed. From up the stairwell, he heard voices and then the sound of a scuffle. Things went quiet, then came the sound of footsteps hurriedly descending.

He glanced around, desperately looking for anything that might be used as a weapon, but there was nothing with which to defend himself. His next thought was to hide, but even that was impossible, for there was no place to do so. Instead, he was forced to wait in plain sight and accept whatever came his way. A silent prayer to Saint Mathew was all he could manage before Lord Emmett reappeared.

Ludwig let out a sigh of relief. "You had me worried there. I assume someone was at the top?"

"There was indeed, but he shall trouble us no further."

"You killed him?"

"Saints, no, but it will be some time before he awakens. Now come. We must move quickly before someone discovers him."

The guard lay at the top of the steps, slumped against the wall, a large bruise already forming on his cheek. Ludwig took the man's sword and belt, feeling safer for having a weapon in hand.

The stairs opened into a corridor just off the great hall, and for a moment, he was afraid they'd be seen.

"Don't worry," said Emmett, sensing his fear. "Everyone is outside the city getting the army underway."

"Where to now?"

"We shall cross the great hall. On the opposite side is a door leading to the stables."

"So we are to just ride out of here?"

Lord Emmett grinned. "My horse is there, and I think it is only proper that the king allows you to take yours, don't you? After all, it's the least he can do for an honoured guest."

"But surely this will get you into trouble?"

"I doubt a missing horse will pique the king's interest, especially not once the campaign had started. Now quickly, before our sleeping friend back there draws unwanted attention."

The stables were almost empty by the time they arrived. Many of the stable hands had left to accompany the army. Those who remained appeared ill-disposed to lend any help. Their behaviour worked to Ludwig and Emmett's advantage, allowing them to saddle their mounts in peace.

They rode out into the city as if nothing unusual had occurred. Most of the townsfolk ignored them, but as the sun broke from behind the clouds, more and more took an interest in Ludwig.

He looked down at his clothes, quickly realizing blood had seeped through his tunic. "It appears I'm drawing attention."

"Yes," agreed Emmett. "We must look after your wounds and get you another change of clothes." He came to a halt and looked around, getting his bearings. "I have a cousin with a house near here. We shall see what they can do for us."

"Won't that put him in danger?"

"I don't believe we have a choice. If you turn up at the city gates looking like that, we'll both end up back in that pit."

"And your cousin?"

"He'll be off with the army, but his wife will look after us."

"How can you be so sure?"

"Liesel is all about family. She couldn't give two figs for this war."

"Figs?"

"Yes. You know, the fruit?"

"I've never had them. Do they grow here in Neuhafen?"

"They do, although I'm told they're more common down by the Shimmering Sea. Liesel is from Corassus, you see."

Emmett led them down a side street, quickening his pace.

"Corassus," mused Ludwig. "That's a city-state, isn't it?"

"It is, and the home to the Holy Fleet. You know, they had a large-scale battle a few years back. They defeated Halvaria; at least that's what they're telling everyone."

"It's true."

"How would you know?"

"It just so happens I know someone who was there."

Emmett turned to look at him, his eyebrows raised. "You do?"

"Yes, but now is not the time to speak of such things. Hopefully, when this war is over, we'll have a chance to sit down and talk more of it."

"You mean after I captured you on the battlefield?"

Ludwig grinned. "Or I, you."

"Fair enough." Emmett looked ready to say more but then stopped and stared at the house to his right. "This is it." He dismounted and led his horse down an alleyway. "There's a stable out back."

The sound of horseshoes on the cobblestones drew the servants' attention, and a pair of young men quickly arrived to take their mounts. A woman's voice could be heard as they handed over the reins. "Do my eyes deceive me, or is that Emmett Kuhn I see standing before me?"

Emmett turned, a large grin spreading across his features. "Cousin Liesel, so good to see you!"

The woman was slightly older than her cousin, enough to show a few streaks of grey in her hair, but the wrinkles around her eyes told of someone who enjoyed life.

Emmett moved closer, embracing the woman. She squeezed him tightly, patting him on the back before holding him at arm's length. "By the Saints, you look much older than last I saw you. How long has it been?"

"Far too long, in my opinion, but the duty of running a barony has kept me busy."

"I was so sorry to hear of your father's passing. He was a good man." She turned her attention to Ludwig. "And who do we have here? Don't tell me you're now picking people up off the streets?"

"No. This is Ludwig, a friend of mine. I'm afraid he was set upon by ruffians. I wondered if we might impose on your hospitality to allow him to get cleaned up?"

"Of course. Come inside, the both of you. I'll have the servants fetch you some food. Are you on your way to join the army?"

"Eventually, but I have some business to attend to first."

"And would this business have something to do with your friend here?"

"Best if you didn't know."

She paused only a moment before continuing. "Very well. I shall ask no further questions." She led them into a dining room. "Have a seat, and I'll send in some food. As for you"—she looked at Ludwig—"we'll need to find you a change of clothes. I'll also provide some soap and water so you can wash up. I suppose I should fetch you some bandages too. Saints know you can't go out looking like that." She disappeared through the doorway.

"She's quite the woman," said Ludwig. "Does she always take charge that way?"

"Oh yes. You should see her at family get-togethers. She always has to be the one in charge." Emmett leaned in closer, lowering his voice. "And she doesn't like people poking their noses where they don't belong, so you can rest assured she'll say naught of our visit."

It was noon by the time they departed. Now clean and sporting a freshly trimmed beard, Ludwig looked nothing like the vagabond who'd escaped imprisonment. This new guise left him so confident that they rode without fear of discovery, no longer drawing the attention of passersby.

The soldiers at the gates were the last obstacle, but they were uninterested in the duo, waving them through without so much as a second glance. Horses had churned up the fields beyond, evidence that the army had left their encampment. The trail led westward along the road, although perhaps path was a better description, considering its poor condition.

Emmett brought his horse to a halt. "I'm afraid this is where I must leave you. Down that road is the Royal Army, and my own companies need their baron. I wish you a safe journey home, Ludwig, although I can't, in good conscience, wish you a victory. Rest assured, if we do happen to win this war, I shall do my best to ensure you are treated with dignity and respect."

"If you do win this war, I shan't be remaining in Hadenfeld," said Ludwig. "I'll seek employment elsewhere, likely as a mercenary."

"Then maybe you'll end up serving Neuhafen after all? I know King Diedrich has larger plans for a reunited kingdom."

"And here I thought this was about old grievances. You must tell me more."

"Not now. We don't have the time. In any case, you must head west, back to Verfeld, while I go to Arnsbach."

"Arnsbach?"

"Yes. It's across the river from Hasdorf and possesses the only bridge into Hadenfeld. I'm surprised you didn't know that."

"Oh, I know Hasdorf," said Ludwig. "It's the other side that I'm unfamiliar with."

37

FLIGHT

SUMMER 1100 SR

Ludwig's original intention was to head due west until he found the river, then cross over into his lands. The more he thought about it, though, the more he became convinced that such was not the best course of action.

He decided to follow in the wake of the army of Neuhafen, to try and learn as much about its makeup as possible. Once they drew closer to Arnsbach, he would find a ford and cross over into Hadenfeld, confident his newfound knowledge could be put to good use.

He tried to determine how large an army Diedrich might've raised as he rode along. In Hadenfeld, the king had called upon his barons to increase their garrisons in recent years. If one assumed they'd followed his own increase at Verfeld, that was likely to mean two hundred men, not including any militia that might accompany them. Seven barons meant at least fourteen hundred men, possibly double that with a poorly armed militia. On top of that were Otto's own forces, of which at least one hundred and fifty were knights and a similar number of trained footmen.

It was reasonable to assume King Diedrich had similar numbers at his disposal, but he had no idea if Diedrich had his own personal warriors or if he employed mercenaries, as Lord Emmett seemed to imply.

They'd been planning this invasion for some time, leading Ludwig to believe they numbered more than Hadenfeld. At the Battle of Chermingen, the Duke of Erlingen fielded nearly two thousand men, but that was on relatively short notice. Neuhafen, on the other hand, had been plotting this for years. It was imperative he find out as much as possible before returning home.

He caught up to the army at the end of the second day but elected to avoid any direct contact. He camped up the road, scouting out the enemy from a distance, trying to count their fires. This proved too difficult, especially considering the number of guards posted as pickets. Still, he discovered, almost by accident, how easy it was to pass by these people without notice.

As the army approached Dornbruck, Ludwig decided to try something more daring. He chose the early morning hours, before sunrise, to infiltrate the camp. Getting in was surprisingly easy. He wandered amongst the warriors, avoiding the nobles and their personal retinues lest they recognize him.

He soon discovered the army of Neuhafen shared the same general organization as that of Erlingen. Each noble commanded their own warriors, effectively dividing the camp into districts. Those under the king's direct command were stationed in the centre, the barons' pavilions within easy reach.

Ludwig's time as a mercenary served him well, and he found it simple enough to blend in. It was odd to think that he, a noble, could so easily fit in with enemy warriors. But then again, all were men from Hadenfeld, or at least they would've been had they not rebelled all those years ago.

Adding to the charade was the fact that everyone here spoke the same dialect. Thus, he chatted as he went, sharing stories of past deeds and feigning eagerness to take vengeance on Hadenfeld.

It soon became evident that this army was similar in size to his homeland's. However, what differed was their quality. King Diedrich's army wore more armour, and even their lighter spearmen were better trained than his own Verfeld militia. When it came time for these two armies to face each other, he feared Neuhafen might gain the upper hand.

He kept up his meanderings night after night, becoming a familiar face amongst the warriors. He called himself Armon, a common enough name and one they accepted without question. In this guise, he joined them by the campfire, even sharing meals with them occasionally, all the while counting their numbers.

In terms of companies, the makeup of each baron's forces was roughly the same as his own, with three-quarters consisting of footmen, the remainder archers. The one thing that set them well apart from Hadenfeld was their cavalry. Whereas Otto possessed only a small number of knights, King Diedrich had obviously spent considerable time training and equipping a much larger force. Ludwig wondered if some of them might be foreign knights but failed to get close enough to confirm his suspicions. Instead, he had to be content with observing from a distance, for it was one thing to chat with the common soldier, quite another to move amongst the nobility of Neuhafen, mainly since most of them had likely been present when he'd arrived in Eisen.

Perhaps of greater import was the quality of leadership. His interaction with the King of Neuhafen had been brief, making an accurate assessment of the royal's military capabilities impossible. The fact that this army marched for the bridge of Hasdorf told him little was new in terms of strategy. They intended to march directly to Harlingen and face off against Otto's army, but did Diedrich have the skills to back up such a move? There was also the matter of his barons. Would he give them free rein when it came to battle or dictate their movements himself? Only time would tell.

The army, along with Ludwig, travelled through Langeven before taking a day to rest weary soldiers, then continued on southward to their next objective. Passing through friendly territory left little need for guards or scouts, but Ludwig knew all that would change once they crossed the border into Hadenfeld. He needed to make his move soon before that happened. The question was, when? He would just have to put his faith in the Saints and wait for some sign that the time was upon him.

A few days later, they passed a road sign indicating they were closing in on Arnsbach, the town across the river from Hasdorf. The proximity of the border would soon force Ludwig to make his move.

A rainstorm brewed up that very morning, leaving everyone drenched by late afternoon. Ludwig, eager to exploit the reduced visibility, decided this was the best time to depart. He left the road, heading directly west towards the river, while the army continued on to the bridge at Arnsbach. He was close to the border by his own reckoning, yet he couldn't be sure without a map. Picking his way through the trees, he took care to avoid stumbling across any signs of civilization.

When the rain finally let up late in the day, the sound of running water drifted towards him. He sped up, sure the border was close, but as he reached the edge of the woods, he spied a group of warriors watering their horses down by the river. He cursed his luck and was about to turn around when a shout revealed they'd discovered him.

Ludwig briefly considered brazening it out. After all, he'd spent enough time amongst the enemy. Why not carry on with the ruse? Unfortunately, these horsemen wore plate armour, sure evidence that they were knights, making recognition much more likely.

He urged his mount into the woods, determined to distance himself from his pursuers. Behind him, the shouting grew louder, and he glanced over his shoulder to spot a trio of riders coming after him.

He snapped his head around just in time for a low-hanging branch to knock him to the forest floor, forcing the breath from his lungs even as his mount continued on into the underbrush.

Ludwig sat up, shaking his head in a vain attempt to clear it. With the approaching sound of horses, he crawled out of the way, huddling behind a tree, hoping they wouldn't spot him.

The sounds of pursuit advanced, then slowed. A horse snorted. Ludwig held his breath, not daring to move. The riders were muttering something, and then a distant crash of twigs demanded their attention. They rode off, lured by his now riderless mount.

Ludwig peered around the tree, ensuring they were well out of sight before leaving his hiding place. Rather than stumble off to what he assumed was north, he decided to backtrack. Hopefully, he could then devise some way to cross without being seen.

It didn't take long to find the river again, but a pair of horsemen remained there, letting their comrades do all the chasing. Now he faced a tough decision. His best option was to swim, easy enough considering he lacked any armour to weigh him down. The problem was how to get in the water before the knights cut him down. He watched them for some time, hoping they would grow bored, but they appeared determined to await their companions' return.

To the south, he could just make out faint trails of smoke, evidence the army of Neuhafen was setting up camp. However, the land grew wilder to the north, with little more than trees and wild grass. The view gave him hope, for if he could reach the river, his escape was all but guaranteed.

He got to his feet, creeping along the edge of the woods, trying to remain as quiet as possible. The songs of birds and insects filled the air, but the farther north he travelled, the quieter things became.

Eventually, the sounds of the woods ceased altogether, and the hair on the back of his neck stood on end. He froze, then heard a huff off to his right, along with the crackling of underbrush.

Turning, he saw a giant creature, its coarse brown hair standing out in stark contrast to the lush greenery of the surrounding vegetation. Rising to its hind legs, it growled as if to announce it was, in fact, precisely what he feared.

Ludwig was no coward, but even he knew it was suicidal to fight a bear with only a sword. He did the only thing he could—he ran, breaking through the treeline at full speed. His actions drew the attention of not only the bear but the knights who'd regrouped and were still searching for him.

They put spurs to their horses as soon as they spotted him, thundering hooves announcing their pursuit. Long before he reached the safety of the water, they would have him. What they hadn't counted on, however, was the bear.

The creature emerged from his woodland habitat, letting out a roar that echoed off the trees. A couple of the knights slowed their advance, but the other three continued, two riding for the bear while the third rode to intercept Ludwig.

Adrenaline coursed through his veins, giving him a boost of strength to help him outdistance his pursuers, both two and four-footed.

A deep-throated growl came from behind him. A horse reared up in panic, though he was too busy to turn and see which one. On and on, he ran, expecting a sword to slice into his back at any moment.

When his feet finally hit the water, he glanced over his shoulder. One knight was down, his head crushed, presumably by the bear's teeth. A second knight struggled to control his horse while the third, who'd chased Ludwig, had turned around, rushing to the aid of his companions.

Ludwig waded waist-deep into the water before diving in, swimming for all he was worth. The current took hold of him, carrying him quite a distance northward before he closed in on the far bank. He grabbed a fallen tree, pulling himself towards the Hadenfeld side of the river.

He looked over at the eastern bank, watching the knights collect their dead comrade as the bear lumbered back into the forest.

Ludwig collapsed when he finally exited the water. Across the river and now unable to catch him, the knights watched, waving. It was a curious moment, for not so long ago, these men had been trying to kill him.

He lay in the sun for some time, regaining his strength, safe for the moment, but he knew it wouldn't last. Eventually, the enemy would cross the river, cutting him off from any help. The question now was what he should do. His original plan was to ride for Harlingen, bringing news of the invasion to the king. However, without a mount, that option was no longer viable. Also, the Neuhafen Army's arrival across the river from Hasdorf would inevitably result in someone else undertaking that task. Determined to do something, anything, to aid his king, he decided to follow the water south until he reached Hasdorf. There, he could at least offer his support to its baron, Lord Egan.

The farther he travelled, the more enemy warriors he spotted on the far bank. They could have crossed easily had they a boat, but with the strong current, armoured men made poor swimmers.

Eventually, he encountered farmland, and then the roofs of Hasdorf were visible off in the distance. As he approached, a low rumbling came to his ears, informing him the fight for the bridge was already underway.

Folks clogged the city streets, trying to escape the coming carnage. He fought to get past them, every step bringing him closer to the sounds of battle. A group of warriors headed towards him, fear on their faces and the crest of Lord Egan emblazoned upon their tunics.

He grabbed a man in the front by the arm. "Stand!" he shouted. "Or they'll kill all these people."

"Better them than us!"

Ludwig slapped the warrior with all the strength he could muster. "Stand," he repeated, this time brandishing his sword.

The fellow's comrades halted, watching the exchange.

"I am Lord Ludwig of Verfeld."

"There are too many of them, Lord!"

"Form a line here, across the street. As men try to withdraw, push them to the sides until there is a solid wall of steel."

The men shuffled into a rough line while Ludwig stood before them. More came running, and these he directed to either side. Slowly, the line grew until almost two dozen men were shoulder to shoulder.

Someone who looked like an officer appeared, his sash soaked with blood. Ludwig quickly seized the fellow's arm. "Where is Lord Egan?" he demanded.

"I... I don't know. I think he's dead."

"You think? Did you see him go down?"

"No, but they overran his position. He couldn't possibly have survived."

"Who's his second?"

"Second?"

"His second-in-command," shouted Ludwig. "Surely he must have one?"

The man looked around in panic. "Isn't he here? Who took charge of these men?"

"I did. Lord Ludwig of Verfeld."

The man's eyes revealed a glint of hope. "You bring reinforcements?"

"No. I came from Neuhafen, and that army"—he pointed at the bridge —"outnumbers your men by at least ten to one."

"What do we do?"

"We hold the line here and try to buy time for these people to evacuate."

"But they'll kill us all!"

"Not so," said Ludwig. "Darkness will soon descend, and then we can make our escape, but only if we slow them down here. This is the only road west, is it not?"

"It is, Lord."

"Good. Then take up a position behind these men and pray we can hold on till then."

A cheer rose from the east, signifying the enemy had taken the bridge. The Neuhafen army marched through, forming a line on the Hadenfeld side, allowing room for cavalry to form up behind them.

"By the Saints," muttered someone from behind him. "They have knights."

Ludwig turned to face the warriors of Hasdorf. "Those horsemen are coming after you," he said, "but even a heavily armoured knight has a weakness. Does anyone know what that is?"

"A tremendous ego?" came a voice.

Ludwig spotted the source, a rough-looking fellow with an axe. "What's your name?"

"Kandam, Lord."

"Kandam? What kind of name is that?"

"Kurathian, Lord. On my father's side."

"Well, you have a good point, Kandam. They do indeed have a large ego. They also have horses, and their legs are particularly vulnerable, as are their feet. If a knight comes after you, don't try to hit him; aim for his horse instead, and try to force him from his saddle."

"But all that armour?" complained another.

"Yes, they have a lot of armour, but those helmets restrict their vision. Get them off their horses, and they're at a disadvantage." He knew it was an exaggeration, yet now was not the time to waver.

A group of knights crossed the bridge and formed a line, ready to run down the road.

"Those who carry spears, plant them as best you can. A horse won't intentionally try to impale itself."

"And those of us who don't?"

"Be prepared to rush forward after the initial impact. Some of you may go down, but if anyone panics, we're all doomed." He drew his sword and moved to stand amongst the men. The knights advanced, horseshoes clattering on the cobblestones. They rode close together, almost stirrup to stirrup, and Ludwig saw little hope of holding them back for long. One knight raised his weapon on high before he swept it down, signalling the charge.

38

WITHDRAWAL

SUMMER 1100 SR

There were at least a dozen enemy riders, yet the clatter of their hooves echoing off the buildings made it sound like many more.

Ludwig braced, but a gap appeared to his right as the horsemen crossed the halfway point. He felt a flash of fear until a group of men pushed a cart forward, its bed bristling with spears. The horses of Neuhafen, spooked by this unexpected development, tried to veer off to either side, throwing their neatly formed line into one of confusion and chaos.

Ludwig saw his chance and ordered the attack. He rushed forward, at a crouch, staying close to the protection the cart offered.

The knights of Neuhafen struggled to control their mounts in the face of these unusual tactics. Ludwig struck out at a horse, his sword drawing blood. The terrified beast reared up, its rider doing all he could to remain mounted.

Ludwig tempted fate by rushing alongside, pulling at the knight's leg. The fellow's foot slipped from the stirrup, causing him to lose his balance, and he came crashing onto the road. One warrior ran forward and thrust out his spear, sliding it along the man's breastplate to lodge under the helmet. Had the knight of Neuhafen worn a gorget, he would've been safe, for it prevented precisely this form of attack. Instead, the tip drove in deep. The attacker pulled back his spear, and blood pumped out from beneath the knight's helmet.

The men of Hadenfeld took Ludwig's advice to heart and struck out at the horses. The beasts' screams, mixed with the sounds of sword against armour, created a cacophony of sounds that only grew in intensity.

Ludwig smacked the now riderless horse with his hand, sending it galloping off and freeing up some space. Another knight bore down on him. He backed up slightly, trying to prepare for the impact, but his legs went out from under him when his foot slipped on something wet. His knee smashed into the cobblestones, pain lancing up his leg, but the stumble saved his life, for the attacker's sword passed over his head.

The knight slowed, then twisted to look back at where his intended target now crouched. Other men of Hadenfeld took advantage of the rider's distraction, plunging forth with spears to send the fellow's horse to the ground, pinning its rider beneath. The beast writhed around, the knight screaming out in agony as it crushed the very life out of him.

Two of the knights who'd attacked were down, with a third limping back to where they'd started their charge. Concerned, lest the defenders overwhelm them, the remainder wisely withdrew, wheeling about, heedless of the danger, and galloping off to safety.

A cheer erupted from the defenders, but as Ludwig looked at them, he discovered they'd suffered greatly. Five men died in the chaos of the fight, with another two nursing wounds. A second charge would destroy them.

"Whose idea was it to push out that cart?" asked Ludwig.

"Mine," said Kandam.

"Well, it was a stroke of genius and, more importantly, bought us some time. They'll think twice about resuming the attack, but we can't stay here and wait for their reinforcements. Time to withdraw westward and hope to meet up with King Otto."

Ludwig took stock of these men. "You two," he said, "take the lead. I want the four of you with spears to bring up the rear. If any horses threaten, give a yell and plant your spears. We'll come running. The rest of you help bind the injured but make it quick. We've got little time."

The men nodded and set to work. Those in the lead assumed their positions, then waited while the wounded were tended to. Ludwig took a step and almost fell over as his knee buckled.

Kandam came to his rescue, clutching his arm and steadying him. "You're injured, Lord."

Ludwig looked down at his leg. "It's only a bruise; others are much worse off."

"Their legs are intact, Lord. Yours is not. You should ride a horse."

"I'd love to," said Ludwig, "but I haven't got one."

Kandam grinned. "But you do." He nodded off to the side where the very horse Ludwig had wounded stood in an alleyway. One of the men, Ludwig's men now, moved closer to the beast, talking in soothing tones. Moments later, he led the creature from its place of refuge.

Ludwig climbed into the saddle.

"Here. Take this," said Kandam. "It's the dead knight's sword—a far better weapon than that old thing."

The blade was quite a prize, easily worth more than what this foot soldier made in a year, yet he handed it over with no hesitation. A lump formed in Ludwig's throat. In the heat of battle, he'd acted without conscious thought, taking charge of the situation because he had to. Now, looking down at Kandam and the rest, he realized he'd done far more than simply fight—he'd given them hope. The weight of responsibility felt heavy on his soul, but he promised himself he would do his best to get these men to safety. He cast his old sword to the ground, took this new weapon and held it high in the air. For the second time today, the men of Hasdorf cheered.

Kandam handed him the belt and scabbard, then waited while Ludwig buckled it on. Satisfied all was as it should be, he nodded at the Lord of Verfeld before marching westward.

The sounds of fighting had long since ceased. Ludwig briefly considered returning to Hasdorf to help in its defence, but from what he'd seen of the enemy army, a few more men would make little difference. Better, instead, to reach Otto and report what he knew about the invading army.

Grienwald was the closest town of any consequence, so they followed the road to the northwest. That night, Ludwig sat by a fire, examining his knee, which had swollen considerably, and was a mass of purple bruising.

"How is it, Lord?"

He looked up to see Kandam. "It's swollen, but I'll survive."

The Kurathian knelt to get a better view. "It needs to be bound. Were we not in the middle of nowhere, I would recommend you elevate and rest it."

"I doubt the enemy will allow us the time."

"Then at least permit me to bind it. You'll find walking difficult, but you still have that horse."

"I do," said Ludwig, "but I wounded the poor beast."

"Have no fear," said Kandam. "They're little more than surface wounds. He will bear your weight for the time being."

Ludwig stared off into the darkness, deep in thought. He'd posted sentinels to watch for any signs of the enemy, yet they'd spotted nothing. Were they being encircled as he sat here? He quickly dismissed the idea, for it was far more likely they were sacking Hasdorf.

"The leg, Lord? Shall I bind it?"

"Very well."

Kandam produced some strips of cloth and got to work. Once done, he propped up the knee, and then Ludwig drifted off to sleep.

They set off early the next day, determined to put as much distance behind them as possible. Ludwig wasn't exactly sure how far away Grienwald was, but after two long days on the road, they passed by some farmland. The distant spires of the town soon came into view, and the men quickened their pace, eager to be amongst friends.

As they approached, they spotted the banner of the Baron of Grienwald, Lord Morgan. Evidently, the noble had seen fit to gather his men, but the manner of their assembly gave the impression of little concern. They meandered around their field in no rush, not even deigning to post sentries or take an interest in Ludwig and his men's arrival.

It took actually entering their camp to warrant a response. A fashionably attired fellow, a knight by his look, sat out in front of his pavilion, drink in hand.

"Where is the baron?" called out Ludwig.

The knight took offence at the lack of deference from the new arrivals. "Mind your manners, cur. You are speaking to Sir Emril of Valaran."

Ludwig was tired, hungry, and in no mood for such treatment. He wanted to lash out at this absurd scene but kept his anger contained as much as possible.

"I am Lord Ludwig, Baron of Verfeld, you dolt. It is you who should show deference to me. Now answer my question, or I shall be forced to demand your apology at the end of my sword."

The knight's look of shock was impossible to miss. "You mean the same Lord Ludwig who fought in the north? King Otto's cousin?"

"The very same."

Emril stood so quickly that his cup dropped from his hand. "My apologies, Lord. I meant no offence."

"And yet you were content to insult me when you believed me to be a mere commoner?"

The man looked ready to faint. "That was different, Lord. The common man needs to be shown their place."

"And what place is that?"

Sir Emril's mouth opened, but no sound issued forth. Instead, it just flapped around, reminding Ludwig of a fish.

"Lord Morgan?" he repeated.

"Over there," the knight replied, pointing.

Ludwig turned to his warriors. "Come along, lads. We have work to do." He ignored Sir Emril's protestations and set a course for the baron.

As they drew closer, the sight of what he could only describe as a garden party shocked Ludwig. Lords and ladies sipped drinks while servants wandered around with trays of food.

He dismounted, handing the reins over to Kandam. "You lot wait here while I have words with His Lordship." They looked uncomfortable, shifting their feet, keeping their gaze downcast, but they held their ground.

Lord Morgan was easy to spot, for he sat in a uniquely carved, ornate chair, holding out his golden chalice to let a servant refill it.

Ludwig pushed his way past the guests. Many turned at the interruption, ready to complain, but the disgust in his eyes kept them silent. He halted before the baron.

"My lord," he began, "I bring news from Hasdorf."

They'd met in Harlingen at Ludwig's induction, but the man's eyes held no recognition, likely because of the beard growth and unkempt wardrobe Ludwig now wore.

"Do I know you?"

"Lord Ludwig, Baron of Verfeld."

"Ludwig? By the Saints, man. I thought you went to Neuhafen?"

"I did. They threw me in a dungeon, then I escaped, but that is of little consequence right now. King Diedrich has crossed the river and taken Hasdorf!"

"Are you positive?"

"As sure as I'm standing here. We fought them two days ago. They could be here at any moment."

The baron paled. "How many?"

"I followed them for some time. I'd estimate their numbers at close to four thousand."

"Come now. You must be exaggerating?"

"I wish I were. The last I saw, their lead warriors had taken the bridge. Crossing the river will slow them down a little, but we must make an effort to oppose them."

Lord Morgan rose, his cup forgotten in the rush of news. A servant ran forward to take it while all his guests stared at the two barons, captivated by the conversation.

"All captains to me," shouted Morgan. "And someone fetch me my armour." He turned his attention to Ludwig. "Have you men?"

"Only a handful. Not nearly enough to stand in battle with your own warriors."

Lord Morgan grabbed the arm of a nearby warrior. "See Lord Ludwig's men fed, then round up any captains who might still be in town. Have them assemble here as soon as possible." His attendant ran off, and the baron turned to his guests. "Lords and ladies, I apologize for the inconvenience, but it appears the King of Neuhafen has finally invaded. Therefore, I suggest you get to your carriages and head for Harlingen."

"Are we in danger?" called out a woman's voice.

"Not at present, but any further delay on your part could change that. Now, you must excuse me. I have military matters to attend to. Come, Lord Ludwig. I shall need your counsel."

"Mine?" said Ludwig.

"Of course. You're one of the few leaders in Hadenfeld who has seen battle."

"I led a company of mercenaries, not an entire army."

"Yet still you snatched victory from the jaws of certain defeat, or so I'm told. Was it not your actions that saved the day at Chermingen?"

Ludwig struggled to answer. He'd tried to give credit to the late Sir Galrath, but the true story eventually came out somewhere along the line. "We must get word to the king," he finally said.

"I'll take care of that." Lord Morgan beckoned a servant. "Bring a quill and ink for Lord Ludwig and paper, mind you. He can't very well write on thin air." He turned back to Ludwig. "It's so hard to find dependable servants these days. Now, I shall need you to record anything you believe of import. My riders will have it in the king's hands as quickly as possible."

"And how long will that be?"

"It's over sixty miles to the capital, and we don't know if the king is already on his way. I'm sure you can do the calculations yourself."

"And your plan?"

"I would've said to line up my troops and block the road, but with the numbers they have at their disposal, that would be suicidal."

"What's the terrain like in these parts?" asked Ludwig.

"Mostly flat, although the Greenwood lies just to our north."

"The Greenwood, you say? Does that extend to the west?"

"It does. Why do you ask?"

"It seems to me it might offer us an alternative to battle. I suggest we head back towards Harlingen and take a position overlooking the road."

"You mean to abandon the town? That's unthinkable!"

"Better that than face annihilation."

The words sobered Lord Morgan. "Yes, I suppose there is that. Very well. We shall withdraw westward in hopes of meeting up with the king."

"Spare me two companies of men, and I'll slow down the invaders as much as possible."

"And how do you expect to do that?"

"I shall use hit-and-run tactics," explained Ludwig. "Archers would be best if you have them."

"That would leave me with none. What if I give you half of my bowmen and a company of foot?"

"That would suffice, I think."

"You think? For Saint's sake, Ludwig. You better be sure about this. I shan't throw away my men on a whim. Is it enough or not?"

"It is. I don't suppose you have horsemen?"

"No, I'm afraid not. They're far too expensive to maintain. Listen, there's more at stake here, Ludwig. You and I are both cousins to the king."

"Meaning?"

"By the time this war is over, we may both be closer to inheriting the Crown. Don't do anything foolish to ruin that."

"And by foolish, you mean dying?"

Lord Morgan cleared his throat to cover up his emotions. "I shall have my men form up over there by that stream. Will that suffice?"

"It will."

"Good. I'll arrange for a local to help, someone who knows the area hereabouts. I'm not suggesting the soldiers are witless, but most of them spend their time in town rather than out in the countryside."

"That would be much appreciated. Thank you."

"Ah, here comes the paper. I'll leave you to your work. When your letter's done, this fellow will take charge of it."

"Understood," said Ludwig.

Much to Lord Morgan's credit, the captains under his command assembled even as their pickets moved into position to warn of the enemy's approach.

With his letter sent off, Ludwig joined them beneath a huge awning. After the briefest of introductions and salutations, Lord Morgan spoke. "Gentlemen. We've received word from Lord Ludwig that the army of Neuhafen has captured the bridge at Hasdorf. As I speak, King Diedrich is crossing into Hadenfeld with nearly four thousand warriors. Now, I needn't tell you they badly outnumber us, so I won't." He waited a moment as his audience forced a chuckle. "My intention is to march westward, back towards Harlingen, joining the army of King Otto. Once we do that, we can return in larger numbers and exact revenge. However, we'll need some of you to remain behind to slow the enemy's advance. "

A voice called out. "My lord, any idea of the makeup of these invaders?"

"A good question and one Lord Ludwig is better suited to address, having seen it first-hand. Ludwig?"

Ludwig stepped forward, turning to face the audience. "The composition of their army is similar to our own. By my estimation, each baron fields between four and five hundred warriors, mostly footmen."

"And their horsemen?"

"All knights, I'm afraid, and under the direct command of King Diedrich. I would say they have double King Otto's numbers, not that I would expect that to make too much of a difference."

"Why would you say that?"

"From what I saw at Chermingen, they typically use knights for the final charge. We've already lost the battle if we get to that point."

"Do you honestly believe we can beat them?" asked Lord Morgan.

"I know we can," replied Ludwig. "Winning a battle isn't only about numbers; it's about breaking the enemy's will. One way is by killing them, but it's far from the only thing we can do."

"What is it you're proposing?" came another voice, this one slightly higher in tone.

"Nothing is as fierce as a warrior who's defending his home. Add to that our leaders' expertise, and there isn't an army on the Continent who can defeat us."

"Except for Halvaria," someone shouted.

"I readily admit that should the empire come, they'd brush us aside like a fly, but this is not Halvaria who's coming for our homes—it's Neuhafen, traitors from our own kingdom. We shall not yield!"

39

SKIRMISH

SUMMER 1100 SR

A stray dog wandered along the road, sniffing at a discarded boot, then something to the east grabbed its attention. Letting out a bark, it ran north to the safety of the forest. It was almost beneath its boughs when it caught a whiff of the men who lingered there. A growl escaped its lips, and then Kandam sprinted out and grabbed the poor creature by the scruff of the neck, carrying it back into the treeline.

"They're close," he said to Ludwig as he set the dog down, trying to calm it.

The archers of Lord Morgan hid amongst the trees while five paces behind them stood the foot soldiers, prepared to rush forward should the enemy attack.

"You may nock when ready," said Ludwig, "but no one looses an arrow until I give the command. Understood? We only get one chance to surprise them with a volley. We must make it count."

He turned his attention to the outskirts of Grienwald. A low rumbling came from the direction of the town, growing more distinct as time passed —the footsteps of many men marching along the cobblestone roads. They soon came into view, the packed dirt of the country road now muffling the sound of their march. As they left the narrow streets behind them, their voices rose, drowning out any chance of their discovering Ludwig's men.

The Neuhafen men leading the march appeared to be a levy or a militia, for they had little in the way of defences save for shields and the occasional helmet. Armed with spears and wearing simple tunics bearing no baronial insignia, many had shoes instead of boots, marking them as city folk.

Ludwig took little interest in such men, as they were not the ones who would decide a battle. In most cases, they only formed part of the battle line, leaving the actual fighting to the professional warriors. Still, on rare occasions, the knights would target them because they were easy to break.

Today, however, he let them pass, content that they would most likely avoid getting into the fray if fighting broke out. Instead, he watched with great interest as the next company emerged from Grienwald, wearing mail and carrying swords or axes. They also wore a blue surcoat over their armour and a coat of arms, although he couldn't identify whose from this distance. No doubt it denoted which baron of Neuhafen they served, and for a moment, Ludwig wondered if it wasn't Lord Emmett's men.

He quickly dismissed the thought as irrelevant. It mattered little who these men served; they were invaders. His men waited patiently, for they'd spent half the morning marking off ranges with small stones. They watched as the enemy marched down the road, confident they'd soon be perfectly placed to receive a devastating volley.

The dog yelped, then ran out of the woods, growling and barking at the distant warriors. They, in turn, laughed at the creature's antics. To them, it was a moment of entertainment, a break from the march's endless boredom.

That all changed as Ludwig gave the signal, and arrows flew forth, striking the line of enemy warriors. Men cried out in both fear and pain, with half a dozen killed outright while twice that fell screaming. The footmen, to their credit, rallied quickly, charging the woods.

One more volley came from Ludwig's men before he ordered them deeper into the forest. The thick underbrush made progress difficult, but he'd picked this spot with the help of local farmers, for they knew the area better than any invader.

The warriors of Neuhafen entered the treeline, their weapons eager for blood. The sounds of Ludwig's retreat drew them, then the bushes erupted as the warriors of Grienwald rose from the dense underbrush, screaming out in defiance.

The tactic took the enemy completely by surprise. Those who didn't die in the initial counterattack fell back, desperate to escape the very same woods where they'd sought revenge.

As they ran for the road, Ludwig brought his archers to the forefront, once more unleashing dangerous volleys. The enemy footmen lost all cohesion, running in all directions to avoid the perilous arrows.

The Grienwald archers loosed arrow after arrow but proved less effective as the enemy fled, and finally, Ludwig ordered them to cease. The woods fell silent, save for the cries of the wounded. His own men finished off the enemy warriors who still lay in the woods. Ludwig thought it a barbaric practice, but he could do little to stop it. These foreigners came to plunder and kill, and the men of Grienwald would spare no mercy for them.

He kept his eyes on the town. He knew those witnessing his attack wouldn't tolerate it for long. Sure enough, the sound of marching feet echoed off the trees once again as more men exited Grienwald.

This time, rather than follow the road, they moved south, keeping out of arrow range while they formed up. Ludwig knew his tactic would not work again.

"Fall back," he ordered. "We must withdraw."

Most of his men obeyed, but half a dozen remained, intent on continuing the fight. He had to physically shove them to get moving. One, in particular, tried to stare him down, but the fire in Ludwig's eyes told him it would be a poor choice. The fellow finally acquiesced, following his comrades in their trek northward.

By the time Ludwig lowered himself from the saddle, the moon was high in the sky. He walked over to a fire, slumping down against an uprooted tree beside Kandam.

"How is that knee of yours?" asked Kandam.

It ached terribly, but Ludwig didn't want to complain. "Well enough," he replied.

Kandam came forward, producing a knife which he used to cut away the bandage. Beneath, the skin had yellowed.

"Why hasn't it healed?" asked Ludwig.

"Healed?" said Kandam. "You only hurt it a few days ago, and you haven't exactly been resting it."

"Yes, but you bandaged it. Surely—"

"It takes more than simple bandages to heal a bruise like that. You've been riding a horse; that's a strain on your knee, especially when it's already bruised."

"Then be honest with me. How long until it stops aching?"

The Kurathian shrugged. "A week, maybe two? If you were resting, as I suggested, I could be more precise."

"Look around you," said Ludwig. "We're not exactly in a place where I can rest. There is a war on, you know."

"Try bending it," suggested Kandam.

"How will that help?"

"We must determine whether or not the hit damaged the joint."

"Of course it's damaged," said Ludwig. "That's why it hurts."

"Nonsense. It's more likely just bruising. Trust me, if you'd broken your knee, you'd be in no end of pain."

Ludwig stared back. "That's hardly reassuring." Despite his protestations, he gritted his teeth and lifted the leg, bending it fully. "There. Satisfied?"

"Did that hurt?"

"A little."

"Good. It means the joint is undamaged. Once the swelling goes down, your leg should be back to normal."

"Lucky for me, you're a healer."

"I don't know where you got that idea," said Kandam. "True, I possess some skill with bandaging and such, but I'm no expert."

"You could have fooled me," said Ludwig.

"You know, it's funny you say that. I always wondered what it would take to become a healer."

"Then I'll make you a deal. If we get out of here alive, I'll send you to the Brothers of Saint Mathew."

"I bear no desire to take Holy Orders."

"And I'm not suggesting you do, merely that you learn what they can teach you about healing."

"And then?"

"If you're willing, I'd have you come back and serve as my official healer. I'd suitably compensate you, of course."

"Compensate?"

"Yes," said Ludwig. "A healer is a highly sought-after individual. Who knows, you might even end up serving the king one day. How would you like that? Living a life of luxury in Harlingen?"

"I would prefer to go where I'm needed. I will consider your offer, Lord Ludwig, but let us first worry about how we'll survive the next few days."

"I have some ideas on that. I think it's about time we head west. This forest butts up against the Harlingen Hills, doesn't it?"

"I believe so, but we're a little too far north for that. Still, if we find the edge of the woods, we can follow it south until the hills come into view. We just need to be careful we don't stumble into the enemy."

"Excellent. We'll set out at first light. In the meantime, I must ensure I post the sentries." Ludwig tried to rise, but his knee complained.

"I shall see to the sentries," said Kandam. "You may be the leader of these men, but when it comes to healing, you are under my care with strict orders to rest that leg."

"Very well, I accept your rules. Say, whatever happened to that stray dog?"

"He ran off at the first sign of bloodshed. Why?"

"Your actions surprised me, that's all. Not every soldier would try to save such a beast."

Kandam smiled. "Every life has value, even a stray dog."

Ludwig let his gaze drift over the camp. Is that what they were, stray dogs? Suddenly the image of a pack of dogs descending on the enemy struck him. "We are like dogs," he said out loud. "Dogs of war that bring fear and destruction to our enemies."

"I like that. It has a certain poetic imagery to it."

"Poetic imagery? And here I thought you a commoner."

"Can a common man not read? Can he not embrace the words of the poets?"

"Sorry. You told me your father was Kurathian. I just assumed he was a mercenary."

"A merchant, actually, a dealer of imports. He used to buy goods off Kurathian ships on the Shimmering Sea, then bring them farther inland. His travels took him all over the Continent."

"And he settled in Hadenfeld?"

"He did, for it is here he met my mother."

"Was he a nobleman?"

"Only in his beliefs. He was what you might call a merchant prince, not true royalty, but wealthy and influential in his own way. When he finally settled down, he used his wealth to build a modest home and start a trading hall, although I suppose that's all gone."

"Why would you say that?"

"He would've had it stocked with goods, just the sort of thing an invading army would plunder."

"How is it you now wield an axe?"

"My father taught me a person must be willing to fight for what they believe in. I cannot stand by while those around me are dying. I am no great warrior, that much is true, but I can at least stand beside my fellow towns-folk and help defend what is rightfully ours. How about you? Have you ever wielded an axe?"

"I've trained with them, but I prefer a sword. My father hired an expert swordsman by the name of Kurt Wasser to teach me how to fight."

"And where is he now?"

"Up north, serving the Duke of Erlingen."

"Erlingen? I've heard of it. My father used to say it was full of greedy nobles and an indifferent duke."

"He wasn't far off the mark. Did he tell stories about the other Petty Kingdoms?"

"Many, but such tales are best reserved for another time. You need to get some sleep while I see to the sentries."

Ludwig awoke with a start. Men shuffled around the camp, gathering their gear and dousing fires. They were ready to march while Ludwig was still struggling to rise. Someone helped him to his feet, and he staggered towards his horse. Thankfully, the beast was already saddled, so he hauled himself up, ignoring the hunger pangs wracking his stomach.

The line of men streamed westward, led by people familiar with the area. Ludwig fell in behind, watching for stragglers or any signs of pursuit. The thick forest's heavy underbrush dampened the sounds of their progress, while the air within had a cloying effect, almost suffocating in its intensity as if this were the height of summer, not the beginning.

He wondered if he might be suffering from a fever, but a quick glance at those nearby assured him everyone was sweating up a storm. Ludwig tried to relax in the saddle, but his knee protested when he shifted to adjust his position. He was miserable, at least from a physical point of view, and all he could think about was lying down and resting.

The day wore on. Endless miles of forest passed by, the sound of birds his constant companion. He completely lost track of time, even drifting off to sleep, only to awaken in a sudden panic, scrambling to avoid falling from his saddle. To occupy his mind, he thought of Clay, the horse he'd inherited from the Earth Mage Linden Herzog. He was a gentle beast, easy on the backside and calm even in the face of danger. It would've been nice to have him here, but he would still be back in Eisen had he brought him to Neuhafen.

So lost in thought was he that he wandered away, jerking back to reality to note he was all alone in the woods. He halted, trying to get his bearings, then listened. It didn't take long to locate his men, and he urged his horse on, his exhaustion suddenly forgotten in a rush of adrenalin.

There was no telling how far they travelled, but as the sky darkened, they reached the western end of the forest. Ahead of them lay the Harlingen Hills. King Otto was assembling his army somewhere out there, but Ludwig had no idea how many of his barons had marched to his aid. He tried to envision a map of Hadenfeld so he could calculate the distances, but his fatigue got the better of him. His men elected to camp at the edge of the Greenwood to conceal their presence, and he lacked the energy to object. Instead, he slid from the saddle and was soon asleep.

· · ·

The Harlingen Hills, as the name suggested, was a hilly region lying to the east of the capital. More importantly, the route from Grienwald to Harlingen wound through these hills, making it the perfect avenue for an ambush. All they need do was find the road, and to this end, they proceeded south, hoping to locate it before the enemy. Ludwig knew that if they miscalculated, they might stumble directly into the middle of King Diedrich's army.

To avoid this potential disaster, he sent half a dozen men ahead to scout the area and return once they knew more about the enemy's disposition.

As noon approached, he spotted them coming back at a run. Fearing the worst, he gave the order to prepare for battle, but it proved an unnecessary precaution. His men had indeed reached the road, but they'd not discovered the enemy, rather the outlying scouts of Otto's army.

Ludwig ordered the rest of his men to pick up their pace, hoping they would reach safety before the enemy arrived. He then galloped off, intent on bringing news about the invasion to whoever commanded the scouts.

As only one of two barons who had mounted men-at-arms, the Baron of Luwen's warriors blocked the road. Despite Ludwig's bedraggled appearance, Lord Meinhard immediately recognized him, waving him over to where he sat on his horse, armoured up and ready for battle.

"Lord Ludwig. I must say this is a bit of a surprise. I believed you to be in Neuhafen, but then we got word you were fighting at Grienwald."

"Both are true, but I fear the invaders will soon be upon you and in greater numbers than I see here."

"We are sentries only, on the lookout for King Diedrich's arrival. I'm told you sent the king a detailed description of their army. How in the name of the Saints did you manage that?"

"After I escaped from Eisen, I shadowed them, even entering their camp to gain some idea of their numbers and composition."

"Remarkable. Wait, did you say you escaped? Surely Diedrich didn't imprison an envoy?"

"He did precisely that, right after he tried to have me killed in a duel."

"Astounding. Clearly, we can't trust him to follow the rules of civilized warfare."

"I don't know that anyone can consider war civilized," said Ludwig. "To my mind, it's exactly the opposite."

"I'm surprised to hear you say that. You, of all people, should understand that battle is the playground of an educated man. The finest test of wills we can ever face."

"War is not a game, especially to those who must sacrifice their lives."

"Come now. It is their lot. Ours is to lead, while theirs is to fight and, if necessary, die. It has always been thus, and always shall be."

"No," said Ludwig. "With all due respect, you're wrong. War is sometimes the only way to settle a conflict, but it's not there purely for the entertainment of the wealthy and powerful. You talk of fighting and dying as the lot of the common man, but what do you know of warfare? I've been there, Lord Meinhard, right in the middle of a battle, where each swing of your sword might be your last. It's not something to be celebrated; rather, we should all strive to avoid it as much as possible."

The Baron of Luwen straightened in his saddle. "I never took you for a coward."

Ludwig bristled. He wanted to lash out but knew it would solve nothing. "You may believe what you want, Meinhard, but when the battle comes, it's men like me who you'll need to keep you alive."

40

THE HILLS OF HARLINGEN
SUMMER 1100 SR

F ifty years earlier, the army of Hadenfeld had assembled before the eastern gates of Harlingen. The newly crowned King Otto led men of the western baronies, who rallied around their ruler to stave off the rebellion from the east. That battle saved the city and the Crown, but at a tremendous cost. Suffering from heavy casualties, Otto could not pursue his defeated opponent, leading to the eventual creation of the breakaway region now known as Neuhafen.

Today, Ludwig led the battered and bruised men of Grienwald onto that very same field. As they approached the army of King Otto, they straightened their backs and picked up the pace. Upon spotting the banner of Verfeld, he angled his men towards it. They'd quickly noticed his arrival, for the baritone voice of Sigwulf boomed out a greeting as he and Cyn trotted forward. Ludwig halted his men, and his friends gathered around.

"By the Saints," said Cyn. "We were wondering if you'd ever get here."

"I knew you'd arrive eventually," said Sigwulf. "It's not like you to miss the opportunity for a good fight." He glanced at the men behind Ludwig. "Who are these folks?"

"Men of Grienwald and Hasdorf who I picked up along the way."

"I'll see them fed." Sigwulf moved to face the small force. "You lot, come with me. Let's get some food into your bellies, shall we?"

"Have you news of Charlotte?" asked Ludwig.

"She's in fine health," replied Cyn. "That reminds me, I have something for you." She dug into her belt and pulled forth a ragged note. "Sorry for its condition. It's been a hurried march."

He took the note, opening it eagerly, devouring the words as a starving man might wolf down food. Tears came to his eyes. "She is well," he said. "Thank the Saints."

"Did you think she wouldn't be?"

"It's silly, I know, but when they imprisoned me in Eisen, I feared I might never see her again."

Cyn lowered her voice. "You know, it's not a sin to love your wife."

Ludwig wiped away the tears. "Look at me, blathering like a newborn when I should be preparing for battle."

"You're a great leader, Ludwig, but you still have a lot to learn about married life."

"Then I shall make it a priority from now on, providing we survive this invasion."

"Clearly, you've been through much," said Cyn. "Anything else you want to share?"

"Lots, but I need to see the king first. The enemy will soon be here, and we have to prepare."

"Already done. Otto briefed us all this morning. He means to make a stand here, amongst the hills."

Ludwig shook his head. "He's making the same mistake he made fifty years ago."

"Which is?"

"He'll waste his men trading lives one for one. He can't afford to do that this time."

"What else can he do? Hold up in Harlingen?"

"He needs to go on the offensive."

"But they have the advantage of numbers, don't they?"

"They do," said Ludwig, "but we can counter that by a judicial use of a few raids. The secret is to break their spirit. Do that, and their army will crumble."

"Spoken like a true general," said Cyn. "It's just too bad you weren't here this morning."

"So what is his plan, precisely?"

"Come with me, and I'll show you." She turned her horse around and headed back to the men of Verfeld. "Each baron commands their own men, with Otto commanding the reserve. That, by the way, consists of all his men, including the knights."

"What of his other horsemen?"

"You mean the mounted men-at-arms? He doesn't think they'll be useful, so he's ignored them." She pointed off to the east. "Those hills on either side of the road will be where we make our stand. Our specific location is on the far section of the northern flank. I assume he was loathe to let Siggy command a more important position. He seems to have a low opinion of those he considers commoners."

"A view the Baron of Luwen agrees with, in my experience."

"The Baron of Luwen? That's Alexandra's father, isn't it?"

"It is. Why? She isn't here, is she?"

"Not that I noticed, but there've been a few come out from the city to watch. I don't believe they realize how truly horrific battle can be."

"Nor do half the nobles here," said Ludwig. "Otto's probably the only one who was around for the rebellion all those years ago, and his memory isn't what it used to be."

"How do you think the enemy will attack?"

"They'll come straight down the road; they have little choice. Those hills make anything else extremely difficult."

"So maybe the king's plan isn't so bad after all?"

"I'll wait till I see the area to decide. Who advised him?"

"I wouldn't know. No one divulged that, but I heard he leaned heavily on his cousin, Lord Morgan. He arrived late yesterday afternoon."

"Yes, I have some of his men. I suppose I should return them now we're here."

"And the men of Hasdorf?"

"Once they're fed, put them in with our own. Speaking of which, how many did you bring?"

"Four hundred, although over half of that is militia. Mind you, compared to what I've seen around here, I'd say they're better trained than those your fellow barons brought."

Ludwig laughed. "You're only saying that because you're the one who trained them."

"Hey now. I'm only telling the truth. Have you seen what the others are fielding?"

"What about Drakenfeld? Did you pick up their men?"

"Yes, and thank the Saints for that. They provide a good core of warriors, more than us, if the truth be told. Lord Merrick sends his regards. He will visit Verfeld in our absence and monitor things."

"And Lady Gita?"

"She'll remain in Drakenfeld to oversee it. The good news is their complement triples our archers."

The men of Verfeld cheered as they rode by.

"They're in high spirits," said Cyn.

"Excellent. We'll need that in the coming days." He halted, then dismounted, shaking out the stiffness in his leg.

"Are you injured?"

"Only a bruised knee, a result of our clash with a small group of knights back in Hasdorf. That reminds me, there's a fellow named Kandam amongst those men I brought with me. He has some skill as a healer. You might want to keep him behind the men to help with casualties."

"I'll bear that in mind," she said.

"Have you thought about how you'll deploy our archers?"

"We have a height advantage, so I thought to deploy the foot on the forward slope with archers behind. That way, they can rain arrows down on our attackers."

"A good choice," said Ludwig. "Was that your idea?"

"It was. After all, you did put me in charge of the bowmen. Now, sit down and rest that leg of yours."

Someone produced a wooden chair with canvas stretched across it. Not much to look at, but after days of sitting on the hard ground, it was magnificent. For the first time in a long while, Ludwig's back didn't ache.

"It seems you and Sig managed quite well without me. Maybe I should go into Harlingen and drink myself into a stupor."

Cyn laughed. "You'd have a hard time. Otto ordered all the taverns to turn away any warriors. He wants the men in fighting shape, not hungover. That includes you."

"It seems our king has a terrible sense of timing. Many men would fight better with a little ale in their blood."

"You and I both know that's not true. Liquid courage passes quickly. To win a battle, you need grit."

"Grit? Is that what you call it?"

"You can call it stubbornness if you prefer, but it amounts to the same thing. In any case, the men of Verfeld aren't here to fight for King Otto."

Ludwig looked up in shock. "They aren't?"

"No. They're here to fight for you!"

"And what have I done to earn that?"

"What haven't you done, Ludwig? You're a hero! The men know you won't throw away their lives like leaves on the wind. Show them they have a chance to survive this battle, and they'll follow you into the Afterlife."

"You realize that's a contradiction of terms, don't you?"

"Is it?" She laughed. "Yes, I suppose it is. In any event, you're their baron. They'll do anything for you."

"I'm just a warrior."

"Oh, you're far more than that. I was there in Chermingen, remember? Without you, we would have perished."

"I wasn't alone."

"That's true, you weren't, but they would've overwhelmed us without your presence."

"That was sheer luck."

"Maybe," said Cyn, "but I'd rather follow a lucky leader than one who has no concern for the lives of others."

Ludwig watched as a group of men rode past. "There'll be a battle tomorrow."

"How can you be so sure?"

"Those are Lord Meinhard's men. They were guarding the road."

"Perhaps they were relieved by others?"

"No. Something has shaken them. My guess is they spotted Diedrich's army and withdrew. When are we to take up our positions?"

"At first light tomorrow," said Cyn. "Why? What are you thinking?"

"It might be a good idea to get into place sooner."

"You believe they might try a night attack?"

"Not in force, no, but they may send in a small expedition to gather information."

"Like we did before Chermingen," said Cyn. "But we're only one element of the army. We can't possibly watch the entire line of battle?"

"True, but if we utilize Lord Merrick's men, we can at least keep the area north of the road clear of any such threats."

"And the south?"

"I can try talking to the other barons. Who is to stand south of the road?"

"Lords Morgan and Jurgen, leaving Meinhard to block the road."

"Just my luck."

"Is there a problem?"

"Perhaps," said Ludwig. "Lord Meinhard and I may have had words."

"Over what?"

"Let's just say he has little regard for the lives of commoners."

"And you don't believe he'll listen to you?"

"Perhaps I can help?" came a familiar voice.

Ludwig looked up in surprise. "Alexandra? What are you doing here? You should be back in Harlingen."

"Nonsense. My place is here, amongst my father's men. A friendly face, if you will, to help lift their spirits."

"Then you've made a right mess of it," said Cyn. "You're in the middle of Verfeld companies, not those of your father."

"Perhaps I should clarify, then," said Alexandra. "I was with the warriors of Luwen, but then I heard Ludwig had returned to us. They say you went to the court of King Diedrich. Is that true?"

"Yes," he replied.

She glanced at Cyn.

"It's all right," said Ludwig. "She knows the entire story."

"Very well," said Alexandra. "I wondered if you'd seen Lord Emmett?"

"I did, as a matter of fact. He released me from my imprisonment."

A flush came to her cheeks. "He's here?"

"No, I'm afraid not, at least not how you mean." He pointed eastward. "He's over there, leading his men in the army of Neuhafen, even though his heart's not in it."

"How would you know that?"

"He told me so himself, just before we parted ways."

"So it has come to this," said Alexandra. "We are doomed to fight on opposite sides."

"Tomorrow, there'll be a great battle," said Ludwig. "A battle which will decide the fate of both our kingdoms. Should King Diedrich win, he'll likely execute the nobles of Hadenfeld, including your father."

"And if we win? Will not Otto insist on the same fate for the nobles of Neuhafen?"

"Likely, but if that should come to pass, I'll plead for leniency for Lord Emmett."

"You would do that for an enemy?"

"He saved my life. I can at least return the favour, but there's more to it than that."

"Then, for Saint's sake, explain it to me!"

"Much depends on tomorrow's battle. When the rebel barons rose up against Otto's rule, we fought in these very same hills. Yes, we won the battle, but we lost so many men, none remained to take the war to the enemy."

"I know my history."

"What I'm trying to say is this," said Ludwig. "We can't afford another victory like that. We must defeat this menace once and for all, not just by destroying their army, but by bringing them back into the fold."

"And how would we go about doing that?"

"By offering amnesty."

"Amnesty? You can't be serious?"

"I'm deadly serious," said Ludwig, "but hear me out before you judge my words. Ours is a land divided. We spent the last five decades preparing for war with our own people, turning our attention inward. If Hadenfeld or any other Petty Kingdom is to survive, we must look at the future of the entire Continent."

"We are about to fight for our lives. What more is there than that?"

"The Continent is on the brink of a great war. Fighting amongst ourselves will only weaken us in the long run. We must stand united against the threat that draws ever closer."

"What threat?"

"The Halvarian Empire."

"That," said Alexandra, "is a distant and empty menace. They wouldn't dare invade the Petty Kingdoms."

"You're wrong. They've proven time and again, that they have no reservations about doing exactly that. Only by standing with our neighbours can we ever hope to counter them."

"You are a dreamer if you think the Petty Kingdoms could ever stand together."

"It is a dream I cannot let die," insisted Ludwig.

"Halvaria is thousands of miles away."

"So thought the kingdoms that the empire has already absorbed."

"But how does the coming battle work into that? You talk of standing beside the other kingdoms, yet we are about to battle them." A look of understanding crossed her face as if a candle had just been lit. "They want us weak," she said. "Saints alive, do you believe they orchestrated all of this?"

"I don't know if they originated the rebellion, but I'm sure they took advantage of it. Before our split with Neuhafen, ours was one of the largest armies in the Petty Kingdoms."

"How do you know all this?"

Ludwig smiled. "Let's just say a friend warned me about the empire. That and the Stormwinds."

"The Stormwinds? Do you mean the mages? They're in courts all over the Petty Kingdoms. What's their part in all of this?"

Ludwig was at a crossroads. Did he reveal all he suspected and risk sounding unhinged? He looked at Alexandra but saw only her desire to know the truth.

"There are rumours," he finally said.

"What rumours?"

"There's a chance they might be working with Halvaria." He saw her look of scorn. "Hear me out. I'm not making this up."

"Very well," said Alexandra. "Go on."

"When I was in Eisen, I met a woman named Mina Stormwind. She offered her support to guarantee Otto's victory."

"She is only one person. How could she do that?"

"Through influence, I would suspect."

"And you turned her down?"

"I did. Better to die an honest man than survive under the yoke of another."

"But you could've avoided all this bloodshed!"

Ludwig looked around at all the warriors making preparations for tomorrow's battle. "No. Mina Stormwind's offer said nothing about stopping the war, only guaranteeing victory. Many still would have died, and she would've had command over the victors, regardless of who won. This battle is not about Hadenfeld and Neuhafen; it's about control. It will decide who controls our future—the Petty Kingdoms or this family of mages."

"And you really believe they're that powerful?"

"I do. I also have confirmation they were behind a Halvarian plot to foment war in the north between other Petty Kingdoms. So you see, it's not a tactic they're unfamiliar with."

"And do you think King Diedrich is aware of this?"

"No, nor do I think he cares, or Otto, for that matter. They are both consumed with the desire to reunite our two kingdoms on their own terms."

"Who knows all of this?"

"Very few. Cyn and Sig know most of it, along with a few people up north, and now you. Beyond that, I can't truly say."

"So, how do we fight this?"

"We start by winning this battle, then rebuild our relationship with Neuhafen, what little there was of it."

"And the Stormwinds?"

"We work to reduce their influence. I don't believe it would take much for Otto to refuse their offers, but I doubt Diedrich would willingly part with Mina Stormwind."

"Have you tried warning him?"

"No, but then again, I wasn't well received at the court of Eisen. It's too late now, although a parley might afford us the opportunity."

"You really think they'll parley?" said Alexandra.

"It's a common courtesy, especially before an imminent battle. It gives the illusion of actually desiring peace. In essence, it's all theatre, designed to calm the nerves of common soldiers."

"And does it work?"

"Not in my experience, although perhaps Cyn might have a better idea."

"Don't look at me," said Cyn. "I was a mercenary, remember? We never got to participate in any parleys."

Ludwig stood. "Much as I'd like to stay and chat, I must try talking some sense into my fellow barons."

"Perhaps I can help?" offered Alexandra. "What is it you want them to do?"

"Move into position tonight rather than in the morning."

"He thinks Neuhafen might try sending in scouts," added Cyn.

"I'll bring your concerns to my father," said Alexandra. "At the very least, I should be able to convince him of the necessity for additional sentries."

"Good. Then I'll talk to Lords Jurgen and Morgan. Perhaps between us, we'll be able to stop the enemy from learning more about our numbers." He turned to Cyn. "You know your orders?"

"Aye. I'm to march the men up to the hills and have them take their positions for tomorrow's battle. If it's all right with you, I'll put the footmen in front with the militia to the rear."

"Surely you mean the opposite," said Alexandra. "My father always puts the militia to the front. It keeps them from running."

"It's a poor tactic," replied Cyn. "Militia is, for the most part, poorly trained and woefully unprotected. Putting them out front makes them more likely to break and send them running for cover amongst your troops. I shouldn't have to tell you how badly that would disrupt a defence."

41

SHOWDOWN

SUMMER 1100 SR

The army of Neuhafen marched across the field. Each baron led his own group of companies, his ceremonial arms emblazoned on a banner, announcing to all that battle would soon be joined.

Ludwig watched from the saddle, bedecked in the armour Cyn and Sigwulf had thought to bring with them. Sigwulf moved his horse beside Ludwig's and stared out across the hills. "Quite the sight, isn't it?"

"How many would you say they have?" asked Ludwig.

"You're the one who counted them."

"I did, but I meant the men directly opposite us. Doubtless, there are more to the south, but we need to know how many our own men will face."

"Hard to say," said Sigwulf. "Maybe a third more than us? They appear to be better equipped, if that armour is any indication."

"I would agree, although I'd like to know where their knights are."

"In reserve, most likely."

"Did they try anything last night?"

"About a half a dozen tried to sneak up on our camp, but we warned them off. Have you heard from anybody else?"

"No," said Ludwig, "but then again, they're likely far too consumed by the enemy's presence. Like them, it appears we have little choice but to watch them line up their warriors opposite ours."

Sigwulf grunted. "That will take half the morning, at least. It's too bad Otto wouldn't consider a cavalry charge. That could have driven them into chaos."

"He doesn't have the numbers." Ludwig spotted the banner of King Diedrich. "It looks as if our guest of honour has arrived."

"So it would seem. Perhaps we'll get lucky and capture him like we did the King of Andover?"

"I doubt we'd be so lucky twice."

Cyn came up alongside them. "You're wanted, Ludwig. The king desires your presence."

"Now?"

"I hardly think he would've sent Sir Petrus otherwise."

Ludwig looked over his shoulder to where the knight waited. "Very well. It's not as if I can ignore a king's summons. Any idea what this is about?"

Cyn shrugged. "It's not as if they discussed this with me. Anyway, you won't miss much. This lot will be marching into position till well past noon."

Ludwig turned his horse around, trotting over to Sir Petrus. "I understand the king has summoned me?"

"He has, my lord. He wishes to consult with you about the coming battle. Well, that and the inevitable parley."

"Why in the name of the Saints would he want me? I'm the most junior baron he's got."

"True," said the knight, "but you are his cousin, even if a distant one."

"Very well. Take me to His Majesty."

They rode along the crest of the hill, the enemy still visible in the distance.

"Exciting, isn't it?" said the knight. "I can hardly wait to sink my steel into those rebels."

"I presume you haven't seen battle before?"

"Why would you say that?"

"You seem eager to fight."

"I've trained my whole life for this. It is the most glorious of men's pursuits."

"Actually, it's a stinking mess of entrails and blood, but don't let me dampen your spirits."

The knight grimaced. "Is it truly that bad?"

"In my experience, battle consists of a lot of waiting followed by short durations of pure terror, where you'll do anything to escape the horror of what's happening around you."

"Didn't you distinguish yourself in the north?"

"Aye, I did, but I fought because I had no choice, just as we do here. You speak of glory, but a battlefield is anything but. I'm not saying we shouldn't fight. Saints alive, Diedrich has given us few options in the matter, but you shouldn't revel in it."

The knight sobered. "Thank you, Lord. I shall remember your words."

"Good. Now tell me what kind of mood Otto was in when last you saw him?"

"I would describe him as nervous. He was pacing as he is wont to do when wrestling with a difficult decision."

"And he asked for all his nobles? Or just me?"

"Just you, Lord. He said it was a matter of life and death, though he didn't see fit to elaborate."

"Just out of curiosity, how much did you tell him about our time in the north?"

"I told him everything, save for Lady Charlotte's illness. Why? Was I not supposed to? Please don't tell me I angered you, Lord."

"I can't be angry with you for carrying out your duty. I just wish I'd been the one to report on our adventures."

"Indeed, Lord, but upon our return, you headed straight to Verfeld Keep with your new bride while I, in turn, came home to Harlingen. I could hardly put off reporting to the king."

"How does he feel about the coming battle?"

"It's hard to tell," said Sir Petrus. "He seems of good spirits, but he's definitely not his usual jovial self."

"Come now. I would never describe Otto as jovial."

"Yet there is precedent for it. I'm told he was most good-natured at the last Midwinter Feast. They say it's his favourite time of year, likely because of the food."

"He does have a healthy appetite," said Ludwig.

The king's standard came into view as they entered the camp. Two knights stood outside his tent, looking splendid in their plate armour. Ludwig and Sir Petrus dismounted, then passed their reins over to an attendant, making their way to the entrance.

Ludwig halted a moment, looking over the knights. They both wore brightly polished mail, leaving him wondering if either had ever seen any real battle. He shook his head, then went inside, Sir Petrus following.

Still pacing as the knight had indicated, Otto had his back to the door upon their entry. He reached the far end of the tent, then turned abruptly and immediately spotted the new arrivals.

"Ah, Ludwig. There you are. Just the man I wanted to see. Would you care for some wine?" He waved a hand at a servant who lifted a tray bearing two cups and handed them to Ludwig and Sir Petrus. A woman entered with an urn which she used to fill the cups with a golden-hued liquid.

"Mead," explained the king. "I hope you like it."

Ludwig sipped sparingly, but the knight tipped his back, draining the cup.

"What did you want to see me about, m'lord?" said Ludwig, remembering the king's preference.

"I'm having doubts, Ludwig, and that's not good."

"Doubts?"

"Yes. About making a stand here. Perhaps it would be better if I withdrew into Harlingen?"

"And abandon the countryside to these men? I think not, Majesty. You have your army assembled. I say it's time to use it."

"Yes, but you would, wouldn't you? After all, you're a veteran of numerous battles."

"I would hardly say numerous, m'lord. By my count, there's only been the two: one at Chermingen, the other at Regnitz, and all I did there was get captured."

"You fought at Hasdorf only a few days ago, not to mention Grienwald. You're one of only a handful of my men who have seen battle."

Ludwig wanted to argue the point but then thought better of it. Otto had summoned him because of some need. He'd best get to the root of it as quickly as possible. He changed tactics. "How can I help?"

"What are your thoughts on the coming battle?"

"You fought them to a standstill all those years ago. Do you not believe you can do so again?"

"Fifty years ago, I was a newly crowned king. Now I'm an old man. Tell me, and be honest with me, have I lost my wits?"

"In what way?"

"Dealing with this invasion in the same way as last time. Is it folly to do the same thing and expect anything different?"

"You don't believe you can win?"

"No," said Otto. "That's not it. I'm not worried about whether or not I can win; I'm concerned about the cost. Am I mad to make a stand here and watch a generation of young men throw their lives away?"

"What's the alternative? To sit idly by and let them ravage the countryside? Or would you prefer to submit to their rule?"

Otto bristled. "No! I'll never do that."

"Then it appears you have little choice. Might I ask your plan of attack?"

"I have none. That is to say, I shall leave the attacking up to our adversary."

"Are you sure that's wise?"

"We have the advantage of the terrain. I would not so easily give that up."

"A wise move," said Ludwig. "Yet we must be prepared to act, should the opportunity present itself."

"What are you suggesting?"

"What advantage do they possess?"

"Hah," said Otto. "You answer a question with a question. How does that help?"

"Indulge me."

"Very well. Their advantage would be in numbers."

"True," said Ludwig, "but we have the advantage of position. Anything else?"

"Their knights outnumber ours, though how they achieved that is beyond me."

"I suspect we may find out many of them are foreign. Many knights in the Petty Kingdoms are looking for someone to serve."

"Yes, but where do the funds to equip and pay such individuals come from? They have no more land than we do."

Ludwig shrugged. "Think of them as mercenaries—warriors bought and paid for by outside coins."

"Outside?" said Otto. "Are you suggesting someone's been helping Diedrich?"

"How else would you explain such numbers? The question is not so much about their quantity than it is about quality."

"I'm not sure what you're suggesting?"

"I fought several knights at Hasdorf. Would it surprise you that some of them were missing pieces of armour?"

"Missing? What do you mean, missing?"

"I saw a spear go into the neck of a knight who wore no gorget to prevent such a wound. To me, that speaks of inexperience, either that or poverty."

"Could the design of armour be so different in other regions?"

"I wouldn't think so," said Ludwig, "at least not in the places I saw on the way to Reinwick. And then there's the example of the Temple Knights. You wouldn't catch one without a full suit of mail."

"So their quality is lacking. I like where this is going. Anything else you can tell me?"

"Yes. Knights are the only horsemen they have, aside from their captains, of course."

"I'm not sure that helps us. We have mounted men-at-arms, but not many. I doubt they'd fare well against knights."

"Might I make a suggestion?"

"Of course," said Otto. "It's refreshing to see someone offering something, rather than just agreeing with what I say. What is it you'd like to propose?"

"Combine all your men-at-arms into one group."

"Hard to do that. They're not mine to command."

"But you are the king. Your orders take precedence over a mere baron, surely?"

"Yes, in theory, but the last thing I want is for a baron to refuse. They know I need them more than they need me."

Ludwig straightened. "There is no time for such games, m'lord. Give me the orders to mass the men-at-arms, and I shall command them."

"And if they refuse you?"

"They won't."

"How can you be so sure?"

"Because the future of Hadenfeld depends on it."

"Surely you're being melodramatic. It's only two companies."

"Two companies at the right time and place can make all the difference. Consider this, Your Majesty; we are in a fight for our very lives. Can we allow petty squabbles over power to destroy everything we hold dear?"

"You're right, of course. If I were thirty years younger, I'd have the strength to lead them myself. As it is, I'll have to content myself with leading my knights."

"You're going to lead them in person?"

"Naturally," said Otto. "I am their king after all."

"Might I suggest you reconsider?"

"And why would I do that?"

"You are our king, Majesty, and we need your guidance to lead us through these trying times."

"For Saint's sake, Ludwig, I'm leading a charge, not a garden party. I have done this before, you know."

"And I don't mean to suggest otherwise, but there are younger men better suited, don't you agree?"

"I shall hear no more of it." Otto smiled. "However, I will write this letter designating you commander over the men-at-arms. Is that agreeable to you?"

"It is, m'lord."

"Good. Now give me a moment to get the thing written, then you can be on your way." The king called for a servant and then began composing his orders.

Ludwig wandered around the tent as he waited. Otto was not known for extravagant tastes, yet somehow, this modestly furnished abode said volumes about his character. He'd ruled Hadenfeld for over fifty years, the longest reigning monarch in the kingdom's history. Was his rule now coming to an end? Ludwig found it hard to imagine the Throne without

Otto on it, then an odd thought struck him. "Excuse me, m'lord? Might I ask a question?"

Otto chuckled. "You may indeed, although I cannot guarantee an answer. What is it you'd like to know?"

"Who will command the army should you meet with ill fortune?"

"That would be Lord Morgan. He is my heir after all."

The answer caught Ludwig off balance. "Are you suggesting Morgan is the prince?"

"I suppose he is, although that is a recent development."

"How recent, if I may be so bold as to ask?"

"Within the last week, if you must know. Clarence succumbed to his illness, moving everyone up the list."

"Clarence?"

"Yes, my grandnephew. He was always a sickly child, but we all thought he'd grow out of it as he got older. Unfortunately, such was not the case. I suppose it was probably for the better in the grand scheme of things. Hadenfeld needs a strong ruler, not a sickly one. You must remember that when I'm gone."

"Me? I'm far down the list."

"At the moment, yes, but we are about to fight for our very existence. There's a good chance some of us might die. You could even end up as king by the time this battle is decided."

His words sobered Ludwig, and his heart tightened. Would there be that much bloodshed? He'd seen death on the battlefield before at Chermingen, but the losses were mainly confined to his own company and the king's knights. Suddenly the direness of their situation pressed in against him, leaving him struggling to breathe.

Otto, sensing his distress, placed his hand on his shoulder. The effect was immediate; a calmness flowed into Ludwig, restoring him to his former self.

"I know this is a lot to bear," said the king, "but I would have you prepared for what is to come. Chances are you won't become king, at least not for some time, but Morgan, my heir designate, has no children of his own, and the rest of my family is ill-suited to the challenges of being king."

"Then why name them as heirs?"

"I have little choice. It is how our laws work. Were I a younger man, I would take action to change how things are done, but it's too late now. We must lie in the bed we have made."

"We are not ready to be rid of you yet, m'lord."

Otto smiled. "I like you, Ludwig. You remind me of myself when I was much younger, although I daresay you have a better head on your shoulders than I ever did. I'm an old man now, and even if I survive tomorrow's battle, it shall not be much longer before I make that final journey to the Afterlife. I would ask that you do all you can to support Morgan."

"And if someone else ends up becoming king?"

"Then you must do what you can to support and guide him. You haven't been baron for very long, yet you gained the respect of all, except possibly for Lord Harvald. It appears his eldest took offence at you for your attention to Lady Alexandra." Otto chuckled. "Well, that and the fact you humiliated him in what was almost a duel. By the Saints, man, what were you thinking?"

"That's just it. I wasn't thinking. It just happened. I will admit, when I returned to Hadenfeld, I was unprepared for what lay waiting for me. Word had reached me that my father was ill, and I hoped we could mend the rift between us. When I learned of his death, all that came crashing to a halt."

"It is not easy to lose a father," said the king. "And even less so when one is not present at their passing. Having said that, maybe it was better you weren't there. I watched my own father waste away during his final days, and the vision still haunts me. I'd prefer to remember him as a vibrant and decisive king."

A rider appeared, a herald, if his clothes were any indication, followed by two of Otto's knights.

"Your Majesty," the fellow began without any introduction. "I bring greetings from King Diedrich of Neuhafen. He invites you to settle your differences by parley."

"Does he, now? Well then, we'd best see what he has to say for himself."

"I shall let you go, m'lord," said Ludwig. "I should get back to my men."

Otto shot him a quick look. "Not quite yet, I think. I need you to help keep my temper in check." He smiled. "I'm also curious to see how he reacts when he learns you escaped his dungeon!"

42

PARLEY

SUMMER 1100 SR

L udwig and Otto rode onto the battlefield, the knights maintaining a respectful distance. The Neuhafen herald guided them to King Diedrich, who waited on the road, halfway between where the armies lined up to face one another. An ominous backdrop against which the fate of two kingdoms would be decided.

Otto slowed as they approached, his gaze locked on the King of Neuhafen. In stark contrast, Ludwig stared at Mina Stormwind, the king's advisor.

Diedrich smiled, although it appeared forced. "Greetings, Uncle."

That simple greeting shocked Ludwig. He knew the barons of Neuhafen had rebelled, but he had no idea the late King Ruger was a part of Otto's actual family.

Diedrich's smile died as his gaze took in Ludwig. "You! How in the name of the Saints did you escape?"

Ludwig merely smiled as he shrugged his shoulders.

"This," explained Otto, "is Diedrich, my sister's son. Like her, he is prone to fits of excitement."

"Do not speak ill of my mother!"

"Or what? You'll invade my country? It's a bit late for that, don't you think?"

The King of Neuhafen closed his eyes, fighting to keep his temper under control.

"Well, Nephew?" said Otto. "You're the one who called for this parley. What is it you propose?"

"You're an old man, Uncle. Name me as your heir, and I'll march back to Eisen, and we can avoid all this bloodshed."

There it was—a flicker of annoyance from Mina Stormwind. She definitely hadn't anticipated this development.

"I wouldn't name you as my heir if you were the last man alive in all the Petty Kingdoms. You dare to come here, with an army no less, and make demands of me? Well, I offer you a counterproposal. Lay down your arms and swear fealty to the true King of Hadenfeld, and I shall spare all your lives."

"And have you award our lands to others? I think not."

"Then it appears we are at a standstill."

"If I may?" said Ludwig. "We are on the brink of a war that will cost the lives of hundreds, if not thousands. Surely there is a way to come to an agreement and avoid such a tragedy?"

Mina Stormwind's eyes bore into him. The sight was unsettling, to say the least, but he ignored it as much as possible, focusing instead on each of the kings. "This battle will solve nothing. Better, I think, to continue with the way things are: two kingdoms sharing a border in relative peace, each content with his own lands?"

"No!" shouted Otto. "It's time I corrected my mistakes. I allowed your father to withdraw from battle fifty years ago, an error I shall not repeat. Neuhafen belongs to Hadenfeld. It always has, and it always will."

Diedrich reddened. "Our history paints a different tale, one of oppression and subjugation. You enslaved our people, working them to the bone to support your feeble Crown."

"Enslaved? The men of Hadenfeld are here to protect their lands. Their land, Diedrich, not the land of their masters. What slave would do that? And as for your history, I couldn't care less what lies it contains. We are a free people who will fight to protect what is ours."

"Come now," said Ludwig. "We could say the same of Neuhafen. Such arguing serves no one's purposes." He held the gaze of Mina Stormwind. "The men of both lands share a common ancestry; to fight would be to pit cousin against cousin. I urge you to consider an alternative. Let us find a third party to host a meeting where both of you can sit down and hash out your differences in a civilized manner."

"And who would host?" said Mina Stormwind. "All the Petty Kingdoms are locked into alliances. There is no such thing as a neutral third party, Lord Ludwig. Of all people, I would have thought you would understand that."

She tried to goad him, but it failed. "I'm sure the Church would be willing to host it, with Temple Knights to guard it. Unless such an august organization makes you feel threatened?"

"We fear nothing," said Diedrich.

"He intends to trap you, Lord," said Mina. "Even as we speak, the army of Otto seeks to gain the upper hand."

Diedrich looked at her in a panic. "A trap, you say?"

She pointed to the north. "Those men moved up while we were talking."

"They did no such thing," said Ludwig. "Those are the men of Verfeld, and they've been there all night."

"Of course, you'd say that. You'd do anything to get your way. You are nothing but a vainglorious fool. A moment of fame in the north, and now you're trying to stretch it out to last a lifetime. He is nothing but a mercenary, my king—a man driven by war to take what he wants."

"And are you any different?" replied Ludwig. "You claim to represent King Diedrich, but you serve only your own interests. Ask yourself this, Your Majesty; who amongst your advisors has been most vocal in their support for this war?"

Diedrich appeared to waver, clearly out of his depth, leaving Ludwig to wonder how firm her grasp was upon the king?

Mina Stormwind reached out to place her hand on Diedrich's forearm. "You must do what you believe is right, my king. If you feel my counsel is detrimental to your rule, dismiss me. I give you my word I shall never again set foot in Neuhafen."

The king stiffened in the saddle. "The choice to invade, or rather liberate, Hadenfeld was mine and mine alone. Surrender your army, Uncle, and name me king, or see me lay waste to this entire land."

Otto shook his head. "So now you would have me surrender my Throne to you? Couldn't even wait for my death? Well, you're out of luck, you ungrateful brat. My men will stand and fight to the death to prevent the likes of you from ever setting foot in Harlingen. Go back to your army and say your prayers, Diedrich. You're going to need all the help you can get. To the Underworld with you!"

"It shall not be me who feeds the worms, Uncle. When I'm done with you, I'll execute every man who even dares to utter your name." Diedrich wheeled his horse around in a fury, tearing off for the safety of his own men.

"It appears," said Otto, "that the parley is over."

The Neuhafen herald bowed respectfully, then turned towards his own lines, Mina Stormwind copying his actions.

"Come," said Otto. "We must prepare for the onslaught."

. . .

Not including this campaign, Ludwig's experience with battles was limited to taking part in the siege of Regnitz Keep and the fight at Chermingen. He'd been immersed in the melee in those, with very little understanding of the battle's overall organization. Today, however, things were quite different.

The army of Neuhafen regrouped to the north, trying to line up against his own companies. The troops of Verfeld occupied a hill, forcing the enemy to advance across an open field.

He had to admit the sight was impressive, for Diedrich held the advantage in numbers. Of course, there was more to a battle than simply numbers, but he couldn't shake the fear that the enemy would overwhelm them.

From Ludwig's limited vantage point, the enemy's line stretched away to the south. The hills opposite him obstructed much of his view, but if Diedrich's pickets were any indication, a flank attack would decide the outcome this day. As he mulled this over, he realized his own men might very well bear the brunt of the battle.

He dispatched Sigwulf to take command of Lord Merrick's men, leaving Cyn to watch over those of Verfeld should he fall.

"I don't like the looks of this," he said, more to himself than anyone else.

"Good," said Cyn. "If you start liking battle, then we're all lost."

"Are you becoming a philosopher now?"

"No, merely a realist. It's fine to feel proud of fighting after the battle. That's how we deal with all that death, but before? They say it's a sign of madness."

"Who's they?"

Cyn shrugged. "No idea, but my father certainly believed it. He hated bloodshed."

"But he was the captain of a mercenary company; that's their stock in trade."

"It is, yet he would've been content serving as a garrison somewhere. Don't get me wrong, he loved warfare, studied it all his life, but he loathed the death associated with it."

"A complex man, to be sure."

"He was," said Cyn.

"And did he teach you everything he knew?"

"He did. Why?"

"I'm curious if your understanding of warfare tells you anything about this battle?"

She gazed out over the enemy troops still trying to get into their positions. "What would you like to know?"

"Are they going to attack us here, on the flank?"

"I don't think so."

"Why would you say that?"

"They had ample opportunity to outflank us, yet they're only now moving into a position opposite us. That tells me they're only there to pin us in place. I suspect the real attack will be against the middle of our line. That's where Otto is, isn't it?"

"It is, just behind the men of Lord Meinhard. What makes you think that's his objective?"

"I don't know Diedrich," said Cyn, "but his deployment is predictable and unimaginative. What was he like at the parley?"

"Angry," said Ludwig, "and headstrong, although perhaps stubborn is a more apt description. Does that help support your theory?"

"It does indeed. There's nothing quite so direct as an attack on the centre of your enemy. The risk is that the enemy's flanks envelop you as you attack, hence the need for these men to oppose us. Trust me, this will not be a battle involving anything grand in the way of tactics, merely a bloodbath where both sides keep pouring in men until one side or the other gives way. I only hope we come out on the winning side."

"Well," said Ludwig. "There are two companies of mounted men-at-arms behind the men of Verfeld, if that helps."

She smiled. "Yes. I see you have them hidden by the hill to keep them from the enemy's sight. Very clever of you, Ludwig."

"Still, it remains to be seen if there'll be a chance for me to use them." He glanced at his own men, curious to know how they were holding up. They looked nervous but eager, a good sign amongst warriors. "Do we have lots of arrows?"

"As many as we could find," said Cyn. "Each man has an extra bundle within easy reach, should they need it. All we must do now is hope the enemy comes close enough for us to use them."

Gustavo, one of his men, approached on foot.

"Problem?" said Ludwig.

The warrior bowed his head briefly. "The men were wondering, Lord, if you would lead them in prayer before the battle begins."

"I am no Holy Man."

"And they no saints, Lord, but they respect you, and a word of prayer would hurt no one."

"Don't look at me," said Cyn. "It wasn't my idea to leave Father Vernan back in Verfeld. It was Siggy's."

"Very well. I shall address them."

Ludwig rode out in front, remaining on his horse to ensure he was visible to all. The men of Verfeld chatted amongst themselves, but as Ludwig removed his helmet, they all fell silent.

When praying before a battle, it was common to invoke the name of Saint Cunar, the patron Saint of battle. As Ludwig mulled over what to say, he thought of Mathew and remembered how he'd brought him peace of mind in Eisen's dungeon.

"Blessed Saint Mathew," he began, trying to remember the exact words. "Watch over us this day and protect us in our time of need. Give us strength that we might endure what is to come and the serenity to accept our fate, whatever that may be. Guide us, oh blessed Saint, that we may pass to the Afterlife, knowing you wait to guide us to a better place." He paused a moment, satisfied with his own interpretation of the prayer. "Saints be with us."

"Saints be with us all," came the reply, echoing off the Hills of Harlingen. Ludwig lifted his helmet, preparing to don it once more, but then his men cheered, leading him to change his mind. Instead, he raised the helmet high into the air. "For Verfeld, Hadenfeld, and the king!"

A roar of defiance replaced the cheer, again echoing off the hills. Ludwig looked on with pride, knowing these men would do their duty. He waited for the shouts to die down before returning to where Cyn was, his face revealing his pleasure at their exuberance.

"That was quite the performance," she said. "Ever considered going into the theatre?"

He grinned. "No. I'm perfectly content as the Baron of Verfeld."

"I wouldn't have taken you for someone to pray."

"I've been praying ever since I left home. I've just chosen to keep it to myself."

"Tell me you're not considering becoming a Temple Knight?"

"No, of course not, but a little faith can go a long way towards comforting a person in battle."

"I noticed you prayed to Saint Mathew. That's very clever."

"Clever? I did that because I found comfort in his words, nothing more. Why do you consider it clever?"

"Mathew is the Saint of the common man. As such, he's seen as their protector. Saint Cunar, on the other hand, wants a man to give up his life in service to something higher. If you ask me, it all smacks of fanaticism. I'd much rather fight behind someone who doesn't take chances."

Ludwig couldn't help but laugh. "Doesn't take chances? That's precisely the opposite of what we did at Chermingen."

"That was different," said Cyn.

"Was it? It looks the same to me."

"That's because you're not looking at it objectively. At Chermingen, you led a desperate attack, but not out of a desire to die gloriously. You honestly thought you had a chance of success. A fanatic would have resigned themselves to death and charged out anyway."

"So it's better to be desperate than fanatical?"

"Precisely. Now, don't let your newfound religion control you. That road only leads to ruin."

"Don't worry, I won't. Someone once told me the Saints offer guidance to help us get the most out of life. They're not there to dictate anything, merely suggest."

"Do the Temple Knights understand that?"

"I'm sure they do," said Ludwig. "Well, the good ones, at least."

"Like Sister Charlaine?"

"You mean Temple Captain Charlaine," he corrected. "And yes, she's a perfect example of all that's right with the Holy Orders. Unfortunately, the same cannot be said for all."

"It's a pity they're not here to help us fight off the enemy," said Cyn. "Then again, it's probably good they're not, considering they might join the other side."

"The Church tries to remain above politics, but you can only do that for so long. Sooner or later, everyone is forced to take sides in a conflict."

"Speaking of taking sides, what about all our alliances we have across the Petty Kingdoms? Why aren't they here?"

"That's an easy one to answer," said Ludwig. "Otto would have sent word as soon as he heard about an invasion, but even our closest ally is at least a week away, and then they'd need time to assemble their army. By the time they're ready to march, this war will be over and done with."

"Do you know if Neuhafen has any allies with them?"

"I noticed no evidence of any amongst his army, but he definitely has foreign knights hired into his service."

"That's a relief. We'll have our hands full just dealing with this lot. I'd hate to imagine how many more of them there'd be if they had allies."

Ludwig glanced to his right, trying to see how the men of Drakenfeld fared, but trees blocked his view.

"Siggy's fine," said Cyn. "And he knows how to handle them. He won't let you down."

"I never suggested he would."

"True, but you thought it."

"Can you read minds now?"

"Whoever said I couldn't before? Seriously, though, he knows what to do. He was born to this."

"You were the one raised by mercenaries," said Ludwig.

"Yes, but he has it in him to be a great leader. His father had a claim to the Throne of Abelard, although distant. If it hadn't been for their defeat at Krosnicht, he might've become heir to their Crown."

"Didn't he have an older brother?"

"He did, and a sister as well, but it still would've made him royalty. Not that he was ready for that, as he wasn't yet an adult when they fled to Braymoor. Of course, it's interesting to imagine how his life would have been different."

"Perhaps," said Ludwig, "but then he wouldn't have met you."

"And is that a good thing? Sometimes I wonder if I'm not holding him back."

"You're not. Quite the opposite. In fact, you give him strength. Without you, he wouldn't be the man he is today. That works both ways, of course. The two of you, together, are more than the sum of your parts."

"Well," said Cyn, "my parts thank you for that, and especially for Siggy. And thanks to you too for—"

"Me? What did I do?"

"You brought us to Verfeld and gave us a home. You can't ask for much more than that."

"Oh, I don't know—maybe a home that isn't subject to invasion?"

"But that's good news; don't you see? The very fact someone wants to conquer us illustrates how desirable our home truly is."

"You're amazing, Cyn. Only you could find a rainbow in amongst the storm of this war."

"That's what I'm here for."

43

BATTLE IS JOINED
SUMMER 1100 SR

E ven from his vantage point atop the northernmost hill, Ludwig could see little of the battle, but horns blaring from the south informed him that the enemy was advancing. Diedrich was doing precisely what Cyn predicted—attacking the centre of Otto's line. It galled Ludwig to be stuck here doing nothing while enemy warriors bore down on his king, but he knew his time would come.

His men waited, gripping their weapons as if death itself was coming for them. Ludwig took a deep breath, trying to calm his nerves. It wasn't that he was afraid, but the endless waiting was almost too much to bear.

His mind wandered, spurred on by the afternoon sun casting its spell over everyone until the sounds of battle drifted towards them. The centre of Otto's line was likely now engaged in combat, while the flanks would hold their position to ensure the king was not encircled.

Mesmerized by the noise, Ludwig tried to envision the fight going on, but Cyn broke his reverie.

"Look," she said, pointing. "Over there!"

Directly opposite, a mass of footmen had just cleared the woods and were heading straight for them. They were still some distance off but moving quickly.

"Bring up the archers," said Ludwig. "The trees are too thick on the left, so place them on our right. And move the militia into support positions. We may need them after all."

It felt good to finally do more than just stand and watch. He cast aside all thoughts of Otto's fight to concentrate on what was about to happen.

Cyn moved the archers up, but they held their volleys until the enemy came closer. Lightly armoured men led the Neuhafen advance, likely the local militia. Their steady pace conveyed an impression of disciplined troops, yet their overall lack of armour left them at a distinct disadvantage. When they were within fifty paces, Cyn gave the order, and the volleys flew forth. Many arrows fell short on the first try, but subsequent volleys didn't take long to find their mark.

The attackers entered the refuge of the woods at the base of the hills, only to be met by Ludwig's foot soldiers. Already weakened by the archers, the militia of Neuhafen broke, rushing eastward in an attempt to find safety.

The warriors of Verfeld wanted to pursue, but Ludwig ordered them to hold their positions, for he'd spotted the banner of Ramfelden. Although he couldn't recall who their lord was, he knew experienced soldiers were about to descend on him.

Despite the woods, the enemy charged forward, the heavily armoured warriors eager to engage his men. The wall of troops struck his line, and the battle was on.

A warrior of Neuhafen cut his way through the line, and Ludwig urged his mount onward, his sword at the ready. The man's axe made contact with his shin, but his grieve deflected the blade. Ludwig countered with a strike of his own, smashing against his opponent's helmet, sending him sprawling. He ignored the man, his horse trampling the unmoving foe as he pushed forward into the thick of the fighting. He struck out many times before they surrounded him, and then he was fighting for his very life.

Someone to his right tugged on his leg, and he feared being pulled from the saddle. He turned to knock the man down, but Edwig rushed forward, striking out with his axe before he could act. Ludwig shifted his attention to his other side, where a spearman stabbed out, taking his mount in the flank. His horse reared up, roaring in pain, sending Ludwig tumbling off his mount. He freed his feet from the stirrups, but the fall knocked the wind from him.

Something splattered against his helmet as he lay there. He threw up his visor to see Edwig standing over him, his axe carving a crimson arc. A spear jabbed out, but the axe caught it on the shaft, pushing it aside. Another foe stabbed his sword into the Therengian's chest, but his mail stopped it short of killing him. Edwig fell back with a cry, his feet tripped up by his lord's body.

Ludwig rose, even as spears struck out at him. One scraped off his chest while another grazed his arm, screeching as the steel scraped across his armour. He'd lost his sword as he fell, but catching sight of Edwig's axe, he tore it from the youth's hand, then turned to face his foes, his anger building.

With a snarl, he lunged forward, ignoring the feeble attempts to penetrate his armour. His axe took off an arm, then plunged it into another's flesh. The battle came down to just him and the men in his immediate vicinity. No longer was it a clash of kingdoms; it was a matter of self-preservation, tearing flesh from his enemies before they did the same to him.

A swordsman appeared before him, and Ludwig struck out again, hoping to end the fight. His foe, however, used his own shield to deflect the axe.

At that moment, Ludwig knew he'd miscalculated. An axe is a slow weapon, much more so than a sword. He would have little time to recover before he could strike again. This flashed through his mind in an instant, and then a spear came out of nowhere, taking his opponent in the face.

Edwig appeared at his side. "Your sword, my lord."

"Thank you, and here's your axe, although I fear it may require some cleaning."

Gustavo, the Calabrian, joined them, his sword dripping blood. "They're falling back," he said.

Ludwig tried to make sense of it all. They stood their ground, but he was at a loss as to why the enemy fled. He heard his name and turned to see Cyn approaching.

"What happened?" he called out.

She waited until she was beside him to answer. "It was Siggy," she yelled. "He brought the men of Drakenfeld up on their flanks. We defeated them."

"No. That attack was only one small part of a much larger battle. What I want to know is why he didn't commit more men to the assault?"

"Perhaps I can answer that." They both turned to see Rikal leading a man in plate armour who limped along at the end of a rope. "I went down to retrieve some arrows and found this one amongst the dead."

The prisoner straightened himself. "I am Lord Jonas Goswald, Baron of Ramfelden. I demand you treat me with the dignity and respect my title confers."

"Do you know who I am?" asked Ludwig.

The man squinted through his blood-soaked eyes. "I'm afraid I do not, sir. Have we met before?"

"I am Lord Ludwig Altenburg, Baron of Verfeld."

"Impossible! Lord Ludwig died in the dungeons of Eisen."

Ludwig looked at Cyn. "Am I alive?"

She poked him in the arm with the tip of her sword. "Near as I can tell."

Ludwig turned his attention back to his prisoner. "It appears I am very much alive, Lord Jonas." He moved closer, taking a better look at the noble. "I shall have someone care for your wounds, Lord, provided you give me your word to no longer take up arms against us."

"I do, sir. I swear."

"Bring him back to Kandam, and see if he can do something for His Lordship. At the very least, he can clean the wound."

"Aye, sir," said Rikal. The archer paused as if unsure.

"Something wrong?" said Ludwig.

"It's just that... well... he had this on him, sir." He produced a small pouch. "It has coins in it, Lord."

"Indeed? How many, might I ask?"

"Ten golden sovereigns, my lord, along with an assortment of lesser coins."

"I see no purse."

"That is my property," said Lord Jonas, "and I demand you return it to me."

Rikal looked at Ludwig, clearly expecting the worst.

"Oh, very well," said Ludwig. "Hand it over." He took the purse. "Hold out your hands, Rikal." The archer did as he was told, then the Baron of Verfeld emptied the pouch's contents into them. He finished by tossing the now empty purse to Lord Jonas. "There. You have your property back. Is there anything else you'd care to complain about, or shall I execute you now for high treason and spare us a trial?"

The Neuhafen lord paled.

"I am curious about one thing," said Ludwig. "Why did you attack my men and not hold your position like the others?"

"I thought to win fame by defeating your men. Of course, that was when we believed you dead back in Eisen."

"So you expected my men to be leaderless?"

The baron nodded his head. "Obviously, I now see the mistake, but King Diedrich will soon destroy your precious King Otto, and I shall be free once more."

"You're not exactly making a convincing argument to keep you alive." Ludwig nodded to Rikal. "All right, I've heard enough. Get him back behind our lines and keep a close eye on him. You have my permission to kill him if he gives you any trouble. Understood?"

"Aye, my lord."

Ludwig watched them lead Lord Jonas away.

"Well," said Cyn, "I suppose that's one down and seven to go. There were only eight of them, right?"

"Yes," replied Ludwig. "I daresay we won't be that lucky a second time."

Sigwulf rode across the battlefield, picking his way amongst the dead. He climbed the hill and came to rest before his friends. "That was fun," he said. "What's next?"

"Otto will be hard-pressed in the centre," said Ludwig. "We need to send help."

"What are you proposing?"

"I thought to hit Diedrich from the side, but I require you to pin down his forces to the east."

"You take the men-at-arms and ride straight for Diedrich," said Sigwulf. "Cyn and I will take care of the rest." The huge northerner dismounted. "Here, use my horse. Yours has seen better days."

Ludwig hauled himself into the saddle. "I'll see you on the battlefield," he said, then rode off to gather his horsemen.

The men-at-arms were eager to do their part. Ludwig organized them into a long column, the better for them to manoeuvre through the battlefield. Once formed up, they paused, waiting for the men of Drakenfeld and Verfeld to begin their advance.

Ludwig trusted Cyn and Sig to lead his men but felt guilty for not being by their side. Part of him recognized Otto was in danger, yet it still felt like a betrayal to leave the command of his men to others. He shook it off, concentrating instead on the task at hand.

He followed along behind Sigwulf until the great northerner started climbing the enemy's hill. Ludwig then cut south, riding between the armies, his objective the road where the two kings struggled for dominance. He fought off panic as the main attack came into view, for Diedrich had pushed Otto much farther back than he'd expected. For the first time, the prospect of defeat loomed before his eyes.

A group of Neuhafen archers rushed across the valley, intent on catching up to Diedrich's assault. Ludwig's men-at-arms rode in amongst them, sending them scattering, but he didn't stop, leading them straight through the hapless bowmen and out the other side.

He took a moment to reform and then turned his men to face westward. Off in the distance, the knights of King Diedrich fought those of Otto. There was little in the way of reserves, a testament to the attack's ferocity. A trail of dead and dying men led straight to the King of Neuhafen's banner, where even now, the man's army pressed forward, threatening to engulf his uncle.

Ludwig wanted to use a wedge formation, but the men-at-arms had no such training, so he formed a line instead. He had one hundred men at his disposal, a scant few compared to the masses before him, but what he lacked in numbers he more than made up for in surprise. His men would come from the rear, throwing Diedrich's attack into chaos.

He advanced, slowly at first, the better to preserve the horses' strength, but as the distance closed, their pace quickened. One or two knights noted their approach but made no sign of reacting, likely believing them simply reinforcements.

Closer and closer, they rode, and then he waved them on, the horses exploding into a full gallop, striking the enemy from behind, carving into their formation with wild abandon.

Ludwig swung, taking a knight in the back of the head, his sword bouncing off the helmet with a clang, quickly absorbed by the swirl of melee. He stabbed again, hitting his opponent in the armpit. The fellow fell from the saddle to be lost amongst the other horsemen.

Ludwig almost dropped his weapon as a blade smashed against his forearm but quickly struck back, the tip nicking his attacker's reins as it scraped along the top of the knight's gauntlet. He raised his sword in time to block another blow before counterattacking, only to have it career off a shield. All around him, his men lashed out, but their swords did little damage against their enemies' heavy mail. Ludwig wished for an axe or, better yet, a hammer, anything to help penetrate the knights' armour.

As if in answer, an axe descended, but the attacker overreached, the edge missing his forearm, the shaft striking instead. He ran his own blade up the handle and into his attacker's hand. The knight lacked the mail such gauntlets typically employed, wearing leather gloves instead. The edge sliced through his fingers, blood spurting out. He quickly pulled back, leaving his axe behind.

Ludwig dropped his own sword in favour of the axe, then ducked just as another knight stabbed at his face. He brought his new weapon down in a mighty overhand blow that sliced into a pauldron, splitting the metal asunder. A firm tug released the head of his weapon, and then the rider toppled, screaming as he fell from the saddle.

Ludwig urged his horse alongside one of his men to keep up a solid formation, but things rapidly deteriorated. King Diedrich's knights, having realized their predicament, turned around to meet this new menace. Soon, the men-at-arms were beset on all sides.

Ludwig felt panic rising and fought to keep it at bay. All he could think about was Verfeld in flames, the people driven from their homes, Charlotte and his son lying in pools of blood. He wrestled with the urge to scream, then gave in, rage surging through him. His axe swung out, slicing into a thigh, mail tearing apart as he withdrew the blade and struck again. Blood surged up as he nearly severed the knight's leg.

Something bounced off his helm. He turned to see a knight, mace in hand, pulling back for another blow. With a quick jab, Ludwig drove his axe into the knight's visor. It failed to penetrate but twisted the helm slightly to one side, obscuring the man's vision.

The knight's mace swung around wildly to little effect other than to cause him to overextend himself. Ludwig slammed the head of the axe into his foe's armoured arm, failing to penetrate. Still, the resulting impact bent the elbow back at an obscene angle, and the mace went limp, the knight withdrawing into the melee.

Ludwig stood in the middle of a lull in the fighting, aware of only the blood coursing through his veins. Time stopped for a moment before his gaze locked on the banner of King Diedrich. He was close, no more than fifty feet, yet it seemed an impossible distance to cross.

He cast his eyes around, flipping up his visor to get an unobstructed view. His quest to save King Otto had driven him deep into the enemy formation, with none of his own men in sight, yet a calm befell him.

In that instant, he found clarity as if his eyes had opened after a long sleep. His surroundings snapped into sharp focus, and somewhere, deep inside him, arose a strength the likes of which he'd never before experienced.

A trio of knights bore down on him, yet strangely, he knew exactly what they would do. He pulled down his visor and gripped the axe, ready to meet this new menace.

The three knights slowed. The tallest one saluted Ludwig with his sword before charging forth, holding the blade out with the tip aimed straight for Ludwig's head, but he didn't flinch. Instead, he let the attack come, waiting until the last possible moment before impact to knock the sword aside with his axe. He followed the block with a backhand that caught the fellow in the chest. The poor fool's horse rode on even as the knight toppled, his foot catching in the stirrup. Ludwig tore his eyes from the sight, concentrating on the remaining combatants.

44

VICTORY

SUMMER 1100 SR

E ven as their comrade was dragged from the scene, the other two knights charged Ludwig. He swung his axe, leaning over his mount's neck to avoid the swords coming straight for him. His pauldron protected his shoulder from one blade while his own weapon carved through the wrist of the other, denying him the opportunity to strike. The man clutched the wound and spurred on his horse, desperate to get out of Ludwig's reach.

Another blow landed on his shoulder, the force threatening to unseat him. He swung his axe overhead, but before he could bring it crashing down, a lance tip emerging from the man's own belly transfixed him. Ludwig stared in disbelief as the rider toppled from the saddle.

The lance's owner flipped up his visor, revealing the face of Sir Petrus. "I hope I'm not interrupting," he called out.

"Not at all," said Ludwig. "You arrived just in time. Where is the king?"

The knight turned his horse around. "This way, but we must hurry. He is hard-pressed."

They raced past dozens of enemy horsemen, rushing to escape. The battle was winding down, now broken into small clumps fighting it out man to man. One group, their armour soaked in blood, their swords stained crimson, stood amidst a pile of the dead.

Men on foot faced them, including one who could only be King Diedrich. Even caked with blood, his golden armour stood out amongst his personal retinue of knights. He lumbered forward, limping slightly, although Ludwig saw no sign of wounds.

Sir Petrus tried to charge in, but his horse balked, for the ground held too many obstacles. Seeing his chance, Ludwig dismounted, picking his way through the carnage.

"Diedrich!" he screamed.

The King of Neuhafen, mistaking him for an ally, waved him forward, then resumed his advance on Otto's last remaining guard. Ludwig drew close enough to push the king, trying to gain his attention.

Diedrich turned, his eyes opened wide in surprise. "You!" he shouted, lifting his sword, but Ludwig was faster, shoving the head of his axe into His Majesty's breastplate and knocking him to the ground.

The King of Neuhafen scrambled to escape, but his hand slipped on the blood-soaked earth. In desperation, he swung out, his blade crashing into Ludwig's thigh but failing to penetrate the thick armoured plate.

Diedrich looked up in horror as Ludwig brought his axe crashing down. The King of Neuhafen twitched in a last spasm before his lifeless body lay still.

Word of his fate spread fast, and while some warriors ran, the majority tossed their weapons to the ground in surrender.

Someone slapped Ludwig on the back, and he turned to see the face of Sir Petrus beaming at him.

"You did it!" roared the knight. "You killed Diedrich. The war is over!"

Overcome with exhaustion, Ludwig fell to his knees as his legs gave out. "Thank the Saints." A great weariness weighed down upon him, his head spinning, and then he toppled over amongst the dead and dying. The last thing he saw was Sir Petrus, staring down at him, a look of concern written on his face.

Ludwig opened his eyes to a darkened sky. "Where am I?" he called out.

Shoes squished through mud, and then Lady Alexandra stared down at him. "Ludwig? Can you hear me?"

"I'm fine," he said. "What's happened?"

"You collapsed after killing King Diedrich."

"And the rest of his army?"

"Those who didn't flee surrendered. The war is over. You saved us from destruction."

He sat up, only to have his head swim once more.

"You're exhausted," she said. "You should rest."

"I can't, at least not yet. Where's King Otto?"

"Why? What's wrong?"

"I must stop him before he makes a terrible mistake."

"The battle is over. There are no mistakes to make."

Ludwig struggled to his feet. "That's just it. There are plenty. I must speak with Otto before it's too late."

"I don't understand?"

"He'll kill all the barons. Don't you see? And that includes Lord Emmett!"

"Then come. Let us find him before the executions begin."

Before King Otto knelt the barons of Neuhafen, at least the six who survived, their heads bared, their hands tied behind their backs. Knights watched over them with drawn swords, ready to carry out the king's command. Otto's words drifted towards Ludwig as he approached.

"You all deserve a traitor's death." The king looked at a nearby knight holding a great two-handed axe, then nodded.

"Wait!" called out Ludwig. "I beg of you."

The axeman remained still while Otto turned to face the new arrival. "Lord Ludwig? I'm glad to see you up and about. You had me worried there for a while." He shifted his gaze to the prisoners. "What do you think of the great nobles of Neuhafen now?"

"I think, m'lord, executing them would be a mistake."

"You dare to cross your king?"

"Please, Majesty, hear me out. If you should then desire to kill them, then I will object no further."

"Very well. Speak your mind."

"These barons are descended from men of Hadenfeld, m'lord. If we hope to rebuild this kingdom, we must learn to forgive, else we'll forever be at war with those who live to the east."

"But these men rebelled against me!"

"No, Majesty. Their fathers did, but can you blame these men for following their king? They've lived their whole lives in an independent realm, separate from the court of Harlingen. None of them were even born at the time of the rebellion."

"All true," said Otto, "but that doesn't change that they fought against us. I cannot let that go unpunished."

"Then force them to swear allegiance to Hadenfeld, m'lord, under threat of forfeiting their land."

"And how do I know they won't simply rebel at the first opportunity?"

Ludwig walked down the line of prisoners. "You must secure their loyalty through marriage, Majesty." He paused before Lord Emmett.

"Marriage?" said Otto. "Who would want to marry a traitor?"

Ludwig held out his hand to Alexandra. She moved without hesitation.

"Would you agree," Ludwig asked, "to marry Lord Emmett to secure the kingdom?"

"Yes," she replied.

"And would you, Lord Emmett, Baron of Dornbruck, consent to such an agreement?"

"I would," replied the prisoner, "with all my heart."

"And would you henceforth pledge allegiance to King Otto and his heirs and become one with the Kingdom of Hadenfeld?"

"I would."

Ludwig looked at Otto. "The choice you make today, Majesty, determines the future of our land. Will you accept these men into your service and bring peace and prosperity, or blacken your kingdom with their deaths, sowing further distrust and rebellion?"

Otto stepped forward, coming to rest face to face with Ludwig. "Do you truly believe this will bring peace?"

"I do, m'lord, as the Saints are my witnesses."

The king grunted, his ashen face looking as if his very life was fleeing his body. For a moment, Ludwig wondered if Otto would collapse, but then the king spoke. "Well, if the Saints are looking down on us, what else can we do? Very well, I shall spare these men, provided they take an oath to serve me." He looked at the executioner. "Put your axe down. You won't be needed today."

The king's attention turned to the prisoners. "You live this day because of the generous spirit of Lord Ludwig, but let me make this clear: if even one of you break your oath, I shall execute the lot of you. Now stand before your king."

They all rose, Otto's knights moving in to untie the barons' hands.

"Shall you hear their oaths now, m'lord?" asked Ludwig.

"No. We'll take them back to Harlingen and do it there."

"And the rest of their army?"

"Those who take an oath never to raise arms against the Crown are free to leave. Those who don't will be executed tomorrow morning."

"You are most generous, Your Majesty."

"If you say so. Now, go and leave me in peace." Otto turned and made his way back towards camp.

"I must thank you," said Lord Emmett. "I know you risked much by interceding."

"I'm just glad this whole thing's over," said Ludwig. "As for Otto, once you get to know him, he's not such a bad sort."

"Still, you spoke on my behalf"—he grasped Alexandra's hand—"our behalf, and I am truly thankful for that."

"Do you think the other barons of Neuhafen will keep their word?"

"Doubtless, there will be some malcontents amongst their followers, but I think the barons see the wisdom in doing so. For them, the most important thing is that their voices are heard at Otto's court."

"Then I shall work tirelessly to ensure that occurs."

"What do you think will happen now?" asked Alexandra.

"That's a good question," said Ludwig. "Most likely, Otto will send the army home, although I expect a small force to accompany them to Eisen to watch over things."

"Any idea who he'll choose?"

"No, but I suspect there are plenty who would volunteer." He cast his gaze around the area. "To tell the truth, I don't even know who survived the battle?"

"My father did," said Alexandra, "and I saw Lord Morgan wandering the camp, but aside from that, I know nothing. I expect someone should inform my father I am to be married." She looked at Ludwig. "You don't suppose you could do that, do you?"

"Me? I don't think he ever forgave me for not marrying you myself."

"Come now, I'm sure there are no hard feelings."

"How can you say that? And how am I to broach the subject of you marrying Emmett?" Suddenly he began laughing.

"What's so funny?"

"Sorry," said Ludwig, trying to regain his breath. "It just occurred to me I've become a matchmaker. First Lady Rosalyn, and now you."

"Lady Rosalyn? Who's that?"

Ludwig sobered. "The Baron of Regnitz's daughter, but that's a long story."

"Then perhaps," said Lord Emmett, "we might discuss it over a drink?"

"Fair enough, but I must see to my men first. Somewhere out there, I have two captains who are probably worried sick over my absence."

"You mean Captains Marhaven and Hoffman?" said Lady Alexandra. "They're fine."

"What do you mean? Have you seen them?"

"Indeed. They were informed of your injuries when you were brought back to camp to recuperate. The king looks after his loyal subjects."

"And how are they?"

"Uninjured, as far as I could tell, although they both looked exhausted."

"Well then, it appears I have no further excuse to avoid the inevitable. Let's go and talk to your father, shall we?"

"Of course." The two of them were walking away, but Ludwig halted, looking back at Lord Emmett. "You'd better come, too, my friend. That way, you can answer any questions he has."

The Baron of Dornbruck hesitated.

"Something wrong?" asked Ludwig.

"You know, it's strange. I have no fear of fighting on the battlefield, yet the very prospect of talking to my future father-in-law has me shaking in my boots."

"Come now," said Alexandra. "He's not that bad. You tell him, Ludwig."

Ludwig decided not to answer, feeling a bit mischievous after all the stress of battle.

"Ludwig?" she repeated.

He simply shrugged, enjoying the look of dismay upon the Baron of Dornbruck's face, but finally relented. "I'm only teasing. Lord Meinhard is a stern man but fair."

Anyone of import, including those who'd avoided court for years, filled the king's hall in Harlingen. The Second Battle of Harlingen, as it was now called, had broken the power of Neuhafen and reunited Hadenfeld, making it, by all accounts, the largest of the Petty Kingdoms, although much remained an unexplored wilderness.

"Did you ever think you'd see this?" asked Cyn.

"Oh, I don't know," said Sigwulf. "How else could it end with Ludwig back home?"

Ludwig almost choked on his wine.

"Now look what you've done," chided Cyn. "He's gone and made a mess of his new clothes."

"I can hear you both," said Ludwig. "I'm not deaf, and for your information, I didn't get any wine on me."

"So, what happens now?"

"That part's easy. The barons of Neuhafen, or perhaps I should say former barons, will officially swear allegiance to King Otto."

"And then?"

"There'll be a big celebration, and then they'll march home."

"And that's it?" said Sigwulf. "Everyone will be nice and happy now?"

"I doubt it'll be that easy, but yes, that's the eventual hope."

"And us?"

"We'll march home, by way of Drakenfeld, so we can return their warriors. Oh, that reminds me, did I mention we'll have company?"

"I'm pretty sure I would've remembered if you had," said Sigwulf. "Why? Who's coming with us?"

"Lord Emmett and his men."

"You can't be serious?"

"Come now," said Cyn. "It makes perfect sense. Dornbruck is just across the river from Verfeld, and this way, we can keep an eye on them as they march."

"I travelled to Dornbruck, remember?" said Sigwulf. "It's thick forest the entire way."

"Then we should clear a road, shouldn't we? What do you think, Ludwig?"

"I think that's a marvellous idea, but we'd need to build a bridge, wouldn't we?"

"Not a bridge," said Cyn. "That would interfere with river traffic. A ferry would be better."

"Very well," said Ludwig. "A ferry it shall be. You know, I'm beginning to suspect you're a reincarnation of an engineer."

"What makes you say that?"

"You jumped at the chance to design the expansion to Verfeld Keep, and now you're eager to start building roads. Anything else you'd care to tackle?"

"Not just at the moment, but if I think of something, I'll be sure to let you know."

A familiar figure wandered over towards them.

"Lord Meinhard," said Ludwig. "I trust there are no hard feelings?"

"About Alexandra marrying that baron? No, although I can't help but feel there's more to this story than political expediency. I must admit I was hesitant to agree to this proposal when you suggested it. Still, the arrangement will make my daughter a baroness, so I can't really complain. Speaking of baronesses, how's that wife of yours?"

"Lady Charlotte is well, the last I heard," said Ludwig, "although that was before all this invasion nonsense took centre stage."

"Invasion nonsense? You make the entire war sound like child's play."

"But it is when you think of it," said Cyn. "A bunch of grown men arguing over who has the bigger weapons."

"Humph," said Lord Meinhard. "You're a foreigner and a woman, so I'll excuse your ignorance."

"Father!" called out Alexandra. "I heard that."

The Baron of Luwen blushed. "This is none of your concern, my dear."

"Captain Hoffman is an experienced military commander," she persisted. "I would wager that makes her opinion as important as any other in this room."

"Very well. I concede the point." He bowed ever so slightly. "My apologies, Lady Cynthia. It is lady, isn't it?"

"Yes," jumped in Sigwulf. He looked at his love. "Now accept the nice apology, Cyn."

"Apology accepted, Lord Meinhard."

The baron turned to his daughter. "Where is Lord Emmett?"

"Still talking to King Otto. He stood first in line to give his oath, although I would've thought he'd be done by now." She scanned the crowd. "Ah, here he comes."

The Baron of Dornbruck smiled as he approached, an expression his soon-to-be bride mirrored. "That wasn't nearly as terrifying as I thought it would be."

"So you're one of us now," said Lord Meinhard.

"Not quite. The king has ordered each of us to pay a special tax. He said it represents years of lost revenue to Hadenfeld. It'll be a struggle, to be sure, but at least it won't bankrupt us. In the meantime, we're to limit our garrison to no more than fifty men."

"Did he mention Eisen?" asked Ludwig. "It seems to me, without Diedrich, someone has to take over running the place."

"Are you volunteering?" replied Meinhard.

"Most assuredly not. I have plenty to do just looking after Verfeld. In any case, Otto has enough relatives to take care of such things."

"I must say," added Emmett, "it rather surprised me to see that young fellow taking his oath."

"Young fellow?"

"Yes, Lord Darrian."

"Darrian Forst?"

"That's the one. Why? Do you know him?"

"He's from Glosnecke, the barony to the west of Verfeld." His gaze went to Alexandra. "He had his eyes set on your future wife."

"Oh yes," added Sigwulf. "I heard his father was killed in the battle. He's the new Baron of Glosnecke. Didn't I mention that?"

"No," replied Ludwig. "You most certainly did not."

"You don't look happy."

"I'm not. He and I haven't exactly seen eye to eye on things, and now you're telling me he's my neighbour."

"Cheer up," said Lord Emmett. "If you run into trouble with him, you can always call on me for help. Not that I'll have very many men to respond with, mind you, but at least I would be there for moral support."

"Yes," added Alexandra, "but you must be sure to invite us to visit Verfeld. I've yet to meet Lady Charlotte, not to mention young Frederick."

"Frederick?" said Emmett.

"Yes, his son and heir."

"Speaking of heirs," interrupted Lord Meinhard, "I expect you to do your duty, my dear, and give me many grandsons."

Alexandra blushed profusely.

"Somehow," said Ludwig, "I doubt that will be much of a problem."

EPILOGUE

SPRING 1101 SR

The beam dropped down on the pylon. Sigwulf and Ludwig waded back to the riverbank now that their work was complete.

"Are you sure about this?" called out the northerner.

"Of course," replied Cyn. "Haven't you ever seen a ferry?"

"A ferry, I understand, but this... thing? I don't know what to make of it."

"This forms the dock on this side. Once it's done, we'll cross the river and build another one on the other bank for the ferry master to pole over to."

"Can't they pull it with a rope?"

"They could if it wasn't for the riverboats."

"I suppose that makes sense."

Exhausted by his ordeal, Ludwig threw himself on the grass, intent on soaking in the sun. His son, however, interrupted his plans by toddling over, laughing hysterically.

"He's just like his father," called out Charlotte.

Ludwig stood, scooping up his heir in his arms. "What are you doing all the way out here, Master Frederick?"

"He decided the keep was lonely without you."

"And you?"

She smiled. "I felt the need to embrace my husband, but it appears he's been up to his neck in water for most of the morning."

Ludwig moved towards her, eliciting a shriek of glee from his son. "Come, my darling, and let me give you a hug, a nice big, wet one!"

Kandam interrupted their frivolity. "Someone's coming, Lord."

"Anyone we know?" replied Ludwig.

"No, but he bears the king's colours."

"That means little in these parts. It's probably an update from Harlingen."

"I think it's more than that, Lord."

"What makes you say that?"

"The two knights who accompany him."

Ludwig waited as the trio approached. They halted only a few paces from the group, then the herald dismounted and came forward, making a deep bow.

"My lord," he said. "I bear sad tidings?"

"Why?" asked Ludwig. "What's happened?"

"I'm afraid there's no easy way to put this. The king is dead."

Ludwig felt the loss keenly. He hadn't known Otto in his youth, but the old king had embraced him as family upon his return from the north. "How did he die?"

"In bed, my lord. The Archprior had time to prepare him for his journey into the Afterlife."

"He was ill? That comes as a surprise. I always thought he had a robust constitution."

"A countenance he sought to reinforce at every opportunity. In reality, he was wracked with pains, particularly in his last few years. He took to his bed some weeks ago and passed a few days later."

"Is that why they sent you, to inform me of his demise?"

"No, Lord. My primary purpose in coming here is to summon you to Harlingen for the crowning of the new king."

"Who is?"

"Lord Morgan. He is to be crowned at the end of the month. He sends word that all barons must attend."

"I would assume that would include our families?"

"No doubt, although it is not specifically mentioned."

Ludwig turned, staring across the river as a tear came to his eye. Sensing his mood, Charlotte moved closer, taking his hand in hers.

"Will you be all right, my love?"

He looked at her and squeezed her hand. "It is the passing of an age," he said. "Otto has left an indelible mark on the kingdom, one that will be sorely missed."

"And King Morgan? Will he follow in Otto's footsteps, do you think?"

"That remains to be seen."

"Where does that put you in the line of succession?"

"That, my dear, is an excellent question."

<<<<>>>>

REVIEW WARRIOR LORD

ONTO BOOK FIVE: TEMPLE COMMANDER

If you liked *Warrior Lord,* then *Ashes,* the first book in *The Frozen Flame* series awaits.

START ASHES

A FEW WORDS FROM PAUL

Unlike its predecessors, Warrior Lord takes place over a span of years rather than months, an important distinction when looking at the series as a whole. It also overlaps with what occurs in Temple Captain, with that story's events profoundly affecting Ludwig's life.

Whereas Charlaine knew from the very beginning she wanted to serve Saint Agnes, Ludwig recognized his faith much later. Within this tale, he finds his true calling: thwarting the Halvarian Empire or their agents, the Stormwinds.

I can't end these notes without mentioning the character of Charlotte. She was originally meant to be a one-off character with a short life, but I found her so interesting I just couldn't help but keep her around. As I delved more into her character, I discovered that, like many people in our present-day society, she's dealing with mental health challenges. I owe a debt of gratitude to my advisor, whose identity will remain anonymous for obvious reasons.

Meanwhile, the saga of Power Ascending will continue with book 5, Temple Commander, in which Charlaine deShandria is up against her old nemesis Halvaria once more.

As usual, I must thank the tireless efforts of my wife, Carol, who acts as both my editor-in-chief and biggest supporter. None of these stories would have seen the light of day without her.

In addition, I would like to thank Stephanie Sandrock, Christie Bennett, and Amanda Bennett for their encouragement and support.

My BETA team has been most helpful, giving encouraging feedback and suggestions that helped improve the tale. Thanks to: Rachel Deibler, Michael Rhew, Phyllis Simpson, Don Hinckley, Charles Mohapel, Lisa Hanika, Debra Reeves, Mitchell Schneidkraut, Susan Young, Joanna Smith, James McGinnis, Keven Hutchinson, and Anna Ostberg.

Last but certainly not least, I must thank you, the reader, for without you, there would never have been any additional stories to write. Your emails and book reviews drive me to create these stories. So thank you, and I look forward to providing you with more tales to entertain and delight.

ABOUT THE AUTHOR

Paul J Bennett (b. 1961) emigrated from England to Canada in 1967. His father served in the British Royal Navy, and his mother worked for the BBC in London. As a young man, Paul followed in his father's footsteps, joining the Canadian Armed Forces in 1983. He is married to Carol Bennett and has three daughters who are all creative in their own right.

Paul's interest in writing started in his teen years when he discovered the roleplaying game, Dungeons & Dragons (D & D). What attracted him to this new hobby was the creativity it required; the need to create realms, worlds and adventures that pulled the gamers into his stories.

In his 30's, Paul started to dabble in designing his own roleplaying system, using the Peninsular War in Portugal as his backdrop. His regular gaming group were willing victims, er, participants in helping to playtest this new system. A few years later, he added additional settings to his game, including Science Fiction, Post-Apocalyptic, World War II, and the all-important Fantasy Realm where his stories take place.

The beginnings of his first book 'Servant to the Crown' originated over five years ago when he began running a new fantasy campaign. For the world that the Kingdom of Merceria is in, he ran his adventures like a TV show, with seasons that each had twelve episodes, and an overarching plot. When the campaign ended, he knew all the characters, what they had to accomplish, what needed to happen to move the plot along, and it was this that inspired to sit down to write his first novel.

Paul now has four series based in his fantasy world of Eiddenwerthe, and is looking forward to sharing many more books with his readers over the coming years.

Made in the USA
Coppell, TX
03 July 2022

79530611R00229